McBain's Ladies

Ed McBain was born in Manhattan, but fled to the Bronx at the age of twelve. He went through elementary and high school in the New York school system, and the Navy claimed him in 1944. When he returned two years later, he attended Hunter College. After a variety of jobs, he worked for a literary agent, where he learnt about plotting stories. When his agent-boss started selling them regularly to magazines, and sold a mystery novel and a juvenile science-fiction title as well, they both decided that it would be more profitable for him to stay at home and write full time. Under his own name, Evan Hunter, he is the author of a number of novels, including *The Blackboard Jungle*, *Come Winter* and *Every Little Crook and Nanny*. As Ed McBain he has written the highly popular '87th Precinct' series of crime novels, including *Shotgun*, *Jigsaw*, *Sadie When She Died*, *Axe*, *Like Love*, *Blood Relatives*, *Ghosts*, *Lightning* and *Poison*, all of which are available in Pan.

D0755187

Also by Ed McBain in Pan Books

Shotgun

Jigsaw

Sadie When She Died

Ten Plus One

Axe

Let's Hear It For the Deaf Man

Like Love

Doll

Blood Relatives

See Them Die

So Long As You Both Shall Live

Long Time No See

The Empty Hours

Ghosts

Heat

Ice

Lightning

Eight Black Horses

Another Part of the City

Poison

Tricks

Ed McBain

McBain's Ladies

Pan Books
in association with Hamish Hamilton

First published in Great Britain 1988 by
Hamish Hamilton Ltd

This edition published 1989 by Pan Books Ltd,
Cavaye Place, London SW10 9PG
in association with Hamish Hamilton Ltd

9 8 7 6 5 4 3 2 1

© Hui Corporation 1988

ISBN 0 330 30821 1

Printed and bound in Great Britain by
Richard Clay Ltd, Bungay, Suffolk

This is for
JACK AND MIRIAM PAAR

The city in these pages is imaginary.
The people, the places are all fictitious.
Only the police routine is based on established
investigatory technique.

TEDDY CARELLA

He had not seen Teddy Franklin since Mike took the slugs.

Generally, in the course of running down something, he would drop in to see her, spending a few minutes with her before rushing off again. And, of course, he spent all his free time with her because he was in love with the girl.

He had met her less than six months ago, when she'd been working addressing envelopes for a small firm on the fringe of the precinct territory. The firm reported a burglary, and Carella had been assigned to it. He had been taken instantly with her buoyant beauty, asked her out, and that had been the beginning. He had also, in the course of investigation, cracked the burglary—but that didn't seem important now. The important thing now was Teddy. Even the firm had gone the way of most small firms, fading into the abyss of a corporate dissolution, leaving her without a job but with enough saved money to maintain herself for a while. He honestly hoped it would only be for a while, a short while at that. This was the girl he wanted to marry. This was the girl he wanted for his own.

Thinking of her, thinking of the progression of slow traffic lights which kept him from racing to her side, he cursed ballistics reports

3

and coroner's reports, and people who shot cops in the back of the head, and he cursed the devilish instrument known as the telephone and the fact that the instrument was worthless with a girl like Teddy. He glanced at his watch. It was close to midnight, and she didn't know he was coming, but he'd take the chance, anyway. He wanted to see her.

When he reached her apartment building in Riverhead, he parked the car and locked it. The street was very quiet. The building was old and sedate, covered with lush ivy. A few windows blinked wide-eyed at the stifling heat of the night, but most of the tenants were alseep or trying to sleep. He glanced up at her window, pleased when he saw the light was still burning. Quickly, he mounted the steps, stopping outside her door.

He did not knock.

Knocking was no good with Teddy.

He took the knob in his hand and twisted it back and forth, back and forth. In a few moments, he hears her footsteps, and then the door opened a crack, and then the door opened wide.

She was wearing prisoner pajamas, white-and-black-striped cotton top and pants she'd picked up as a gag. Her hair was raven black, and the light in the foyer put a high sheen onto it. He closed the door behind him, and she went instantly into his arms, and then she moved back from him, and he marveled at the expressiveness of her eyes and her mouth. There was joy in her eyes, pure soaring joy. Her lips parted, edging back over small white teeth, and then she lifted her face to his, and he took her kiss, and he felt the warmth of her body beneath the cotton pajamas.

"Hello," he said, and she kissed the words on his mouth, and then broke away, holding only his hand, pulling him into the warmly lighted living room.

She held her right index finger alongside her face, calling for his attention.

"Yes?" he said, and then she shook her head, changing her mind, wanting him to sit first. She fluffed a pillow for him, and he sat in the easy chair, and she perched herself on the arm of the chair and cocked her head to one side, repeating the extended index finger gesture.

"Go ahead," he said, "I'm listening."

She watched his lips carefully, and then she smiled. Her index finger dropped. There was a white tag sewed onto the prisoner pajama top close to the mound of her left breast. She ran the extended finger across the tag. He looked at it closely.

"I'm not examining your feminine attributes," he said, smiling, and she shook her head, understanding. She had inked numbers onto the tag, carrying out the prison garb motif. He studied the numbers closely.

4

"My shield numbers," he said, and the smile flowered on her mouth. "You deserve a kiss for that," he told her.

She shook her head.

"No kiss?"

She shook her head again.

"Why not?"

She opened and closed the fingers on her right hand.

"You want to talk?" he asked.

She nodded.

"What about?"

She left the arm of the chair suddenly. He watched her walking across the room, his eyes inadvertently following the swing of her small, rounded backside. She went to an end table and picked up a newspaper. She carried it back to him and then pointed to the picture of Mike Reardon on page one, his brains spilling out onto the sidewalk.

"Yeah," he said dully.

There was sadness on her face now, an exaggerated sadness because Teddy could not give tongue to words, Teddy could neither hear words, and so her face was her speaking tool, and she spoke in exaggerated syllables, even to Carella, who understood the slightest nuance of expression in her eyes or on her mouth. But the exaggeration did not lie, for there was genuineness to the grief she felt. She had never met Mike Reardon, but Carella had talked of him often, and she felt that she knew him well.

She raised her eyebrows and spread her hands simultaneously, asking Carella *"Who?"* and Carella, understanding instantly, said, "We don't know yet. That's why I haven't been around. We've been working on it." He saw puzzlement in her eyes. "Am I going too fast for you?" he asked.

She shook her head.

"What then? What's the matter?"

She threw herself into his arms and she was weeping suddenly and fiercely, and he said, "Hey, hey, come on, now," and then realized she could not read his lips because her head was buried in his shoulder. He lifted her chin.

"You're getting my shirt wet," he said.

She nodded, trying to hold back the tears.

"What's the matter?"

She lifted her hand slowly, and she touched his cheek gently, so gently that it felt like the passing of a mild breeze, and then her fingers touched his lips and lingered there, caressing them.

"You're worried about me?"

She nodded.

"There's nothing to worry about."

5

She tossed her hair at the first page of the newspaper again.

"That was probably some crackpot," Carella said.

She lifted her face, and her eyes met his fully, wide and brown, still moist from the tears.

"I'll be careful," he said. "Do you love me?"

She nodded, and then ducked her head.

"What's the matter?"

She shrugged and smiled, an embarrassed, shy smile.

"You missed me?"

She nodded again.

"I missed you, too."

She lifted her head again, and there was something else in her eyes this time, a challenge to him to read her eyes correctly this time, because she had truly missed him but he had not uncovered the subtlety of her meaning as yet. He studied her eyes, and then he knew what she was saying, and he said only, "Oh."

She knew that he knew then, and she cocked one eyebrow saucily, and slowly gave one exaggerated nod of her head, repeating his "Oh," soundlessly rounding her lips.

"You're just a fleshpot," he said jokingly.

She nodded.

"You only love me because I have a clean, strong, young body."

She nodded.

"Will you marry me?"

She nodded.

"I've only asked you about a dozen times so far."

She shrugged and nodded, enjoying herself immensely.

"When?"

She pointed at him.

"All right, I'll set the date. I'm getting my vacation in August. I'll marry you then, okay?"

She sat perfectly still, staring at him.

"I mean it."

She seemed ready to cry again. He took her in his arms and said, "I mean it, Teddy. Teddy, darling, I mean it. Don't be silly about this, Teddy, because I honestly, truly mean it. I love you, and I want to marry you, and I've wanted to marry you for a long, long time now, and if I have to keep asking you, I'll go nuts. I love you just the way you are, I wouldn't change any of you, darling, so don't get silly, please don't get silly again. It . . . it doesn't matter to me, Teddy. Little Teddy, little Theodora, it doesn't matter to me, can you understand that? You're more than any other woman, so much more, so please marry me."

She looked up at him, wishing she could speak because she could not trust her eyes now, wondering why someone as beautiful as Steve

6

Carella, as wonderful as Steve Carella, as brave and as strong and as marvelous as Steve Carella would want to marry a girl like her, a girl who could never say, "I love you, darling. I adore you." But he had asked her again, and now, close in the circle of his arms, now she could believe that it didn't really matter to him, that to him she was as whole as any woman, "more than any other woman," he had said.

"Okay?" he asked. "Will you let me make you honest?"

She nodded. The nod was a very small one.

"You mean it this time?"

She did not nod again. She lifted her mouth, and she put her answer into her lips, and his arms tightened around her, and she knew that he understood her. She broke away from him, and he said "Hey!" but she trotted away from his reach and went to the kitchen.

When she brought back the champagne, he said, "I'll be damned!"

She sighed, agreeing that he undoubtedly would be damned, and he slapped her playfully on the fanny.

She handed him the bottle, did a deep curtsy which was ludicrous in the prisoner pajamas and then sat on the floor cross-legged while he struggled with the cork.

The champagne exploded with an enormous pop, and though she did not hear the sound, she saw the cork leave the neck of the bottle and ricochet off the ceiling, and she saw the bubbly white fluid overspilling the lip and running over his hands.

She began to clap, and then she got to her feet and went for glasses, and he poured first a little of the wine into his, saying, "That's the way it's done, you know. It's supposed to take off the skim and the bugs and everything," and then filling her glass, and then going back to pour his to the brim.

"To us," he toasted.

She opened her arms slowly, wider and wider and wider.

"A long, long, happy love," he supplied.

She nodded happily.

"And our marriage in August." They clinked glasses, and then sipped at the wine, and she opened her eyes wide in pleasure and cocked her head appreciatively.

"Are you happy?" he asked.

Yes, her eyes said, yes, yes.

"Did you mean what you said before?"

She raised one brow inquisitively.

"About . . . missing me?"

Yes, yes, yes, yes, her eyes said.

"You're beautiful."

She curtsied again.

"Everything about you. I love you, Teddy. Jesus, how I love you."

She put down the wineglass and then took his hand. She kissed the

7

palm of the hand, and the back, and then she led him into the bedroom, and she unbuttoned his shirt and pulled it out of his trousers, her hands moving gently. He lay down on the bed, and she turned off the light and then, unself-consciously, unembarrassedly, she took off the pajamas and went to him.

She stood by the window when the rain stopped.

She swore mentally, and she reminded herself that she would have to teach Steve sign language, so that he'd know when she was swearing. He had promised to come tonight, and the promise filled her now, and she wondered what she should wear for him.

"Nothing" was probably the best answer. She was pleased with her joke. She must remember it. To tell him when he came.

The street was suddenly very sad. The rain had brought gaiety, but now the rain was gone, and there was only the solemn gray of the street, as solemn as death.

Death.

Two dead, two men he worked with and knew well. Why couldn't he have been a streetcleaner or a flagpole sitter or something, why a policeman, why a cop?

She turned to look at the clock, wondering what time it was, wondering how long it would be before he came, how long it would be before she spotted the slow, back-and-forth twisting of the knob, before she rushed to the door to open it for him. The clock was no comfort. It would be hours yet. If he came, of course. If nothing else happened, something to keep him at the station house, another killing, another . . .

No, I mustn't think of that.

It's not fair to Steve to think that.

If I think of harm coming to him . . .

Nothing will happen to him . . . no. Steve is strong, Steve is a good cop, Steve can take care of himself. But Reardon was a good cop, and Foster, and they're dead now. How good can a cop be when he's shot in the back with a .45? How good is any cop against a killer in ambush?

No, don't think these things.

The murders are over now. There will be no more. Foster was the end. It's done. Done.

Steve, hurry.

She sat facing the door, knowing it would be hours yet, but waiting for the knob to turn, waiting for the knob to tell her he was there.

The bar was air-conditioned, a welcome sanctuary from the stifling heat outdoors. They ordered their drinks and then sat opposite each other at the booth alongside the left-hand wall.

"All I want to know," Savage said, "is what you think."

8

"Do you mean me personally, or the department?"

"You, of course. I can't expect you to speak for the department."

"Is this for publication?" Carella asked.

"Hell, no. I'm just trying to jell my own ideas on it. Once this thing is broken, there'll be a lot of feature coverage. To do a good job, I want to be acquainted with every facet of the investigation."

"It'd be a little difficult for a layman to understand every facet of police investigation," Carella said.

"Of course, of course. But you can at least tell me what you think."

"Sure. Provided it's not for publication."

"Scout's honor," Savage said.

"The department doesn't like individual cops trying to glorify . . ."

"Not a word of this will get into print," Savage said. "Believe me."

"What do you want to know?"

"We've got the means, we've got the opportunity," Savage said. "What's the motive?"

"Every cop in the city would like the answer to that one," Carella said.

"A nut maybe."

"Maybe."

"You don't think so?"

"No. Some of us do. I don't."

"Why not?"

"Just like that."

"Do you have a reason?"

"No, just a feeling. When you've been working on a case for any length of time, you begin to get feelings about it. I just don't happen to believe a maniac's involved here."

"What do you believe?"

"Well, I have a few ideas."

"Like what?"

"I'd rather not say right now."

"Oh, come on, Steve."

"Look, police work is like any other kind of work—except we happen to deal with crime. If you run an import-export business, you play certain hunches and others you don't. It's the same with us. If you have a hunch, you don't go around making a million-dollar deal on it until you've checked it."

"Then you do have a hunch you want to check?"

"Not even a hunch, really. Just an idea."

"What kind of an idea?"

"About motive."

"What about motive?"

Carella smiled. "You're a pretty tenacious guy, aren't you?"

"I'm a good reporter. I already told you that."

"All right, look at it this way. These men were cops. Three of them were killed in a row. What's the automatic conclusion?"

"Somebody doesn't like cops."

"Right. A cop hater."

"So?"

"Take off their uniforms. What have you got then?"

"They weren't wearing uniforms. None of them were uniform cops."

"I know. I was speaking figuratively. I meant, make them ordinary citizens. Not cops. What do you have then? Certainly not a cop hater."

"But they *were* cops."

"They were men first. Cops only coincidentally and secondarily."

"You feel, then, that the fact that they were cops had nothing to do with the reason they were killed."

"Maybe. That's what I want to dig into a little deeper."

"I'm not sure I understand you."

"It's this," Carella said. "We knew these men well, we worked with them every day. Cops. We knew them as cops. We didn't know them as *men*. They may have been killed because they were men, and not because they were cops."

"Interesting," Savage said.

"It means digging into their lives on a more personal level. It won't be fun because murder has a strange way of dragging skeletons out of the neatest closets."

"You mean, for example . . ." Savage paused. "Well, let's say Reardon was playing around with another dame, or Foster was a horseplayer, or Bush was taking money from a racketeer, something like that."

"To stretch the point, yes."

"And somehow, their separate activities were perhaps tied together to one person who wanted them all dead for various reasons. Is that what you're saying?"

"That's a little complicated," Carella said. "I'm not sure the deaths are connected in such a complicated way."

"But we do know the same person killed all three cops."

"Yes, we're fairly certain of that."

"Then the deaths are connected."

"Yes, of course. But perhaps . . ." Carella shrugged. "It's difficult to discuss this with you because I'm not sure I know what I'm talking about. I only have this idea, that's all. This idea that motive may go deeper than the shields these men wore."

"I see." Savage sighed. "Well, you can console yourself with the knowledge that every cop in the city probably has his own ideas on how to solve this one."

Carella nodded, not exactly understanding Savage, but not willing to get into a lengthier discussion. He glanced at his watch.

"I've got to go soon," he said. "I've got a date."

"Your girlfriend?"

"Yes."

"What's her name?"

"Teddy. Well, Theodora really."

"Theodora what?"

"Franklin."

"Nice," Savage said. "Is this a serious thing?"

"As serious as they come."

"These ideas of yours," Savage said. "About motive. Have you discussed them with your superiors?"

"Hell, no. You don't discuss every little pang of inspiration you get. You look into it, and then if you turn up anything that looks remotely promising, well, then you air the idea."

"I see. Have you discussed it with Teddy?"

"Teddy? Why, no, not yet."

"Think she'll go for it?"

Carella smiled uneasily. "She thinks I can do no wrong."

"Sounds like a wonderful girl."

"The best. And I'd better get to her before I lose her."

"Certainly," Savage said understandingly. Carella glanced at his watch again. "Where does she live?"

"Riverhead," Carella said.

"Theodora Franklin of Riverhead," Savage said.

"Yes."

"Well, I've appreciated listening to your ideas."

Carella rose. "None of that was for print, remember," he said.

"Of course not," Savage assured him.

"Thanks for the drink," Carella said.

The man in the black suit stood outside the apartment door, listening. A copy of the afternoon newspaper stuck up from the right-hand pocket of his jacket. His left shoulder throbbed with pain, and the weight of the .45 automatic tugged at the other pocket of his jacket, so that—favoring the wound, bearing the weight of the gun—he leaned slightly to his left while he listened.

There was no sound from within the apartment.

He had read the name very carefully in the newspaper, Theodora Franklin, and then he had checked the Riverhead directory and come up with the address. He wanted to talk to this girl. He wanted to find out how much Carella knew. He had to find out.

She's very quiet in there, he thought. *What's she doing?*

Cautiously, he tried the doorknob. He wiggled it slowly from side to side. The door was locked.

He heard footsteps. He tried to back away from the door too late. He reached for the gun in his pocket. The door was opening, wide, wider.

The girl stood there, surprised. She was a pretty girl, small, dark-haired, wide brown eyes. She wore a white terry robe. The robe was damp in spots. He assumed she had just come from the shower. Her eyes went to his face, and then to the gun in his hand. Her mouth opened, but no sound came from it. She tried to slam the door, but he rammed his foot into the wedge and then shoved it back.

She moved away from him, deeper into the room. He closed the door and locked it.

"Miss Franklin?" he asked.

She nodded, terrified. She had seen the drawing on the front pages of all the newspapers, had seen it broadcast on all the television programs. There was no mistake, this was the man Steve was looking for.

"Let's have a little talk, shall we?" he asked.

His voice was a nice voice, smooth, almost suave. He was a good-looking man, why had he killed those cops? Why would a man like this . . . ?

"Did you hear me?" he asked.

She nodded. She could read his lips, could understand everything he said, but . . .

"What does your boyfriend know?" he asked.

He held the .45 loosely, as if he were accustomed to its lethal power now, as if he considered it a toy more than a dangerous weapon.

"What's the matter, you scared?"

She touched her hands to her lips, pulled them away in a gesture of futility.

"What?"

She repeated the gesture.

"Come on," he said, "talk, for Christ's sake! You're not that scared!"

Again, she repeated the gesture, shook her head this time. He watched her curiously.

"I'll be damned," he said at last. "A dummy!" He began laughing. The laugh filled the apartment, reverberating from the walls. "A dummy! If that don't take the cake! A dummy!" His laughter died. He studied her carefully. "You're not trying to pull something, are you?"

She shook her head vigorously. Her hands went to the opening of her robe, clutching the terry to her more tightly.

"Now this has definite advantages, doesn't it?" he said, grinning. "You can't scream, you can't use the phone, you can't do a damned thing, can you?"

Teddy swallowed, watching him.

"What does Carella know?" he asked.

She shook her head.

"The paper said he's got a lead. Does he know about me? Does he have any idea who I am?"

Again, she shook her head.

"I don't believe you."

She nodded, trying to convince him that Steve knew nothing. What paper was he referring to? What did he mean? She spread her hands wide, indicating innocence, hoping he would understand.

He reached into his jacket pocket and tossed the newspaper to her.

"Page four," he said. "Read it. I've got to sit down. This goddamn shoulder . . ."

He sat, the gun leveled at her. She opened the paper and read the story, shaking her head as she read.

COP DEFIES DEPARTMENT
'MAY KNOW MURDERER,'
DETECTIVE SAYS

The bar was cool and dim.

We sat opposite each other, Detective Stephen Carella and I. He toyed with his drink, and we talked of many things, but mostly we talked of murder.

"I've got an idea I know who killed those three cops," Carella said. "It's not the kind of idea you can take to your superiors, though. They wouldn't understand."

And so came the first ray of hope in the mystery which has baffled the masterminds of Homicide North and tied the hands of stubborn, opinionated Detective-Lieutenant Peter Byrnes of the 87th Precinct.

"I can't tell you very much more about it right now," Carella said, "because I'm still digging. But this cop-hater theory is all wrong. It's something in the personal lives of these three men, of that I'm sure. It needs work, but we'll crack it."

So spoke Detective Carella yesterday afternoon in a bar in the heart of the Murder Belt. He is a shy, withdrawn man, a man who—in his own words—is "not seeking glory."

"Police work is like any other kind of work," he told me, "except that we deal in crime. When you've got a hunch, you dig into it. If it pans out, then you bring it to your superiors, and maybe they'll listen, and maybe they won't."

Thus far, he has confided his "hunch" only to his fiancée, a lovely young lady named Theodora Franklin, a girl from Riverhead. Miss Franklin feels that Carella can "do no wrong," and is certain he will crack the case despite the inadequate fumblings of the department to date.

"There are skeletons in the closets," Carella said. "And

those skeletons point to our man. We've got to dig deeper. It's just a matter of time now."

We sat in the cool dimness of the bar, and I felt the quiet strength emanating from this man who has the courage to go ahead with this investigation in spite of the cop-hater theory which pervades the dusty minds of the men working around him.

This man will find the murderer, I thought.

This man will relieve the city of its constant fear, its dread of an unknown killer roaming the streets with a wanton .45 automatic in his bloodstained fist. This man . . .

"Well?" he asked.

She kept shaking her head. *No, this is not true. No, Steve would never say things like these. Steve would . . .*

"What'd he tell you?" the man asked.

Her eyes opened wide with pleading. *Nothing, he told me nothing.*

"The newspaper says . . ."

She hurled the paper to the floor.

"Lies, huh?"

Yes, she nodded.

His eyes narrowed. "Newspapers don't lie," he said.

They do, they do!

"When's he coming here?"

She stood motionless, controlling her face, not wanting her face to betray anything to the man with the gun.

"Is he coming?"

She shook her head.

"You're lying. It's all over your face. He's coming here, isn't he?"

She bolted for the door. He caught her arm and flung her back across the room. The robe pulled back over her legs when she fell to the floor. She pulled it together quickly and stared up at him.

"Don't try that again," he said.

Her breath came heavily now. She sensed a coiled spring within this man, a spring which would unleash itself at the door the moment Steve opened it. But he'd said he would not be there until midnight. He had told her that, and there were a lot of hours between now and midnight. In that time . . .

"You just get out of the shower?" he asked.

She nodded.

"Those are good legs," he said, and she felt his eyes on her. "Dames," he said philosophically. "What've you got on under that robe?"

Her eyes widened.

He began laughing. "Just what I thought. Smart. Good way to beat the heat. When's Carella coming?"

She did not answer.

"Seven, eight, nine? Is he on duty today?" He watched her. "Nothing from you, huh? What's he got, the four to midnight? Sure, otherwise he'd probably be with you right this minute. Well, we might as well make ourselves comfortable, we got a long wait. Anything to drink in this place?"

Teddy nodded.

"What've you got? Gin? Rye? Bourbon?" He watched her. "Gin? You got tonic? No, huh? Club soda? Okay, mix me a Collins. Hey, where you going?"

Teddy gestured to the kitchen.

"I'll come with you," he said. He followed her into the kitchen. She opened the refrigerator and took out an opened bottle of club soda.

"Haven't you got a fresh one?" he asked. Her back was to him, and so she could not read his lips. He seized her shoulder and swung her around. His hand did not leave her shoulder.

"I asked you if you had a fresh bottle," he said.

She nodded and knelt, taking an unopened bottle from the lowest shelf of the refrigerator. She took lemons from the fruit drawer, and then went to the cupboard for the bottle of gin.

"Dames," he said again.

She poured a double shot of gin into a tall glass. She spooned sugar into the glass, and then she went to one of the drawers.

"Hey!"

He saw the knife in her hand.

"Don't get ideas with that. Just slice the lemon."

She sliced the lemon and squeezed both halves into the glass. She poured club soda until the glass was three-quarters full, and then she went back to the refrigerator for the ice cubes. When the drink was finished, she handed it to him.

"Make one for yourself," he said.

She shook her head.

"I said make one for yourself! I don't like to drink alone."

Patiently, wearily, she made herself a drink.

"Come on. Back in the living room."

They went into the living room, and he sat in an easy chair, wincing as he adjusted himself so that his shoulder was comfortable.

"When the knock comes on that door," he said, "you just sit tight, understand? Go unlock it now."

She went to the door and unlocked it. And now, knowing that the door was open, knowing that Steve would enter and be faced with a blazing .45, she felt fear crawl into her head like a nest of spiders.

"What are you thinking?" he asked.

She shrugged. She walked back into the room and sat opposite him, facing the door.

"This is a good drink," he said. "Come on, drink."

She sipped at the Collins, her mind working ahead to the moment of Steve's arrival.

"I'm going to kill him, you know," he said.

She watched him, her eyes wide.

"Won't make any difference now, anyway, will it? One cop more or less. Make it look a little better, don't you think?"

She was puzzled, and the puzzlement showed on her face.

"It's the best way," he explained. "If he knows something, well, it won't do to have him around. And if he doesn't know anything, it'll round out the picture." He struggled in the chair. "Jesus, I've got to get this shoulder fixed. How'd you like that lousy doctor? That was something, wasn't it? I thought they were supposed to be healers."

He talks the way anyone does, she thought. *Except that he talks so casually of death. He is going to kill Steve.*

"We were figuring on Mexico, anyway. Going to leave this afternoon, until your boyfriend came up with his bright idea. We'll take off in the morning, though. Soon as I take care of this." He paused. "Do you suppose I can get a good doctor in Mexico? Jesus, the things a guy will do, huh?" He watched her face carefully. "You ever been in love?"

She studied him, puzzled, confused. He did not seem like a killer. She nodded.

"Who with? This cop?"

She nodded again.

"Well, that's a shame." He seemed sincerely sorry. "It's a damn shame, honey, but what hasta be hasta be. There's no other way, you can see that, can't you? I mean, there was no other way right from the start, from the minute I started this thing. And when you start something, you've got to see it through right to the finish. It's a matter of survival now, you realize that? Jesus, the things a guy will do. Well, you know." He paused. "You'd kill for him, wouldn't you?"

She hesitated.

"To keep him, you'd kill for him, wouldn't you?" he repeated.

She nodded.

"So? So there." He smiled. "I'm not a professional, you know. I'm a mechanic. That's my line. I'm a damn good mechanic, too. Think I'll be able to get work in Mexico?"

Teddy shrugged.

"Sure, they must have cars down there. They've got cars everywhere. Then, later, when things have cooled down, we'll come back to the States. Hell, things should cool down sooner or later. But what I'm trying to tell you, I'm not a professional killer, so don't get that idea. I'm just a regular guy."

Her eyes did not believe him.

"No, huh? Well, I'm telling you. Sometimes, there's no other way

16

out. If you see something's hopeless, and somebody explains to you where there's some hope, okay, you take it. I never harmed nobody until I killed those cops. You think I wanted to kill them? Survival, that's all. Some things, you've got to do. Agh, what the hell do you understand? You're just a dummy."

She sat silent, watching him.

"A woman gets under your skin. Some women are like that. Listen, I've been around. I've been around plenty. I had me more dames than you could count. But this one—different. Different right from the beginning. She just got under my skin. Right under it. When it gets you like that, you can't eat, you can't sleep, nothing. You just think about her all day long. And what can you do when you realize you can't really have her unless . . . well . . . unless you . . . hell, didn't she ask him for a divorce? Is it my fault he was a stubborn son of a bitch? Well, he's still stubborn—only now he's dead."

Teddy's eyes moved from his face. They covered the door behind him, and then dropped to the doorknob.

"And he took two of his pals with him." He stared into his glass. "Those are the breaks. He should've listened to reason. A woman like her . . . Jesus, you'd do anything for a woman like her. Anything! Just being in the same room with her, you want to . . ."

Teddy watched the knob with fascination. She rose suddenly. She brought back her glass and then threw it at him. It grazed his forehead, the liquid splashing out of the glass and cascading over his shoulder. He leaped to his feet, his face twisted in fury, the .45 pointed at her.

"You stupid bitch!" he bellowed. "Why the hell did you do that?"

Carella left the precinct at six-thirty on the button. Havilland had not yet come back from supper, but he could wait no longer. He did not want to leave Teddy alone in that apartment, not after the fool stunt Savage had pulled.

He drove to Riverhead quickly. He ignored traffic lights and full stop signs. He ignored everything. There was an all-consuming thought in his mind, and that thought included a man with a .45 and a girl with no tongue.

When he reached her apartment building, he glanced up at her window. The shades were not drawn. The apartment looked very quiet. He breathed a little more easily, and then entered the building. He climbed the steps, his heart pounding. He knew he shouldn't be alarmed but he could not shake the persistent feeling that Savage's column had invited danger for Teddy.

He stopped outside her door. He could hear the persistent drone of what sounded like the radio going inside. He reached for the knob. In his usual manner, he twisted it slowly from side to side, waiting for

17

her footsteps, knowing she would come to the door the moment she saw his signal.

He heard the sound of a chair scraping back and then someone shouted, "You stupid bitch! Why the hell did you do that?"

His brain came alive. He reached for his .38 and snapped the door open with his other hand.

The man turned.

"You . . . !" he shouted, and the .45 bucked in his hand.

Carella fired low, dropping to the floor the instant he entered the room. His first two shots took the man in the thigh. The man fell face forward, the .45 pitching out of his fist. Carella kicked back the hammer on the .38, waiting.

"You bastard," the man on the floor said. "You bastard."

Carella got to his feet. He picked up the .45 and stuck it into his back pocket.

"Get up," he said. "You all right, Teddy?"

Teddy nodded. She was breathing heavily, watching the man on the floor.

"Thanks for the warning," Carella said. He turned to the man again. "Get up!"

"I can't, you bastard. Why'd you shoot me? For Christ's sake, why'd you shoot me?"

"Why'd you shoot three cops?"

The man went silent.

"What's your name?" Carella asked.

"Mercer. Paul Mercer."

"Don't you like cops?"

"I love them."

"What's the story, then?"

"I suppose you're going to check my gun with what you've already got."

"Damn right," Carella said. "You haven't got a chance, Mercer."

"She put me up to it," Mercer said, a scowl on his dark face. "She's the real murderer. All I done was pull the trigger. She said we had to kill him, said it was the only way. We threw the others in just to make it look good, just to make it look as if a cop hater was loose. But it was her idea. Why should I take the rap alone?"

"Whose idea?" Carella asked.

"Alice's," Mercer said. "You see . . . we wanted to make it look like a cop hater. We wanted . . ."

"It was," Carella said.

When they brought Alice Bush in, she was dressed in gray, a quiet gray. She sat in the squad room, crossing her legs.

"Do you have a cigarette, Steve?" she asked.

Carella gave her one. He did not light it for her. She sat with the cigarette dangling from her lips until it was apparent she would have to light it herself. Unruffled, she struck a match.

"What about it?" Carella asked.

"What about it?" she repeated, shrugging. "It's all over, isn't it?"

"You must have really hated him. You must have hated him like poison."

"You're directing," Alice said. "I'm only the star."

"Don't get glib, Alice!" Carella said angrily. "I've never hit a woman in my life, but I swear to God . . ."

"Relax," she told him. "It's all over. You'll get your gold star, and then you'll . . ."

"Alice . . ."

"What the hell do you want me to do? Break down and cry? I hated him, all right? I hated his big, pawing hands and I hated his stupid red hair, and I hated everything about him, all right?"

"Mercer said you'd asked for a divorce. Is that true?"

"No, I didn't ask for a divorce. Hank never would've agreed to one."

"Why didn't you give him a chance?"

"What for? Did he ever give me a chance? Cooped up in that goddamn apartment, waiting for him to come off some burglary or some knifing or some mugging? What kind of life is that for a woman?"

"You knew he was a cop when you married him."

Alice didn't answer.

"You could've asked for a divorce, Alice. You could've tried."

"I didn't want to, damnit. *I wanted him dead.*"

"Well, you've got him dead. Him and two others. You must be tickled now."

Alice smiled suddenly. "I'm not too worried, Steve."

"No?"

"There have to be *some* men on the jury." She paused. "Men like me."

There were, in fact, eight men on the jury.

The jury brought in a verdict in six minutes flat.

Mercer was sobbing as the jury foreman read off the verdict and the judge gave sentence. Alice listened to the judge with calm indifference, her shoulders thrown back, her head erect.

The jury had found them both guilty of murder in the first degree, and the judge sentenced them to death in the electric chair.

On August 19, Stephen Carella and Theodora Franklin listened to their own sentence.

"Do either of you know of any reason why you both should not be legally joined in marriage, or if there be any present who can show any just cause why these parties should not be legally joined together, let him now speak or hereafter hold his peace."

Lieutenant Byrnes held his peace. Detective Hal Willis said nothing. The small gathering of friends and relatives watched, dewy-eyed.

The city clerk turned to Carella.

"Do you, Stephen Louis Carella, take this woman as your lawfully wedded wife to live together in the state of matrimony? Will you love, honor, and keep her as a faithful man is bound to do, in health, sickness, prosperity, and adversity, and forsaking all others keep you alone unto her as long as you both shall live?"

"Yes," Carella said. "Yes, I will. I do. Yes."

"Do you, Theodora Franklin, take this man as your lawfully wedded husband to live together in the state of matrimony? Will you love, honor, and cherish him as a faithful woman is bound to do, in health, sickness, prosperity, and adversity, and forsaking all others keep you alone unto him as long as you both shall live?"

Teddy nodded. There were tears in her eyes, but she could not keep the ecstatic smile off her face.

"For as you both have consented in wedlock and have acknowledged it before this company, I do by virtue of the authority vested in me by the laws of this state now pronounce you husband and wife. And may God bless your union."

Carella took her in his arms and kissed her. The clerk smiled. Lieutenant Byrnes cleared his throat. Willis looked up at the ceiling. The clerk kissed Teddy when Carella released her. Byrnes kissed her. Willis kissed her. All the male relatives and friends came up to kiss her.

Carella smiled idiotically.

"You hurry back," Byrnes said to him.

"Hurry back? I'm going on my honeymoon, Pete!"

"Well, hurry anyway. How are we going to run that precinct without you? You're the only cop in the city who has the courage to buck the decisions of stubborn, opinionated Detective-Lieutenant Byrnes of the . . ."

"Oh, go to hell," Carella said, smiling.

Willis shook his hand. "Good luck, Steve. She's a wonderful gal."

"Thank you, Hal."

Teddy came to him. He put his arm around her.

"Well," he said, "let's go."

They went out of the room together.

Byrnes stared after them wistfully.

"He's a good cop," he said.

"Yeah," Willis answered.

Cop Hater, 1956

He was bushed when he got home that night. Teddy greeted him at the door, and he kissed her in a perfunctory, most unnewlywedlike way. She looked at him curiously, led him to a drink waiting in the living room, and then, attuned to his uncommunicative mood, went out to the kitchen to finish dinner. When she served the meal, Carella remained silent.

She looked at him often, wondering if she had offended him in some way, longing to see words on his lips, words she could read and understand. And finally, she reached across the table and touched his hand, and her eyes opened wide in entreaty, brown eyes against an oval face.

"No, it's nothing," Carella said gently.

But still her eyes asked their questions. She cocked her head to one side, the short raven hair sharply detailed against the white wall behind her.

"This case," he admitted.

She nodded, waiting, relieved that he was troubled with his work and not with his wife.

"Well, why the hell would anyone leave a perfect set of fingerprints on a goddamn murder weapon, and then leave the weapon where every rookie cop in the world could find it?"

Teddy shrugged sympathetically, and then nodded.

"And why try to simulate a hanging afterward? Does the killer think he's dealing with a pack of nitwits, for Christ's sake?" He shook his head angrily. Teddy shoved back her chair and then came around the table and plunked herself down in his lap. She took his arm and wrapped it around her waist, and then she snuggled up close to him and kissed his neck.

"Stop that," he told her, and then—realizing she could not see his lips because her face was buried in his throat—he caught her hair and gently yanked back her head, and repeated, "Stop it. How can I think about the case with you doing that?"

Teddy gave an emphatic nod of her head, telling her husband that he had exactly understood her motivations.

"You'll destroy me," Carella said, smiling. "Do you think . . ."

Teddy kissed his mouth.

Carella moved back gently. "Do you think you'd leave a . . ."

She kissed him again, and this time he lingered awhile before moving away.

". . . syringe with fingerprints all over it on a mmmmmmmm. . . ."

Her face was very close to his, and he could see the brightness in her eyes, and the fullness of her mouth when she drew back.

21

"Oh God, woman," he said.

She rose and took his hand and as she was leading him from the room he turned her around and said, "The dishes. We have to . . ." and she tossed up her back skirts in reply, the way cancan dancers do. In the living room, she handed him a sheet of paper, neatly folded in half.

"I didn't know you wanted to answer the mail," Carella said. "I somehow suspected I was being seduced."

Impatiently, Teddy gestured to the paper in his hand. Carella unfolded it. The white sheet was covered with four typewritten stanzas. The stanzas were titled "Ode for Steve."

"For me?" he asked.

Yes, she nodded.

"Is this what you do all day, instead of slaving around the house?" She wiggled her forefinger, urging him to read the poem.

> Ode for Steve
>
> I love you, Steve,
> I love you so.
> I want to go
> Where'er you go.
>
> In counterpoint,
> And conversely,
> When you return
> 'Twill be with me.
>
> So darling boy,
> My message now
> Will follow with
> A courtly bow:
>
> You go, I go;
> Return, return I;
> Stay, go, come—
> Together.

"The last stanza doesn't rhyme," Carella said.

Teddy pulled a mock mask of stunned disgust.

"Also, methinks I read sexual connotations into this thing," Carella added.

Teddy waved one hand airily, shrugged innocently, and then—like a burlesque queen imitating a high-priced fashion model—walked gracefully and suggestively into the bedroom, her buttocks wiggling exaggeratedly.

Carella grinned and folded the sheet of paper. He put it into his wallet, walked to the bedroom door, and leaned against the jamb.

"You know," he said, "you don't have to write poems."

Teddy stared at him across the length of the room.

"All you have to do is ask," he said huskily.

The only warning was the tightening of Gonzo's eyes. Carella saw them squinch up, and he tried to move sideways, but the gun was already speaking. He did not see it buck in the boy's fist. He felt searing pain lash at his chest, and he heard the shocking declaration of three explosions and then he was falling, and he felt very warm, and he also felt very ridiculous because his legs simply would not hold him up, how silly, how very silly, and his chest was on fire, and the sky was tilting to meet the earth, and then his face struck the ground. He did not put out his arms to stop his fall because his arms were somehow powerless. His face struck the loose stones, and his body crumpled behind it, and he shuddered and felt a warm stickiness beneath him, and only then did he try to move and then he realized he was lying in a spreading pool of his own blood. He wanted to laugh and he wanted to cry at the same time. He opened his mouth, but no sound came from it. And then the waves of blackness came at him, and he fought to keep them away, unaware that Gonzo was running off through the trees, aware only of the engulfing blackness, and suddenly sure that he was about to die.

Teddy sat in the room with her husband, watching him. The blinds were drawn, but she could see his face clearly in the dimness, the mouth open, the eyes closed. Beside the bed, the plasma ran from an upturned bottle, slid through a tube, and entered Carella's arm. He lay without stirring, the blankets pulled up over the jagged wounds in his chest. The wounds were dressed now, but they had leaked their blood, they had done their damage, and he lay pale and unmoving, as if death were already inside him.

No, she thought, *he won't die.*

Please, God, please, dear God, don't let this man die, please.

Her thoughts ran freely, and she didn't realize she was praying because her thoughts sounded only like thoughts to her, simple thoughts, the thoughts a girl thinks. But she was praying.

She was remembering how she'd met Carella. She could remember exactly how he had come into the room, he and another man, a detective who was later transferred to another precinct, a detective whose face she could no longer remember. She had been concerned only with the face of Steve Carella that day. He had entered the office, and he was tall, and he walked erect, and he wore his clothes as if he were a high-priced men's fashion model rather than a cop. He had shown her his shield and introduced himself, and she had scribbled on a sheet of paper, explaining that she could neither hear nor speak, explaining that the receptionist was out, that she was hired as a typist, but that her employer would see him in a moment, as soon as she went to tell him the police were there. His face had registered mild surprise. When she rose from her desk and went to the boss's office, she could feel his eyes on her all the way.

She was not surprised when he asked her out.

She had seen interest in his eyes, and so the surprise was not in his asking, the surprise was that he could find her interesting at all. She supposed, of course, that there were men who would try anything once, just for kicks. Why not a girl who couldn't hear or talk? Might be interesting. She supposed, at first, that this was what had motivated Steve Carella, but after their first date, she knew this wasn't the case at all. He was not interested in her ears or her tongue. He was interested in the girl Teddy Franklin. He told her so, repeatedly. It took her a long while to believe it, even though she intuitively suspected its truth. And then one day, belief came, the way belief suddenly comes, and she realized he really and truly did want her for his wife. And now he lay in a hospital bed, and it seemed he might die, it seemed possible he might die, the doctors had told her that her husband might die.

She did not concern herself with the unfairness of the situation. The situation was shockingly unfair, her husband should not have been shot, her husband should not now be fighting for his life on a hosptial bed. The unfairness shrieked within her, but she did not concern herself with it, because what was done was done.

But he was good, and he was gentle, and he was her man, the only man in the world for her. There were those who held that any two people can make a go of it. If not one, then another. Throw them in bed together and things will work out all right. There's always another streetcar. Teddy did not believe this. Teddy did not believe that there was another man anywhere in the world who was as right for her as Steve Carella. Somehow, quite miraculously, he had been delivered to her doorstep, a gift, a wonderful gift.

She could not now believe he would be torn rudely from her. She could not believe it, she would not believe it. She had told him what she wanted for Christmas. She wanted him. She had said it earnestly, knowing he took it as jest, but she had meant every word of it. And now, her words were being hurled back into her face by a cruel wind. Because now she really wanted him for Christmas, now he was the only thing she really wanted for Christmas. Earlier, she had been secure when she asked for him, knowing she would certainly have him. But now the security was gone, now there was left only a burning desire for her man to live. She would never again want anything more than Steve Carella.

* * *

Byrnes hung up and then put on his overcoat. He was suddenly feeling quite good about everything. He was sure Carella would pull through. Damnit, you can't shoot a good cop and expect him to die! Not a cop like Carella!

He walked all the way to the hospital. The temperature was dipping close to zero, but he walked all the way, and he shouted "Merry Christmas!" to a pair of drunks who passed him. When he reached the hospital, his face was tingling, and he was out of breath, but he was more sure than ever before that everything would work out all right.

He took the elevator up to the eighth floor, and the doors slid open and he stepped into the corridor. It took a moment to orient himself and then he started off toward Carella's room, and it took another moment for the new feeling to attack him. For here in the cool antiseptic sterility of the hospital, he was no longer certain about Steve Carella. Here he had his first doubts, and his step slowed as he approached the room.

He saw Teddy then.

At first she was only a small figure at the end of the corridor, and then she walked closer and he watched her. Her hands were wrung together at her waist, and her head was bent, and Brynes watched her and felt a new dread, a dread that attacked his stomach and his mind. There was defeat in the curve of her body, defeat in the droop of her head.

Carella, he thought. *Oh God, Steve, no . . .*

He rushed to her, and she looked up at him, and her face was streaked with tears, and when he saw the tears on the face of Steve Carella's wife, he was suddenly barren inside, barren and cold, and he wanted to break from her and run down the corridor, break from her and escape the pain in her eyes.

And then he saw her mouth.

And it was curious, because she was smiling. She was smiling and the shock of seeing that smile opened his eyes wide. The tears coursed down her face, but they ran past a beaming smile, and he took her shoulders and he spoke very clearly and very distinctly and he said, "Steve? Is he all right?"

She read the words on his mouth, and then she nodded, a small nod at first, and then an exaggerated delirious nod, and she threw herself into Byrnes's arms, and Byrnes held her close to him, feeling for all the world as if she were his daughter, surprised to find tears on his own face.

Outside the hospital, the church bells tolled.

It was Christmas Day, and all was right with the world.

The Pusher, 1956

The beauty of being a shoemaker, Teddy Carella thought, is that you don't take your work home with you. You cobble so many shoes, and then you go home to your wife, and you don't think about soles and heels until the next day.

A cop thinks about heels all the time.

A cop like Steve Carella thinks about souls, too.

She would not, of course, have been married to anyone else but it pained her nonetheless to see him sitting by the window brooding His brooding position was almost classical, almost like the Rodin statue. He sat slumped in the easy chair, his chin cupped in one large hand, his legs crossed. He sat barefoot, and she loved his feet, that was ridiculous, you don't love a man's feet, well the hell with you, I love his feet. They've got good clean arches and nice toes, sue me.

She walked to where he was sitting.

She was not a tall girl, but she somehow gave an impression of height. She held her head high, and her shoulders erect, and she walked lightly with a regal grace that added inches to her stature.

Standing spread-legged before her brooding husband, she put her hands on her hips and stared down at him. She wore a red wraparound skirt, a huge gold safety pin fastening it just above her left knee. She wore red Capezio flats, and a white blouse swooped low at the throat to the first swelling rise of her breasts. She had caught her hair back with a bright red ribbon, and she stood before him now and defied him to continue with his sullen brooding.

Neither spoke. Teddy because she could not, and Carella because he would not. The silent skirmish filled the small apartment.

At last, Carella said, "All right, all right."

Teddy nodded and cocked one eyebrow.

"Yes," he said, "I'm emerging from my shell."

She hinged her hands together at the wrist and opened them slowly, and then snapped them shut.

"You're right," Carella said. "I'm a clam."

She pointed a pistol-finger at him and squeezed the trigger.

"Yes, my work," he said.

Abruptly, without warning, she moved onto his lap. His arms circled her, and she cuddled up into a warm ball, pulling her knees up, snuggling her head against his chest. She looked up at him, and her eyes said, *Tell me.*

"This girl," he said. "Mary Louise Proschek."

Teddy nodded.

"Thirty-three years old, comes to the city to start a new life. Turns up floating in the Harb. Letter to her folks was full of good spirits.

26

Even if we suspected suicide, which we don't, the letter would fairly well eliminate that. The M.E. says she was dead before she hit the water. Cause of death was acute arsenic poisoning. You following me?"

Teddy nodded, her eyes wide.

"She's got a tattoo mark right here . . ." He showed the spot on his right hand. ". . . the word 'Mac' in a heart. Didn't have it when she left Scranton, her hometown. How many Macs do you suppose there are in this city?"

Teddy rolled her eyes.

"You said it. Did she come here to meet this Mac? Did she just run into him by accident? Is he the one who threw her in the river after poisoning her? How do you go about locating a guy named Mac?"

Teddy pointed to the flap of skin between her thumb and forefinger.

"The tattoo parlors? I've already started checking them. We may get a break because not many women wear tattoos.

What'd *you* do all day?" he asked, holding her close, beginning to relax, succumbing to the warmth of her.

Teddy opened her hands like a book.

"Read?" Carella watched while she nodded. "What'd you read?"

Teddy scrambled off his lap and then clutched her middle, indicating that she had read something that was very funny. She walked across the room and he watched her when she stooped alongside the magazine rack.

"If you're not careful," he said, "I'm going to undo that damn safety pin."

She put the magazines on the floor, stood up, and undid the safety pin. The skirt hung loose, one flap over the other. When she stooped to pick up the magazine again, it opened in a wide slit from her knee to almost her waist. Wiggling like the burlesque queen Carella had described, she walked back to him and dumped the magazines in his lap.

"Pen pal magazines?" Carella asked, astonished.

Teddy hunched up her shoulders, grinned, and then covered her mouth with one hand.

"My God!" he said. "Why?"

With her hands on her hips, Teddy kicked at the ceiling with one foot, the skirt opening over the clean line of her leg.

"For kicks?" Carella asked, shrugging. "What kind of stuff is in here? *'Dear Pen Pal: I am a cocker spaniel who always wanted to be in the movies . . .'*"

Teddy grinned and opened one of the magazines for him. Carella thumbed through it. She sat on the arm of his chair, and the skirt opened again. He looked at the magazine, and then he looked at his woman, and then he said, "The hell with this noise," and he threw the magazine to the floor and pulled Teddy onto his lap.

The magazine fell open to the Personals column.

It lay on the floor while Steve Carella kissed his wife. It lay on the floor when he picked her up and carried her into the next room.

There was a small ad in the Personals column.

It read:

> Widower. Mature. Attractive. 35 years old. Seeks alliance with understanding woman of good background. Write P.O. Box 137.

The idea was to combine business with pleasure.

It was an idea Steve Carella didn't particularly relish, but he'd promised Teddy he'd meet her downtown at eight on the button, and the call from the tattoo parlor had been clocked in at seven forty-five, and he knew it was too late to reach her at the house. He couldn't have called her in any case because the telephone was one instrument Carella's wife could never use. But he had, on other occasions, illegally dispatched a radio motor patrol car to his own apartment with the express purpose of delivering a message to Teddy. The police commissioner, even while allowing that Carella was a good cop, might have frowned upon such extracurricular squad car activity. So Carella, sneak that he was, never told him.

He stood now on the corner under the big bank clock, partially covered by the canopy which spread out over the entrance, shielding the big metal doors. He hoped there would not be an attempted bank robbery. If there was anything he disliked, it was foiling attempted bank robberies when he was off duty and waiting for the most beautiful woman in the world. Naturally, he was never off duty. A cop, as he well knew, is on duty twenty-four hours a day, three hundred and sixty-five days a year, three hundred and sixty-six days in leap year. Then, too, there was the tattoo parlor to visit, and he couldn't consider himself officially clocked out until he'd made that call, and then reported the findings back to whoever was catching at the squad.

He hoped there would not be an attempted bank robbery, and he also hoped it would stop drizzling because the rain was seeping into his bones and making his wounds ache, oh, my aching wounds!

He put his aches out of his mind and fell to woolgathering. Carella's favorite form of woolgathering was thinking about his wife. He knew there was something hopelessly adolescent about the way he loved her, but those were the facts, ma'm, and there wasn't much he could do to change his feelings. There were probably more-beautiful women in the world, but he didn't know who they were. There were probably sweeter, purer, warmer, more-passionate women, too. He doubted it. He very strongly doubted it. The simple truth was that she pleased him. Hell, she delighted him. She had a face he would never tire of watching, a face which was a thousand faces, each linked subtly by a slender chain of beauty. Fully made up, her brown eyes glowing, the lashes darkened with mascara, her lips cleanly stamped with lipstick, she was one person—and he loved the meticulously calculated beauty, the freshly combed, freshly powdered veneer of that person.

In the morning, she was another person. Warm with sleep, her eyes would open, and her face would be undecorated, her full lips swollen, the black hair tangled like wild weeds, her body supple and pliable. He loved her this way, too, loved the small smile on her mouth and the sudden eager alertness of her eyes.

Her face was a thousand faces, quiet and introspective when they walked along a lonely shore barefoot and the only sound was the distant sound of breakers on the beach, a sound she could not hear in her silent world. Alive with fury, her face could change in an instant, the black brows swooping down over suddenly incandescent eyes, her lips skinning back over even white teeth, her body taut with invective she could not hurl because she could not speak, her fists clenched. Tears transformed her face again. She did not cry often, and when she did cry it was with completely unself-conscious anguish. It was almost as if, secure in the knowledge of her beauty, she could allow her face to be torn by agony.

Many men longed for the day when their ship would come in.

Carella's ship *had* come in—and it had launched a thousand faces.

There were times, of course, like *now* when he wished the ship could do a little more than fifteen knots. It was eight twenty, and she'd promised to be there at eight on the dot, and whereas he never grew weary of her mental image he much preferred her in person.

Now! For the first time! Live! On our stage! In person! Imported from the Cirque d'Hiver in Paris . . .

There must be something wrong with me, Carella thought. *I'm never really here. I'm always . . .*

He spotted her instantly. By this time, he was not surprised by what the sight of her could do to him. He had come to accept the instant quickening of his heart and the automatic smile on his face. She had not yet seen him, and he watched her from his secret vantage point, feeling somewhat sneaky, but what the hell!

· She wore a black skirt and a red sweater, and over that a black cardigan with red piping. The cardigan hung open, ending just below her hips. She had a feminine walk which was completely unconscious, completely uncalculated. She walked rapidly because she was late, and he heard the steady clatter of the black pumps on the pavement and he watched with delighted amusement the men who turned for a second look at his wife.

When she saw him, she broke into a run. He did not know what it was between them that made the shortest separation seem like a ten-year stretch at Alcatraz. Whatever it was, they had it. She came into his arms, and he kissed her soundly, and he wouldn't have given a damn if 20th Century-Fox had been filming the entire sequence for a film titled *The Mating Season Jungle*.

"You're late," he said. "Don't apologize. You look lovely. We have to make a stop, do you mind?"

Her eyes questioned his face.

"A tattoo parlor downtown. Guy thinks he may remember Mary Louise Proschek. We're lucky. This is business, so I was able to check out a sedan. Means we don't have to take the train home tonight. Some provider, your husband, huh?"

Teddy grinned and squeezed his arm.

"The car's around the corner. You look beautiful. You smell nice, too. What've you got on?"

Teddy dry-washed her hands.

"Just soap and water? You're amazing! Look how nice you can make soap smell. Honey, this won't take more than a few minutes. I've got some pictures of the Proschek girl in the car, and maybe we can get a make on them from this guy. After that, we'll eat and whatever you like. I can use a drink, can't you?"

Teddy nodded.

"Why do people always say they can 'use' a drink? What, when you get right down to it, can they use it for?" He studied her and added, "I'm too talkative tonight. I guess I'm excited. We haven't had a night out in a long while. And you look beautiful. Don't you get tired of my saying that?"

Teddy shook her head, and there was a curious tenderness in the movement. He had grown used to her eyes, and perhaps he missed what they were saying to him, over and over again, repeatedly. Teddy Carella didn't need a tongue.

They walked to the car, and he opened the door for her, went around to the other side, and then started the motor. The police radio erupted into the closed sedan.

"Car 21, Car 21, Signal 1. Silvermine at North 40th . . ."

"I'll be conscientious and leave it on," Carella said to Teddy. "Some pretty redhead may be trying to reach me."

Teddy's brows lowered menacingly.

"In connection with a case, of course," he explained.

Of course, she nodded mockingly.

"God, I love you," he said, his hand moving to her thigh. He squeezed her quickly, an almost unconscious gesture, and then he put his hand back on the wheel.

They drove steadily through the maze of city traffic. At one stoplight, a traffic cop yelled at Carella because he anticipated the changing of the light from red to green. The cop's rain gear was slick with water. Carella felt suddenly like a heel.

The windshield wipers snicked at the steady drizzle. The tires whispered against the asphalt of the city. The city was locked in against the rain. People stood in doorways, leaned out of windows. There was a gray quietness to the city, as if the rain had suspended all activity, had caused the game of life to be called off. There was a rain smell to the city, too, all the smells of the day captured in the steady canopy of water and washed clean by it. There was, too, and strange for the city, a curious sense of peace.

"I love Paris when it drizzles," Carella said suddenly, and he did not have to explain the meaning of his words because she knew at once what he meant, she knew that he was not talking about Paris or Wichita, that he was talking about this city, his city, and that he had been born in it and into it and that it, in turn, had been born into him.

The expensive apartment houses fell away behind them, as did the line of high-fashion stores, and the advertising agency towers, and the publishing shrines, and the gaudy brilliance of the amusement area, and the stilled emptiness of the garment district at night, and the tangled intricacy of the narrow side streets far downtown, the pushcarts lining the streets, filled with fruits and vegetables, the store windows behind them, the Italian salami, and the provolone, and the pepperoni hanging in bright red strings.

The tattoo parlor nestled in a side street on the fringe of Chinatown, straddled by a bar and a laundromat. The combination of the three was somewhat absurd, ranging from the exotica of tattooing into the netherworld of intoxication and from there to the plebeian task of laundering clothes. The neighborhood had seen its days of glory perhaps, but they were all behind it. Far behind it. Like an old man with cancer, the neighborhood patiently and painfully awaited the end—and the end was the inevitable city housing project. And in the meantime, nobody bothered to change the soiled bedclothes. Why bother when something was going to die anyway?

The man who ran the tattoo parlor was Chinese. The name on the plate-glass window was Charlie Chen.

"Everybody call me Charlie Chan," he explained. "Big detective, Charlie Chan. But me *Chen*, Chen. You know Charlie Chan, detective?"

"Yes," Carella said, smiling.

"Big detective," Chen said. "Got stupid sons." Chen laughed. "Me got stupid sons, too, but me no detective." He was a round fat man, and everything he owned shook when he laughed. He had a small mustache on his upper lip, and he had thick fingers, and there was an oval jade ring on the forefinger of his left hand. "You detective, huh?" he asked.

"Yes," Carella said.

"This lady police lady?" Chen asked.

"No. This lady's my wife."

"Oh. Very good. Very good," Chen said. "Very pretty. She wants tattoo, maybe? Do nice butterfly for her on shoulder. Very good for strapless gowns. Very pretty. Very decorative."

Teddy shook her head, smiling.

"Very pretty lady. You very lucky detective," Chen said. He turned to Teddy. "Nice yellow butterfly maybe? Very pretty?" He opened his eyes seductively. "Everybody say very pretty."

Teddy shook her head again.

"Maybe you like red better? Red your color, maybe? Nice red butterfly?"

Teddy could not keep herself from smiling. She kept shaking her head and smiling, feeling very much a part of her husband's work, happy that he'd had to make the call, and happy that he'd taken her with him. It was curious, she supposed, but she did not know him as a cop. His function as a cop was something almost completely alien to her, even though he talked about his work. She knew that he dealt with crime, and the perpetrators of crime, and she often wondered what kind of man he was when he was on the job. Heartless? She could not imagine that in her man. Cruel? No. Hard, tough? Perhaps.

"About this girl," Carella said to Chen. "When did she come in for the tattoo?"

"Oh, long time ago," Chen said. "Maybe five months, maybe six. Nice lady. Not so pretty like your lady, but very nice."

"Was she alone?"

"No. She with tall man." Chen scrutinized Carella's face. "Prettier than you, detective."

Carella grinned. "What did he look like?"

"Tall. Movie star. Very handsome. Muscles."

"What color was his hair?"

"Yellow," Chen said.

"His eyes?"

Chen shrugged.

"Anything you remember about him?"

"He smile all the time," Chen said. "Big white teeth. Very pretty teeth. Very handsome man. Movie star."

"Tell me what happened."

"They come in together. She hold his arm. She look at him, stars in her eyes." Chen paused. "Like your lady. But not so pretty."

"Were they married?"

32

Chen shrugged.

"Did you see an engagement ring or a wedding band on her finger?"

"I don't see," Chen said. He grinned at Teddy. Teddy grinned back. "You like black butterfly? Pretty black wings? Come, I show you." He led them into the shop. A beaded curtain led to the back room. The walls of the shop were covered with tattoo designs. A calendar with a nude girl on it hung on the wall near the beaded curtain. Someone had jokingly inked tattoos onto her entire body. The tattooer had drawn a pair of clutching hands on the girl's full breasts. Chen pointed to a butterfly design on one of the walls.

"This butterfly. You like? You pick color. Any color. I do. I put on your shoulder. Very pretty."

"Tell me what happened with the girl," Carella said, gently insistent. Teddy looked at him curiously. Her husband was enjoying the byplay between herself and Chen, but he was not losing sight of his objective. He was here in this shop for a possible lead to the man who had killed Mary Louise Proschek. She suddenly felt that if the byplay got too involved, her husband would call a screaming halt to it.

"They come in shop. He say the girl want tattoo. I show them designs on wall. I try to sell her butterfly. Nobody like butterfly. Butterfly my own design. Very pretty. Good for shoulder. I do butterfly on one lady's back, near base of spine. Very pretty, only nobody see. Good for shoulder. I try to sell her butterfly, but man say he wants heart. She say she wants heart, too. Stars in eyes, you know? Big love, big thing, shining all over. I show them big hearts. Very pretty hearts, very complicated, many colors."

"They didn't want a big heart?"

"Man wants small heart. He show me where." Chen spread his thumb and forefinger. "Here. Very difficult. Skinny flesh, needle could go through. Very painful. Very difficult. He say he wants it there. She say if he wants it there, she wants it there. Crazy."

"Who suggested what lettering to put into the heart?"

"Man. He say you put M, A, C in heart."

"He said to put the name Mac into that heart?"

"He no say name Mac. He say put M, A, C."

"And what did she say?"

"She say yes, M, A, C."

"Go on."

"I do. Very painful. Girl scream. He hold her shoulders. Very painful. Tender spot." Chen shrugged. "Butterfly on shoulder better."

"Did she mention his name while she was here?"

"No."

"Did she call him Mac?"

"She call him nothing." Chen thought a moment. "Yes, she call him darling, dear, sweetheart. Love words. No name."

Carella sighed. He lifted the flap of the manila envelope in his hands and drew out the glossy prints that were inside it. "Is this the girl?" he asked Chen.

Chen looked at the pictures. "That she," he said. "She dead, huh?"

"Yes, she's dead."

"He kill her?"

"We don't know."

"She love him," Chen said, wagging his head. "Love very special. Nobody should kill love."

Teddy looked at the little round Chinese, and she suddenly felt very much like allowing him to tattoo his prize butterfly design on her shoulder. Carella took the pictures back and put them into the envelope.

"Has this man ever come into your shop again?" Carella asked. "With another woman perhaps?"

"No, never," Chen said.

"Well," Carella said, "thanks a lot, Mr. Chen. If you remember anything more about him, give me a call, won't you?" He opened his wallet. "Here's my card. Just ask for Detective Carella."

"You come back," Chen said, "you ask for Charlie Chan, big detective with stupid sons. You bring wife. I make pretty butterfly on shoulder." He extended his hand and Carella took it. For a moment, Chen's eyes went serious. "You lucky," he said. "You not so pretty, have very pretty lady. Love very special." He turned to Teddy. "Someday, if you want butterfly, you come back. I make very pretty." He winked. "Detective husband like. I promise. Any color. Ask for Charlie Chan. That's me."

He grinned and wagged his head, and Carella and Teddy left the shop, heading for the police sedan up the street.

"Nice guy, wasn't he?" Carella said.

Teddy nodded.

"I wish they were all like him. A lot of them aren't. With many people, the presence of a cop automatically produces a feeling of guilt. That's the truth, Teddy. They instantly feel that they're under suspicion, and everything they say becomes defensive. I guess that's because there are skeletons in the cleanest closets. Are you very hungry?"

Teddy made a face which indicated she was famished.

"Shall we find a place in the neighborhood, or do you want to wait until we get uptown?"

Teddy pointed to the ground.

"Here?"

Yes, she nodded.

"Chinese?"

No.

"Italian?"

Yes.

"You shouldn't have married a guy of Italian descent," Carella said. "Whenever such a guy eats in an Italian restaurant, he can't help comparing his spaghetti with what his mother used to cook. He then becomes dissatisfied with what he's eating, and the dissatisfaction spreads to include his wife. The next thing you know, he's suing for divorce."

Teddy put her forefingers to her eyes, stretching the skin so that her eyes became slitted.

"Right," Carella said. "You should have married a Chinese. But then, of course, you wouldn't be able to eat in Chinese restaurants." He paused and grinned. "All this eating talk is making me hungry. How about that place up the street?"

They walked to it rapidly, and Carella looked through the plate-glass window.

"Not too crowded," he said, "and it looks clean. You game?"

Teddy took his arm, and he led her into the place.

It was, perhaps, not the cleanest place in the world. As sharp as Carella's eyes were, a cursory glance through a plate-glass window is not always a good evaluation of cleanliness. And, perhaps, the reason it wasn't too crowded was that the food wasn't too good. Not that it mattered very much, since both Carella and Teddy were really very hungry and probably would have eaten sautéed grasshoppers if they were served.

The place did have nice checkered tablecloths and candles stuck into the necks of old wine bottles, the wax frozen to the glass. The place did have a long bar which ran the length of the wall opposite the dining room, bottles stacked behind it, amber lights illuminating the bottles. The place did have a phone booth, and Carella still had to make his call back to the squad.

The waiter who came over to their table seemed happy to see them.

"Something to drink before you order?" he asked.

"Two martinis," Carella said. "Olives."

"Would you care to see a menu now or later, sir?"

"Might as well look at it now," Carella said. The waiter brought them two menus. Carella glanced at his briefly and then put it down. "I'm bucking for a divorce," he said. "I'll have spaghetti."

While Teddy scanned the menu, Carella looked around the room. An elderly couple were quietly eating at a table near the phone booth. There was no one else in the dining room. At the bar, a man in a leather jacket sat with a shot glass and a glass of water before him. The man was looking into the bar mirror. His eyes were on Teddy.

Behind the bar, the bartender was mixing the martinis Carella had ordered.

"I'm so damn hungry I could eat the bartender," Carella said.

When the waiter came with their drinks, he ordered spaghetti for himself and then asked Teddy what she wanted. Teddy pointed to the lasagna dish on the menu, and Carella gave it to the waiter. When the waiter was gone, they picked up their glasses.

"Here's to ships that come in," Carella said.

Teddy stared at him, puzzled.

"All loaded with treasures from the East," he went on, "smelling of rich spices, with golden sails."

She was still staring at him, still puzzled.

"I'm drinking to you, darling," he explained. He watched the smile form on her mouth. "Poetic cops this city can do without," he said, and he sipped at the martini and then put the glass down. "I want to call the squad, honey. I'll be back in a minute." He touched her hand briefly, and then went toward the phone booth, digging in his pocket for change as he walked away from the table.

She watched him walk from her, pleased with the long athletic strides he took, pleased with the impatience of his hand as it dug for change, pleased with the way he held his head. She realized abruptly that one of the first things that had attracted her to Carella was the way he moved. There was an economy and simplicity of motion about him, a sense of directness. You got the feeling that before he moved he knew exactly where he was going and what he was going to do, and so there was a tremendous sense of security attached to being with him.

Teddy sipped at the martini and then took a long swallow. She had not eaten since noon, and so she was not surprised by the rapidity with which the martini worked its alcoholic wonders. She watched her husband enter the phone booth, watched as he dialed quickly. She wondered how he would speak to the desk sergeant and then to the detective who was catching in the squad room. Would they know he'd been talking of treasure ships just a few moments before? What kind of a cop was he? What did the other cops think of him? She felt a sudden exclusion. Faced with the impenetrable privacy which was any man's work, she felt alone and unwanted. Quickly, she drained the martini glass.

A shadow fell over the table.

At first she thought it was only a trick of her eyes, and then she looked up. The man who'd been sitting at the bar, the man in the leather jacket, was standing at the table, grinning.

"Hi," he said.

She glanced hastily at the phone booth. Carella had his back to the dining room.

"What're you doing with a creep like that?" the man said.

Teddy turned away from him and fastened her eyes to the napkin in her lap.

"You're just about the cutest doll that ever walked into this dump," the man in the leather jacket said. "Why don't you ditch that creep and meet me later. How about it?"

She could smell whiskey on the man's breath. There was something frightening about his eyes, something insulting about the way they roamed her body with open candor. She wished she were not wearing a sweater. Unconsciously, she pulled the cardigan closed over the jutting cones of her breasts.

"Come on," the man said, "don't cover them up."

She looked up at him and shook her head. Her eyes pleaded with him to go away. She glanced again to the phone booth. Carella was talking animatedly.

"My name's Dave," the man said. "That's a nice name, ain't it? Dave. What's your name?"

She could not answer him. She would not have answered him even if she could.

"Come on, loosen up," Dave said. He stared at her, and his eyes changed, and he said, "Jesus, you're beautiful, you know that? Ditch him, will you? Ditch him and meet me."

Teddy shook her head.

"Let me hear you talk," Dave said.

She shook her head again, pleadingly this time.

"I want to hear your voice. I'll bet it's the sexiest goddamn voice in the world. Let me hear it."

Teddy squeezed her eyes shut tightly. Her hands were trembling in her lap. She wanted this man to go away, wanted him to leave her alone, wanted him to be gone before Steve came out of that booth, before Steve came back to the table. She was slightly dizzy from the martini, and her mind could only think that Steve would be displeased, Steve might think she had invited this.

"Look, what do you have to be such a cold tomato for, huh? I'll bet you're not so cold. I'll bet you're pretty warm. Let me hear your voice."

She shook her head again, and then she saw Carella hang up the phone and open the door of the booth. He was grinning, and then he looked toward the table and the grin dropped from his mouth, and she felt a sudden sick panic at the pit of her stomach. Carella moved out of the booth quickly. His eyes had tightened into focus on the man with the leather jacket.

"Come on," Dave said, "what you got to be that way for, huh? All I'm asking . . ."

"What's the trouble, mister?" Carella said suddenly. She looked up at her husband, wanting him to know she had not asked for this, hoping it was in her eyes. Carella did not turn to look at her. His eyes were riveted to Dave's face.

"No trouble at all," Dave said, turning, facing Carella with an arrogant smile.

"You're annoying my wife," Carella said. "Take off."

"Oh, was I annoying her? Is the little lady your wife?" He spread his legs wide and let his arms dangle at his sides, and Carella knew instantly that he was looking for trouble and wouldn't be happy until he found it.

"You were, and she is," Carella said. "Go crawl back to the bar. It's been nice knowing you."

Dave continued smiling. "I ain't crawling back nowhere," he said. "This is a free country. I'm staying right here."

Carella shrugged and pulled out his chair. Dave continued standing by the table. Carella took Teddy's hand.

"Are you all right?" he asked.

Teddy nodded.

"Ain't that sweet?" Dave said. "Big handsome hubby comes back from . . ."

Carella dropped his wife's hand and stood suddenly. At the other end of the dining room, the elderly couple looked up from their meal.

"Mister," Carella said slowly, "you're bothering the hell out of me. You'd better . . ."

"Am I bothering you?" Dave said. "Hell, all I'm doing is admiring a nice piece of . . ." and Carella hit him.

He hit him suddenly with the full force of his arm and shoulder behind the blow. He hit him suddenly and full in the mouth, and Dave staggered back from the table and slammed into the next table, knocking the wine bottle candle to the floor. He leaned on the table for a moment, and when he looked up his mouth was bleeding, but he was still smiling.

"I was hoping you'd do that, pal," he said. He studied Carella for a moment, and then he lunged at him.

Teddy sat with her hands clenched in her lap, her face white. She saw her husband's face, and it was not the face of the man she knew and loved. The face was completely expressionless, the mouth a hard tight line that slashed it horizontally, the eyes narrowed so that the pupils were barely visible, the nostrils wide and flaring. He stood spread-legged with his fists balled, and she looked at his hands and they seemed bigger than they'd ever seemed before, big and powerful, lethal weapons which hung at his sides, waiting. His entire body seemed to be waiting. She could feel the coiled-spring tautness of him as he waited for Dave's rush, and he seemed like a smoothly functioning, well-oiled machine in that moment, a machine which would react automatically as soon as the right button was pushed, as soon as the right lever was pressed. There was nothing human about the machine. All humanity had left Steve Carella the moment his fist had lashed out at Dave. What Teddy saw now was a highly trained and a highly skilled technician about to do his work, waiting for the response buttons to be pushed.

Dave did not know he was fighting a machine. Ignorantly, he pushed out at the buttons.

Carella's left fist hit him in the gut, and he doubled over in pain and then Carella threw a flashing uppercut which caught Dave under the chin and sent him sprawling backward against the table again. Carella moved quickly and effortlessly, like a cue ball under the hands of an expert pool player, sinking one ball and then rolling to position for a good shot at the next ball. Before Dave clambered off the table, Carella was in position again, waiting.

When Teddy saw Dave pick up the wine bottle, her mouth opened in shocked anguish. But she knew somehow this did not come as a surprise to her husband. His eyes, his face did not change. He watched dispassionately while Dave hit the bottle against the table. The jagged shards of the bottle neck clutched in Dave's fist frightened her until she wanted to scream, until she wished she had a voice so that she could scream until her throat ached. She knew her husband would be cut, she knew that Dave was drunk enough to cut him, and she watched Dave advancing with the broken bottle, but Carella did not budge an inch, he stood there motionless, his body balanced on the balls of his feet, his right hand open, the fingers widespread, his left hand flat and stiff at his side.

Dave lunged with the broken bottle. He passed low, aiming for Carella's groin. A look of surprise crossed his face when he felt Carella's right hand clamp onto his wrist. He felt himself falling forward suddenly, pulled by Carella who had stepped back lightly on his right foot, and who was raising his left hand high over his head, the hand still stiff and rigid.

And then Carella's left hand descended. Hard and straight, like the sharp biting edge of an ax, it moved downward with remarkable swiftness. Dave felt the impact of the blow. The hard calloused edge of Carella's hand struck him on the side of his neck, and then Dave bellowed and Carella swung his left hand across his own body and again the hand fell, this time on the opposite side of Dave's neck, and he fell to the floor, both arms paralyzed for the moment, unable to move.

Carella stood over him, waiting.

"Lay . . . lay off," Dave said.

The waiter stood at the entrance to the dining room, his eyes wide. "Get the police," Carella said, his voice curiously toneless.

"But . . ." the waiter started.

"I'm a detective," Carella said. "Get the patrolman on the beat. Hurry up!"

"Yes," the waiter said. "Yes, sir."

Carella did not move from where he stood over Dave. He did not once look at Teddy. When the patrolman arrived, he showed his shield and told him to book Dave for disorderly conduct, generously neglecting to mention assault. He gave the patrolman all the information he needed, walked out with him to the squad car, was gone for some five minutes. When he came back to the table, the elderly couple had gone. Teddy sat staring at her napkin.

"Hi," he said, and he grinned.

She looked across the table at him.

"I'm sorry," he said. "I didn't want trouble."

She shook her head.

"He'll be better off locked up for the night. He'd only have picked on someone else, hon. He was spoiling for a fight." He paused. "The next guy he might have succeeded in cutting."

Teddy Carella nodded and sighed heavily. She had just had a visit to her husband's office and seen him at work. And she could still remember the terrible swiftness of his hands, hands which she had only known tenderly before.

And so she sighed heavily because she had just discovered the world was not populated with gentle little boys playing games.

And then she reached across the table, and she took his right hand and brought it to her mouth, and she kissed the knuckles, and she kissed the palm, and Carella was surprised to feel the wetness of her tears against his flesh.

To say that Charlie Chen was surprised to see Teddy Carella would be complete understatement.

The door to his shop had been closed, and he heard the small tinkle of the bell when the door opened, and he glanced up momentarily and then lifted his bulk from the chair in which he sat smoking and went to the front of the shop.

"Oh!" he said, and then his round face broke into a delighted grin. "Pretty detective lady come back," he said. "Charlie Chen is much honored. Charlie Chen is much flattered. Come, sit down, Mrs. . . ." He paused. "Charlie Chen forget name."

Teddy touched her lips with the tips of her fingers and then shook her head. Chen stared at her, uncomprehending. She repeated the gesture.

"You can't talk maybe?" he asked. "Laryngitis?"

Teddy smiled, shook her head, and then her hand traveled swiftly from her mouth to her ears, and Chen at last understood.

"Oh," he said. "Oh." His eyes clouded. "Very sorry, very sorry."

Teddy gave a slight shake of her head and a slight lift of her shoulders and a slight twist of her hands, explaining to Chen that there was nothing to be sorry for.

"But you understand me?" he asked. "You know what I say?"

Yes, she nodded.

"Good. You most beautiful lady ever come into Charlie Chen's poor shop. I speak this from my heart. Beauty is not plentiful in the world today. There is not much beauty. To see true beauty, this gladdens me. Makes me very happy, very happy. I talk too fast for you?"

Teddy shook her head.

"You read my lips?" He nodded appreciatively. "That very clever. Very clever. Why you come visit Charlie Chen?"

Teddy looped her thumbs together and then moved her hands as if they were in flight.

"The butterfly?" Chen asked, astounded. "You want the butterfly?"

Yes, she nodded, delighted by his response.

"Oh," he said, "ohhhhhh," as if her acknowledgment were the fulfillment of his wildest dream. "I make very pretty. I make big pretty butterfly."

Teddy shook her head.

"No big butterfly? Small butterfly?"

Yes.

"Ah, very clever, very clever. Delicate butterfly for pretty lady. Big butterfly no good. Small, little, pretty butterfly better. You very smart. You very beautiful, and you very smart. I do. Come. Come in. Please. Come in."

He parted the curtains leading to the back of the shop, and then gallantly bowed and stepped aside while Teddy passed through. She went directly to the butterfly design pinned to the wall. Chen smiled, and then seemed to notice for the first time the calendar with its naked woman on the other wall.

"Excuse other pretty lady, please," he said. "Stupid sons do."

Teddy glanced at the calender and smiled.

"You decide color?" Chen asked.

She nodded.

"Which?"

Teddy touched her hair.

"Black? Ah, good. Black very good. Little black butterfly. Come, sit. I do. No pain. Charlie Chen be very careful."

He sat her down, and she watched him, beginning to get a little frightened now. Deciding to get one's shoulder decorated was one thing. Going ahead with it was another thing again. She watched his movements as he walked around the shop preparing his tools. Her eyes were saucer wide.

"You frightened?" he asked.

She gave a very small nod.

"No be. Everything go hunky-dory. I promise. Very clean, very sanitary, very harmless." He smiled. "Very painless, too."

Teddy kept watching him, her heart in her mouth.

"I use very deep black. Black no good unless really black. Otherwise is gray. Life is all full of grays, pretty lady. No sharp whites, no sharp blacks. All grays. Very sad, life is." Chen brought a pencil and a sheet of paper to the table. He drew several circles on it, one the size of a dime, the next the size of a nickel, then the size of a quarter, and lastly the size of a half-dollar.

"Which size you want butterfly?" he asked.

Teddy studied the circles.

"Biggest one too big, no?" Chen asked.

Teddy nodded.

"Okay. We disintegrate." He made a large cross over the half-dollar circle.

"Littlest one too little, yes?" he asked.

Again, Teddy nodded.

"Poof!" Chen said, and he crossed out the dime-sized circle. "Which of these two?" he asked, pointing to the nickel and the quarter.

Teddy shrugged.

"I think bigger one, no? Then Charlie can do nice lace on wings. Too small, is difficult. Can do, but is difficult. Bigger one, we get nice effect, all lacy. Very pretty." He cocked his head to one side and extended his forefinger. "But not too big. Too big, no good." He nodded. "Most things in life too big. Gray, and too big. People forget blacks and whites, people forget little things. I tell you something."

Teddy watched him, wondering if he was talking to put her at ease, realizing at the same time that he was succeeding. The panic she had felt just a few moments earlier was rapidly dissolving.

"You want listen?" Chen asked.

Teddy nodded.

"I was married very pretty lady. Shanghai. You know Shanghai?"

Teddy nodded again.

"Very nice city, Shanghai. I was tattoo there, too. Very skill art in China, tattoo. I tattoo many people. Then I marry very pretty lady. Prettiest lady in all Shanghai. Prettiest lady in all China! She give me three sons. She make me very happy. Life blacks and whites with her. Sharp good contrast. Everything clear and bright. Everything clean. No grays. Big concern for little things. Very joyous, very happy," Chen was nodding, lost in his reminiscence. His eyes had glazed somewhat, and Teddy watched him, feeling a sadness in the man even before he spoke his next words.

"She die," he said. "Life very funny. Good things die early, bad ones never die. She die, life is gray again. Have three sons, but no laughter.

No more lights in Shanghai. No more people talking. No more happiness. Only empty Charlie Chen. Empty."

He paused, and she wanted to reach out to touch his hand, to comfort him.

"I come here America. Very good country. I have trade, tattoo." He wagged his head. "I get by, make living. Send oldest son to college, he not so stupid as I say. Younger ones good in school, too. I learn to live. Only one thing missing. Beauty. Very hard to find beauty." Chen smiled. "You bring beauty to my shop. I am very grateful. I do beautiful butterfly. My fingers wither and dry if I do not do beautiful butterfly. This I promise. I promise, too, no pain. This, too, I promise. You relax, yes? You unbutton blouse just a little, move off shoulder." He paused. "Which shoulder? Left or right? Very important to decide."

Teddy touched her left shoulder.

"Ah, no, butterfly on left shoulder bad omen. We do right, okay? You no mind? We put small pretty black lacy butterfly on right shoulder, okay?"

Teddy nodded. She unbuttoned the top button of her blouse, and then slipped the blouse off her shoulder.

Chen looked up from his needle suddenly.

The bell over his front door had just sounded.

Someone had entered the shop.

Chen may not have recognized the tall blond man were it not for the fact that Teddy Carella was in the back of his shop, waiting to be tattooed.

For whereas the handsome blond had been an impressive figure, Chen had only seen him once and that had been a long time ago. But now, with Teddy in the rear of the shop, with Chen keenly reminded of Teddy's relationship to a husband who was a cop, he recognized the blond man the instant he stepped through the beaded curtains to confront him.

"Yes?" he said, and he saw the man's face and, curiously, he automatically began thinking in Chinese. *This is the man the detective seeks*, he thought. *The husband of the beauty who now waits to be tattooed. This is the man.*

"Hello, there," Donaldson said. "We've got some work for you."

Chen's eyes fled to the girl beside Donaldson. She was not pretty. Her hair was a mousy brown, and her eyes were a faded brown, and she wore glasses, and she peered through the glasses, she was not pretty at all. She also looked a little sick. There was a tight drawn expression to her face, and her skin was pallid, she did not look good at all.

"What kind of work, please?" Chen asked.

"A tattoo," Donaldson said, smiling.

Chen nodded. "A tattoo for the gentleman, yessir," he said.

"No," Donaldson corrected, "a tattoo for the lady," and there was no longer the slightest doubt in Chen's mind. This was the man. A girl was dead, perhaps because of this man. Chen eyed him narrowly. This man was dangerous.

"You will sit down, please?" he asked. "I be with you in one minute."

"Hurry, won't you?" Donaldson said. "We haven't got much time."

"I be with you two shakes," Chen said, and he parted the curtains and moved quickly to the back of the shop. He walked directly to Teddy. She saw the anxiety on his face immediately. She gave him her complete attention at once. Something had happened, and Chen was very troubled.

In a whisper, he said, "Man here. One your husband wants. Do you understand?"

For a moment, she didn't understand. *Man here? One my husband . . . ?* And then the meaning became clear, and she felt a sudden chill at the base of her spine, felt her scalp begin to prickle.

"He here with girl," Chen said. "Want tattoo. You understand?"

She swallowed hard, and then she nodded.

"What I should do?" Chen asked.

"I . . . I don't feel too well," Priscilla Ames said.

"This won't take but a moment," Donaldson assured her.

"Chris, I really don't feel well. My stomach . . ." She shook her head. "Do you suppose that food was all right?"

"I'm sure it was, darling. Look, we'll get the tattoo, and then we'll stop for a bromo or something, all right? We have a long drive ahead, and I wouldn't want you to be sick."

"Chris, do we . . . do we have to get the tattoo? I feel awful. I've never felt like this before in my life."

"It'll pass, darling. Perhaps the food was a little too rich."

"Yes, it must have been something. Chris, I feel awful."

Carella opened the door to his apartment.

"Teddy?" he called, and then he realized that calling her name was useless if she could not see his lips. He closed the door behind him and walked into the living room. He took off his jacket, threw it onto one of the easy chairs, and then walked through to the kitchen.

The kitchen was empty.

Carella shrugged, went back to the living room, and then opened the door leading to their bedroom. Teddy wasn't in the bedroom, either.

He stood looking into the room for several moments, then he sighed, went into the living room again, and opened the window wide. He picked up the newspaper, kicked off his shoes, loosened his tie, and then sat down to read and wait for his wayward wife.

He was dog-tired.

In ten minutes, he was sound asleep in the easy chair.

"I adore you, Chris," Priscilla said, "and I want to do this for you, but I just . . . don't . . . feel well."

"You'll feel better in a little while," Donaldson said. He paused and smiled. "Would you like some chewing gum?" he asked pleasantly.

"Call him, would you, Chris? Please call him. Let's get this over with."

Call him, Teddy wrote on the sheet of paper under the circles Chen had drawn. *My husband, Detective Carella. Call him. FRederick 7-8024. Tell him.*

"Now?" Chen whispered.

Teddy nodded urgently. On the paper, she wrote, *You must keep that man here. You must not allow him to leave the shop.*

"The phone," Chen said. "The phone is out front. How I can call?"

"Hey there!" Donaldson said. "Are you coming out?"

The beaded curtains parted. Chen stepped through them. "Sorry, sir," he said. "Slight delay. Sit a moment, please. Must call friend."

"Can't that wait?" Donaldson asked. "We're in something of a hurry."

"No can wait, sir, sorry. Be with you one moment. Promised dear friend to call. Must do." He moved toward the phone quickly. Quickly, he dialed. FR7-8024. He waited. He could hear the phone ringing on the other end. Then . . .

"87th Precinct, Sergeant Murchison."

"I speak to Mr. Carella, please?" Chen said. Donaldson stood not three feet from him, impatiently toeing the floor. The girl sat in the chair opposite the phone, her head cradled in her hands.

"Just a second," the desk sergeant said. "I'll connect you with the Detective Division."

Chen listened to the clicking on the line.

A voice said, "87th Squad, Havilland speaking."

"Mr. Carella, please," Chen said.

"Carella's not here right now," Havilland said. "Can I help you?"

Chen looked at Donaldson. Donaldson looked at his watch. "The . . . ah . . . the tattoo design he wanted," Chen said. "Is in the shop now."

"Just a minute," Havilland said. "Let me take that down. Tattoo design he wanted, in shop now. Okay. Who's this, please?"

"Charlie Chen."

"Charlie Chan? What is this, a gag?"

"No, no. You tell Mr. Carella. You tell him call me back soon as he get there. Tell him I try to hold design."

"He may not even come back to the squad," Havilland said. "He's . . ."

"You tell him," Chen said. "Please."

"Okay," Havilland said, sighing. "I'll tell him."

"Thank you," Chen said, and he hung up.

Bert Kling walked over to Havilland's desk.

"Who was that?" he asked.

"Charlie Chan," Havilland said. "A crackpot."

"Oh," Kling said. He had half hoped it was Claire, even though he'd talked to her not five minutes earlier.

"Guys got nothing to do but bug police stations," Havilland said. "There ought to be a law against some of the calls we get!"

"Was your friend out?" Donaldson asked.

"Yes. He call me back. What kind tattoo you want?"

"A small heart with initials in it," Donaldson said.

"What initials?"

"P, A, C."

"Where you want heart?"

"On the young lady's hand." Donaldson smiled. "Right here between the thumb and forefinger."

"Very difficult to do," Chen said. "Hurt young lady."

Priscilla Ames looked up. "Chris," she said, "I . . . I don't feel well, honestly I don't. Couldn't we . . . couldn't we let this wait?"

Donaldson took one quick look at Priscilla. His face grew suddenly hard. "Yes," he said, "it will have to wait. Until another time. Come, Pris." He took her elbow, pulled her to her feet, held her arm in a firm grip. He turned to Chen. "Thank you," he said, "We'll have to go now."

"Can do now," Chen said desperately. "You sit lady down, I make tattoo. Do very pretty heart with initials. Very pretty."

"No," Donaldson said. "Not now."

Chen grabbed Donaldson's arm. "Take very quick. I do good job."

"Take your hand off me," Donaldson said, and he opened the door. The tinkle of the bell was loud in the small shop. The door slammed. Chen rushed into the back room.

"They go!" he said. "Can't keep them! They go!"

Teddy was buttoning her blouse. She scooped the pencil and paper from the tabletop and threw them into her bag.

"His name Chris," Chen said. "She call him Chris."

Teddy nodded and started for the door.

"Where you go?" Chen shouted. "Where you go?"

She turned and smiled at him fleetingly. Then the door slammed again, and she was gone.

Chen stood in the middle of his shop, listening to the reverberating tinkle of the bell.

"What I do now?" he said aloud.

She followed behind them closely. They were not easy to lose, he as tall as a giant, his blond hair catching the afternoon sunlight. She, unsteady on her feet, his arm circling her waist, holding her. She followed behind them closely, and she could feel her heart hammering inside her rib cage.

What do I do now? she wondered, but she kept following because this was the man her husband wanted.

When she saw them stop before an automobile, she suddenly lost heart. The chase seemed to be a futile one. He opened the door for the girl and helped her in, and Teddy watched as he walked to the other side of the car and then the taxicab appeared and she knew the chase was not over but that it was just beginning. She hailed the cab, and it pulled to the side of the curb, and the cabbie flicked open the rear door, and Teddy climbed in. He turned to face her and quickly she gestured to her ears and her mouth, and miraculously he understood her at once. She pointed through the windshield where Donaldson was just entering his car. She took a long hard look at the rear of the car.

"What, lady?" the cabbie asked.

Again, she pointed.

"You want me to follow him?" The cabbie watched Teddy nod, watched the door of Donaldson's car slam shut, and then watched as the sedan pulled away from the curb. The cabbie couldn't resist the crack.

"What happened, lady?" he asked. "That guy steal your voice?"

He gunned away from the curb, following Donaldson, and then he glanced over his shoulder to see if Teddy had appreciated his humor.

Teddy wasn't even looking at him.

She had taken Chen's pencil and paper from her purse and was scribbling furiously.

He hoped she would not die in the car.

It did not seem possible or likely that she would, but he planned ahead for the eventuality because if it happened he didn't want to be caught short. It would be difficult getting her out of the car. This had never happened to him before, and he felt a tenseness in his hands as he gripped the wheel and navigated the car through the afternoon traffic. He must not panic. Whatever happened, he must not panic. Things had gone too well up to now. Panic could throw everything out the window. Whatever happened, he had to keep a clear head. Whatever happened, there was too much at stake, too much to lose. He had to think clearly and coolly. He had to face each situation as it presented itself. He had to face it and handle it.

"I'm sick, Chris," Priscilla said. "I'm very sick."

You don't know just how sick, he thought. He kept his eyes on the road and his hands on the wheel. He did not answer her.

"Chris, I'm . . . I'm going to throw up."

"Can't you . . . ?"

"Please stop the car, Chris. I'm going to throw up."

"I can't stop the car," he said. He looked at her briefly, a side glance that took in the pale white face, the watery eyes. Roughly, he pulled a neatly folded white handkerchief from his breast pocket, thrusting it at her, "Use this," he said.

"Chris, can't you stop? Can't you please . . ."

"Use the handkerchief," he said, and there was something strange and new in his voice, and she was suddenly frightened. She could not think of her fright very long. In the next moment, she was violently ill and violently ashamed of herself for being ill.

"That guy's going to Riverhead," the cabbie said, turning to Teddy. "See, he's crossing the bridge. You sure you want me to follow him?"

Teddy nodded. Riverhead. She lived in Riverhead. She and Steve lived in Riverhead, but Riverhead was a big part of the city, where in Riverhead was the man taking the girl? And where was Steve? Was he at the squad? Was he home? Was he still out canvassing tattoo parlors? Was it possible he'd visit Charlie Chen again? She tore off a slip of paper, put it with the growing pile of slips beside her on the seat. Then she began writing again.

And then, as if to check the accuracy of her first observation, she looked at the rear of Donaldson's car again.

"Are you a writer or something?" the cabbie asked.

It bothered Kling.

He got up and walked to where Havilland was reading a true-detective magazine, his feet propped up on the desk.

"What'd you say that guy's name was?"

"What?" Havilland asked, looking up from the magazine. "Here's a case about a guy who cut up his victims. Put them in trunks."

"This guy who called for Steve," Kling said. "What'd you say his name was?"

"A crackpot. Sam Spade or something."

"Didn't you say Charlie Chan?"

"Yeah, Charlie Chan. A crackpot "

"What'd he say to you?"

48

"Said Carella's tattoo design was in the shop. Said he'd try to keep it there."

"Charlie Chen," Kling said thoughtfully. "Carella questioned him. Chen. He was the man who tattooed Mary Proschek." He thought again. Then he said, "What's his number?"

"He didn't leave any," Havilland said.

"It's probably in the book," Kling said, starting back for his own desk.

"The hell of this thing is that the cops didn't tip to this guy for three years," Havilland said, wagging his head. "Cutting up dames for three years, and they didn't tip." He wagged his head again. "Jesus, how could they be so stupid!"

"It looks like he's pulling over, lady," the cabbie said. "You want I should pull in right behind him?"

Teddy shook her head.

The cabbie sighed. "So where, then? Right here okay?" Teddy nodded. The cabbie pulled in and stopped his meter. Up ahead, Donaldson had parked and was helping Priscilla from the car. Teddy watched them as she fished in her purse for money to pay the cabbie. She paid him, and then she scooped up the pile of paper slips from the seat beside her. She handed one to the cabbie, stepped out, and began running because Donaldson and Priscilla had just turned the corner.

"What . . . ?" the cabbie said, but his fare was gone.

He looked at the narrow slip of paper. In a hurried hand, Teddy had written:

Call Detective Steve Carella, FRederick 7-8024. Tell him license number is DN1556. Hurry, please!

The cabbie stared at the note.

He sighed heavily.

"Women writers!" he said aloud, and he crumpled the slip, threw it out the window, and gunned away from the curb.

Kling found the number in the yellow pages. He asked the desk sergeant for a line, and then he dialed.

He could hear the phone ringing on the other end. Methodically, he began counting the rings.

Three . . . four . . . five . . .

Kling waited.

Six . . . seven . . . eight . . .

Come on, Chen, he thought. *Answer the damn thing!*

And then he remembered the message Chen had given Havilland. *He would try to keep the tattoo design in the shop.* Jesus, had something happened to Chen?

He hung up on the tenth ring.

"I'm checking out a car," he shouted to Havilland. "I'll be back later."

Havilland looked up from his magazine. "What?" he asked.

But Kling was already through the gate in the slatted railing and heading for the steps leading to the first floor.

Besides, the phone on Havilland's desk was ringing.

Chen was walking away from the shop when he heard the telephone. He had left the shop a moment earlier, fired with the decision to go directly to the 87th Precinct, find Carella, and tell him what had happened. He had locked up, and was walking toward his car when the telephone began ringing.

Perhaps there is no difference in the way a telephone rings. It does not ring differently for sweethearts making lover's calls, it does not ring differently when it carries bad news, or when it carries news of a big deal being closed.

Chen was in a hurry. He had to see Carella, had to talk to him.

So perhaps the ring of the telephone in his closed and locked shop was not really so urgent. Perhaps it did not really sound so terribly important. It was, after all, only a telephone ring.

It was, nonetheless, urgent-sounding enough to pull him back from the curb and over to the locked door. It sounded urgent enough to force him to reach for his keys rapidly, find the right key, shove it into the hanging padlock, snap open the lock, and then throw open the door and rush to the phone.

It sounded urgent as hell until it stopped ringing.

By the time Chen lifted the receiver, all he got was a dial tone.

And since he had a dial tone, he used it.

He called FRederick 7-8024.

"87th Precinct, Sergeant Murchison," the voice said.

"Detective Carella, please," Chen said.

"Second," the desk sergeant answered. Chen waited. He was right, then. Carella was back. He listened to the clicking on the line.

"87th Squad, Detective Havilland," Havilland said.

"I speak to Detective Carella, please?"

"Not here," Havilland said. "Who's this?" From the corner of his eye, he saw Kling disappear into the stairwell leading to the first floor.

"Charlie Chen. When he be back?"

"Just a second," Havilland said. He covered the mouthpiece. "Hey, Bert!" he shouted. "Bert!" There was no answer from the stairwell. Into the phone, Havilland said, "I'm a cop, too, mister. What's on your mind?"

"Man who tattoo girl," Chen said. "He was here shop. With Mrs. Carella."

"Slow down," Havilland said. "What man? What girl?"

"Carella knows," Chen said. "Tell him man's name is Chris. Big blond man. Tell him wife follows. When he be back? Don't you know when he be back?"

"Listen . . ." Havilland started, and Chen impatiently said, "I come. I come tell him. You ask him wait."

"He may not even . . ." Havilland said, but he was talking to a dead line.

The girl was bent over double, the handkerchief pressed to her mouth. The tall blond man kept his arm around her waist, holding her up, half walking her, half dragging her down the street.

Behind them, Teddy followed.

She knew very little about con men.

She knew, though, that you could stand on a corner and offer to sell five-dollar gold pieces for ten cents, and you wouldn't get a buyer all day. She knew that the city was an inherently distrustful place, that strangers did not talk to strangers in restaurants, that people somehow did not trust people.

And so she had taken out insurance.

If she had a tongue, she'd have shouted her message.

She could not speak, and so she'd taken insurance that would shout her message, a dozen narrow slips of paper, with the identical message on each slip:

Call Detective Carella, FRederick 7-8024. Tell him license number is DN1556. Hurry, please!

And now, as she followed along behind Donaldson and the girl, she began to shout her message. She could not linger long with each passerby because she could not afford to lose sight of the pair. She could only touch the sleeve of an old man and hand him the paper, and then walk off. She could only gently press the slip into the hand of a matron in a gray dress, and leave her puzzled and somewhat amused. She could only stop a teenager, avoid the open invitation in his eyes, and hand him the message. She left behind her a trail of people with a scrap of paper in their hands. She hoped that one of them would call the 87th. She hoped the license number would reach her husband. In the meantime, she followed a sick girl and a killer, and she didn't know what she would do if her husband didn't reach her, if her husband didn't somehow reach her.

"Sick . . . I . . ." Priscilla Ames could barely speak. She clung to the reassurance of his arm around her waist, and she staggered along the street with him, wondering where he was taking her, wondering why she was so deathly ill.

"Listen to me," he said. There was a hard edge to his voice. He was breathing heavily, and she did not recognize his voice. Her throat burned, and she could only think of the churning in her stomach, why should she be so sick, why, why, "I'm talking to you, do you hear me?" she'd never been sick in her life, never a day's serious illness, why then this sudden "Goddamnit, listen to me! You start throwing up again, I swear to Christ I'll leave you here in the gutter!"

"Wh . . . wh . . ." She swallowed. She was ashamed of herself, the food, it must have been the food, that and the fear of the needle, he shouldn't have asked her to be tattooed, always afraid of needles . . .

"It's the next house," he said, "the big apartment house. I'm taking you in the back way. We'll use the service elevator. I don't want anyone to see you like this. Do you hear me? Can you understand me?"

She nodded, swallowing hard, wondering why he was telling her all this, squeezing her eyes shut tightly, knowing only excruciating pain, feeling weak all over, suddenly so very weak, my purse, my purse, Chris, I've . . .

She stopped.

She gestured limply with one hand

"What is it?" he snapped. "What . . . ?" His eyes followed her gesture. He saw her purse where she'd dropped it to the sidewalk. "Oh, goddamnit," he said, and he braced her with one arm and stooped, half turning, for the purse.

He saw the pretty brunette then.

She was not more than fifty feet behind them, and when he stooped to pick up the purse, the girl stopped, stared at him for a moment, and then quickly turned away to look into one of the store windows.

Slowly, he picked up the purse, his eyes narrowed with thought. He began walking again.

Behind him, he could hear the clatter of the girl's heels.

"87th Precinct, Sergeant Murchison."

"Detective Carella, please," the young voice said.

"He's not here right now," Murchison answered. "Talk to anyone else?"

"The note said Carella," the young voice said.

"What note, son?"

"Aw, never mind," the boy replied. "It's probably a gag."

"Well, what . . . ?"

The line went dead.

A fly was buzzing around the nose of Steve Carella. Carella swatted at it in his sleep.

The fly zoomed up toward the ceiling, and then swooped down again. Sssssszzzzzzzzz. It landed on Carella's ear.

Still sleeping, Carella brushed at it.

* * *

"87th Precinct, Sergeant Murchison."

"Is there a Detective Carella there?" the voice asked.

"Just a minute," Murchison said. He plugged into the bull's wire. Havilland picked up the phone.

"87th Detective Squad, Havilland," he said.

"Rog, this is Dave," Murchison said. "Has Carella come back yet?"

"Nope," Havilland said.

"I've got another call for him. You want to take it?"

"I'm busy," Havilland said.

"Doing what? Picking your nose?"

"All right, give me the call," Havilland said, putting down the magazine and the story about the trunk murderer.

"Here's the Detective Division," he heard Murchison say.

"This is Detective Havilland," Havilland said. "Can I help you?"

"Some dame handed me a note," the voice said.

"Yeah?"

"Said to call Detective Carella and tell him the license number is DN1556. Is this on the level? Is there really a Carella?"

"Yeah," Havilland said. "What was that number again?"

"What?"

"The license number."

"Oh. DN1556. What's it all about?"

"Mister," Havilland said, "your guess is as good as mine. Thanks for calling."

Kling sat in the squad car alongside the patrolman.

"Can't you make this thing go any faster?" he asked.

"I'm sorry, *sir*," the patrolman said with broad sarcasm, somewhat miffed with the knowledge that not too many months ago Kling had been a patrolman, too. "I wouldn't want to get a speeding ticket."

Kling studied the patrolman with an implacable eye. "Put on your goddamn siren," he said harshly, "and get this thing to Chinatown or your ass is going to be in a great big sling!"

The patrolman blinked.

The squad car's siren suddenly erupted. The patrolman's foot came down onto the accelerator.

Kling leaned forward, staring through the windshield.

Charlie Chen leaned forward, staring through the windshield.

He did not like to drive in city traffic.

Doggedly, he headed uptown.

When he heard the siren, he thought it was a fire engine, and he started to pull over to his right.

Then he saw that it was a police car, and not even on his side of the avenue. The police car sped by him, heading downtown, its siren blaring.

It strengthened Chen's resolve. He gritted his teeth, leaned over the wheel, and stepped on the accelerator more firmly.

Carella swatted at the fly, and then sat upright in his chair, suddenly wide awake. He blinked.

The apartment was very silent.

He stood and yawned. What the hell time was it, anyway? Where the hell was Teddy? He looked at his watch. She was usually home by this time, preparing dinner. Had she left a note? He yawned again and began looking through the apartment for a note.

He could find none. He looked at his watch again, then he went to his jacket and fished for his cigarettes. He reached into the package. It was empty. His fingers explored the sides. It was still empty.

Wearily, he sat down and put on his shoes.

He took his pad from his back pocket, slid the pencil out from under the leather loop, and wrote, *"Dear Teddy: I've gone down for some cigarettes. Be right back. Steve."* He propped the note on the kitchen table. Then he went into the bathroom to wash his face.

"87th Squad, Detective Havilland."

"I wanted Carella," the woman's voice said.

"He's out," Havilland said.

"A young lady stopped me and gave me a note," the woman said. "I really don't know whether or not it's serious, but I felt I should call. May I read the note to you?"

"Please do," Havilland said.

"It says, *'Call Detective Steve Carella, FRederick 7-8024. Tell him license number is DN1556. Hurry, please!'* Does that mean anything?"

"You say a young lady gave this to you?" Havilland asked.

"Yes, a quite beautiful young lady. Dark hair and dark eyes. She seemed rather in a hurry herself."

For the first time that afternoon, Havilland forgot his trunk murderer. He remembered instead that the Chinaman who'd called had said, "Man who tattoo girl. He was here shop. With Mrs. Carella."

And now a girl who answered the description of Steve's wife was going around handing out messages. That made sense. Carella's wife was a deaf-mute.

"I'll get on it right away," Havilland said. "Thanks for calling."

He hung up, consulted his list of numbers, and then dialed the Bureau of Motor Vehicles. He gave them the license number and asked them to check it. Then he hung up and looked up another number.

He was dialing Steve Carella's home when Charlie Chen walked down the corridor and came to a breathless stop outside the slatted rail divider.

Carella put on his jacket.

He went into the kitchen again to check the note and then, because he was there, he checked the handles on the gas range, to make sure all the jets were out.

He walked out of the kitchen and into the living room and then to the front door. He was in the corridor and closing the door behind him when the telephone rang. He cursed mildly, went to the phone, and lifted the receiver.

"Hello?" he said.

"Steve?"

"Yeah."

"Rog Havilland."

"What's up, Rog?"

"Got a man here named Charlie Chen who says your killer was in his shop this afternoon. Teddy was there at the time, and . . ."

"What!"

"Teddy. Your wife. She trailed the guy when he left. Chen says the girl with him was very sick. I've gotten half a dozen phone calls in the past half hour. Girl who answers Teddy's description has been handing out notes asking people to call you with a license number. I've got the MVB checking it now. What do you think?"

"Teddy!" Carella said, and that was all he could think. He heard a phone ringing someplace, and then Havilland said, "There's the other line going now. Might be the license information. Hold on, Steve."

He heard the click as the "hold" button was pressed, and he waited, squeezing the plastic of the phone, thinking over and over again, *Teddy, Teddy, Teddy.*

Havilland came back on in a minute.

"It's a black 1955 Cadillac hardtop," Havilland said. "Registered to a guy named Chris Donaldson."

"That's the bird," Carella said, his mind beginning to function again. "What address have you got for him?"

"4118 Ranier. That's in Riverhead."

"That's about ten minutes from here," Carella said. "I'm starting now. Get a call in to whichever precinct owns that street. Get an ambulance going, too. If that girl is sick, it's probably from arsenic."

"Right," Havilland said. "Anything else, Steve?"

"Yeah. Start praying he hasn't spotted my wife!"

He hung up, slapped his hip pocket to make sure he still had his .38, and then left the apartment without closing the door.

* * *

Standing in the concrete and cinder block basement of the building, Teddy watched the indicator needle of the service elevator. She could see the washing machines going in another part of the basement, and beyond that she could feel the steady thrum of the apartment building's oil burner, and she watched the needle as it moved numeral to numeral and then stopped at 4.

She pressed the "down" button.

Donaldson and the girl had entered that service elevator and had got off at the fourth floor. And now, as the elevator dropped to the basement again, Teddy wondered what she would do when she discovered what apartment he was in, wondered, too, just how sick the girl was, just how much time she had. The elevator door slid open.

Teddy got in, pressed the number 4 in the panel. The door slid shut. The elevator began its climb. Oddly, she felt no fear, no apprehension. She wished only that Steve were with her, because Steve would know what to do. The elevator climbed and then shuddered to a stop. The door slid open. She started out of the car, and then she saw Donaldson.

He was standing just outside the elevator, waiting for the door to open, waiting for her. In blind panic, she jabbed her palm at the floor buttons. Donaldson's arm lashed out. His fingers clamped on her wrist, and he pulled her out of the car.

"Why are you following me?" he asked.

She shook her head dumbly. Donaldson was pulling her down the hallway. He stopped before apartment 4C, threw open the door, and then shoved her into the apartment. Priscilla Ames was lying on the couch facedown. The apartment smelled of human waste.

"There she is," Donaldson said. "Is that who you're looking for?"

He snatched Teddy's purse from her hands and began going through it, scattering lipstick, change, mascara, address book onto the floor. When he came upon her wallet, he unsnapped it and went through it quickly.

"Mrs. Stephen Carella," he read from the identification card. "Resident of Riverhead, eh? So we're neighbors. Meet Miss Ames, Mrs. Carella. Or have you already met?" He looked at the card again. "In case of emergency, call . . ." His voice stopped. Then, like the slow trickle of a faulty water spout, it came on again. "Detective Steve Carella, 87th Precinct, FRederick 7-802 . . ." He looked up at Teddy. "Your husband's a cop, huh?"

Teddy nodded.

"What's the matter? Too scared to speak?" He studied her again. "I said . . ." He stopped, watching her. "Is something wrong with your voice?"

Teddy nodded.

"What is it? Can you talk?"

She shook her head. Her eyes lingered on his mouth, and following her gaze he suddenly knew.

"Are you deaf?" he asked.

Teddy nodded.

"Good," Donaldson said flatly. He was silent again, watching her. "Did your husband put you up to following me?"

Teddy made no motion, no gesture. She stood as silent as a stone.

"Does he know about me?"

Again no answer.

"Why were you following me?" Donaldson asked, moving closer to her. "Who put you on to me? Where'd I slip up?" He took her wrist. "Answer me, goddamnit!"

His fingers were tight on her wrist. On the couch, Priscilla Ames moaned weakly. He turned abruptly.

"She's been poisoned, you know that, don't you?" he said to Teddy. "*I* poisoned her. She'll be dead in a little while, and tonight she goes into the river." He saw Teddy's involuntary shudder. "What's the matter? Does that frighten you? Don't be frightened. She's in pain, but she hardly knows what the hell's happening anymore. All she can think about right now is her own sickness. Christ, it smells vile in here! How can you stand it?" He laughed a short harsh laugh. The laugh was over almost before it began. His voice grew hard again. There was no compromise in it now. "What does your husband know?" he asked. *"What does your husband know?"*

Teddy made no motion. Her face remained expressionless.

Donaldson watched her. "All right," he said. "I'll assume the worst. I'll assume he's headed here right now with a whole damn battalion of police. Okay?"

Again, there was nothing on Teddy's face, nothing in her eyes.

"He won't find a damn thing when he gets here. I'll be gone, and Miss Ames'll be gone, and you'll be gone. He'll find the four walls." He went to the closet, opened it quickly, and pulled out a suitcase. "Come with me," he said. He shoved Teddy ahead of him, into the bedroom. "Sit down," he said. "On the bed. Hurry up."

Teddy sat.

Donaldson went to the dresser, threw open the top drawer. He began shoveling clothes into the suitcase. "You're a pretty one," he said. "If I came onto something like you . . ." He didn't complete the sentence. "The trouble with my business is that you can't enjoy yourself," he said vaguely. "Plain girls are good. They buy whatever you sell. Get involved with a beauty, and your secret's in danger. Murder is a big secret, don't you think? It pays well, too. Don't let anyone tell you crime doesn't pay. It pays excellently. If you don't get caught." He grinned. "I have no intention of getting caught." He looked at her again. "You're a pretty one. And you can't talk. A secret could be told to you." He shook his head. "It's too bad we haven't got more time." He shook his head again. "You're a pretty one," he repeated.

Teddy sat on the bed, motionless.

"You must know how it is," he said. "Being good-looking. It's a pain sometimes, isn't it? Men get to hate you, distrust you. Me, I mean. They don't like a man who's too good-looking. Makes them feel uncomfortable. Too much virility for them. Points up their own petty quarrels with the world, makes them feel inadequate." He paused. "I can get any girl I want, do you know that? Any girl. I just flutter my lashes, they fall down dead." He chuckled. "Dead. That's a laugh, isn't it? You must know, I guess. Men fall all over you, don't they?" He looked at her questioningly. "Okay, sit there in your shell. You're coming with me, you know that, don't you? You're my insurance." He laughed again. "We'll make a good couple. We'll really give the spectators something to ogle. We offset each other. Blond and brunette. That's very good. It won't be bad, being seen with a pretty girl for a change. I get tired of these goddamn witches. But they pay well. I've got a nice bank balance."

On the couch, Priscilla Ames moaned. Donaldson went to the doorway and looked into the living room. "Relax, lover," he called. "In a little while, you'll go for a nice refreshing swim." He burst out laughing and turned to Teddy. "Nice girl," he said. "Ugly as sin. Nice." He went back to packing the bag, silent now, working rapidly. Teddy watched him. He had not packed a gun, so perhaps he didn't own one.

"You'll help me downstairs with her," he said suddenly. "The service elevator again. In and out, and whoosh, we're on our way. You'll stay with me for a while. You can't talk, that's good. No phone calls, no idle gossip to waiters, good, good. Just have to keep you away from pen and paper, I guess, huh?" He studied her again, his eyes changing. "Be good to have a ball for a change," he said. "I get so goddamn tired of these witches, and you can't trust the beauties. If you want to know something, you can't trust *any*body. The world is full of con men. But we'll have a ball." He looked at her face. "Don't like the idea, huh? That's rough. It'll make it more interesting. You should consider yourself lucky. You *could* be scheduled for a swim with Miss Ames, you know. You should consider yourself lucky. Most women fall down when I come into a room. Consider yourself lucky. I'm pleasant company, and I know the nicest places in town. That's my business, you know. My avocation. I'm really an accountant. Actually, *accounting* is my avocation, I suppose. Women are my business. The lonely ones. The plain Janes. You're a surprise. I'm glad you followed me." He grinned boyishly. "Nice having somebody to talk to who doesn't talk back. That's the secret of the Catholic confession, and also the secret of psychoanalysis. You can tell the truth and the worst that'll happen to you is twelve Hail Marys or the discovery that you hate your mother. With you, there's no punishment. I can talk, and you can listen, and I don't have to spout the love phrases or the undying bliss bit. You look sexy, too. Still water. Deep, deep."

He heard the sudden sharp snap of the front door lock. He whirled quickly and ran into the living room.

Carella saw a blond giant appear in the doorframe, eyes alert, fists clenched. The giant took in the .38 in Carella's fist, took in the unwavering glint in Carella's eye, and then lunged across the room.

Carella was no fool. This man was a powerhouse. This man could rip him in two.

Steadily, calmly, Carella leveled the .38.

And then he fired.

The working day was over.

There was May mixed in the April air. It touched the cheeks mildly, it lingered on the mouth. Carella walked and drank of it, and the draught was heady.

When he opened the door to his apartment, he was greeted with silence. He turned out the light in the living room and went into the bedroom.

Teddy was asleep.

He undressed quietly and then got into bed beside her. She wore a fluffy white gown, and he lowered the strap of the gown from her right shoulder and kissed the warm flesh there. A cloud passed from the moon, filling the room with pale silver. Carella moved back from his wife's shoulder and blinked. He blinked again.

"I'll be goddamned!" he said.

The April moonlight illuminated a small, lacy black butterfly on Teddy's shoulder.

"I'll be goddamned!" Carella said again, and he kissed her so hard that she woke up.

And, big detective that he was, he never once suspected she'd been awake all the while.

The Con Man, 1957

Carella was nervous.

Sitting alongside Teddy, he could feel nervousness ticking along the backs of his hands, twitching in his fingers. Clean-shaved, his high cheekbones and downward-slanting eyes giving him an almost Oriental appearance, he sat with his mouth tensed, and the doctor smiled gently.

"Well, Mr. Carella," Dr. Randolph said, "your wife is going to have a baby."

The nervousness fled almost instantly. The cork had been pulled, and the violent waters of his tension overran the tenuous walls of the dike, leaving only the muddy silt of uncertainty. If anything, the uncertainty was worse. He hoped it did not show. He did not want it to show to Teddy.

"Mr. Carella," the doctor said, "I can see the prenatal jitters erupting all over you. Relax. There's nothing to worry about."

Carella nodded, but even the nod lacked conviction. He could feel the presence of Teddy beside him, his Teddy, his Theodora, the girl he loved, the woman he'd married, her brown eyes gleaming with pride now, the silent red lips slightly parted.

I mustn't spoil it for her, he thought.

And yet he could not shake the doubt.

"May I reassure you on several points, Mr. Carella?" Randolph said.

"Well, I really . . ."

"Perhaps you're worried about the infant. Perhaps, becuse your wife is a deaf-mute, born that way . . . perhaps you feel the infant may also be born handicapped. This is a reasonable fear, Mr. Carella."

"I . . ."

"But a completely unfounded one." Randolph smiled. "Medicine is in many respects a cistern of ignorance—but we *do* know that deafness, though sometimes congenital, is not hereditary. For example, perfectly normal offspring have been produced by *two* deaf parents. Lon Chaney is the most famous of these offspring, I suppose. With the proper care and treatment, your wife will go through a normal pregnancy and deliver a normal baby. She's a healthy animal, Mr. Carella. And if I may be so bold, a very beautiful one."

Teddy, reading the doctor's lips, came close to blushing. Her beauty, like a rare rose garden which a horticulturist has come to take for granted, was a thing she'd accepted for a long time now. It always came as a surprise, therefore, when someone referred to it in glowing terms. These were the face and the body with which she had been living for a good many years. She could not have been less concerned over whether or not they pleased the strangers of the world. She wanted them to please one person alone: Steve Carella. Now, with

Steve's acceptance of the idea coupling with her own thrilled anticipation, she felt a soaring sense of joy.

"Thank you, Doctor," Carella said.

"Not at all," Randolph answered. "Good luck to you both. I'll want to see you in a few weeks, Mrs. Carella. Now take care of her."

"I will," Carella answered, and they left the obstetrician's office. In the corridor outside, Teddy threw herself into his arms and kissed him violently.

"Hey!" he said. "Is that any way for a pregnant woman to behave?"

Teddy nodded, her eyes glowing mischievously. With one sharp twist of her dark head, she gestured toward the elevators.

"You want to go home, huh?"

She nodded.

"And then what?"

Teddy was eloquently silent.

"It'll have to wait," he said. "There's a little suicide I'm supposed to be covering."

He pressed the button for the elevator.

"I behaved like a jerk, didn't I?"

Teddy shook her head.

"I did. I was worried. About you, and about the baby . . ." He paused. "But I've got an idea. First of all, to show my appreciation for the most wonderfully fertile and productive wife in the city . . ."

Teddy grinned.

". . . I would like us both to have a drink. We'll drink to you and the baby, darling." He took her into his arms. "You because I love you so much. And the baby because he's going to share our love." He kissed the tip of her nose. "And then off to my suicide. But is that all? Not by a long shot. This is a day to remember. This is the day the most beautiful woman in the United States, nope, the world, hell, the universe, discovered she was going to have a baby! So . . ." He looked at his watch. "I should be back at the squad room by about seven, latest. Will you meet me there? I'll have to do a report, and then we'll go out to dinner, some quiet place where I can hold your hand and lean over to kiss you whenever I want to. Okay? At seven?"

Teddy nodded happily.

"And then home. And then . . . is it decent to make love to a pregnant woman?"

Teddy nodded emphatically, indicating that it was not only decent but perfectly acceptable and moral and absolutely necessary.

"I love you," Carella said gruffly. "Do you know that?"

She knew it. She did not say a word. She would not have said a word even if she could have. She looked at him, and her eyes were moist, and he said, "I love you more than life."

Killer's Wedge, 1959

Carella blinked at the early Sunday morning sunshine, cursed himself for not having closed the blinds the night before, and then rolled over onto his left side. Relentlessly, the sunlight followed him, throwing alternating bars of black and gold across the white sheet. Like the detention cells at the 87th, he thought. God, my bed has become a prison.

No, that isn't fair, he thought. And besides, it'll all be over soon—but Teddy, I wish to hell you'd hurry.

He propped himself on one elbow and looked at his sleeping wife. Teddy, he thought. Theodora. Whom I used to call my *little* Theodora. How you have changed, my love. He studied her face, framed with short black hair recklessly cushioned against the stark-white pillow. Her eyes were closed, thick-fringed with long black lashes. There was a faint smile on the full pout of her lips. Her throat swept in an immaculate arc to breasts covered by the sheet—and then the mountain began.

Really, darling, he thought, you do look like a mountain.

It is amazing how much you resemble a mountain. A very beautiful mountain, to be sure, but a mountain nonetheless. I wish I were a mountain climber. I wish, honey, oh how I wish I could get *near* you! How long has it been now? Cut it out, Steve-o, he told himself. Just cut it out because this sort of erotic rambling doesn't do anyone a damn bit of good, least of all me.

Steve Carella, the celebrated celibate.

Well, he thought, the baby is due at the end of the month, by God, that's next week! Is it the end of June already? Sure it is, my how the time flies when you've got nothing to do in bed but sleep. I wonder if it'll be a boy. Well, a girl would be nice, too, but oh would Papa raise a stink, he'd probably consider it a blot on Italy's honor if his only son Steve had a girl child first time out.

What were those names we discussed?

Mark if it's a boy and April if it's a girl. And Papa will raise a stink about the names, too, because he's probably got something like Rodolfo or Serafina in mind. Stefano Luigi Carella, that's me, and thank you, Pop.

Today is the wedding, he thought suddenly, and that makes me the most inconsiderate big brother in the world because all I can think of is my own libido when my kid sister is about to take the plunge. Well, if I know Angela, the prime concern on her mind today is probably *her* libido, so we're even.

The telephone rang.

It startled him for a moment, and he turned sharply toward Teddy, forgetting, thinking the sudden ringing would awaken her, and then remembering that his wife was immune to little civilized annoyances like the telephone.

"I'm coming," he said to the persistent clamor. He swung his long legs over the side of the bed. He was a tall man with wide shoulders and narrow hips, his pajama trousers taut over a flat hard abdomen. Bare-chested and barefoot, he walked to the phone in nonchalant athletic ease, lifted the receiver, and hoped the call was not from the precinct. His mother would have a fit if he missed the wedding.

"Hello?" he said.

"Steve?"

"Yes. Who's this?"

"Tommy. Did I wake you?"

"No, no, I was awake." He paused. "How's the imminent bride-groom this morning?"

"I . . . Steve, I'm worried about something."

"Uh-oh," Carella said. "You're not planning on leaving my sister waiting at the altar, are you?"

"No, nothing like that. Steve, could you come over here?"

"Before we go to the church, you mean?"

"No. No. I mean now."

"Now?" Carella paused. A frown crossed his face. In his years with the police department, he had heard many anxious voices on the telephone. He had attributed the tone of Tommy's voice to the normal preconjugal jitters at first, but he sensed now that this was something more. "What is it?" he asked. "What's the matter?"

"I . . . I don't want to talk about it on the phone. Can you come over?"

"I'll be right there," he said, "As soon as I dress."

"Thank you, Steve," Tommy said, and he hung up.

Carella cradled the phone. He stared at it thoughtfully for a moment, and then went into the bathroom to wash. When he came back into the bedroom, he tilted the blinds shut so that the sunshine would not disturb his sleeping wife. He dressed and wrote a note for her and then—just before he left—he caressed her breast with longing tenderness, sighed, and propped the note up against his pillow. She was still sleeping when he went out of the apartment.

Teddy sat at the table alongside the bride's table, sipping disconsolately at a Manhattan, watching her husband cavort in the arms of a redheaded sexpot from Flemington, New Jersey.

This is not fair, she thought angrily. There is no competition here. I don't know who that damn girl is, or what she wants—although what she wants seems pretty apparent—but I do know that she is svelte and trim and wearing a dress designed for a size 8. Since she is at least a

63

10, and possibly a 12, the odds are stacked against me to begin with. I am at least a size 54 right now. When will this baby come? Next week, did the doctor say? Yes, next week. Next week and four thousand years from now. I've been big forever. I hope it's a boy. Mark if it's a boy. Mark Carella. That's a good name.

Steve, you don't have to hold her so damn close!

I mean, *really*, goddamnit!

And April if it's a girl.

I wonder if I should faint or something. That would bring him back to the table in a hurry, all right. Although I can't really say that *he's* holding her close because *she* seems to be doing all the holding. But I guess holding works both ways, and don't think this has been easy on me, Steve, my pet, and you really needn't . . . Steve! If your hand moves another inch, I am going to crown you with a champagne bottle!

A boy or a girl, the baby was kicking up a storm.

Sitting with her father-in-law, who had surely had too much to drink, Teddy could not remember the heir apparent ever having raised such a fuss.

It was difficult for her to appreciate the oncoming dusk with her son- or daughter-to-be doing his early evening calisthenics. Every now and then the baby would kick her sharply, and she'd start from the sudden blow, certain that everyone at the reception was witnessing her wriggling fidgets. The baby seemed to have a thousand feet, God forbid! He kicked her high on the belly, close under her breasts, and then he kicked her again, lower in the pelvic region, and she was sure he'd turned a somersault, so widely diverse had the kicks been.

It'll be over next week, she thought, and she sighed. No more backaches. No more children pointing fingers at me in the street. *Hey, lady, what time does the balloon go up?* Ha-ha, very funny. She glanced across the dance floor. The redhead from Teaneck or Gowanus or wherever had latched onto a new male, but it hadn't helped Teddy very much. Steve hadn't been anywhere near her for the past few hours, and she wondered now what it was that could possibly be keeping him so occupied. Of course, it was his sister's wedding, and she supposed he was duty bound to play the semi-host. But why had Tommy called him so early this morning? And what were Bert and Cotton doing here? With the instincts of a cop's wife, she knew that something was in the wind—but she didn't know quite what.

The baby kicked her again.

Damn, she thought, I do wish you'd stop that.

"Steve! Steve!"

He hesitated, one foot inside the car, the other on the pavement.

"What is it, Mama?"

"Teddy! It's Teddy! It's her time!"

"What?"

"Her time! The baby, Steve!"

"But the baby isn't due until next—"

"It's her time!" Louisa Carella said firmly. "Get her to the hospital!"

Carella slammed the car door shut. He thrust his head through the open window and shouted, "Bert! My wife's gonna have a baby!" and he ran like hell up the path to the house.

"Can't you drive any faster?" Carella said to the cabdriver.

"I'm driving as fast as I can," the cabbie answered.

"Damnit! My wife's about to have a baby!"

"Well, mister, I'm . . ."

"I'm a cop," Carella said. "Get this heap moving."

"What are you worried about?" the cabbie said, pressing his foot to the accelerator. "Between a cop and a cabbie, we sure as hell should be able to deliver a baby."

Carella paced the floor of the hospital waiting room. Meyer, Hawes, and O'Brien paced the floor behind him.

"What's taking so long?" Carella asked. "My God, does it always take this long?"

"Relax," Meyer said. "I've been through this three times already. It gets longer each time."

"She's been up there for close to an hour," Carella moaned.

"She'll be all right, don't worry. What are you going to name the baby?"

"Mark if it's a boy, and April if it's a girl. Meyer, it shouldn't be taking this long, should it?"

"Relax."

"Relax, relax."

"Relax," Meyer said.

"Here comes a nurse," O'Brien said.

Carella whirled. With starched precision, the nurse marched down the corridor. He walked rapidly to greet her, his heels clicking on the marble floor.

"Is she all right?" the detectives heard him ask, and the nurse nodded and then took Carella's arm and brought him to the side of the corridor where they entered into a whispered consultation. Carella kept nodding. The detectives watched him. Then, in a louder voice, Carella asked, "Can I go see her now?"

"Yes," the nurse answered. "The doctor's still with her. Everything's fine."

Carella started down the hallway, not looking back at his colleagues.

"Hey!" Meyer shouted.

Carella turned.

"What is it?" Meyer said. "Mark or April?"

And Carella, a somewhat mystified grin on his face, shouted *"Both!"* and then broke into a trot for the elevators.

'Til Death, 1959

It was a great little holiday, Halloween.

Cops just loved it.

Nevertheless, at six o'clock on All Hallows Even, after a tiring day of inactivity on the Leyden case and all sorts of activity in the streets preventing and discouraging mayhem, not to mention arresting people here and there who had allowed their celebrating to become a bit too uninhibited, Carella watched his wife as she painted the face of his son, and prepared to go out into the streets once again.

"I got a great idea, Pop," Mark said. He was the older of the twins by seven minutes, which gave him seniority as well as masculine superiority over his sister, April. It was Mark who generally had the "great" ideas and April who invariably put him down with something sweet like, "That's the stupidest idea I ever heard in my life."

"What's your idea?" Carella asked.

"I think we should go to Mr. Oberman's house . . ."

"Oberman the Creep," April observed.

"That's not a nice way to talk about an old man," Carella said.

"But he *is* a creep, Daddy."

"That doesn't matter," Carella said.

"Anyway," Mark said, "I think we should go to his house, and April and me'll knock on the door . . ."

"April and *I*," Carella corrected.

Mark looked up at his father, wondering whether he should try the joke about, "Oh, are *you* going to knock on the door too?" and decided in his infinite wisdom that he'd better not risk it, even though it had gone over pretty well once with Miss Rutherford, who taught the third grade at the local elementary school. "April and *I*," he said, and smiled at his father angelically, and then beamed at his mother as she continued drawing a black mustache under his nose, and then said,

"April and I will knock on Mr. Oberman's door and yell, 'Trick or treat,' and when he opens it, you stick your gun in his face."

Teddy, who was watching her son's lips as he talked, shook her head violently, and looked up at her husband. Before Carella could answer, April said, "That's the stupidest idea I ever heard in my life," her life to date having consisted of eight years, four months, and ten days.

Mark said, "Shut up, who asked *you?*" and Teddy scowled at her husband, warning him to put an end to this before it got out of hand, and then grasping both of Mark's shoulders to turn him toward her so that she could properly finish the job. She was using felt-tipped watercolor markers, and whereas her makeup artistry might not have passed muster with the National Repertory, it looked pretty good to her from where she knelt beside her son. She had enlarged and angled Mark's eyebrows with the black marker, and had then used green eye shadow on his lids, and the black marker again to draw a sinister, drooping mustache and an evil-looking goatee. Her son was supposed to be Dracula, who did not have either a mustache or a beard, but she felt he looked far too cherubic without them, and had taken artistic license with the Bram Stoker character. She was now using the bright-red marker to paint in a few drops of blood under his lip, and since her back was to Carella, she did not hear him admonish Mark first for his idiotic idea about brandishing a real gun, and next for yelling at his sister. She dotted a last tiny dribble of blood below the other three larger drops, and then rose and stepped back to admire her handiwork.

"How do I look?" Mark asked Carella.

"Horrible."

"Great!" Mark shouted, and ran out of the room to search for a mirror.

"Make me pretty, Mommy," April said, looking directly up at her mother. Teddy smiled, and then slowly and carefully moved her fingers in the universal language of the deaf-mute while Carella and the little girl watched.

"She says she doesn't *have* to make you pretty," Carella said. "You *are* pretty."

"I could read almost all of it," April said, and hugged Teddy fiercely. "I'm the Good Princess, you know," she said to her father.

"That's true, you *are* the Good Princess."

"Are there *bad* princesses, too?"

Teddy was replacing the caps on the felt-tipped markers to keep them from drying out. She smiled at her daughter, shook her head, reached into her purse for a lipstick tube, and then carried it to where April waited patiently for the touches that would transform her into a true Good Princess. Kneeling before her, Teddy expertly began to apply the lipstick. The two looked remarkably alike, the same brown eyes and black hair, the clearly defined widow's peak, the long lashes and generous mouth. April wore a long gown and cape fashioned of hunter-green velvet by Fanny, their housekeeper. Teddy wore tight blue jeans and a white T-shirt, her hair falling onto her cheek now as she bent her head, concentrating on the line of April's mouth. She touched her fingertip to the lipstick and brushed a bit of it onto each of April's cheeks, blending it, and then reached for the eye shadow she had used on her son, using it more subtly on April's lids, mindful of the fact that her daughter was not supposed to be a bloodthirsty vampire. Using a mascara brush, she darkened April's lashes and then turned her to face Carella.

"Beautiful," Carella said. "Go look at yourself."

"Am I, Mommy?" April asked and, without waiting for an affirming nod, scurried out of the room.

Fanny came in not a moment later, grinning.

"There's a horrid little beast rushing all about the kitchen with blood dripping from his mouth," she said, and then, pretending to notice Carella for the first time even though he'd been home for more than half an hour, added, "Well, it's himself. And will you be taking the children out for their mischief?"

"I will," Carella said.

"Mind you're back by seven, because that's when the roast'll be done."

"I'll be back by seven," Carella promised. To Teddy, he said, "I thought you said there were no bad princesses."

"And what is *that* supposed to mean?" Fanny asked.

She had come to the Carellas' more than eight years ago as a one-month gift from Teddy's father, who had felt his daughter needed at least that much time to rearrange the household after the birth of twins. In those days Fanny's hair was blue, and she wore a pince-nez, and she weighed a hundred and fifty pounds. The prepaid month had gone by all too quickly, and Carella had regretfully informed her that he could not afford a full-time housekeeper on his meager salary. But Fanny was an indomitable broad who had never had a family of her own, and who rather liked this one. So she told Carella he could pay her whatever he might scrape up for the time being, and she would supplement her income with night jobs, she being a trained nurse and a very strong healthy woman to boot. Carella had flatly refused, and Fanny had put her hands on her hips and said, "Are you going to throw me out into the street, is that it?" and they had argued back and forth, and Fanny had stayed. She was still with them. Her hair was now bleached red, and she wore harlequin glasses with black frames, and her weight was down to a hundred and forty as a result of chasing after two very lively children. Her influence on the family unit was perhaps best reflected in the speech of the twins. As infants, they'd been alone with her and their mother for much of the day, and since Teddy could not utter a word, much of their language had been patterned after Fanny's. It was not unusual to hear Mark referring to someone as a lace-curtain, shanty-Irish son of a B, or little April telling a playmate to go scratch her arse. It made life colorful, to say the least.

Fanny stood now with her hands on her ample hips, daring Carella to explain what he meant by his last remark. Carella fixed her with a menacing detective-type stare and said, "I was referring, dear, to the fact that you are sometimes overbearing and raucous and could conceivably be thought of as a *bad* princess, *that* is what it's supposed to mean," and Fanny burst out laughing.

"How can you live with such a beast?" she asked Teddy, still laughing, and then went out of the room, wagging her head.

"Daddy, are you coming?" Mark shouted.

"Yes, son," he answered.

He folded Teddy into his arms and kissed her. Then he went out into the living room and took his children one by each hand, and went out into the streets to ring doorbells with them.

Shotgun, 1969

In bed with Teddy that night, holding her close in the dark, the rain lashing the windowpanes, Carella was aware all at once that she was not asleep, and he sat up and turned on the bed lamp and looked at her, puzzled.

"Teddy?" he said.

Her back was to him, she could not see his lips. He touched her shoulder and she rolled over to face him, and he was surprised to see that there were tears in her eyes.

"Hey," he said, "hey, honey . . . what . . . ?"

She shook her head and rolled away from him again, closing herself into her pillow, closing him out—if she could not see him, she could not hear him. Her eyes were her ears; her hands and her face were her voice. She lay sobbing into the pillow, and he put his hand on her shoulder again, gently, and she sniffed and turned toward him again.

"Want to talk?" he said.

She nodded.

"What's the matter?"

She shook her head.

"Did I do something?"

She shook her head again.

"What is it?"

She sat up, took a tissue from the box on the bedside table, blew her nose, and then put the tissue under her pillow. Carella waited. At last, her hands began to speak. He watched them. He knew the language, he had learned it well over the years, he could now speak it better than hesitantly with his own hands. As she spoke to him, the tears began rolling down her face again, and her hands fluttered and then stopped completely. She sniffed again, and reached for the crumpled tissue under her pillow.

"You're wrong," he said.

She shook her head.

"I'm telling you you're wrong."

She shook her head again.

"Honey, she likes you very much."

Her hands began again. This time they spilled out a torrent of words and phrases, speaking to him so rapidly that he had to tell her to slow down, and even then continuing at a pace almost too fast for him to comprehend. He caught both her hands in his own, and said, "Now come on, honey. If you want me to listen . . ." She nodded, and sniffed, and began speaking more slowly now, her fingers long and fluid, her dark eyes glistening with the tears that sat upon them as she told him again that she was certain Augusta Kling didn't like her, Augusta had said things and done things tonight—

"What things?"

Teddy's hands moved again. *The wine*, she said.

"The wine? What about the wine?"

When she toasted.

"I don't remember any toast."

She made a toast.

"To what?"

To you and Bert.

"To the case, you mean. To solving the case."

No, to you and Bert.

"Honey—"

She left me out. She drank only to you and Bert.

"Now, why would she do a thing like that? She's one of the sweetest people—"

Teddy burst into tears again.

He put his arms around her and held her close. The rain beat steadily on the windowpanes. "Honey," he said, and she looked up into his face, and studied his mouth, and watched the words as they formed on his lips. "Honey, Augusta likes you very much." Teddy shook her head. "Honey, she *said* so. Do you remember when you told the story about the kids . . . about April falling in the lake at that

PBA picnic? And Mark jumping in to rescue her when the water was only two feet deep? Do you remember telling . . . ?"

Teddy nodded.

"And then you went to the ladies' room, do you remember?"

She nodded again.

"Well, the minute you were gone, Augusta told me how terrific you were."

Teddy looked up at him.

"That's just what she said. She said, 'Jesus, Teddy's terrific, I wish I could tell a story like her.'"

The tears were beginning to flow again.

"Honey, why on earth *wouldn't* she like you?"

She looked him dead in the eye. Her hands began to move. *Because I'm a deaf-mute,* she said.

"You're the most wonderful woman in the world," he said, and kissed her, and held her close again. And then he kissed the tears from her face and from her eyes, and told her again how much he loved her, told her what he had told her that day years and years ago when he'd asked her to marry him for the twelfth time and had finally convinced her that she was so much *more* than any other woman when until that moment she had considered herself somehow less. He told her again now, he said, "Jesus, I love you, Teddy, I love you to death," and then they made love as they had when they were younger, much younger.

Calypso, 1979

She tried to remember how long ago it had been. Years and years, that was certain. And would he think her frivolous now? Would he accept what she had done (what she was *about* to do, actually, since she hadn't yet done it, and could still change her mind about it) as the gift she intended it to be, or would he consider it the self-indulgent whim of a woman who was no longer the young girl he'd married years and years ago? Well, who *is*? Teddy thought. Even Jane Fonda is no longer the young girl she was years and years ago. But does Jane Fonda worry about such things? Probably, Teddy thought.

The section of the city through which she walked was thronged with people, but Teddy could not hear the drifting snatches of their conversations as they moved past her and around her. Their exhaled breaths pluming on the brittle air were, to her, only empty cartoon balloons floating past in a silent rush. She walked in an oddly hushed

71

world, dangerous to her in that her ears could provide no timely warnings, curiously exquisite in that whatever she saw was unaccompanied by any sound that might have marred its beauty. The sight (and aroma) of a bluish-gray cloud of carbon monoxide, billowing onto the silvery air from an automobile exhaust pipe, assumed dreamlike proportions when it was not coupled with the harsh mechanical sound of an automobile engine. The uniformed cop on the corner, waving his arms this way and that, artfully dodging as he directed the cross-purposed stream of lumbering traffic, became an acrobat, a ballet dancer, a skilled mime the moment one did not have to hear his bellowed, *"Move it, let's keep it moving!"* And yet—

She had never heard her husband's voice.

She had never heard her children's laughter.

She had never heard the pleasant wintry jingle of automobile skid chains on an icy street, the big-city cacophony of jackhammers and automobile horns, street vendors and hawkers, babies crying. As she passed a souvenir shop whose window brimmed with inexpensive jade, ivory (illegal to import), fans, dolls with Oriental eyes (like her husband's), she did not hear drifting from a small window on the side wall of the shop the sound of a stringed instrument plucking a sad and delicate Chinese melody, the notes hovering on the air like ice crystals—she simply did not hear.

The tattoo parlor was vaguely anonymous, hidden as it was on a narrow Chinatown side street. The last time she'd been here, the place had been flanked by a bar and a laundromat. Today, the bar was an offtrack betting parlor and the laundromat was a fortune-telling shop run by someone named Sister Lucy. Progress. As she passed Sister Lucy's emporium, Teddy looked over the curtain in the front window and saw a Gypsy woman sitting before a large phrenology poster hanging on the wall. Except for the poster and the woman, the shop was empty. The woman looked very lonely and a trifle cold, huddled in her shawl, looking straight ahead of her at the entrance door. For a moment, Teddy was tempted to walk into the empty store and have her fortune told. What was the joke? Her husband was very good at remembering jokes. What was it? Why couldn't women remember jokes? Was that a sexist attitude? What the hell was the *joke*? Something about a Gypsy band buying a chain of empty stores?

The name on the plate-glass window of the tattoo parlor was Charlie Chen. Beneath the name were the words, "Exotic Oriental Tattoo." She hesitated a moment, and then opened the door. There must have been a bell over the door, and it probably tinkled, signaling Mr. Chen from the back of his shop. She had not heard the bell, and at first she did not recognize the old Chinese man who came toward her. The last time she'd seen him, he had been a round fat man with a small mustache on his upper lip. He had laughed a lot, and each time he laughed, his fat little body quivered. He had thick fingers, she remembered, and there had been an oval jade ring on the forefinger of his left hand.

"Yes, lady?" he said.

It was Chen, of course. The mustache was gone, and so was the jade ring, and so were the acres of flesh, but it was surely Chen, wizened and wrinkled and shrunken, looking at her now out of puzzled brown eyes, trying to place her. She thought, *I've* changed, too, he doesn't recognize me, and suddenly felt foolish about what she was here to do. Maybe it was too late for things like garter belts and panties, ribbed stockings and high-heeled, patent-leather pumps, merry widows and lacy teddies, too late for Teddy, too late for silly, sexy playfulness. Was it? Oh my God, *was* it?

She had asked Fanny to call yesterday, first to find out if the shop would be open today, and next to make an appointment for her. Fanny had left the name Teddy Carella. Had Chen forgotten her name as well? He was still staring at her.

"You Missa Carella?" he said.

She nodded.

"I know you?" he said, his head cocked, studying her.

She nodded again.

"You know me?"

She nodded.

"Charlie Chen," he said, and laughed, but nothing about him shook, his laughter was an empty wind blowing through a frail old body. "Everybody call me Charlie *Chan*," he explained. "Big detective Charlie Chan. But me Chen, *Chen*. You know Charlie Chan, detective?"

The same words he had spoken all those years ago.

Oddly, she felt like weeping.

"Big detective," Chen said. "Got stupid sons." He laughed again. "Me got stupid sons, too, but me no detec—" And suddenly he stopped, and his eyes opened wide, and he said, "Detective wife, you detective *wife*! I make butterfly for you! Black lacy butterfly!"

She nodded again, grinning now.

"You no can talk, right. You read my lips, right?"

She nodded.

"Good, everything hunky-dory. How you been, lady? You still so pretty, most beautiful lady ever come my shop. You still got butterfly on shoulder?

She nodded.

"Best butterfly I ever make. Nice small butterfly. I want to do *big* one, remember? You say no, small one. I make tiny delicate black butterfly, very good for lady. Very sexy in strapless gown. You husband think was sexy?"

Teddy nodded. She started to say something with her hands, caught

73

herself—as she so often had to—and then pointed to a pencil and a sheet of paper on Chen's counter.

"You wanna talk, right?" Chen said, smiling, and handed her the pencil and paper.

She took both, and wrote: *How have you been, Mr. Chen?*

"Ah, well, not so good," Chen said.

She looked at him expectantly, quizzically.

"Old Charlie Chen gotta Big C, huh?" he said.

She did not understand him for a moment.

"Cancer," he said, and saw the immediate shocked look on her face and said, "No, no, lady, don't worry, old Charlie be hunky-dory, yessir." He kept watching her face. She did not want to cry. She owed the old man the dignity of not having to watch her cry for him. She opened her hands. She tilted her head. She raised her eyebrows ever so lightly. She saw on his face and in his eyes that he knew she was telling him how sorry she was. "Thank you, lady," he said, and impulsively took both her hands between his own, and, smiling, said, "So, why you come here see Charlie Chen? You write down what you like, yes?"

She picked up the pencil and began writing again.

"Ah," he said, watching. "Ah. Very smart idea. Very smart. Okay, fine."

He watched the moving pencil.

"Very good," he said, "come, we go in back. Charlie Chen so happy you come see him. My sons all married now, I tell you? My oldest son a doctor Los Angeles. A *head* doctor!" he said, and burst out laughing. "A shrink! You believe it? My oldest *son*! My other two sons . . . come in back, lady . . . my other two sons . . ."

Carella said good night to Meyer at ten minutes past six, and only then remembered he had not yet bought Teddy a present. He shopped the Stem until he found an open lingerie shop, only to discover that it featured panties of the open-crotch variety and some that could be eaten like candy, decided this was not quite what he had in mind, thank you, and then shopped fruitlessly for another hour before settling on a heart-shaped box of chocolates in a drugstore. He felt he was letting Teddy down.

Her eyes and her face showed no disappointment when he presented the gift to her. He explained that it was only a temporary solution, and that he'd shop for her *real* present once the pressure of the case let up a little. He had no idea when that might be, but he promised himself that he would buy her something absolutely mind-boggling tomorrow, come hell or high water. He did not yet know that the case had already taken a peculiar turn or that he would learn about it tomorrow, when once again it would postpone his grandiose plans.

At the dinner table, ten-year-old April complained that she had received only one Valentine's card, and that one from a doofus. She pronounced the word with a grimace her mother might have used more suitably, managing to look very much like Teddy in that moment—the dark eyes and darker hair, the beautiful mouth twisted in an expression of total distaste. Her ten-year-old brother, Mark, who resembled Carella more than he did either his mother or his twin sister, offered the opinion that anyone who would send a card to April *had* to be a doofus, at which point April seized her half-finished pork chop by its rib, and threatened to use it on him like a hatchet. Carella calmed them down. Fanny came in from the kitchen and casually mentioned that these were the same pork chops she'd taken out of the freezer the night before and she hoped they tasted okay and wouldn't give the whole family trichinosis. Mark wanted to know what trichinosis was. Fanny told him it was related to a cassoulet and winked at Carella.

They put the children to bed at nine.

They watched television for a while, and then they went into the bedroom. Teddy was in the bathroom for what seemed an inordinately long time. Carella guessed she was angry. When she came into the bedroom again, she was wearing a robe over her nightgown. Normally, she wasn't quite so modest in their own bedroom. He began to think more and more that his gift of chocolates without even a selection chart under the lid had truly irritated her. So deep was his own guilt ("Italians and Jews," Meyer was fond of saying, "are the guiltiest people on the face of the earth") that he did not remember until she pulled back the covers in the dark and got into bed beside him that *she* hadn't given *him* anything at *all*.

He snapped on the bedside lamp.

"Honey," he said, "I'm really sorry. I know I should have done it earlier, it was stupid of me to leave it for the last minute. I promise you tomorrow I'll. . ."

She put her fingers to his lips, silencing him.

She sat up.

She lowered the strap of her nightgown.

In the glow of the lamplight, he saw her shoulder. Where previously there had been only a single black butterfly tattoo, put there so long ago he could hardly remember when, he now saw *two* butterflies, the new one slightly larger than the other, its wings a bright yellow laced with black. The new butterfly seemed to hover over the original, as though kissing it with its outstretched wings.

His eyes suddenly flooded with tears.

He pulled her to him and kissed her fiercely and felt his tears mingling with hers as surely as did the butterflies on her shoulder.

Ice, 1983

75

Teddy was talking to him now.

They had just made love.

The first words she said to him were, "I love you."

She used the informal sign, a blend of the letters "i," "l," and "y," her right hand held close to her breast, the little finger, index finger, and thumb extended, the remaining two fingers folded down toward her palm. He answered with the more formal sign for "I love you": first touching the tip of his index finger to the center of his chest; then clenching both fists in the "a" hand sign, crossing his arms below the wrists, and placing his hands on his chest; and finally pointing at her with his index finger—a simple "I" plus "love" plus "you."

They kissed again.

She sighed.

And then she began telling him about her day.

He had known for quite some time now that she was interested in finding a job. Fanny had been with them since the twins were born, and she ran the house efficiently. The twins—Mark and April—were now eleven years old, and in school much of the day. Teddy was bored with playing tennis or lunching with the "girls." She signed "girl" by making the "a" hand sign with her right fist, and dragging the tip of her thumb down her cheek along the jawline; to make the word plural, she rapidly indicated several different locations, pointing with her extended forefinger. More than *one* girl. Girls. But her eyes and the expression on her face made it clear that she was using the word derogatively; she did not consider herself a "girl," and she certainly didn't consider herself one of the "girls."

Well, I went to this real estate agency on Cumberland Avenue this morning, Teddy was saying with her hands and her eyes and her face. I'd written them a letter answering an ad in the newspaper, telling them what my experience had been before we got married and before I became a mother, and they wrote back setting up an appointment for an interview. So I got all dolled up this morning, and went over there.

To express the slang expression "dolled up," she first signed "x," stroking the curled index finger of the hand sign on the tip of her nose, twice. To indicate "doll" was in the past tense, she immediately made the sign for "finished." For "up" she made the same sign anyone who was not a deaf-mute might have made: She simply moved her extended index finger upward. Dolled up. Carella got the message, and visualized her in a smart suit and heels, taking the bus to Cumberland Avenue, some two miles from the house.

And now her hands and her eyes and her mobile face spewed forth a torrent of language. Surprise of all surprises, she told him, the lady is a deaf-mute. The lady cannot *hear*, the lady cannot *speak*, the lady—however intelligent her letter may have sounded, however bright and perky she may appear in person—possesses neither tongue nor ear, the lady simply will not *do*! This despite the fact that the ad called only for someone to type and file. This despite the fact that I was reading that fat bastard's lips and understanding every single word he said—which wasn't easy since he was chewing on a cigar—this despite the fact that I can *still* type sixty words a minute after all these years, ah, the hell with it. Steve, he thought I was *dumb* (she tapped the knuckles of the "a" hand sign against her forehead, indicating someone stupid), the obvious mate to *deaf*, right? (she touched first her mouth and then her ear with her extended index finger), like ham and eggs, right? Deaf and *dumb*, right? Shit, she said, signing the word alphabetically for emphasis, S-H-I-T!

He took her in his arms.

He was about to comfort her, about to tell her that there were ignorant people in this world who were incapable of judging a person's worth by anything but the most obvious external evidence, when suddenly she was signing again. He read her hands and the anger in her eyes.

I'm not quitting, she said. *I'll get a goddamn job.*

She rolled into him, and he felt her small determined nod against his shoulder. Reaching behind him toward the night table, he snapped off the bedside light. He could hear her breathing in the darkness beside him. He knew she would lie awake for a long time, planning her next move.

Teddy's appointment at the law offices was for three o'clock that afternoon. She arrived at twenty minutes to, and waited downstairs until two-fifty, not wanting to seem too eager by arriving early. She really wanted the job; the job sounded perfect to her. She was dressed in what she considered a sedate but not drab manner, wearing a smart suit over a blouse with a stock tie, panty hose color-coordinated with the nubby brown fabric of the suit, brown shoes with French heels. The lobby of the building was suffocatingly hot after the dank drizzle outdoors, and so she took off her raincoat before she got on the elevator. At precisely 3:00 P.M. she presented herself to the receptionist at Franklin, Logan, Gibson and Knowles and showed her the letter she had received from Philip Logan. The receptionist told her Mr. Logan would see her in a few moments. At ten minutes past three the receptionist picked up the phone receiver—it must have buzzed, but Teddy had not heard it—and then said Mr. Logan would see her now. Reading the girl's lips, Teddy nodded.

"First doorway down the hall on your right," the girl said.

Teddy went down the hallway and knocked on the door.

She waited a few seconds, allowing time for Logan inside to have said, "Come in," and then turned the doorknob and went into the office. The office was spacious, furnished with a large desk, several easy chairs, a coffee table, and banks of bookcases on three walls. The fourth wall was fashioned almost entirely of glass that offered a splendid view of the city's towering buildings. Rain slithered down the glass panels. A shaded lamp cast a glow of yellow illumination on the desktop.

Logan rose from behind the desk the moment she entered the room. He was a tall man wearing a dark blue suit, a white shirt, and a striped tie. His eyes were a shade lighter than the suit. His hair was graying. Teddy guessed he was somewhere in his early fifties.

"Ah, Miss Carella," he said, "how kind of you to come. Please sit down."

She sat in one of the easy chairs facing his desk. He sat behind the desk again and smiled at her. His eyes looked warm and friendly.

"I assume you can . . . uh . . . read my lips," he said. "Your letter . . ."

She nodded.

"It was very straightforward of you to describe your disability in advance," Logan said. "In your letter, I mean. Very frank and honest."

Teddy nodded again, although the word *disability* rankled.

"You are . . . uh . . . you *do* understand what I'm saying, don't you?"

She nodded, and then motioned to the pad and pencil on his desk.

"What?" he said. "Oh. Yes, of *course*, how silly of me."

He handed the pad and pencil across to her.

On the pad, she wrote: *I can understand you completely.*

He took the pad again, read what she'd written, and said, "Wonderful, good." He hesitated. "Uh . . . perhaps we should move that chair around here," he said, "don't you think? So we won't have to be passing this thing back and forth."

He rose quickly and came to where she was sitting. Teddy got up, and he shoved the easy chair closer to the desk and to the side of it. She sat again, folding her raincoat over her lap.

"There, that's better," he said. "Now we can talk a bit more easily. Oh, excuse me, was my back to you? Did you get all of that?"

Teddy nodded, and smiled.

"This is all very new to me, you see," he said. "So. Where shall we begin? You understand, don't you, that the job calls for an expert typist . . . I see in your letter that you can do sixty words a minute . . ."

I may be a little rusty just now, Teddy wrote on the pad.

"Well, that all comes back to you, doesn't it? It's like roller skating, I would guess."

Teddy nodded, although she did not think typing was at all like roller skating.

"And you *do* take steno . . ."

She nodded again.

"And, of course, the filing is a routine matter, so I'm sure you can handle that."

She looked at him expectantly.

"We like attractive people in our offices, Miss Carella," Logan said, and smiled. "You're a very beautiful woman."

She nodded her thanks—modestly, she hoped—and then wrote: *It's Mrs. Carella.*

"Of course, forgive me," he said. "Theodora, is it?"

She wrote: *Most people call me Teddy.*

"Teddy? That's charming. Teddy. It suits you. You're extraordinarily beautiful, Teddy. I suppose you've heard that a thousand times . . ."

She shook her head.

". . . but I find that most compliments bear repeating, don't you? Extraordinarily beautiful," he said, and his eyes met hers. He held contact for longer than was comfortable. She lowered her eyes to the pad. When she looked up again, he was still staring at her. She shifted her weight in the chair. He was still watching her.

"So," he said. "Hours are nine to five, the job pays two and a quarter to start, can you begin Monday morning? Or will you need a little time to get your affairs in order?"

Her eyes opened wide. She had not for a moment believed it would be this simple. She was speechless, literally so, but speechless beyond that—as if her mind had suddenly gone blank, her ability to communicate frozen somewhere inside her head.

"You *do* want the job, don't you?" he said, and smiled again.

Oh, yes, she thought, oh God, *yes*! She nodded, her eyes flashing happiness, her hands unconsciously starting to convey her appreciation, and then falling empty of words into her lap when she realized he could not possibly read them.

"*Will* Monday morning be all right?" he asked.

She nodded yes.

"Good, then," he said, "I'll look forward to seeing you then."

He leaned toward her.

"I'm sure we'll get along fine," he said, and suddenly, without warning, he slid his hand under her skirt. She sat bolt upright, her eyes opening wide, too shocked to move for an instant. His fingers tightened on her thigh.

"Don't you think so, Miss Car . . . ?"

She slapped him hard, as hard as she could, and then rose at once from her chair, and moved toward him, her teeth bared, her hand drawn back to hit him again. He was nursing his jaw, his blue eyes looking hurt and a trifle bewildered. Words welled up inside her, words she could not speak. She stood there trembling with fury, her hand still poised to strike.

"That's it, you know," he said, and smiled.

She was turning away from him, tears welling into her eyes, when she saw more words forming on his lips.

"You just blew it, dummy."

And the last word pained her more than he possibly could have known, the last word went through her like a knife.

She was still crying when she came out of the building into the falling rain.

Lightning, 1984

CLAIRE TOWNSEND

In Riverhead—and throughout the city for that matter—but especially in Riverhead, the cave dwellers have thrown up a myriad number of dwellings which they call middle-class apartment houses. These buildings are usually constructed of yellow brick, and they are carefully set on the street so that no wash in seen hanging on the lines, except when an inconsiderate city transit authority constructs an elevated structure that cuts through backyards.

The fronts of the buildings are usually hung with a different kind of wash. Here is where the women gather. They sit on bridge chairs and stools and they knit and they sun themselves, and they talk, and their talk is the dirty wash of the apartment building. In three minutes flat, a reputation can be ruined by these Mesdames Defarges. The ax drops with remarkable abruptness, whetted by a friendly discussion of last night's mah-jongg game. The head, with equally remarkable suddenness, rolls into the basket, and the discussion idles on to topics like "Should birth control be practiced in the Virgin Isles?"

Autumn was a bold seductress on that late Monday afternoon, September 18. The women lingered in front of the buildings, knowing their hungry men would soon be home for dinner, but lingering nonetheless, savoring the tantalizing bite of the air. When the tall blond man stopped in front of 728 Peterson, paused to check the address over the arched doorway, and then stepped into the foyer, speculation ran rife among the women knitters. After a brief period of consultation, one of the women—a girl named Birdie—was chosen to sidle unobtrusively into the foyer and, if the opportunity were ripe, perhaps casually follow the good-looking stranger upstairs.

Birdie, so carefully unobtrusive was she, missed her golden opportunity. By the time she had wormed her way into the inner foyer, Bert Kling was nowhere in sight.

He had checked the name "Townsend" in the long row of brass-plated mailboxes, pushed the bell button, and then leaned on the inner door until an answering buzz released its lock mechanism. He had then climbed to the fourth floor, found apartment 47, and pushed another button.

He was now waiting.

He pushed the button again.

The door opened suddenly. He had heard no approaching footsteps, and the sudden opening of the door surprised him. Unconsciously, he looked first to the girl's feet. She was barefoot.

"I was raised in the Ozarks," she said, following his glance. "We own a vacuum cleaner, a carpet sweeper, a broiler, a set of encyclopedias, and subscriptions to most of the magazines. Whatever you're selling, we've probably got it, and we're not interested in putting you through college."

Kling smiled. "I'm selling an automatic apple corer," he said.

"We don't eat apples," the girl replied.

"This one mulches the seeds, and converts them to fiber. The corer comes complete with an instruction booklet telling you how to weave fiber mats."

The girl raised a speculative eyebrow.

"It comes in six colors," Kling went on. "Toast Brown, Melba Peach, Tart Red—"

"Are you on the level?" the girl asked, puzzled now.

"Proofreader Blue," Kling continued, "Bilious Green, and Midnight Dawn." He paused. "Are you interested?"

"Hell, no," she said, somewhat shocked.

"My name is Bert Kling," he said seriously. "I'm a cop."

"Now you sound like the opening to a television show."

"May I come in?"

"Am I in trouble?" the girl asked. "Did I leave that damn shebang in front of a fire hydrant?"

"No."

And then, as an afterthought, "Where's your badge?"

Kling showed her his shield.

"You're supposed to ask," the girl said. "Even the man from the gas company. Everybody's supposed to carry identification like that."

"Yes, I know."

"So come in," she said. "I'm Claire Townsend."

"I know."

"*How* do you know?"

"The boys at Club Tempo sent me here."

Claire stared at Kling levelly. She was a tall girl. Even barefoot, she reached to Kling's shoulder. In high heels, she would give the average American male trouble. Her hair was black. Not brunette, not brownette, but black, a total black, the black of a starless, moonless night. Her eyes were a deep brown, arched with black brows. Her nose was straight, and her cheeks were high, and there wasn't a trace of makeup on her face, not a tint of lipstick on her wide mouth. She wore a white blouse, and black toreador pants, which tapered down to her naked ankles and feet. Her toenails were painted a bright red.

She kept staring at him. At last, she said, "Why'd they send you here?"

"They said you knew Jeannie Paige."

"Oh." The girl seemed ready to blush. She shook her head slightly, as if to clear it of an erroneous first impression, and then said, "Come in."

Kling followed her into the apartment. It was furnished with good middle-class taste.

"Sit down," she said.

"Thank you." He sat in a low easy chair. It was difficult to sit erect, but he managed it. Claire went to the coffee table, shoved the lid off a cigarette box, took one of the cigarettes for herself, and then asked, "Smoke?"

"No, thanks."

"Your name was Kling, did you say?"

"Yes."

"You're a detective?"

"No. A patrolman."

"Oh." Claire lighted the cigarette, shook out the match, and then studied Kling. "What's your connection with Jeannie?"

"I was about to ask you the same thing."

Claire grinned. "I asked first."

"I know her sister. I'm doing a favor."

"Um-huh." Claire nodded, digesting this. She puffed on the cigarette, folded her arms across her breasts, and then said, "Well, go ahead. Ask the questions. You're the cop."

"Why don't you sit down?"

"I've been sitting all day."

"You work?"

"I'm a college girl," Claire said. "I'm studying to be a social worker."

"Why that?"

"Why not?"

Kling smiled. "This time, *I* asked first."

"I want to get to people before you do," she said.

"That sounds reasonable," Kling said. "Why do you belong to Club Tempo?"

Her eyes grew suddenly wary. He could almost see a sudden film pass over the pupils, masking them. She turned her head and blew out a ball of smoke. "Why shouldn't I?" she asked.

"I can see where our conversation is going to run around in the why/why not rut," Kling said.

"Which is a damn sight better than the why/because rut, don't you think?" There was an edge to her voice now. He wondered what had suddenly changed her earlier friendliness. He weighed her reaction for a moment, and then decided to plunge onward.

"The boys there are a little young for you, aren't they?"

"You're getting a little personal, aren't you?"

"Yes," Kling said. "I am."

"Our acquaintance is a little short for personal exchanges," Claire said icily.

"Hud can't be more than eighteen—"

"Listen—"

"And what's Tommy? Nineteen? They haven't got an ounce of brains between them. Why do you belong to Tempo?"

Claire squashed out her cigarette. "Maybe you'd better leave, Mr. Kling," she said.

"I just got here," he answered.

She turned. "Let's set the record straight. So far as I know, I'm not obliged to answer any questions you ask about my personal affairs, unless I'm under suspicion for some foul crime. To bring the matter down to a fine technical point, I don't have to answer *any* questions a patrolman asks me, unless he is operating in an official capacity, which you admitted you were not. I liked Jeannie Paige, and I'm willing to cooperate. But if you're going to get snotty, this is still my home, and my home is my castle, and you can get the hell out."

"Okay," Kling said, embarrassed. "I'm sorry, Miss Townsend."

"Okay," Claire said. A silence clung to the atmosphere. Claire looked at Kling. Kling looked back at her.

"I'm sorry, too," Claire said finally. "I shouldn't be so goddamn touchy."

"No, you were perfectly right. It's none of my business what you—"

"Still, I shouldn't have—"

"No really, it's—"

Claire burst out laughing, and Kling joined her. She sat, still chuckling, and said, "Would you like a drink, Mr. Kling?"

Kling looked at his watch. "No, thanks," he said.

"Too early for you?"

"Well—"

"It's never too early for cognac," she said.

"I've never tasted cognac," he admitted.

"You haven't?" Her eyebrows shot up onto her forehead. "Ah, monsieur, you are meesing one of ze great treats of life. A little, *oui? Non?*"

"A little," he said.

She crossed to a bar with green Leatherette doors, opened them, and drew out a bottle with a warm, amber liquid showing within.

"Cognac," she announced grandly, "the king of brandies. You can drink it as a highball, cocktail, punch—or in coffee, tea, hot chocolate, and milk."

"Milk?" Kling asked, astonished.

"Milk, yes indeed. But the best way to enjoy cognac is to sip it—neat."

"You sound like an expert," Kling said.

Again, quite suddenly, the veil passed over her eyes. "Someone taught me to drink it," she said flatly, and then she poured some of the liquid into two medium-sized, tulip-shaped glasses. When she turned to face Kling again, the mask had dropped from her eyes.

"Note that the glass is only half filled," she said. "That's so you can twirl it without spilling any of the drink." She handed the glass to Kling. "The twirling motion mixes the cognac vapors with the air in the glass, bringing out the bouquet. Roll the glass in your palms, Mr. Kling. That warms the cognac and also brings out the aroma."

"Do you smell this stuff or drink it?" Kling wanted to know. He rolled the glass between his big hands.

"Both," Claire said. "That's what makes it a good experience. Taste it. Go ahead."

Kling took a deep swallow, and Claire opened her mouth and made an abrupt "Stop!" signal with one outstretched hand. "Good God," she said, "don't gulp it! You're committing an obscenity when you gulp cognac. Sip it, roll it around your tongue."

"I'm sorry," Kling said. He sipped the cognac, rolled it on his tongue. "Good," he said.

"Virile," she said.

"Velvety," he added.

"End of commercial."

They sat silently, sipping the brandy. He felt very cozy and very warm and very comfortable. Claire Townsend was a pleasant person to look at, and a pleasant person to talk to. Outside the apartment, the shadowy grays of autumn dusk were washing the sky.

"About Jeannie," he said. He did not feel like discussing death.

"Yes?"

"How well did you know her?"

"As well as anyone, I suppose. I don't think she had many friends."

"What makes you say that?"

"You can tell. That lost-soul look. A beautiful kid, but lost. God, what I wouldn't have given for the looks she had."

"You're not so bad," Kling said, smiling. He sipped more brandy.

"That's the warm, amber glow of the cognac," Claire advised him. "I'm a beast in broad daylight."

"I'll just bet you are," Kling said. "How'd you first meet her?"

"At Tempo. She came down one night. I think her boyfriend sent her. In any case, she had the name of the club and the address written on a little white card. She showed it to me, almost as if it were a ticket of admission, and then she just sat in the corner and refused dances. She looked . . . It's hard to explain. She was there, but she wasn't there. Have you seen people like that?"

"Yes," Kling said.

"I'm like that myself sometimes," Claire admitted. "Maybe that's why I spotted it. Anyway, I went over and introduced myself and we started talking. We got along very well. By the end of the evening we'd exchanged telephone numbers."

"Did she ever call you?"

"No. I only saw her at the club."

"How long ago was this?"

"Oh, a long time now."

"How long?"

"Let me see." Claire sipped her cognac and thought. "Gosh, it must be almost a year." She nodded. "Yes, just about."

"I see. Go ahead."

"Well, it wasn't hard to find out what was troubling her. The kid was in love."

Kling leaned forward. "How do you know?"

Claire's eyes did not leave his face. "I've been in love, too," she said tiredly.

"Who was her boyfriend?" Kling asked.

"I don't know."

"Didn't she tell you?"

"No."

"Didn't she mention his name ever? I mean, in conversation?"

"No."

"Hell," Kling said.

"Understand, Mr. Kling, that this was a new bird taking wing. Jeannie was leaving the nest, testing her feathers."

"I see."

"Her first love, Mr. Kling, and shining in her eyes, and glowing on

her face, and putting her in this dream world of hers where everything
outside it was shadowy." Claire shook her head. "God, I've seen them
green, but Jeannie—" She stopped and shook her head again. "She
just didn't know anything, do you know? Here was this woman's body
. . . well, had you ever seen her?"

"Yes."

"Then you know what I mean. This was the real item, a woman. But
inside—a little girl."

"How do you figure that?" Kling asked, thinking of the autopsy
results.

"Everything about her. The way she used to dress, the way she
talked, the questions she asked, even her handwriting. All a little
girl's. Believe me, Mr. Kling, I've never—"

"Her handwriting?"

"Yes, yes. Here, let me see if I've still got it." She crossed the room
and scooped her purse from a chair. "I'm the laziest girl in the world. I
never copy an address into my address book. I just stick it in between
the pages until I've . . ." She was thumbing through a little black
book. "Ah, here it is," she said. She handed Kling a white card. "She
wrote that for me the night we met. Jeannie Paige, and then the phone
number. Now, look at the way she wrote."

Kling looked at the card in puzzlement. "This says 'Club Tempo,'"
he said. "'1812 Klausner Street.'"

"What?" Claire frowned. "Oh, yes. That's the card she came down
with that night. She used the other side to give me her number. Turn it
over."

Kling did.

"See the childish scrawl? That was Jeannie Paige a year ago."

Kling flipped the card over again. "I'm more interested in *this* side,"
he said. "You told me you thought her boyfriend might have written
this. Why do you say that?"

"I don't know. I just assumed he was the person who sent her down,
that's all. It's a man's handwriting."

"Yes," Kling said. "May I keep this?"

Claire nodded. "If you like." She paused. "I guess I have no further
use for Jeannie's phone number."

"No," Kling said. He put the card into his wallet. "You said she
asked you questions. What kind of questions?"

"Well, for one, she asked me how to kiss."

"What?"

"Yes. She asked me what to do with her lips, whether she should
open her mouth, use her tongue. And all this delivered with that wide-
eyed, baby-blue stare. It sounds incredible, I know. But, remember,
she was a young bird, and she didn't know how strong her wings
were."

"She found out," Kling said.

"Huh?"

"Jeannie Paige was pregnant when she died."

"No!" Claire said. She put down the brandy glass. "No, you're joking!"

"I'm serious."

Claire was silent for several moments. Then she said, "First time at bat, and she gets beaned. Damnit! Goddamnit!"

"But you don't know who her boyfriend was?"

"No."

"Had she continued seeing him? You said this was a year ago. I mean—"

"I know what you mean. Yes, the same one. She'd been seeing him regularly. In fact, she used the club for that."

"He came to the club?" Kling said, sitting erect.

"No, no." Claire was shaking her head impatiently. "I think her sister and brother-in-law objected to her seeing this fellow. So she told them she was going down to Tempo. She'd stay there a little while, just in case anyone was checking, and then she'd leave."

"Let me understand this," Kling said. "She came to the club, and then left to meet him. Is that right?"

"Yes."

"This was standard procedure? This happened each time she came down?"

"Almost each time. Once in a while she'd stay at the club until things broke up."

"Did she meet him in the neighborhood?"

"No, I don't think so. I walked her down to the El once."

"What time did she generally leave the club?"

"Between ten and ten-thirty."

"And she walked to the El, is that right? And you assume she took a train there and went to meet him."

"I *know* she went to meet him. The night I walked her, she told me she was going downtown to meet him."

"Downtown where?"

"She didn't say."

"What did he look like, this fellow?"

"She didn't say."

"She never described him?"

"Only to say he was the handsomest man in the world. Look, who ever describes his love? Shakespeare, maybe. That's all."

"Shakespeare and seventeen-year-olds," Kling said. "Seventeen-year-olds shout their love to the rooftops."

"Yes," Claire said gently. "Yes."

"But not Jeannie Paige. Damnit, why not her?"

90

"I don't know." Claire thought for a moment. "This mugger who killed her—"

"Um?"

"The police don't think he was the fellow she was seeing, do they?"

"This is the first anyone connected with the police is hearing about her love life," Kling said.

"Oh. Well, he—he didn't sound that way. He sounded gentle. I mean, when Jeannie did talk about him, he sounded gentle."

"But she never mentioned his name?"

"No. I'm sorry."

Kling rose. "I'd better be going. That *is* dinner I smell, isn't it?"

"My father'll be home soon," Claire said. "Mom is dead. I whip something up when I get home from school."

"Every night?" Kling asked.

"What? I'm sorry . . ."

He didn't know whether to press it or not. She hadn't heard him, and he could easily have shrugged his comment aside. But he chose not to.

"I said, 'Every night?'"

"Every night what?"

She certainly was not making it easy for him. "Do you prepare dinner every night? Or do you occasionally get a night off?"

"Oh, I get nights off," Claire said.

"Maybe you'd enjoy dinner out some night?"

"With you, do you mean?"

"Well, yes. Yes, that's what I had in mind."

Claire Townsend looked at him long and hard. At last she said, "No, I don't think so. I'm sorry. Thanks. I couldn't."

"Well . . . uh . . ." Quite suddenly, Kling felt like a horse's ass. "I . . . uh . . . guess I'll be going, then. Thanks for the cognac. It was very nice."

"Yes," she said, and he remembered her discussing people who were there and yet not there, and he knew exactly what she meant because she was not there at all. She was somewhere far away, and he wished he knew where. With sudden, desperate longing, he wished he knew where she was because, curiously, he wanted to be there with her.

"Good-bye," he said.

She smiled in answer, and closed the door behind him.

That Thursday afternoon, Kling called Claire Townsend the first chance he got.

The first chance he got was on his lunch hour. He ordered a western sandwich and a cup of coffee, went to the phone book, looked up Townsend at 728 Peterson in Riverhead, and came up with a listing for Ralph Townsend. He went into the booth, deposited a dime, and dialed the number. He allowed the phone to ring for a total of twelve times, and then he hung up.

There were a lot of things to keep him busy on the beat that afternoon. A woman, for no apparent reason other than that her husband had called her "babe," had struck out at him with a razor, opening a gash the size of a banana on the side of his face. Kling made the pinch. The razor, by the time he had arrived on the scene, had gone the way of all discreet assault weapons—down the nearest sewer.

No sooner was he back on the street than a gang of kids attacked a boy as he was coming home from school. The boy had committed the unpardonable sin of making a pass at a deb who belonged to a rival street gang. Kling arrived just as the gang members were ready to stomp the kid into the pavement. He collared one of them, told him he knew the faces of all the kids who'd participated in the beating, and that if anything happened to the boy they'd jumped from here on in, he'd know just where to look. The gang member nodded solemnly, and then took off after his friends. The boy they'd jumped survived with only a few bumps on his head. This time, fists had been the order of the day.

Kling then proceeded to break up a crap game in the hallway of one of the buildings, listen to the ranting complaints of a shopkeeper who insisted that an eight-year-old boy had swiped a bolt of blue shantung, warn one of the bar owners that his license was kaput the next time any hustlers were observed soliciting in his joint, have a cup of coffee with one of the better-known policy runners in the neighborhood, and then walk back to the precinct house, where he changed into street clothes.

As soon as he hit the street again, he called Claire. She picked up the instrument on the fourth ring.

"Who is it?" she said, "and I hope to hell you apologize for getting me out of the shower. I'm wringing wet."

"I apologize," Kling said.

"Mr. Kling?" she asked, recognizing his voice.

"Yes."

"I was going to call you, but I didn't know where. I remembered something that might help."

"What is it?"

"The night I walked Jeannie down to the train station she said something."

"What?"

"She said she had a half-hour ride ahead of her. Does that help?"

"It might. Thanks a lot." He paused. "Listen, I've been thinking."

"Yes."

"About . . . about this dinner setup. I thought maybe—"

"Mr. Kling," she interrupted, "you don't want to take me to dinner."

"I do," he insisted.

"I'm the dullest girl in the world, believe me. I'd bore you stiff."

"I'd like to take the chance."

"You're only asking for trouble for yourself. Don't bother, believe me. Buy your mother a present with the money."

"I bought my mother a present last week."

"Buy her another one."

"Besides, I was thinking of going Dutch."

Claire chuckled. "Well, now you make it sound more attractive."

"Seriously, Claire—"

"Seriously, Mr. Kling, I'd rather not. I'm a sad sack, and you wouldn't enjoy me one bit."

"I enjoy you already."

"Those were company manners."

"Say, have you got an inferiority complex or something?"

"It's not that I have an inferiority complex, Doctor," she said, "it's that I really *am* inferior." Kling laughed, and she said, "Do you remember that cartoon?"

"No, but it's wonderful. How about dinner?"

"Why?"

"I like you."

"There are a million girls in this city."

"More than that, even."

"Mr. Kling—"

"Bert."

"Bert, there's nothing here for you."

"I haven't said what I want yet."

"Whatever you want, it's not here."

"Claire, let me gamble on it. Let me take you to dinner, and let me spend what may turn out to be the most miserable evening in my entire life. I've gambled with larger stakes involved. In the service, I even gambled with my life once in a while."

"Were you in the service?" she asked.

"Yes."

There seemed to be sudden interest in her voice. "Korea?"

"Yes."

There was a long silence on the line.

"Claire?"

"I'm here."

"What's the matter?"

"Nothing."

"Deposit five cents for the next three minutes, please," the operator said.

"Oh, hell, just a minute," Kling replied. He dug into his pocket and deposited a nickel. "Claire?" he said.

"I'm costing you money already," she told him.

"I've got money to burn," he answered. "How about it? I'll call for you tonight at about six-thirty."

"No, tonight is out of the question."

"Tomorrow night, then."

"I have a late class tomorrow. I don't get out until seven."

"I'll meet you at the school."

"That won't give me any time to change."

"It'll be a come-as-you-are date, okay?"

"I usually wear flats and a dirty old sweater to school."

"Fine!" he said enthusiastically.

"I suppose I could wear a dress and heels, though. It might shock some of the slobs in our hallowed halls, but then again it might set a precedent."

"Seven o'clock?"

"All right," she said.

"Good, I'll see you then."

"Good-bye."

" 'Bye." He hung up, grinning. He was stepping out of the booth when he remembered. Instantly, he reached into his pocket for another dime. He had no change. He went to the proprietor of the candy store, who was busy doling out a couple of two-cent seltzers. By the time he got his change, five minutes had rushed by. He dialed the number rapidly.

"Hello?"

"Claire, this is me again."

"You got me out of the shower again, you know that, don't you?"

"Gee, I'm awfully sorry, but you didn't tell me *which* school."

"Oh." Claire was silent. "Nope, I didn't. It's Women's U. Do you know where that is?"

"Yes."

"Fine. Go to Radley Hall. You'll find the office of our alleged college newspaper there. The paper is called *The Radley Clarion*, but the sign on the door says *The Radley Rag*. I keep my coat in a locker there. Don't let all the predatory females frighten you."

"I'll be there on the dot," Kling said.

"And I, exercising a woman's prerogative, shall be there ten minutes *after* the dot."

"I'll wait."

"Good. Now, you don't mind, do you, but I'm making a big puddle on the carpet."

"I'm sorry. Go wash."

"You said that as if you thought I was dirty."

"If you'd rather talk, I've got all night."

"I'd rather wash. Good-bye, Tenacious."

"Good-bye, Claire."

"You *are* tenacious, you realize that, don't you?"

Kling grinned. "Tenacious, anyone?" he asked.

"Ouch!" Claire said. "Good-bye," and then she hung up.

He sat in the booth grinning foolishly for a good three minutes. A fat lady finally knocked on the glass panel in the door and said, "Young man, that booth isn't a hotel."

Kling opened the doors. "That's funny," he said. "Room service just sent up a sandwich."

The woman blinked, pulled a face, and then stuffed herself into the booth, slamming the door emphatically.

Kling dressed for his date carefully.

He didn't know exactly why, but he felt that extreme care should be exercised in the handling and feeding of Claire Townsend. He admitted to himself that he had never—well, hardly ever—been so taken with a girl, and that he would probably be devastated forever—well, for a long time—if he lost her. He had no ideas on exactly how to win her, except for this intuition which urged him to proceed with caution. She had, after all, warned him repeatedly. She had put out the "Keep off" sign, and then she had read the sign aloud to him, and then she had translated it into six languages, but she had nonetheless accepted his offer.

Which proves beyond doubt, he thought, *that the girl is wildly in love with me.*

Which piece of deduction was about on a par with the high level detective work he had done so far. His abortive attempts at getting anywhere with the Jeannie Paige murder left him feeling a little foolish. He wanted very much to be promoted to Detective 3rd/Grade someday, but he entertained severe doubts now as to whether he really was detective material. It was almost two weeks since Peter Bell had come to him with his plea. It was almost two weeks since Bell had scribbled his address on a scrap of paper, a scrap still tucked in one of the pockets of Kling's wallet. A lot had happened in those nearly two weeks. And those happenings gave Kling reason for a little healthy soul-searching.

He was, at this point, just about ready to leave the case to the men who knew how to handle such things. His amateurish legwork, his fumbling questions, had netted a big zero—or so he thought. The only important thing he'd turned up was Claire Townsend. Claire, he was certain, was important. She was important now, and he felt she would become more important as time went by.

So let's polish our goddamn shoes. You want to look like a slob?

He took his shoes from the closet, slipped them on over socks he would most certainly smear with polish and later change, and set to work with his shine kit.

He was spitting on his right shoe when the knock sounded on the door.

"Who is it?" he called.

"Police. Open up," the voice said.

"Who?"

"Police."

Kling rose, his trouser cuffs rolled up high, his hands smeared with black polish. "Is this a gag?" he said to the closed door.

"Come on, Kling," the voice said. "You know better than that."

Kling opened the door. Two men stood in the hallway. Both were huge, both wore tweed jackets over V-necked sweaters, both looked bored.

"Bert Kling?" one of them asked.

"Yes?" he said, puzzled.

A shield flashed. "Monoghan and Monroe," one of them said. "Homicide. I'm Monoghan."

"I'm Monroe," the other one said.

They were like Tweedledum and Tweedledee, Kling thought. He suppressed his smile. Neither of his visitors was smiling. Each looked as if he had just come from an out-of-town funeral.

"Come in, fellers," Kling said. "I was just dressing."

"Thank you," Monoghan said.

"Thank you," Monroe echoed.

They stepped into the room. They both took off their fedoras. Monoghan cleared his throat. Kling looked at them expectantly.

"Like a drink?" he asked, wondering why they were here, feeling somehow awed and frightened by their presence.

"A short one," Monoghan said.

"A tiny hooker," Monroe said.

Kling went to the closet and pulled out a bottle. "Bourbon okay?"

"When I was a patrolman," Monoghan said, "I couldn't afford bourbon."

"This was a gift," Kling said.

"I never took whiskey. Anybody on the beat wanted to see me, it was cash on the line."

"That's the only way," Monroe said.

"This was a gift from my father. When I was in the hospital. The nurses wouldn't let me touch it there."

"You can't blame them," Monoghan said.

"Turn the place into an alcoholic ward," Monroe said, unsmiling.

Kling brought them their drinks. Monoghan hesitated.

"Ain't you drinking with us?"

"I've got an important date," he said. "I want to keep my head."

Monoghan looked at him with the flat look of a reptile. He shrugged, then turned to Monroe and said, "Here's looking at you."

Monroe acknowledged the toast. "Up yours," he said unsmilingly, and then tossed off the shot.

"Good bourbon," Monoghan said.

"Excellent," Monroe amplified.

"More?" Kling asked.

"Thanks," Monoghan said.

"No," Monroe said.

Kling looked at them. "You said you were from Homicide?"

"Homicide North."

"Monoghan and Monroe," Monroe said. "Ain't you heard of us? We cracked the Nelson-Nichols-Permen triangle murder."

"Oh," Kling said.

"Sure," Monoghan said modestly. "Big case."

"One of our biggest," Monroe said.

"Big one."

"Yeah."

"What are you working on now?" Kling asked, smiling.

"The Jeannie Paige murder," Monoghan said flatly.

A dart of fear shot up into Kling's skull. "Oh?" he said.

"Yeah," Monoghan said.

"Yeah," Monroe said.

Monoghan cleared his throat. "How long you been with the force, Kling?" he asked.

"Just—just a short while."

"That figures," Monoghan said.

"Sure," Monroe said.

"You like your job?"

"Yes," Kling answered hesitantly.

"You want to keep it?"

"You want to go on being a cop?"

"Yes, of course."

"Then keep your ass out of Homicide."

"What?" Kling said.

"He means," Monroe explained, "keep your ass out of Homicide."

"I—I don't know what you mean."

"We mean keep away from stiffs. Stiffs are *our* business."

"We like stiffs," Monroe said.

"We're specialists, you understand? You call in a heart doctor when you got heart disease, don't you? You call in an eye, ear, nose, and throat man when you got laryngitis, don't you? Okay, when you got a stiff, you call in Homicide. That's us. Monoghan and Monroe."

"You don't call in a wet-pants patrolman."

"Homicide. Not a beat-walker."

"Not a pavement-pounder."

"Not *you!*" Monoghan said.

"Not a nightstick-twirler."

"Not a traffic jockey."

"Clear?" Monroe asked.

"Yes," Kling said.

"It's gonna get a lot clearer," Monoghan added. "The lieutenant wants to see you."

"What for?"

"The lieutenant is a funny guy. He thinks Homicide is the best damn department in the city. He runs Homicide, and he don't like people coming in where they ain't asked. I'll let you in on a secret. He don't even like the *detectives* from your precinct to go messing around in murder. Trouble is, he can't refuse their assistance or their cooperation, specially when your precinct manages to stack up so many goddamn homicides each year. So he suffers the dicks—but he don't have to suffer no goddamn patrolman."

"But—but why does he want to see me? I understand now. I shouldn't have stuck my nose in, and I'm sorry I—"

"You shouldn't have stuck your nose in," Monoghan agreed.

"You definitely shouldn't have."

"But I didn't do any harm. I just—"

"Who knows what harm you've done?" Monoghan said.

"You may have done untold harm," Monroe said.

"Ah, hell," Kling said, "I've got a date."

"Yeah," Monoghan said. "With the lieutenant."

"Call your broad," Monroe advised. "Tell her the police are bugging you."

Kling looked at his watch. "I can't reach her," he said. "She's at school."

"Impairing the morals of a minor," Monoghan said, smiling.

"Better you shouldn't mention that to the lieutenant."

"She's in *college*," Kling said. "Listen, will I be through by seven?"

"Maybe," Monoghan said.

"Get your coat," Monroe said.

"He don't need a coat. It's nice and mild."

"It may get chilly later. This is pneumonia weather."

Kling sighed heavily. "All right if I wash my hands?"

"What?" Monoghan asked.

"He's polite," Monroe said. "He has to take a leak."

"No, I have to wash my hands."

"Okay, so wash them. Hurry up. The lieutenant don't like to be kept waiting."

He called Claire at eleven-ten. The phone rang six times, and he was ready to hang up, afraid he'd caught her asleep, when the receiver was lifted.

"Hello?" she said. Her voice was sleepy.

"Claire?"

"Yes, who's this?"

"Did I wake you?"

"Yes." There was a pause, and then her voice became a bit more lively. "Bert? Is that you?"

"Yes. Claire, I'm sorry I—"

"The last time I got stood up was when I was sixteen and had a—"

"Claire, I didn't stand you up, honest. Some Homicide cops—"

"It *felt* like being stood up. I waited in the newspaper office until a quarter to eight, God knows why. Why didn't you call?"

"They wouldn't let me use the phone." Kling paused. "Besides, I didn't know how I could reach you."

Claire was silent.

"Claire?"

"I'm here," she said wearily.

"Can I see you tomorrow? We'll spend the day together. I'm off tomorrow."

Again there was silence.

"Claire?"

"I heard you."

"Well?"

"Bert, why don't we call it quits, huh? Let's consider what happened tonight an ill omen, and just forget the whole thing, shall we?"

"No," he said.

"Bert—"

"No! I'll pick you up at noon, all right?"

Silence.

"Claire?"

"All right. Yes," she said. "Noon."

"I'll explain then. I . . . I got into a little trouble."

"All right."

"Noon?"

"Yes."

"Claire?"

"Yes?"

"Good night, Claire."

"Good night, Bert."

"I'm sorry I woke you."

"That's all right. I'd just dozed off, anyway."

"Well . . . good night, Claire."

"Good night, Bert."

He wanted to say more, but he heard the click of the receiver being replaced in the cradle. He sighed, left the phone booth, and ordered a steak with mushrooms, French fried onions, two baked potatoes, a huge salad with Roquefort dressing, and a glass of milk. He finished off the meal with three more glasses of milk and a slab of chocolate cream pie.

On the way out of the restaurant, he bought a candy bar.

Then he went home to sleep.

He had planned on a picnic in Bethtown, with its attendant ferry ride from Isola across the river. Rain had destroyed that silly notion.

He had drippingly called for Claire at twelve on the dot. The rain had given her a "horrible headache." Would he mind if they stayed indoors for a little while, just until the Empirin took hold?

Kling did not mind.

Claire had put some good records onto the record player, and then had lapsed into a heavy silence which he attributed to the throbbing headache. The rain had oozed against the windowpanes, streaking the city outside. The music had oozed from the record player—Bach's *Brandenburg Concerto No. 5 in D*, Strauss's *Don Quixote*, Franck's *Psyche*.

Kling almost fell asleep.

They left the apartment at two. The rain had let up somewhat, but it had put a knife-edge on the air, and they sloshed along in a sullen, uncommunicative silence, hating the rain with common enmity, but somehow having allowed the rain to build a solid wedge between them. When Kling suggested a movie, Claire accepted the offer eagerly.

The movie was terrible.

The feature was called *Apache Undoing*, or some such damn thing, and it starred hordes of painted Hollywood extras who screeched and whooped down upon a small band of blue-clothed soldiers. The handful of soldiers fought off the wily Apaches until almost the end of the movie. By this time, the hordes flung against the small, tired band must have numbered in the tens of thousands. With five minutes to go in the film, another small handful of soldiers arrived, leaving Kling with the distinct impression that the war would go on for another two hours in a subsequent film to be titled *Son of Apache Undoing*.

The second film on the bill was about a little girl whose mother and father are getting divorced. The little girl goes with them to Reno—Dad conveniently has business there at the same time Mom must establish residence—and through an unvarying progression of mincing postures and bright-eyed, smirking little-girl facial expressions, convinces Mom and Dad to stay together eternally and live in connubial bliss with their mincing, bright-eyed, smirking little smart-assed daughter.

They left the theater bleary-eyed. It was six o'clock.

Kling suggested a drink and dinner. Claire, probably in self-defense, agreed that a drink and dinner would be just dandy along about now.

And so they sat in the restaurant high atop one of the city's better-known hotels, and they looked through the huge windows which faced the river; and across the river there was a sign.

The sign first said: SPRY.

Then it said: SPRY FOR FRYING.

Then it said: SPRY FOR BAKING.

Then it said, again: SPRY.

"What'll you drink?" Kling asked.

"A whiskey sour, I think," Claire said.

"No cognac?"

"Later maybe."

The waiter came over to the table. He looked as romantic as Adolf Hitler.

"Something to drink, sir?" he asked.

"A whiskey sour and a martini."

"Lemon peel, sir?"

"Olive," Kling said.

"Thank you, sir. Would you care to see a menu now?"

"We'll wait until after we've had our drinks, thank you. All right, Claire?"

"Yes, fine," she said.

They sat in silence. Kling looked through the windows.

SPRY FOR FRYING.

"Claire?"

"Yes?"

SPRY FOR BAKING.

"It's been a bust, hasn't it?"

"Please, Bert."

"The rain . . . and that lousy movie. I didn't want it to be this way. I wanted—"

"I knew this would happen, Bert. I tried to tell you, didn't I? Didn't I try to warn you off? Didn't I tell you I was the dullest girl in the world? Why did you insist, Bert? Now you make me feel like a—like a—"

"I don't want you to feel *any* way," he said. "I was only going to suggest that we—we start afresh. From now. Forgetting everything that's—that's happened."

"Oh, what's the use?" Claire said.

The waiter came with their drinks. "Whiskey sour for the lady?" he asked.

"Yes."

He put the drinks on the table. Kling lifted the martini glass.

"To a new beginning," he said.

"If you want to waste a drink," she answered, and she drank.

"About last night—" he started.

"I thought this was to be a new beginning."

"I wanted to explain. I got picked up by two Homicide cops and taken to their lieutenant, who warned me to keep away from the Jeannie Paige potato."

"Are you going to?"

"Yes, of course." He paused. "I'm curious, I admit, but . . ."

"I understand."

"Claire," he said evenly, "what the hell is the matter with you?"

"Nothing."

"Where do you go when you retreat?"

"What?"

"Where do you . . . ?"

"I didn't think it showed. I'm sorry."

"It shows," Kling said. "Who was he?"

Claire looked up sharply. "You're a better detective than I realized."

"It doesn't take much detection," he said. There was a sad undertone to his voice now, as if her confirmation of his suspicions had suddenly taken all the fight out of him. "I don't mind your carrying a torch. Lots of girls—"

"It's not that," she interrupted.

"Lots of girls do," he continued. "A guy drops them cold, or else it just peters out the way romances sometimes—"

"It's not that!" she said sharply, and when he looked across the table at her, her eyes filmed with tears

"Hey, listen, I—"

"Please, Bert, I don't want to—'

"But you said it *was* a guy. You said—"

"All right," she answered. "All right, Bert." She bit down on her lip. "All right, there was a guy. And I was crazy in love with him. I was seventeen—just like Jeannie Paige—and he was nineteen."

Kling waited. Claire lifted her drink and drained the glass. She swallowed hard, and then sighed and Kling watched her, waiting.

"I met him at Club Tempo. We hit it off right away. Do you know how such things happen, Bert? It happened that way with us. We made a lot of plans, big plans. We were young, and we were strong, and we were in love."

"I—I don't understand," he said

"He was killed in Korea."

Across the river, the sign blared, SPRY FOR FRYING.

The table was very silent. Claire stared at the tablecloth. Kling folded his hands nervously.

"So don't ask me why I go down to the Tempo and make a fool of myself with kids like Hud and Tommy. I'm looking for *him* all over again, Bert, can't you see that? I'm looking for his face, and his youth, and—"

Cruelly, Bert Kling said, "You won't find him."

"I—"

"You won't find him. You're a fool for trying. He's dead and buried. He's—"

"I don't want to listen to you," Claire said. "Take me home, please."

"No," he said. "He's dead and buried, and *you're* burying yourself alive, you're making a martyr of yourself, you're wearing a widow's weeds at twenty! What the hell's the matter with you? Don't you know that people die every day? Don't you know?"

"Shut up!" she said.

"Don't you know you're killing yourself? Over a kid's puppy love— over a—"

"Shut up!" she said again, and this time her voice was on the verge of hysteria, and some of the diners around them turned at her outburst.

"Okay!" Kling said tightly. "Okay, bury yourself! Bury your beauty, and try to hide your sparkle! Wear black every day of the week, for all I give a damn! But I think you're a phony! I think you're a fourteen-carat phony!" He paused, and then said angrily, "Let's get the hell out of this goldfish bowl!"

He started to rise, signaling for the waiter at the same time. Claire sat motionless opposite him. And then, quite suddenly, she began to cry. The tears started slowly at first, forcing their way past clenched eyelids, trickling silently down her cheeks. And then her shoulders began to heave, and she sat as still as a stone, her hands clasped in her lap, her shoulders heaving, sobbing silently while the tears coursed down her face. He had never seen such honest misery before. He turned his face away. He did not want to watch her.

"You are ready to order, sir?" the waiter asked, sidling up to the table.

"Two more of the same," Bert said. The waiter started off, and he caught at his arm. "No. Change the whiskey sour to a double shot of Canadian Club."

"Yes, sir," the waiter said, padding off.

"I don't want another drink," Claire muttered.

"You'll have one."

"I don't want one." She erupted into tears again, and this time Kling watched her. She sobbed steadily for several moments, and then the tears stopped as suddenly as they had begun, leaving her face looking as clean as a city street does after a sudden summer storm.

"I'm sorry," she said.

"Don't be."

"I should have cried a long time ago."

"Yes."

The waiter brought the drinks. Kling lifted his glass. "To a new beginning," he said.

Claire studied him. It took her a long while to reach for the double shot before her. Finally, her hand closed around the glass. She lifted it and touched the rim of Kling's glass. "To a new beginning," she said. She threw off the shot quickly.

"That's strong," she said.

"It'll do you good."

"Yes. I'm sorry, Bert. I shouldn't have burdened you with my troubles."

"Offhand, can you think of anyone who'd accept them so readily?"

"No," she said immediately. She smiled tiredly.

"That's better."

She looked across at him as if she were seeing him for the first time. The tears had put a sparkle into her eyes. "It—it may take time, Bert," she said. Her voice came from a long way off.

"I've got all the time in the world," he said. And then, almost afraid she would laugh at him, he added, "All I've been doing is killing time, Claire, waiting for you to come along."

She seemed ready to cry again. He reached across the table and covered her hand with his.

"You . . . you're very good, Bert," she said, her voice growing thin, the way a voice does before it collapses into tears. "You're good, and kind, and gentle, and you're quite beautiful, do you know that? I . . . I think you're very beautiful."

"You should see me when my hair is combed," he said, smiling, squeezing her hand.

"I'm not joking," she said. "You always think I'm joking, and you really shouldn't because I'm—I'm a serious girl."

"I know."

"So—"

He shifted his position abruptly, grimacing.

"Is something wrong?" she asked, suddenly concerned.

"No. This goddamn pistol." He shifted again.

"Pistol?"

"Yes. In my back pocket. We have to carry them, you know. Even off duty."

"Not really? A gun? You have a gun in your pocket?"

"Sure."

She leaned closer to him. Her eyes were clear now, as if they had never known tears or sadness. They sparkled with interest. "May I see it?"

"Sure." He reached down, unbuttoned his jacket, and then pulled the gun with its leather holster from his hip pocket. He put it on the table. "Don't touch it, or it'll go off in your face."

"It looks menacing."

"It *is* menacing. I'm the deadest shot in the 87th Precinct."

"Are you really?"

"'Kling the King,' they call me."

She laughed suddenly.

"I can shoot any damn elephant in the world at a distance of three feet," Kling expanded. Her laugh grew. He watched her laughing. She seemed unaware of the transformation.

"Do you know what I feel like doing?" he said.

"What?"

"I feel like taking this gun and shooting out that goddamn Spry sign across the river."

"Bert," she said, "Bert," and she put her other hand over his, so that three hands formed a pyramid on the table. Her face grew very serious. "Thank you, Bert. Thank you so very, very much."

He didn't know what to say. He felt embarrassed and stupid and happy and very big. He felt about eighty feet tall.

"What—what are you doing tomorrow?" he asked.

"Nothing. What are you doing tomorrow?"

"I'm calling Molly Bell to explain why I can't snoop around anymore. And then I'm stopping by at your place, and we're going on a picnic. *If* the sun is shining."

"The sun'll be shining, Bert."

"I know it will," he said.

She leaned forward suddenly and kissed him, a quick, sudden kiss that fleetingly touched his mouth and then was gone. She sat back again, seeming very unsure of herself, seeming like a frightened little girl at her first party. "You—you must be patient," she said.

"I will," he promised.

The waiter suddenly appeared. The waiter was smiling. He coughed discreetly. Kling watched him in amazement.

"I thought," the waiter said gently, "perhaps a little candlelight at the table, sir? The lady will look even more lovely by candlelight."

"The lady looks lovely just as she is," Kling said.

The waiter seemed disappointed. "But . . ."

"But the candlelight, certainly," Kling said. "By all means, the candlelight."

The waiter beamed. "Ah, yes, sir. Yes, sir. And then we will order, yes? I have some suggestions, sir, whenever you're ready." He paused, his smile lighting his face. "It's a beautiful night, sir, isn't it?"

"It's a wonderful night," Claire answered.

The Mugger, 1956

The department stores on Friday, December 22, were a little crowded. Kling could not honestly say he disliked the crowds because the crowds forced him into close proximity with Claire, and there was no girl he'd rather have been proximately close to. On the other hand, however, the alleged purpose of this excursion was to pick up presents for people like Uncle Ed and Aunt Sarah—whom Kling had never met—and the sooner that task was accomplished, the sooner he and Claire could begin spending an uncluttered afternoon together. This was, after all, a day off and he did not enjoy trudging all over department stores on his day off, even if that trudging were being done with Claire.

He had to admit that of all the trudgers around, he and Claire made the nicest-looking pair of trudgers. There was a tireless sort of energy about her, an energy he usually associated with phys ed majors. Phys ed majors were easily identified by short, squat bodies with muscular legs and bulging biceps. Claire Townsend had none of the attributes of the phys ed major, except the tireless energy.

He wondered when the dynamo would run down, but the dynamo kept right on discharging electrical bolts and buying gifts for Cousin Percy and Grandmother Eloise, and Kling trailed along like a dinghy tied to a schooner in full sail, mixing his metaphors with reckless abandon.

"You should see what I got you," she told him.

"What?" he asked.

"A gold-plated holster for your ridiculous weapon."

"My gun, you mean?" he asked.

"And a carton of soap for your dirty mind."

"I'll bet I could make 2nd/Grade in ten minutes just picking up shoplifters here," he said.

"Don't pick up any who are young or blond."

"Claire . . ."

"Look at those gloves! Only $2.98 and perfect for . . ."

"Cousin Antoinette in Kalamazoo. Claire . . ."

"As soon as I get these gloves, darling."

"How do you know what I was going to say?"

"You want to stop all this nonsense and get some drinks, don't you?"

"Yes."

"Just what I had in mind," Claire said. And then, being in a gay and expansive mood, she added, "You should be delighted. When we're married, *you'll* have to pay for all this junk."

It was the first time the subject of marriage had come up between them and, being towed as he was, Kling almost missed it. Before he became fully aware of the miracle of what she had said, Claire had purchased the $2.98 gloves and was whisking him along to the roof garden of the store. The roof garden was packed with matronly women who were bulging with bundles.

"They only serve those triangular little sandwiches here," Kling announced. "Come on, I'll take you to a shady bar."

The shady bar he took her to was really not quite so shady as all that. It was dim, true, but dimness and shadiness are not necessarily synonymous.

When the waiter tiptoed over, Kling ordered a Scotch on the rocks and then glanced inquisitively toward Claire.

"Cognac," she said, and the waiter crept away.

"Are you really going to marry me someday?" Kling asked.

"Please," Claire told him, "I'll burst. I'm full of Christmas cheer, and a proposal now will just destroy me."

"But you *do* love me?"

"Did I ever say so?"

"No."

"Then what makes you so impetuous?"

"I'm sure you love me."

"Well, confidence is a fine quality, to be sure, but . . ."

"Don't you?"

Claire sobered quite suddenly. "Yes, Bert," she said. "Yes, Bert darling, I do love you. Very much."

"Well, then . . .." He was speechless. He grinned foolishly and covered her hand with his and blinked.

"Now I've spoiled you," she said, smiling. "Now that you know I'm in your power, you'll be unbearable."

"No, no, I won't."

"I know you policemen," she insisted. "You're brutal and cruel and . . ."

"No, Claire, no, really I . . ."

"Yes, yes. You'll take me in for questioning and . . ."

"Oh Jesus, Claire, I love you," he said plaintively.

"Yes," she said, smiling contentedly. "Isn't it wonderful? Aren't we so lucky, Bert?"

The Pusher, 1956

When Kling came back to the table, there was a smile on his face.

"What's up?" Carella asked.

"Oh, nothing much. Claire's father left for New Jersey this morning, that's all. Won't be back until Monday."

"Which gives you an empty apartment for the weekend, huh?" Carella said.

"Well, I wasn't thinking of anything like that," Kling said.

"No, of course not."

"But it might be nice," Kling admitted.

"When are you going to marry that girl?"

"She wants to get her master's degree before we get married."

"Why?"

"How do I know? She's insecure." Kling shrugged. "She's psychotic. How do I know?"

"What does she want after the master's? A doctorate?"

"Maybe." Kling shrugged. "Listen, I ask her to marry me every time I see her. She wants the master's. So what can I do? I'm in love with her. Can I tell her to go to hell?"

"I suppose not."

"Well, I can't." Kling paused. "I mean, what the hell, Steve, if a girl wants an education, it's not my right to say no, is it?"

"I guess not."

"Well, would you have said no to Teddy?"

"I don't think so."

"Well, there you are."

"Sure."

"I mean, what the hell else can I do, Steve? I either wait for her, or I decide not to marry her, right?"

"Right," Carella said.

"And since I want to marry her, I have no choice. I wait." He paused thoughtfully. "Jesus, I hope she isn't one of those perennial schoolgirl types." He paused again. "Well, there's nothing I can do about it. I'll just have to wait, that's all."

"That sounds like sound deduction."

"Sure. The only thing is . . . well, to be absolutely truthful with you, Steve, I'm afraid she'll get pregnant or something, and then we'll *have* to get married, do you know what I mean? And that'll be different than if we just got married because we felt like it. I mean, even though we love each other and all, it'd be different. Oh, Jesus, I don't know what to do."

"Just be careful, that's all," Carella said.

"Oh, I am. I mean, we are, we are. You want to know something, Steve?"

"What?"

"I wish I could keep my hands off her. You know, I wish we didn't have to . . . well, you know, my landlady looks at me cockeyed every time I bring Claire upstairs. And then I have to rush her home because her father is the strictest guy who ever walked the earth. I'm surprised he's leaving her alone this weekend. But what I mean is . . . well, damnit, what the hell does she need that master's for, Steve? I mean, I wish I could leave her alone until we were married, but I just can't. I mean, all I have to do is be with her, and my mouth goes dry. Is it that way with . . . well, never mind, I didn't mean to get personal."

"It's that way," Carella said.

"Yeah," Kling said, and he nodded. He seemed lost in thought for a moment. Then he said, "I've got tomorrow off, but not Sunday. Do you think somebody would want to switch with me? Like for a Tuesday or something? I hate to break up the weekend."

"Where'd you plan to spend the weekend?" Carella asked.

"Well, you know . . ."

"*All* weekend?" Carella said, surprised.

"Well, you know . . ."

"Starting *tonight*?" he asked, astonished.

"Well, you know . . ."

"I'd give you my Sunday, but I'm afraid . . ."

"Will you?" Kling said, leaning forward.

". . . you'll be a wreck on Monday morning." Carella paused. "*All* weekend?" he asked again.

"Well, it isn't often the old man goes away. You know."

"Flaming Youth, where have you gone?" Carella said, shaking his head. "Sure, you can have my Sunday if the Skipper says okay."

"Thanks, Steve."

"Or did Teddy have something planned?" Carella asked himself.

"Now, don't change your mind," Kling said anxiously.

"Okay, okay." He tapped the missing-persons report with his forefinger. "What do you think?"

"He looks good, I would say. He's big enough, anyway. Six-four and weighs two-ten. That's no midget, Steve."

"And that hand belonged to a big man." Carella finished his coffee and said, "Come on, lover man, let's go see Mrs. Androvich."

As they rose, Kling said, "It's not that I'm a great lover or anything, Steve. It's just . . . well . . ."

"What?"

Kling grinned. "I *like* it," he said.

* .* *

109

She kissed him the moment he entered the apartment. She was wearing black slacks and a wide, white, smocklike blouse which ended just below her waist.

"What kept you?" she said.

"Florists," he answered.

"You brought me flowers?"

"No. A lady we talked to said her husband bought her a dozen red roses. We checked about ten florists in the immediate and surrounding neighborhoods. Result? No red roses on Valentine's Day. Not to Mrs. Karl Androvich, anyway."

"So?"

"So Steve Carella is uncanny. Can I take off my shoes?"

"Go ahead. I bought two steaks. Do you feel like steaks?"

"Later."

"How is Carella uncanny?"

"Well, he lit into this skinny, pathetic dame as if he were going to rip all the flesh from her bones. When we got outside, I told him I thought he was a little rough with her. I mean, I've seen him operate before, and he usually wears kid gloves with the ladies. So with this one, he used a sledgehammer, and I wondered why. And I told him I disapproved."

"So what did he say?"

"He said he knew she was lying from the minute she opened her mouth, and he began wondering why."

"How did he know?"

"He just knew. That's what was so uncanny about it. We checked all those damn florists, and nobody made a delivery at six in the morning, and none of them were even *open* before nine."

"The husband could have ordered the flowers anywhere in the city, Bert."

"Sure, but that's pretty unlikely, isn't it? He's not a guy who works in an office someplace. He's a seaman, and when he's not at sea, he's home. So the logical place to order flowers would be a neighborhood florist."

"So?"

"So nothing. I'm tired. Steve sent a meat cleaver to the lab." He paused. "She didn't look like the kind of a dame who'd use a meat cleaver on a man. Come here."

She went to him, climbing into his lap. He kissed her and said, "I've got the whole weekend. Steve's giving me his Sunday."

"Oh? Yes?"

"You feel funny," he said.

"Funny? How?"

"I don't know. Softer."

"I'm not wearing a bra."

"How come?"

"I wanted to feel free. Keep your hands off me!" she said suddenly, and she leaped out of his lap.

"Now, you are the kind of dame who would use a meat cleaver on a man," Kling said, appraising her from the chair in which he sat.

"Am I?" she answered coolly. "When do you want to eat?"

"Later."

"Where are we going tonight?" Claire asked.

"No place."

"Oh?"

"I don't have to be back at the squad until Monday morning," Kling said.

"Oh, is that right?"

"Yes, and what I planned was . . ."

"Yes?"

"I thought we could get into bed right now and stay in bed all weekend. Until Monday morning. How does that sound to you?"

"It sounds pretty strenuous."

"Yes, it does. But I vote for it."

"I'll have to think about it. I had my heart set on a movie."

"We can always see a movie," Kling said.

"Anyway, I'm hungry right now," Claire said, studying him narrowly. "I'm going to make the steaks."

"I'd rather go to bed."

"Bert," she said, "man does not live by bed alone."

Kling rose suddenly. They stood at opposite ends of the room, studying each other. "What did *you* plan on doing tonight?" he asked.

"Eating steaks," she said.

"And what else?"

"A movie."

"And tomorrow?"

Claire shrugged.

"Come here," he said.

"Come get me," she answered.

He went across the room to her. She tilted her head to his and then crossed her arms tightly over her breasts.

"All weekend," he said.

"You're a braggart," she whispered.

"You're a doll."

"Am I?"

"You're a lovely doll."

"You going to kiss me?"

"Maybe."

They stood not two inches from each other, not touching, staring at each other, savoring this moment, allowing desire to leap between them in a mounting wave.

He put his hands on her waist, but he did not kiss her.

Slowly, she uncrossed her arms.

"You really have no bra on?" he asked.

"Big weekend lover," she murmured. "Can't even find out for himself whether or not I have a . . ."

His hands slid under the smock and he pulled Claire to him.

The next time anyone would see Kling would be on Monday morning.

It would still be raining.

Give the Boys a Great Big Hand, 1960

Patterns.

The pattern of October sunlight filtering past barred and grilled windows to settle in an amber splash on a scarred wooden floor. Shadows merge with the sun splash—the shadows of tall men in shirt sleeves; this is October, but the squad room is hot and Indian summer is dying slowly.

A telephone rings.

There is the sound of a city beyond those windows. The sudden shriek in unison of children let out from school, the peddler behind his cart—"Hot dogs, orange drink"—the sonorous rumble of buses and automobiles, the staccato click of high-heeled pumps, the empty rattle of worn roller skates on chalked sidewalks. Sometimes the city goes suddenly still. You can almost hear a heartbeat. But this silence is a part of the city noise, a part of the pattern. In the stillness, sometimes a pair of lovers will walk beneath the windows of the squad room, and their words will drift upward in a whispered fade. A cop will look up from his typewriter. A city is going by outside.

Patterns.

A detective is standing at the water cooler. He holds the cone-shaped paper cup in his hand, waits until it is filled, and then tilts his head back to drink. A .38 Police Special is resting in a holster which is clipped to the left-hand side of his belt. A typewriter is going across the room, hesitantly, fumblingly, but reports must be typed, and in triplicate; cops do not have private secretaries.

Another phone rings.

"87th Squad, Carella."

There is a timelessness to this room. There are patterns overlapping patterns, and they combine to form the classic design that is police work. The design varies slightly from day to day. There is an office routine, and an investigatory routine, and very rarely does a case come along which breaks the classic pattern. Police work is like a bullfight. There is always a ring, and always a bull, and always a matador and picadors and *chulos*, and always, too, the classic music of the arena, the opening trumpet playing *La Virgen de la Macarena*, the ritual music throughout, announcing the various stages of a contest which is not a contest at all. Usually the bull dies. Sometimes, but only when he is an exceptionally brave bull, he is spared. But for the most part he dies. There is no real sport involved here because the outcome is assured before the mock combat begins. The bull will die. There are, to be sure, some surprises within the framework of the sacrificial ceremony—a matador will be gored, a bull will leap the *barrera*—but the pattern remains set and unvaried, the classic ritual of blood.

It is the same with police work.

There are patterns to this room. There is a timelessness to these men in this place doing the work they are doing.

They are all deeply involved in the classic ritual of blood.

"87th Squad, Detective Kling."

Bert Kling, youngest man on the squad, cradled the telephone receiver between his shoulder and his ear, leaned over the typewriter, and began erasing a mistake. He had misspelled "apprehended."

"Who?" he said into the phone. "Oh, sure, Dave, put her on." He waited while Dave Murchison, manning the switchboard in the muster room downstairs, put the call through.

From the water cooler, Meyer Meyer filled another paper cup and said, "He's always got a girl on the phone. The girls in this city, they got nothing else to do, they call Detective Kling and ask him how the crime is going today." He shook his head.

Kling shushed him with an outstretched palm. "Hello, honey," he said into the phone.

"Oh, it's *her*," Meyer said knowingly.

Carella, completing a call at his own desk, hung up and said, "It's who?"

"Who do you think? Kim Novak, that's who. She calls here every day. She wants to know should she buy some stock in Columbia Pictures."

"Will you guys please shut up?" Kling said. Into the phone, he said, "Oh, the usual. The clowns are at it again."

Claire, on the other end of the line, said, "Tell them to stop kibitzing. Tell them we're in love."

113

"They already know that," Kling said. "Listen, are we all set for tonight?"

"Yes, but I'll be a little late."

"Why?"

"I've got a stop to make after school."

"What kind of a stop?" Kling asked.

"I have to pick up some texts. Stop being suspicious."

"Why don't you stop being a schoolgirl?" Kling asked. "Why don't you marry me?"

"When?"

"Tomorrow."

"I can't tomorrow. I'll be very busy tomorrow. Besides, the world needs social workers."

"Never mind the world. *I* need a wife. I've got holes in my socks."

"I'll darn them when I get there tonight," Claire said.

"Well, actually," Kling whispered, "I had something else in mind."

"He's whispering," Meyer said to Carella.

"Shut up," Kling said.

"Every time he gets to the good part, he whispers," Meyer said, and Carella burst out laughing.

"This is getting impossible," Kling said, sighing. "Claire, I'll see you at six-thirty, okay?"

"Seven's more like it," she said. "I'm wearing a disguise, by the way. So your nosy landlady won't recognize me when she peeks into the hall."

"What do you mean? What kind of a disguise?"

"You'll see."

"No, come on. What are you wearing?"

"Well . . . I've got on a white blouse," Claire said, "open at the throat, you know, with a strand of very small pearls. And a black skirt, very tight, with a wide black belt, the one with the silver buckle . . ."

As she spoke, Kling smiled unconsciously, forming a mental picture of her in the university phone booth. He knew she would be leaning over very close to the mouthpiece. She was five feet seven inches tall, and the booth would seem too small for her. Her hair, as black as sin, would be brushed back from her face, her brown eyes intensely alive as she spoke, perhaps with a faint smile on her mouth. The full white blouse would taper to a narrow waist, the black skirt hanging on wide hips, dropping in a straight line over her thighs and her long legs.

". . . no stockings because the weather's so damn hot," Claire said, "and high-heeled black pumps, and that's it."

"So, where's the disguise?"

"Well, I bought a new bra," Claire whispered.

"Oh?"

"You should see what it does for me, Bert." She paused. "Do you love me, Bert?"

"You know I do," he said.

"She just asked him does he love her," Meyer said, and Kling pulled a face.

"Tell me," Claire whispered.

"I can't right now."

"Will you tell me later?"

"Mmmm," Kling said, and he glanced apprehensively at Meyer.

"Wait until you see this bra," Claire said.

"Yes, I'm looking forward to it," Kling said, watching Meyer, phrasing his words carefully.

"You don't sound very interested," Claire said.

"I am. It's a little difficult, that's all."

"It's called Abundance," Claire said.

"What is?"

"The bra."

"That's nice," Kling said.

"What are they doing up there? Standing around your desk and breathing down your neck?"

"Well, not exactly, but I think I'd better say good-bye now. I'll see you at six-thirty, honey."

"Seven," Claire corrected.

"Okay. 'Bye, doll."

"Abundance," she whispered, and she hung up. Kling put the receiver back into the cradle.

"Okay," he said, "I'm going to call the telephone company and ask them to put in a phone booth."

"You're not supposed to make private calls on the city's time," Carella said, and he winked at Meyer.

"I didn't *make* this call. I *received* it. Also, a man is entitled to a certain amount of privacy, even if he works with a bunch of horny bastards. I don't see why I can't talk to my fiancée without—"

"He's sore," Meyer said. "He called her his fiancée instead of his girl. Look, talk to her. Call her back and tell her you sent all us gorillas out of the room and now you can talk to her. Go ahead."

"Go to hell," Kling said. Angrily, he turned back to his typewriter, forgetting that he'd been in the middle of an erasure. He began typing again and then realized he was overscoring what he'd already typed. Viciously, he ripped the almost-completed report from the machine. "See what you made me do?" he shouted impotently. "Now I have to start all over again!" He shook his head despairingly, took a white, a blue, and a yellow Detective Division report from his top drawer, separated the three sheets with carbon paper, and began typing again, banging the keys with a vengeance.

115

* * *

It was 5:15 P.M. when the telephone rang.

Meyer lifted the receiver and said, "87th Squad, Detective Meyer." He moved a pad into place on his desk. "Yeah, go ahead," he said. He began writing on the pad. "Yep," he said. He wrote down an address. "Yep." He continued writing. "Yep, right away." He hung up. "Steve, Bert," he said, "you want to take this?"

"What is it?" Carella asked.

"Some nut just shot up a bookstore on Culver Avenue," Meyer said. "There's three people lying dead on the floor."

The crowd had already gathered around the bookshop. A sign out front read "Good Books, Good Reading." There were two uniformed cops on the sidewalk, and a squad car was pulled up to the curb across the street. The people pulled back instinctively when they heard the wail of the siren on the police sedan. Carella got out first, slamming the door behind him. He waited for Kling to come around the car, and then both men started for the shop. At the door, the patrolman said, "Lot of dead people in there, sir."

"When'd you get here?"

"Few minutes ago. We were just cruising when we took the squeal. We called back the minute we saw what it was."

"Know how to keep a timetable?"

"Yes, sir."

"Come along and keep it, then."

"Yes, sir."

They started into the shop. Not three feet from the door, they saw the first body. The man was partially slumped against one of the book stalls, partially sprawled on the floor. He was wearing a blue seersucker suit, and his hand was still holding a book, and a line of blood had run down his arm, and stained his sleeve, and continued down over the hand holding the book. Kling looked at him and knew instantly that this was going to be a bad one. Just how bad, he did not yet realize.

"Here's another one," Carella said.

The second body was some ten feet away from the first, another man coatless, his head twisted and fitting snugly into the angle formed by the book stall and the floor. As they approached, he moved his head slightly, trying to raise it from its uncomfortable position. A new flow of blood spilled onto his shirt collar. He dropped his head again. The patrolman, his throat parched, his voice containing something like awe, said, "He's alive."

Carella stooped down beside the man. The man's neck had been ripped open by the force of the bullet which had struck him. Carella looked at torn flesh and muscle, and for an instant he closed his eyes, the action coming as swiftly as the clicking shutter of a camera, the eyes opening again at once, a tight hard mask claiming his face.

"Did you call for a meat wagon?" he asked.

"The minute I got here," the patrolman said.

"Good."

"There are two others," a voice said.

Kling turned away from the dead man in the seersucker suit. The man who'd spoken was a small, birdlike man with a bald head. He stood crouched against one of the bookstalls, his hand to his mouth. He was wearing a shabby brown sweater open over a white shirt. There was abject terror on his face and in his eyes. He was sobbing low, muted sobs which accompanied the tears that flowed from his eyes, oddly channeling themselves along either side of his nose. As Kling approached him, he thought, Two others. Meyer said there were three. But it's four.

"Are you the owner of this shop?" he asked.

"Yes," the man said. "Please look at the others. Back there. Is an ambulance coming? A wild man, a wild man. Look at the others, please. They may be alive. One of them is a woman. Please look at them."

Kling nodded and walked to the back of the shop. He found the third man bent double over one of the counters, an open book beside him; he had undoubtedly been browsing when the shots were loosed. The man was dead, his mouth open, his eyes staring sightlessly. Unconsciously, Kling's hand went to the man's eyelids. Gently he closed them.

The woman lay on the floor beside him.

She was wearing a red blouse.

She had undoubtedly been carrying an armful of books when the bullets took her. She had fallen to the floor, and the books had fallen around her and upon her. One book lay just under her extended right hand. Another, open like a tent, covered her face and her black hair. A third leaned against her curving hip. The red blouse had pulled free from the woman's black skirt as she had fallen. The skirt had risen over the backs of her long legs. One leg was bent, the other rigid and straight. A black high-heeled pump lay several inches away from one naked foot. The woman wore no stockings.

Kling knelt beside her. Oddly, the titles of the books registered on his mind: *Patterns of Culture* and *The Sane Society* and *Interviewing: Its Principles and Methods*. He saw suddenly that the blouse was not a red blouse at all. A corner that had pulled free from the black skirt showed white. There were two enormous holes in the girl's side, and the blood had poured steadily from those wounds, staining the white blouse a bright red. A string of tiny pearls had broken when she had fallen, and the pearls lay scattered on the floor now, tiny luminescent islands in the sticky coagulation of her blood. He felt pain looking at her. He reached for the book which had fallen open over her face. He lifted the book, and the pain suddenly became a very personal, very involved thing.

"Oh my Jesus Christ!" he said.

There was something in his voice which caused Steve Carella to run toward the back of the shop immediately. And then he heard Kling's cry, a single sharp anguished cry that pierced the dust-filled, cordite-stinking air of the shop.

"Claire!"

He was holding the dead girl in his arms when Carella reached him. His hands and his face were covered with Claire Townsend's blood, and he kissed her lifeless eyes and her nose and her throat, and he kept murmuring over and over again, "Claire, Claire," and Steve Carella would remember that name and the sound of Kling's voice as long as he lived.

Lady, Lady, I Did It!, 1961

CINDY FORREST

The young blonde who walked into the squadroom while Bert Kling was poring over the files was Cindy Forrest. She was carrying a black tote bag in one hand and a manila folder under her arm, and she was looking for Detective Steve Carella, ostensibly to give him the material in the folder. Cindy—by her own admission—was a nineteen-year-old girl who would be twenty in June and who had seen it all and heard it all, and also done a little. She thought Steve Carella was an attractive man in a glamor profession—listen, some girls have a thing for cops—and whereas she knew he was married and suspected he had four dozen kids, she nonetheless thought it might be sort of interesting to see him again, the marriage contract being a remote and barely understood cultural curiosity to most nineteen-year-olds going on twenty. She didn't know what would happen with Carella when she saw him again, though she had constructed a rather elaborate fantasy in her own mind and knew exactly what she *wished* would happen. The fact that he was married didn't disturb her at all, nor was she very troubled by the fact that he was almost twice her age. She saw in him a man with an appealing animal vitality, not too dumb for a cop, who had just possibly seen and heard even more than she had, and who had most certainly *done* more than she had, her own experience being limited to once in the backseat of an automobile and another time on a bed at a party in New Ashton. She could remember the names of both boys, but they were only boys, that was the thing, and Steve Carella seemed to her to be a man, which was another thing again and something she felt she ought to experience *now*, before she got married herself one day and tied down with kids.

She hadn't consulted Carella on the possibility as yet, but she felt this was only a minor detail. She was extremely secure in her own good looks and in an undeniable asset called youth. She was certain that once Carella understood her intentions, he would be happy to oblige, and they would then enter into a madly delirious and delicious love affair which would end some months from now because, naturally, it could never be; but Carella would remember her forever, the nineteen-year-old going on twenty who had shared those tender moments of passion, who had enriched his life, who had rewarded him with her inquiring young mind and her youthful, responsive body.

Feeling like Héloïse about to keep an assignation with Abelard, she walked into the squad room expecting to find Carella—and instead found Bert Kling.

Kling was sitting at his own desk in a shaft of sunlight that came through the grilled window and settled on his blond head like a halo. He was suntanned and muscular, and he was wearing a white shirt open at the throat, and he was bent over the papers on his desk, the sun touching his hair, looking very healthy and handsome and young.

She hated him on sight.

"I beg your pardon," she said.

Kling looked up. "Yes, miss?"

"I'd like to see Detective Carella, please."

"Not here right now," Kling answered. "Can I help you?"

"Who are *you*?" Cindy asked.

"Detective Kling."

"How do you do?" She paused. "You did say *Detective* Kling?"

"That's right."

"You seem so"—she hesitated on the word, as if it were loathsome to her—"young. To be a detective, I mean."

Kling sensed her hostility immediately, and immediately reacted in a hostile manner. "Well, you see," he said, "I'm the boss's son. That's how I got to be a detective so fast."

"Oh, I see." She looked around the squadroom, obviously annoyed by Kling, and the room, and Carella's absence, and the world. "When will he be back? Carella?"

"Didn't say. He's out making some calls."

With a ghoulishly sweet grin, Cindy said, "And they left *you* to mind the store. How nice."

"Yeah," Kling answered, "they left me to mind the store." He was not smiling, because he was not enjoying this little snotnose who came up here with her *Saturday Evening Post* face and her college-girl talk. "So since I'm minding the store, what is it you want, miss? I'm busy."

"Yes, I can see that."

"What can I do for you?"

"Nothing. I'll wait for Carella, if you don't mind." She was opening the gate in the slatted rail divider when Kling came out of his chair swiftly and abruptly.

"Hold it right there!" he snapped.

"Wh-what?" Cindy asked, her eyes opening wide.

"Just *hold* it, miss!" Kling shouted, and to Cindy's shocked surprise, he pulled a pistol from a holster clipped to his belt and pointed it right at her heart."

"Get in here," he said. "Don't reach into that bag!"

"What? Are you . . . ?"

"*In!*" Kling shouted.

She obeyed him instantly, because she was certain he was going to shoot her dead in the next moment. She had heard stories about cops who lost their minds and went around shooting anything that moved. She was also beginning to wonder whether he really was a cop, and not simply a stray hoodlum who had wandered up here.

"Empty your bag on the desk," Kling said.

"Listen, what the hell do you think you're . . . ?"

"Empty it, miss," he said menacingly.

"I'm going to *sue* you, you know," she said coldly, and turned over her bag, spilling the contents onto the desk.

Kling went through the pile of junk rapidly. "What's in that folder?" he asked.

"Some stuff for Detective Carella."

"On the desk."

She put the folder down. Kling loosened the ties on it, and stuck his hand into it. He kept the gun trained at Cindy's middle, and she watched him with growing exasperation.

"All right?" she asked at last.

"Put your hands up over your head as high as you can get them."

"Listen, I don't have to . . ."

"Miss," he said warningly, and she raised her hands.

"Higher. Stretch."

"Why?"

"Because I'd really like to frisk you, but this'll have to do."

"Oh, boy, are you getting in trouble," she said, and she reached up for the ceiling. He studied her body minutely, looking for the bulge of a gun anywhere under her clothes. He saw only a trim, youthful figure in a white sweater and a straight black skirt. No unexplainable bulges.

"All right, put your hands down. What do you want with Carella?"

"I want to give him what's in that folder. Now, suppose you explain . . ."

"Miss, a couple of years back we had a girl come in here asking for Steve Carella, who happened to be out making a call. None of us could help her. She said she wanted to wait for Steve. So she marched through that gate, just the way you were about to do, and then she pulled out a thirty-eight, and the next thing we knew, she told us she was here to *kill* Carella."

"What's that got to do with . . . ?"

"So, miss, I'm only the boss's son and a very dumb cop, but that dame put us through hell for more hours than I care to remember. And I know enough to come in out of the rain. Especially when there's lightning around."

"I see. And is this what you do with every girl who comes into the squad room? You frisk them?"

"I didn't frisk you, miss."

"Are you finished with me?"

"Yes."

"Then go frisk yourself," Cindy said, and she turned away from him coldly and began putting the junk back into her bag.

"Let me help you with that," Kling said.

"Mister, you'd better just stay as far away from me as possible. I don't have a thirty-eight, but if you take one step closer to me, I'll clonk you right on the head with my shoe."

"Look, you weren't exactly radiating . . ."

"I've never in my entire life dealt with anyone as . . ."

". . . sunshine when you came in here. You looked sore, and I automatically . . ."

". . . suspicious, or as rude, or as overbearing in his manner . . ."

". . . assumed you . . ."

"Shut up when I'm talking!" Cindy shouted.

"Look, miss," Kling said angrily. "This happens to be a police station, and I happen to be a policeman, and I . . ."

"*Some* policeman!" Cindy snapped.

"You want me to kick you out of here?" Kling said menacingly.

"I want you to apologize to me!" Cindy yelled.

"Yeah, you've got a fat chance."

"Yeah, I'm going to tell you something, Mister Big Shot Boss's Son. If you think a citizen . . ."

"I'm not the boss's son," Kling yelled.

"You said you were!" Cindy yelled back.

"Only because you were so snotty!"

"*I* was snotty? *I* was . . ."

"I'm not used to seventeen-year-old brats . . ."

"I'm nineteen! Damn you, I'm *twenty*!"

"Make up your mind!" Kling shouted, and Cindy picked up her bag by the straps and swung it at him. Kling instinctively put up one of his hands, and the black leather collided with the flat palm, and all the junk Cindy had painstakingly put back into the bag came spilling out again, all over the floor.

They both stood stock-still, as if the spilling contents of the bag were an avalanche. Cigarettes, matches, lipstick, eyeshadow, sunglasses, a comb, an address and appointment book, a bottle of APC tablets, a book of twenty-five gummed parcel-post labels, a checkbook, a compact, more matches, a package of Chiclets, an empty cigarette package, a scrap of yellow paper with the handwritten words "Laundry, Quiz Philosophy," a hairbrush, an eyelash curler, two more combs, a package of Kleenex, several soiled Kleenex tissues, more matches, a pillbox without any pills in it, a box of Sucrets, two pencils, a wallet, more matches, a ballpoint pen, three pennies, several empty cellophane wrappers, and a peach pit all came tumbling out of the bag and fell onto the floor to settle in a disorderly heap between them.

Kling looked down at the mess.

Cindy looked down at the mess.

Silently, she knelt and began filling the bag again. She worked without looking up at him, without saying a word. Then she rose, picked up the manila folder from the desk, put it into Kling's hands, and frostily said, "Will you please see that Detective Carella gets this?"

Kling accepted the folder. "Who shall I say left it?"

"Cynthia Forrest."

"Listen, I'm sorry about . . ."

"Detective Kling, I think you are the biggest bastard I've ever met in my life," Cindy said, enunciating every word sharply and distinctly.

Then she turned and walked out of the squad room.

Ten Plus One, 1963

The man was sitting on a bench in the reception room when Miles Vollner came back from lunch that Wednesday afternoon. Vollner glanced at him, and then looked quizzically at his receptionist. The girl shrugged slightly and went back to her typing. The moment Vollner was inside his private office, he buzzed her.

"Who's that waiting outside?" he asked.

"I don't know, sir," the receptionist said.

"What do you mean, you don't know?"

"He wouldn't give me his name, sir."

"Did you ask him?"

"Yes, I did."

"What did he say?"

"Sir, he's sitting right here," the receptionist said, her voice lowering to a whisper. "I'd rather not—"

"What's the matter with you?" Vollner said. "This is *my* office, not *his*. What did he say when you asked him his name?"

"He—he told me to go to hell, sir."

"What?"

"Yes, sir."

"I'll be right out," Vollner said.

He did not go right out because his attention was caught by a letter on his desk, the afternoon mail having been placed there some five minutes ago by his secretary. He opened the letter, read it quickly, and then smiled because it was a large order from a retailer in the Midwest, a firm Vollner had been trying to get as a customer for the past six months. The company Vollner headed was small but growing. It specialized in audiovisual components, with its factory across the River Harb in the next state, and its business and administrative office here on Shepherd Street in the city. Fourteen people worked in the business office—ten men and four women. Two hundred and six people worked in the plant. It was Vollner's hope and expectation that both office and factory staffs would have to be doubled within the next year, and perhaps trebled the year after that. The large order from the Midwest retailer confirmed his beliefs, and pleased him enormously. But then he remembered the man sitting outside, and the smile dropped from his face. Sighing, he went to the door, opened it, and walked down the corridor to the reception room.

The man was still sitting there.

He could not have been older than twenty-three or twenty-four, a sinewy man with a pale narrow face and hooded brown eyes. He was clean-shaven and well dressed, wearing a gray topcoat open over a darker gray suit. A pearl-gray fedora was on top of his head. He sat on the bench with his arms folded across his chest, his legs outstretched, seemingly quite at ease. Vollner went to the bench and stood in front of him.

"Can I help you?" he said.

"Nope."

"What do you want here?"

"That's none of your business," the man said.

"I'm sorry," Vollner answered, "but it is my business. I happen to own this company."

"Yeah?" He looked around the reception room, and smiled. "Nice place you've got."

The receptionist, behind her desk, had stopped typing and was watching the byplay. Vollner could feel her presence behind him.

"Unless you can tell me what you want here," he said, "I'm afraid I'll have to ask you to leave."

The man was still smilling. "Well," he said, "I'm not about to tell you what I want here, and I'm not about to leave, either."

For a moment, Vollner was speechless. He glanced at the receptionist, and then turned back to the man. "In that case," he said, "I'll have to call the police."

"You call the police, and you'll be very sorry."

"We'll see about that," Vollner said. He walked to the receptionist's desk and said, "Miss Di Santo, will you get me the police, please?"

The man rose from the bench. He was taller than he had seemed while sitting, perhaps six feet two or three inches, with wide shoulders and enormous hands. He moved toward the desk and, still smiling, said, "Miss Di Santo, I wouldn't pick up that phone if I was you."

Miss Di Santo wet her lips and looked at Vollner.

"Call the police," Vollner said.

"Miss Di Santo, if you so much as put your hand on that telephone, I'll break your arm. I promise you that."

Miss Di Santo hesitated. She looked again to Vollner, who frowned and then said, "Never mind, Miss Di Santo," and without saying another word, walked to the entrance door and out into the corridor and toward the elevator. His anger kept building inside him all the way down to the lobby floor. He debated calling the police from a pay phone, and then decided he would do better to find a patrolman on the beat and bring him back upstairs personally. It was two o'clock, and the city streets were thronged with afternoon shoppers. He found a patrolman on the corner of Shepherd and Seventh, directing traffic. Vollner stepped out into the middle of the intersection and said, "Officer, I'd—"

"Hold it a minute, mister," the patrolman said. He blew his whistle and waved at the oncoming automobiles. Then he turned to Vollner and said, "Now, what is it?"

"There's a man up in my office, won't tell us what his business is."

"Yeah?" the patrolman said.

"Yes. He threatened me and my receptionist, and he won't leave."

"Yeah?" The patrolman kept looking at Vollner curiously, as though only half believing him.

"Yes. I'd like you to come up and help me get him out of there."

"You would, huh?"

"Yes."

"And who's gonna handle the traffic on this corner?" the patrolman said.

"This man is threatening us," Vollner said. "Surely that's more important than—"

"This is one of the biggest intersections in the city right here, and you want me to leave it."

"Aren't you supposed to—"

"Mister, don't bug me, huh?" the patrolman said, and blew his whistle, and raised his hand, and then turned and signaled to the cars on his right.

"What's your shield number?" Vollner said.

"Don't bother reporting me," the patrolman answered. "This is my post, and I'm not supposed to leave it. You want a cop, go use the telephone."

"Thanks," Vollner said tightly. "Thanks a lot."

"Don't mention it," the patrolman said breezily, and looked up at the traffic light, and then blew his whistle again. Vollner walked back to the curb and was about to enter the cigar store on the corner, when he spotted a second policeman. Still fuming, he walked to him rapidly and said, "There's a man up in my office who refuses to leave and who is threatening my staff. Now, just what the hell do you propose to do about it?"

The patrolman was startled by Vollner's outburst. He was a new cop and a young cop, and he blinked his eyes and then immediately said, "Where's your office, sir? I'll go back there with you."

"This way," Vollner said, and they began walking toward the building. The patrolman introduced himself as Ronnie Fairchild. He seemed brisk and efficient until they entered the lobby, where he began to have his first qualms.

"Is the man armed?" he asked.

"I don't think so," Vollner said.

"Because if he is, maybe I ought to get some help."

"I think you can handle it," Vollner said.

"You think so?" Fairchild said dubiously, but Vollner had already led him into the elevator. They got out of the car on the tenth floor, and again Fairchild hesitated. "Maybe I ought to call this in," he said. "After all . . ."

"By the time you call in, the man may *kill* someone," Vollner suggested.

"Yeah, I suppose so," Fairchild said hesitantly, thinking that if he *didn't* call this in and ask for help, the person who got killed might very well be himself. He paused outside the door to Vollner's office. "In there, huh?" he said.

"That's right."

"Well, okay, let's go."

They entered the office. Vollner walked directly to the man, who had taken his seat on the bench again, and said, "Here he is, Officer."

Fairchild pulled back his shoulders. He walked to the bench. "All right, what's the trouble here?" he asked.

"No trouble, Officer."

"This man tells me you won't leave his office."

"That's right. I came here to see a girl."

"Oh," Fairchild said, ready to leave at once now that he knew this was only a case of romance. "If that's all . . ."

"What girl?" Vollner said.

"Cindy."

"Get Cindy out here," Vollner said to his receptionist, and she rose immediately and hurried down the corridor. "Why didn't you tell me you were a friend of Cindy's?"

"You didn't ask me," the man said.

"Listen, if this is just a private matter—"

"No, wait a minute," Vollner said, putting his hand on Fairchild's arm. "Cindy'll be out here in a minute."

"That's good," the man said. "Cindy's the one I want to see."

"Who are you?" Vollner asked.

"Well, who are *you?*"

"I'm Miles Vollner. Look, young man—"

"Nice meeting you, Mr. Vollner," the man said, and smiled again.

"What's your name?"

"I don't think I'd like to tell you that."

"Officer, ask him what his name is."

"What's your name, mister?" Fairchild said, and at that moment the receptionist came back, followed by a tall blond girl wearing a blue dress and high-heeled pumps. She stopped just alongside the receptionist's desk and said, "Did you want me, Mr. Vollner?"

"Yes, Cindy. There's a friend of yours here to see you."

Cindy looked around the reception room. She was a strikingly pretty girl of twenty-two, full-breasted and wide-hipped, her blond hair cut casually close to her head, her eyes a cornflower blue that

129

echoed the color of her dress. She studied Fairchild and then the man in gray. Puzzled, she turned again to Vollner.

"A friend of *mine*?" she asked.

"This man says he came here to see you."

"Me?"

"He says he's a friend of yours."

Cindy looked at the man once more, and then shrugged. "I don't know you," she said

"No, huh?"

"No."

"That's too bad."

"Listen, what is this?" Fairchild said.

"You're *going* to know me, baby," the man said.

Cindy looked at him coldly, and said, "I doubt that very much," and turned and started to walk away. The man came off the bench immediately, catching her by the arm.

"Just a second," he said.

"Let go of me."

"Honey, I'm *never* gonna let go of you."

"Leave the girl alone," Fairchild said.

"We don't need fuzz around here," the man answered. "Get lost."

Fairchild took a step toward him, raising his club. The man whirled suddenly, planting his left fist in Fairchild's stomach. As Fairchild doubled over, the man unleashed a vicious uppercut that caught him on the point of his jaw and sent him staggering toward the wall. Groggily, Fairchild reached for his gun. The man kicked him in the groin, and he fell to the floor groaning. The man kicked him again, twice in the head, and then repeatedly in the chest. The receptionist was screaming now. Cindy was running down the corridor, shouting for help. Vollner stood with his fists clenched, waiting for the man to turn and attack him next.

Instead, the man only smiled and said, "Tell Cindy I'll be seeing her," and walked out of the office.

Vollner immediately went to the phone. Men and women were coming out of their private offices all up and down the corridor now. The receptionist was still screaming. Quickly, Vollner dialed the police and was connected with the 87th Precinct.

Sergeant Murchison took the call and advised Vollner that he'd send a patrolman there immediately and that a detective would stop by either later that day or early tomorrow morning.

Vollner thanked him and hung up. His hand was trembling, and his receptionist was still screaming.

The man assigned to investigate the somewhat odd incident in Miles Vollner's office was Detective Bert Kling. Early Thursday morning, while Carella and Meyer were still asleep, Kling took the subway down to the precinct, stopped at the squad room to see if there were any messages for him on the bulletin board, and then bused over to Shepherd Street. Vollner's office was on the tenth floor. The lettering on the frosted-glass door disclosed that the name of the firm was Vollner Audiovisual Components, unimaginative but certainly explicit. Kling opened the door and stepped into the reception room. The girl behind the reception desk was a small brunette, her hair cut in bangs across her forehead. She looked up as Kling walked in, smiled, and said, "Yes, sir, may I help you?"

"I'm from the police," Kling said. "I understand there was some trouble here yesterday."

"Oh, *yes*," the girl said, "there *certainly was*!"

"Is Mr. Vollner in yet?"

"No, he isn't," the girl said. "Was he expecting you?"

"Well, not exactly. The desk sergeant—"

"Oh, he doesn't usually come in until about ten o'clock," the girl said. "It's not even nine-thirty yet."

"I see," Kling said. "Well, I have some other stops to make, so maybe I can catch him later on in the—"

"Cindy's here, though," the girl said.

"Cindy?"

"Yes. She's the one he came to see."

"What do you mean?"

"The one he *said* he came to see, anyway."

"The assailant, do you mean?"

"Yes. He said he was a friend of Cindy's."

"Oh. Well, look, do you think I could talk to her? Until Mr. Vollner gets here?"

"Sure, I don't see why not," the girl said, and pressed a button in the base of her phone. Into the receiver, she said, "Cindy, there's a detective here to talk about yesterday. Can you see him? Okay, sure." She replaced the receiver. "In a few minutes, Mr. . . ." She let the sentence hang.

"Kling."

"Mr. Kling. She's got someone in the office with her." The girl paused. "She interviews applicants for jobs out at the plant, you see."

"Oh. Is she in charge of hiring?"

"No, our personnel director does all the hiring."

"Then why does she interview—"

"Cindy is assistant to the company psychologist."

"Oh."

"Yes, she interviews all the applicants, you know, and later our psychologist tests them. To see if they'd be happy working out at the plant. I mean, they have to put together these tiny little transistor things, you know, there's a lot of pressure doing work like that."

"I'll bet there is," Kling said.

"Sure, there is. So they come here, and first she talks to them for a few minutes, to try to find out what their background is, you know, and then if they pass the first interview, our psychologist gives them a battery of psychological tests later on. Cindy's work is very important. She majored in psychology at college, you know. Our personnel director won't even consider a man if Cindy and our psychologist say he's not suited for the work."

"Sort of like picking a submarine crew," Kling said.

"What? Oh, yes, I guess it is," the girl said, and smiled. She turned as a man came down the corridor. He seemed pleased and even inspired by his first interview with the company's assistant psychologist. He smiled at the receptionist, and then he smiled at Kling and went to the entrance door, and then turned and smiled at them both again, and went out.

"I think she's free now," the receptionist said. "Just let me check." She lifted the phone again, pressed the button, and waited. "Cindy, is it all right to send him in now? Okay." She replaced the receiver. "Go right in," she said. "It's number fourteen, the fifth floor on the left."

"Thank you," Kling said.

"Not at all," the girl answered.

He nodded and walked past her desk and into the corridor. The doors on the left-hand side started with the number 8 and then progressed arithmetically down the corridor. The number 13 was missing from the row. In its place, and immediately following 12, was 14. Kling wondered if the company's assistant psychologist was superstitious, and then knocked on the door

"Come in," a girl's voice said.

He opened the door.

The girl was standing near the window, her back to him. One hand held a telephone receiver to her ear, the blond hair pushed away from it. She was wearing a dark skirt and a white blouse. The jacket that matched the skirt was draped over the back of her chair. She was very tall, and she had a good figure and a good voice. "No, John," she said, "I didn't think a Rorschach was indicated. Well, if you say so. I'll call you back later, I've got someone with me. Right. G'bye." She turned to put the phone back into its cradle, and then looked up at Kling.

They recognized each other immediately.

"What the hell are *you* doing here?" Cindy said.

"So you're Cindy," Kling said. "Cynthia Forrest. I'll be damned."

"Why'd they send *you*? Aren't there any other cops in that precinct of yours?"

"I'm the boss's son. I told you that a long time ago."

"You told me a lot of things a long time ago. Now, go tell your captain I'd prefer talking to another—"

"My lieutenant."

"*Whatever* he is. I mean, *really*, Mr. Kling, I think there's such a thing as adding insult to injury. The way you treated me when my father was killed—"

"I think there was a great deal of misunderstanding all around at that time, Miss Forrest."

"Yes, and mostly on your part."

"We were under pressure. There was a sniper loose in the city—"

"Mr. Kling, *most* people are under pressure *most* of the time. It was my understanding that policemen are civil servants, and that—"

"We are, that's true."

"Yes, well, you were anything *but* civil. I have a long memory, Mr. Kling."

"So do I. Your father's name was Anthony Forrest, he was the first victim in those sniper killings. Your mother—"

"Look, Mr. Kling—"

"Your mother's name is Clarice, and you've got—"

"Clara."

"Clara, right, and you've got a younger brother named John."

"Jeff."

"Jeff, right. You were majoring in education at the time of the shootings—"

"I switched to psychology in my junior year."

"Downtown at Ramsey University. You were nineteen years old—"

"Almost twenty."

"—and that was close to three years ago, which makes you twenty-two."

"I'll be twenty-two next month."

"I see you graduated."

"Yes, I have," Cindy said curtly. "Now, if you'll excuse me, Mr. Kling—"

"I've been assigned to investigate this complaint, Miss Forrest. Something of this nature is relatively small potatoes in our fair city, so I can positively guarantee the lieutenant won't put another man on it simply because you don't happen to like my face."

"Among *other* things."

"Yes, well, that's too bad. Would you like to tell me what happened here yesterday?"

"I would like to tell you nothing."

"Don't you want us to find the man who came up here?"

"I do."

"Then—"

"Mr. Kling, let me put this as flatly as I can. I don't like you. I didn't like you the last time I saw you, and I *still* don't like you. I'm afraid I'm just one of those people who never change their minds."

"Bad failing for a psychologist."

"I'm not a psychologist *yet*. I'm going for my master's at night."

"The girl outside told me you're assistant to the company—"

"Yes, I am. But I haven't yet taken my boards."

"Are you allowed to practice?"

"According to the law in this state—I thought you just *might* be familiar with it, Mr. Kling—no one can be licensed to—"

"No, I'm not."

"Obviously. No one can be licensed to practice psychology until he has a master's degree *and* a Ph.D., *and* has passed the state boards. I'm not practicing. All I do is conduct interviews and sometimes administer tests."

"Well, I'm relieved to hear that," Kling said.

"What the hell is that supposed to mean?"

"Nothing," Kling said, and shrugged.

"Look, Mr. Kling, if you stay here a minute longer, we're going to pick up right where we left off. And as I recall it, the last time I saw you, I told you to drop dead."

"That's right."

"So why don't you?"

"Can't," Kling said. "This is my case." He smiled pleasantly, sat in the chair beside her desk, made himself comfortable, and very sweetly said, "Do you want to tell me what happened here yesterday, Miss Forrest?"

Lieutenant Peter Byrnes read Kling's report that Thursday afternoon, and then buzzed the squadroom and asked him to come in. When he arrived, Byrnes offered him a chair (which Kling accepted) and a cigar (which Kling declined) and then lighted his own cigar and blew out a wreath of smoke and said, "What's this 'severe distaste for my personality' business?"

Kling shrugged. "She doesn't like me, Pete. I can't say I blame her. I was going through a bad time. Well, what am I telling you for?"

"Mmm," Byrnes said. He puffed meditatively on his cigar, and then glanced at the report again. "Four teeth knocked out, and three broken ribs," he said. "Tough customer."

"Well, Fairchild's a new cop."

"I know that. Still, this man doesn't seem to have much respect for the law, does he?"

"To put it mildly," Kling said, smiling.

"Your report says he grabbed the Forrest girl by the arm."

"That's right."

"I don't like it, Bert. If this guy can be so casual about beating up a cop, what'll he do if he gets that girl alone sometime?"

"Well, that's the thing."

"I think we ought to get him."

"Sure, but who is he?"

"Maybe we'll get a make downtown. From those mugs shots."

"She promised to call in later, as soon as she's had a look."

"Maybe we'll be lucky."

"Maybe."

"If we're not, I think we ought to smoke out this guy. I don't like cops getting beat up, that's to begin with. And I don't like the idea of this guy maybe waiting to jump on that girl. He knocked out four of Fairchild's teeth and broke three of his ribs. Who knows what he'd do to a helpless little girl?"

"She's about five-seven, Pete. Actually, that's pretty big. For a girl, I mean."

"Still, If we're not careful here, we may wind up with a homicide on our hands."

"Well, that's projecting a little further than I think we have to, Pete."

"Maybe, maybe not. I think we ought to smoke him out."

"How?"

"Well, I'm not sure yet. What are you working on right now?"

"Those liquor store holdups. And also an assault."

"When was the last holdup?"

"Three nights ago."

"What's your plan?"

"He seems to be hitting them in a line, Pete, straight up Culver Avenue. I thought I'd plant myself in the next store up the line."

"You think he's going to hit again so soon?"

"They've been spaced about two weeks apart so far."

"Then there's no hurry, right?"

"Well, he may change the timetable."

"He may change the pattern, too. In which case, you'll be sitting in the wrong store."

"That's true. I just thought—"

"Let it wait. What's the assault?"

"Victim is a guy named Vinny Marino, he's a small-time pusher, lives on Ainsley Avenue. About a week ago, two guys pulled up in a car and got out with baseball bats. They broke both his legs. The neighborhood rumble is that he was fooling around with one of their wives. That's why they went for his legs, you see, so he wouldn't be able to chase around anymore. It's only coincidental that he's a pusher."

"For my part, they could have killed him," Byrnes said. He took his handkerchief from his back pocket, blew his nose, and then said, "Mr. Marino's case can wait, too. I want you to stay with this one, Bert."

"I think we'd do better with another man. I doubt if I'll be able to get any cooperation at all from her."

"Who can I spare?" Byrnes asked. "Willis and Brown are on that knife murder, Hawes is on a plant of his own, Meyer and Carella are on this damn television thing, Andy Parker—"

"Well, maybe I can switch with one of them."

"I don't like cases to change hands once they've been started."

"I'll do whatever you say, Pete, but—"

"I'd appreciate it," Byrnes said.

"Yes, sir."

Byrnes puffed on his cigar, and then said, "She claims she doesn't know him, huh?"

"That's right."

"I thought maybe he was an old boyfriend."

"No."

"Rejected, you know, that kind of crap."

"No, not according to her."

"Maybe he just wants to get in her pants."

"Maybe."

"Is she good-looking?"

"She's attractive, yes. She's not a raving beauty, but I guess she's attractive."

"Then maybe that's it."

"Maybe, but why would he go after her in this way?"

"Maybe he doesn't *know* any other way. He sounds like a hood, and hoods take what they want. He doesn't know from candy or flowers. He sees a pretty girl he wants, so he goes after her—even if it means beating her up to get her. That's my guess."

"Maybe."

"And that's in our favor. Look what happened to Fairchild when he got in this guy's way. He knocked out his teeth and broke his ribs. *Whatever* he wants from this girl—and it's my guess all he wants is her tail—he's not going to let anybody stop him from getting it, law or otherwise. That's where you come in."

"What do you mean?"

"That's how we smoke him out. I don't want to do anything that'll put this girl in danger. I want this punk to make his move against *you*, Bert."

"Me?"

"You. He knows where she works, and chances are he knows where she lives, and I'll bet my life he's watching her every minute of the day. Okay, let's give him something to watch."

"Me?" Kling said again.

"You, that's right. Stay with that girl day and night. Let's—"

"Day and *night*?"

"Well, within reason. Let's get this guy so goddamn sore at you that he comes after you and tries to do exactly what he did to Fairchild."

Kling smiled, "Gee," he said, "suppose he succeeds?"

"Fairchild is a new cop," Byrnes said. "You told me so yourself,"

"Okay, Pete, but you're forgetting something, aren't you?"

"What's that?"

"The girl doesn't like me. She's not going to take kindly to the idea of spending time with me."

"Ask her if she'd rather get raped some night in the elevator after this guy has knocked out her teeth and broken some of her ribs. Ask her that."

Kling smiled again. "She might prefer it."

"I doubt it."

"Pete, she hates me. She *really* . . ."

Byrnes smiled. "Win her over, boy," he said. "Just win her over, that's all."

As Kling had anticipated, Cindy Forrest was not overwhelmed by the prospect of having to spend even an infinitesimal amount of time with him. She reluctantly admitted, however, that such a course might be less repulsive than the possibility of spending an equal amount of time in a hospital. It was decided that Kling would pick her up at the office at noon Friday, take her to lunch, and then walk her back again. He reminded her that he was a city employee and that there was no such thing as an expense account for taking citizens to lunch while trying to protect them, a subtlety Cindy looked upon as simply another index to Kling's personality. Not only was he obnoxious, but he was apparently cheap as well.

Thursday's beautiful weather had turned foreboding and blustery by Friday noon. The sky above was a solemn gray, the streets seemed dimmer, the people less animated. He picked her up at the office, and they walked in silence to a restaurant some six blocks distant. She was wearing high heels, but the top of her head still came only level with his chin. They were both blond, both hatless. Kling walked with his hands in his coat pockets. Cindy kept her arms crossed over her middle, her hands tucked under them. When they reached the restaurant, Kling forgot to hold open the door for her, but only the faintest flick of Cindy's blue eyes showed that this was exactly what she expected from a man like him. Too late, he allowed her to precede him into the restaurant.

"I hope you like Italian food," he said.

"Yes, I do," she answered, "but you might have asked *first*."

"I'm sorry, but I have a few other things on my mind besides worrying about which restaurant you might like."

"I'm sure you're a very busy man," Cindy said.

"I am."

"Yes, I'm sure."

The owner of the restaurant, a short Neapolitan woman with masses of thick black hair framing her round and pretty face, mistook them for lovers and showed them to a secluded table at the rear of the place. Kling remembered to help Cindy off with her coat (she mumbled a polite thank-you) and then further remembered to hold out her chair for her (she acknowledged this with a brief nod). The waiter took their order and they sat facing each other without a word to say.

The silence lengthened.

"Well, I can see this is going to be perfectly charming," Cindy said. "Lunch with you for the next God knows how long."

"There are things I'd prefer doing myself, Miss Forrest," Kling said. "But as you pointed out yesterday, I am only a civil servant. I do what I'm told to do."

"Does Carella still work up there?" Cindy asked.

"Yes."

"I'd much rather be having lunch with him."

"Well, those are the breaks," Kling said. "Besides, he's married."

"I know he is."

"In fact, he's got two kids."

"I know."

"Mmm. Well, I'm sure he'd have loved this choice assignment, but unfortunately he's involved with a poisoning at the moment."

"Who got poisoned?"

"Stan Gifford."

"Oh? Is he working on that? I was reading about it in the paper just yesterday."

"Yes, it's his case."

"He must be a good detective. I mean, to get such an important case."

"Yes, he's very good," Kling said.

The table went silent again. Kling glanced over his shoulder toward the door, where a thickset man in a black overcoat was just entering.

"Is that your friend?" he asked.

"No. And he's *not* my friend."

"The lieutenant thought he might have been one of your ex-boyfriends."

"No."

"Or someone you'd met someplace."

"No."

"You're sure you didn't recognize any of those mug shots yesterday?"

"I'm positive. I don't know who the man is, and I can't imagine what he wants from me."

"Well, the lieutenant had some ideas about that, too."

"What were his ideas?"

"Well, I'd rather not discuss them."

"Why not?"

"Because . . . well, I'd just rather not."

"Is it the lieutenant's notion that this man wants to lay me?" Cindy asked.

"What?"

"I said is it the—"

"Yes, something like that," Kling answered, and then cleared his throat.

"I wouldn't be surprised," Cindy said.

The waiter arrived at that moment, sparing Kling the necessity of further comment. Cindy had ordered the antipasto to start, a supposed specialty of the house. Kling had ordered a cup of minestrone. He carefully waited for her to begin eating before he picked up his spoon.

"How is it?" he asked her.

"Very good." She paused. "How's the soup?"

"Fine."

They ate in silence for several moments.

"What *is* the plan exactly?" Cindy asked.

"The lieutenant thinks your admirer is something of a hothead, a reasonable assumption, I would say. He's hoping we'll be seen together, and he's hoping our man will take a crack at me."

"In which case?"

"In which case I will crack him back and carry him off to jail."

"My hero," Cindy said dryly, and attacked an anchovy on her plate.

"I'm supposed to spend as much time with you as I can," Kling said, and paused. "I guess we'll be having dinner together tonight."

"What?"

"Yes," Kling said.

"Look, Mr. Kling—"

"It's not *my* idea, Miss Forrest."

"Suppose I've made other plans?"

"Have you?"

"No, but—"

"Then there's no problem."

"I don't usually go out for dinner, Mr. Kling, unless someone is escorting me."

"I'll be escorting you."

"That's not what I meant. I'm a working girl. I can't afford—"

"Well, I'm sorry about the financial arrangements, but as I explained—"

"Yes, well, you just tell your lieutenant I can't afford a long, leisurely dinner every night, that's all. I earn a hundred and two dollars a week after taxes, Mr. Kling. I pay my own college tuition and the rent on my own apartment—"

"Well, this shouldn't take too long. If our man spots us, he may make his play fairly soon. In the meantime, we'll just have to go along with it. Have you seen the new Hitchcock movie?"

"What?"

"The new—"

"No, I haven't."

"I thought we'd go see it after dinner."

"Why?"

"Got to stay together." Kling paused. "I could suggest a long walk as an alternative, but it might be pretty chilly by tonight."

"I could suggest your going directly home after dinner," Cindy said. "As an alternative, you understand. Because to tell the truth, Mr. Kling, I'm pretty damned tired by the end of a working day. In fact, on Tuesdays, Wednesdays, and Thursdays, I barely have time to grab a hamburger before I run over to the school. I'm not a rah-rah party girl. I think you ought to understand that."

"Lieutenant's orders," Kling said.

"Yeah, well, tell *him* to go see the new Hitchcock movie. I'll have dinner with you, if you insist, but right after that I'm going to bed." Cindy paused. "And I'm *not* suggesting that as an alternative."

"I didn't think you were."

"Just so we know where we stand."

"I know exactly where we stand," Kling said. "There are a lot of people in this city, Miss Forrest, and one of them is the guy who's after you. I don't know how long it'll take to smoke him out, I don't know when or where he'll spot us. But I *do* know he's not going to see us together if you're safe and cozy in your little bed and I'm safe and cozy in mine." Kling took a deep breath. "So what we're going to do, Miss Forrest, is have dinner together tonight, and then see the Hitchcock movie. And then we'll go for coffee and something afterward, and then I'll take you home. Tomorrow's Saturday, so we can plan on a nice long day together. Sunday, too. On Monday—"

"Oh God," Cindy said.

"You said it," Kling answered. "Cheer up, here comes your lasagna."

He had followed them to the restaurant and the movie theater, and now he stood in the doorway across from her house, waiting for her to come home. It was a cold night, and he stood huddled deep in the shadows, his coat collar pulled high on the back of his neck, his hands thrust into his coat pockets, his hat low on his forehead.

It was ten minutes past twelve, and they had left the movie theater at eleven forty-five, but he knew they would be coming straight home. He had been watching the girl long enough now to know a few things about her, and one of those things was that she didn't sleep around much. Last month sometime, she had shacked up with a guy on Banning Street, just for the night, and the next morning after she left the apartment he had gone up to the guy and had worked him over with a pair of brass knuckles, leaving him crying like a baby on the kitchen floor. He had warned the guy against calling the police, and he had also told him he should never go near Cindy Forrest again, never try to see her again, never even try to call her again. The guy had held his broken mouth together with one bloody hand, and nodded his head, and begged not to be hit again—that was one guy who wouldn't be bothering *her* anymore. So he knew she didn't sleep around too much, and besides he knew she wouldn't be going anyplace but straight home with this blond guy because this blond guy was a cop.

He had got the fuzz smell from him almost the minute he first saw him, early this afternoon when he came to the office to take her to lunch. He knew the look of fuzz and the smell of fuzz, and he realized right off that the very smart bulls of this wonderful city were setting a trap for him, and that he was supposed to fall right into it—here I am, fuzz, take me.

Like fun.

He had stayed far away from the restaurant where they had lunch, getting the fuzz stink sharp and clear in his nostrils and knowing something was up, but not knowing what kind of trap was being set for him, and wanting to make damn sure before he made another move. The blond guy walked like a cop, that was an unmistakable cop walk. And also he had a sneaky way of making the scene, his head turned in one direction while he was really casing the opposite direction, a very nice fuzz trick that known criminals sometimes utilized, but that mostly cops from here to Detroit and back again were very familiar with. Well, he had known cops all across this fine little country of America, he had busted more cops' head than he could count on all his fingers and toes. He wouldn't mind busting another, just for the fun of it, but not until he knew what the trap was. The one thing he wasn't going to do was walk into no trap.

In the wintertime, or like now when it was getting kind of chilly and a guy had to wear a coat, you could always tell when he was heeled because if he was wearing a shoulder harness, the button between the top one and the third one was always left unbuttoned. If he was wearing the holster clipped to his belt, then a button was left undone just above the waist, so the right hand could reach in and draw—that was the first concrete tip-off that Blondie was a cop. He was a cop, and he wore his gun clipped to his belt. Watching him from outside the plate-glass window of the second restaurant later that day, there had been the flash of Blondie's tin when he went to pay his check, opening his wallet, with the shield catching light for just a second. That was the second concrete fact, and a smart man don't need more than one or two facts to piece together a story, not when the fuzz smell is all over the place to begin with.

The only thing he didn't know now was what the trap was, and whether or not he should accommodate Blondie by walking into it and maybe beating him up. He thought it would be better to work on the girl, though. It was time the girl learned what she could do and couldn't do, there was no sense putting it off. The girl had to know that she couldn't go sleeping around with no guys on Banning Street, or for that matter anyplace in the city. And she also had to know she couldn't play along with the cops on whatever trap they were cooking up. She had to know it now, and once and for all; because he wasn't planning on staying in the shadows for long. The girl had to know she was *his* meat and his *alone*.

He guessed he'd beat her up tonight.

He looked at his watch again. It was fifteen minutes past twelve, and he began to wonder what was keeping them. Maybe he should have stuck with them when they came out of the movie house, instead of rushing right over here. Still, if Blondie—

A car was turning into the street.

He pulled back into the shadows and waited. The car came up the street slowly. Come on, Blondie, he thought, you ain't being followed, there's no reason to drive so slow. He grinned in the darkness. The car pulled to the curb. Blondie got out and walked around to the other side, holding open the door for the girl, and then walking her up the front steps. The building was a gray four-story job, and the girl lived on the top floor rear. The name on the bell read "C. Forrest," that was the first thing he'd found out about her, almost two months ago. A little while after that, he'd broken open the lock on her mailbox and found two letters addressed to Miss Cynthia Forrest—it was a good thing she wasn't married, because if she was, her husband would have been in for one hell of a time—and another letter addressed to Miss Cindy Forrest, this one from a guy over in Thailand, serving with the Peace Corps. The guy was lucky he was over in Thailand, or he'd have had a visitor requesting him to stop writing letters to little Sweet-pants.

Blondie was unlocking the inner vestibule door for her now. The girl said good night—he could hear her voice clear across the street—and Blondie gave her the keys and said something with his back turned, which couldn't be heard. Then the door closed behind her, and

Blondie came down the steps, walking with a funny fuzz walk, like a boxer moving toward the ring where a pushover sparring partner was waiting, and keeping his head ducked, though this was a cop trick and those eyes were most likely flashing up and down the street in either direction even though the head was ducked and didn't seem to be turning. Blondie got into the car—the engine was still running—put it into gear, and drove off.

He waited.

In five minutes' time, the car pulled around the corner again and drifted slowly past the gray building.

He almost burst out laughing. What did Blondie think he was playing around with, an amateur? He waited until the car rounded the corner again, and then he waited for at least another fifteen minutes, until he was sure Blondie wasn't coming back.

He crossed the street rapidly then, and walked around the corner and into the building directly behind the girl's. He went straight through the building, opening the door at the rear of the ground floor and stepping out into the backyard. He climbed the clothesline pole near the fence separating the yard from the one behind it, leaped over the fence, and dropped to his knees. Looking up, he could see a light burning in the girl's window on the fourth floor. He walked toward the rear of the building, cautiously but easily, jumping up for the fire-escape ladder, pulling it down, and then swinging up onto it and beginning to climb. He went by each window with great care, especially the other lighted one on the second floor, flitting past it like a shadow and continuing on up to the third floor, and then stepping onto the fourth-floor fire escape, *her* fire escape.

There was a wooden cheese box resting on the iron slats of the fire-escape floor, the dried twigs of dead flowers stuck into the stiff earth it contained. The fire escape was outside her bedroom. He peered around the edge of the window, but the room was empty. He glanced to his right and saw that the tiny bathroom window was lighted; the girl was in the bathroom. He debated going right into the bedroom while she was occupied down the hall, but decided against it. He wanted to wait until she was in bed. He wanted to scare her real good.

The only light in the room came from a lamp on the night table near the girl's bed. The bed was clearly visible from where he crouched outside on the fire escape. There was a single chair on this side of the bed, he would have to avoid that in the dark. He wanted his surprise to be complete; he didn't want to go stumbling over no furniture and waking her up before it was time. The window was open just a trifle at the top, probably to let in some air, she'd probably opened it when she came into the apartment. He didn't know whether or not she'd close and lock it before going to bed, maybe she would. This was a pretty decent neighborhood, though, without any incidents lately—he'd checked on that because he was afraid some cheap punk might bust into the girl's apartment and complicate things for him—so maybe she slept with the window open just a little, at the top, the way it was now. While she was in the bathroom, he studied the simple lock on the sash and decided it wouldn't be a problem, anyway, even if she locked it.

The bathroom light went out suddenly.

He flattened himself against the brick wall of the building. The girl was humming when she came into the room. The humming trailed off abruptly, she was turning on the radio. It came on very loud, for Christ's sake, she was going to wake up the whole damn building! She kept twisting the dial until she found the station she wanted, sweet music, lots of violins and muted trumpets, and then she lowered the volume. He waited. In a moment, she came to the window and pulled down the shade. Good, he thought, she didn't lock the window. He waited a moment longer, and then flattened himself onto the fire escape so that he could peer into the room beneath the lower edge of the shade, where the girl had left a good two-inch gap between it and the windowsill.

The girl was still dressed. She was wearing the tan dress she had worn to dinner with Blondie, but when she turned away and began walking toward the closet, he saw that she had already lowered the zipper at the back. The dress was spread in a wide V, the white elastic line of her brassiere crossing her back, the zipper lowered to a point just above the beginning curve of her buttocks. The radio was playing a song she knew, and she began humming along with it again as she opened the closet door and took her nightgown from a hook. She closed the door and then walked to the bed, sitting on the side facing the window and lifting her dress up over her thighs to unhook first one garter and then the other. She took off her shoes and rolled down her stockings, and then walked to the closet to put the shoes away and to put the stockings into some kind of a bag hanging on the inside doorknob. She closed the door again, and then took off her dress, standing just outside the closet and not moving toward the bed again. In her bra and half-slip, she walked over to the other side of the room, where he couldn't see her anymore, almost as if the lousy little bitch knew he was watching her! She was still humming. His hands were wet. He dried them on the sleeves of his coat and waited.

She came back so suddenly that she startled him. She had taken off her underwear, and she walked swiftly to the bed, naked, to pick up her nightgown. Jesus, she was beautiful! Jesus, he hadn't realized how goddamn beautiful she really was. He watched her as she bent slightly to pull the gown over her head, straightened, and then let it fall down over her breasts and her tilted hips. She yawned. She looked at her watch and then went across the room again, out of sight, and came back to the bed carrying a paperback book. She got into the bed, her legs parting, opening, as she swung up onto it, and then pulled the blanket up over her knees, and fluffed the pillow, and scratched her jaw, and opened the book. She yawned. She looked at her watch again, seemed to change her mind about reading the book, put it down on the night table, and yawned again.

A moment later, she turned out the light.

The first thing she heard was the voice.

It said "Cindy," and for the briefest tick of time she thought she was dreaming because the voice was just a whisper. And then she heard it again, "Cindy," hovering somewhere just above her face, and her eyes popped wide, and she tried to sit up but something pressed her fiercely back against the pillow. She opened her mouth to scream, but a hand clamped over her lips. She stared over the edge of the thick fingers into the darkness, trying to see. "Be quiet, Cindy," the voice said. "Just be quiet now."

His grip on her mouth was hard and tight. He was straddling her now, his knees on the bed, his legs tight against her pinioned arms, sitting on her abdomen, one arm flung across her chest, holding her to the pillow.

"Can you hear me?" he asked.

She nodded. His hand stayed tight on her mouth, hurting her. She wanted to bite his hand, but she could not free her mouth. His weight upon her was unbearable. She tried to move, but she was helplessly caught in the vise of his knees, the tight band of his arm thrown across her chest.

"Listen to me," he said. "I'm going to beat the shit out of you."

She believed him instantly; terror rocketed into her skull. Her eyes were growing accustomed to the darkness. She could dimly see his grinning face hovering above her. His fingers smelled of tobacco. He kept his right hand clamped over her mouth, his left arm thrown across her chest, lower now, so that the hand was gripping her breast. He kept working his hand as he talked to her, grasping her through the thin nylon gown, squeezing her nipple as his voice continued in a slow lazy monotone, "Do you know why I'm going to beat you, Cindy?"

She tried to shake her head, but his hand was so tight against her mouth that she could not move. She knew she would begin to cry within the next few moments. She was trembling beneath his weight. His hand was cruel on her breast. Each time he tightened it on her nipple, she winced with pain.

"I don't like you to go out with cops," he said. "I don't like you to go out with *anybody*, but cops especially."

She could see his face clearly now. He was the same man who had come to the office, the same man who had beaten up the policeman.

She remembered the way he had kicked the policeman when he was on the floor, and she began trembling more violently. She heard him laugh.

"I'm going to take my hand off your mouth now," he said, "because we have to talk. But if you scream, I'll kill you. Do you understand me?"

She tried to nod. His hand was relaxing. He was slowly lifting it from her mouth, cupped, as though cautiously peering under it to see if he had captured a fly. She debated screaming, and knew at once that if she did he would keep his promise and kill her. He shifted his body to the left, relaxing his grip across her chest, lifting his arm, freeing her breast. He rested his hands palms downward on his thighs, his legs bent under him, his knees still holding her arms tightly against her side, most of his weight still on her abdomen. Her breast was throbbing with pain. A trickle of sweat rolled down toward her belly and she thought for a moment it was blood, had he made her bleed somehow? A new wave of fear caused her to begin trembling again. She was ashamed of herself for being so frightened, but the fear was something uncontrollable, a raw animal panic that shrieked silently of pain and possible death.

"You'll get rid of him tomorrow," he whispered. He sat straddling her with his huge hands relaxed on his own thighs.

"Who?" she said. "Who do you—"

"The cop. You'll get rid of him tomorrow."

"All right." She nodded in the darkness. "All right," she said again.

"You'll call his precinct—what precinct is it?"

"The 8 . . . the 87th, I think."

"You'll call him."

"Yes. Yes, I will."

"You'll tell him you don't need a police escort no more. You'll tell him everything is all right now."

"Yes, all right," she said. "Yes, I will."

"You'll tell him you patched things up with your boyfriend."

"My . . ." She paused. Her heart was beating wildly, she was sure he could feel her heart beating in panic. "My *boyfriend*?"

"Me," he said, and grinned.

"I . . . I don't even know you," she said.

"I'm your boyfriend."

She shook her head.

"I'm your lover."

She kept shaking her head.

"Yes."

"I don't *know* you," she said, and suddenly she began weeping. "What do you want from me? Please, won't you go? Won't you please leave me alone? I don't even know you. Please, please."

"Beg," he said, and grinned.

"Please, please, please . . ."

"You're going to tell him to stop coming around."

"Yes, I *am*. I *said* I would."

"Promise."

"I promise."

"You'll keep the promise," he said flatly.

"Yes, I will. I told you—"

He slapped her suddenly and fiercely, his right hand abruptly leaving his thigh and coming up viciously toward her face. She blinked her eyes an instant before his open palm collided with her cheek. She pulled back rigidly, her neck muscles taut, her eyes wide, her teeth clamped together.

"You'll keep the promise," he said, "because this is a sample of what you'll get if you don't."

And then he began beating her.

She did not know where she was at first. She tried to open her eyes, but something was wrong with them, she could not seem to open her eyes. Something rough was against her cheek, her head was twisted at a curious angle. She felt a hundred separate throbbing areas of hurt, but none of them seemed connected with her head or her body, each seemed to pulse with a solitary intensity of its own. Her left eye trembled open. Light knifed into the narrow crack of opening eyelid, she could open it no further. Light flickered into the tentative opening, flashes of light pulsated as the flesh over her eye quivered.

She was lying with her cheek pressed to the rug.

She kept trying to open her left eye, catching fitful glimpses of gray carpet as the eye opened and closed spasmodically, still not knowing where she was, possessing a sure knowledge that something terrible had happened to her, but not remembering what it was as yet. She lay quite still on the floor, feeling each throbbing knot of pain, arms, legs, thighs, breasts, nose, the separate pains combining to form a recognizable mass of flesh that was her body, a whole and unified body that had been severely beaten.

And then, of course, she remembered instantly what had happened.

Her first reaction was one of whimpering terror. She drew up her shoulders, trying to pull her head deeper into them. Her left hand came limply toward her face, the fingers fluttering, as though weakly trying to fend off any further blows.

"Please," she said.

The word whispered into the room. She waited for him to strike her again, every part of her body tensed for another savage blow, and when none came, she lay trembling lest she was mistaken, fearful that

147

he was only pretending to be gone while silently waiting to attack again.

Her eye kept flickering open and shut.

She rolled over onto her back and tried to open the other eye, but again only a crack of winking light came through the trembling lid. The ceiling seemed so very far away. Sobbing, she brought her hand to her nose, thinking it was running, wiping it with the back of her hand, and then realizing that blood was pouring from her nostrils.

"Oh," she said, "oh my God."

She lay on her back, sobbing in anguish. At last, she tried to rise. She made it to her knees, and then fell to the floor again, sprawled on her face. The police, she thought, I must call the police. And then she remembered why he had beaten her. He did not want the police. Get rid of the police, he had said. She got to her knees again. Her gown was torn down the front. Her breasts were splotched with purple bruises. The nipple of her right breast looked as raw as an open wound. Her throat, the torn gown, the sloping tops of her breasts were covered with blood from her nose. She cupped her hand under it, and then tried to stop the flow by holding a torn shred of nylon under the nostrils, struggling to her feet and moving unsteadily toward her dressing table, where she knew she'd left her house keys, Kling had returned her house keys, she had left them on the dresser, she would put them at the back of her neck, they would stop the blood, groping for the dresser top, a severe pain on the side of her chest, had he kicked her the way he'd kicked that policeman, get rid of the police, oh my God, oh God, oh God dear God.

She could not believe what she saw in the mirror.

The image that stared back at her was grotesque and frightening, hideous beyond belief. Her eyes were puffed and swollen, the pupils invisible, only a narrow slit showing on the bursting surface of each discolored bulge. Her face was covered with blood and bruises, a swollen mass of purple lumps, her blond hair was matted with blood, there were welts on her arms, and thighs, and legs.

She felt suddenly dizzy. She clutched the top of the dressing table to steady herself, taking her hand away from her nose momentarily, watching the falling drops of blood spatter onto the white surface. A wave of nausea came and passed. She stood with her hand pressed to the top of the table, leaning on her extended arm, her head bent, refusing to look into the mirror again. She must not call the police. If she called the police, he would come back and do this to her again. He had told her to get rid of the police, she would call Kling in the morning and tell him everything was all right now, she and her boyfriend had patched it up. In utter helplessness, she began crying again, her shoulders heaving, her nose dripping blood, her knees shaking as she clung to the dressing table for support.

Gasping for breath, she stood suddenly erect and opened her mouth wide, sucking in great gulps of air, her hand widespread over her belly like an open fan. Her fingers touched something wet and sticky, and she looked down sharply, expecting more blood, expecting to find herself soaked in blood that seeped from a hundred secret wounds.

She raised her hand slowly toward her swollen eyes.

She fainted when she realized the wet and sticky substance on her belly was semen.

Bert Kling kicked down the door of her apartment at ten-thirty the next morning. He had begun trying to reach her at nine, wanting to work out the details of their day together. He had let the phone ring seven times, and then decided he'd dialed the wrong number. He hung up, and tried it again. This time, he let it ring for a total of ten times, just in case she was a heavy sleeper. There was no answer. At nine-thirty, hoping she had gone down for breakfast and returned to the apartment by now, he called once again. There was still no answer. He called at five-minute intervals until ten o'clock, and then clipped on his gun and went down to his car. It took him a half hour to drive from Riverhead to Cindy's apartment on Glazebrook Street. He climbed the steps to the fourth floor, knocked on the door, called her name, and then kicked it open.

He phoned for an ambulance immediately.

She regained consciousness briefly before the ambulance arrived. When she recognized him, she mumbled, "No, please, get out of here, he'll know," and then passed out again.

Elizabeth Rushmore Hospital was on the southern rim of the city, a complex of tall white buildings that faced the River Dix. From the hospital windows, one could watch the river traffic, could see in the distance the smokestacks puffing up black clouds, could follow the spidery strands of the three bridges that connected the island to Sands Spit, Calm's Point, and Majesta.

A cold wind was blowing off the water. He had called the hospital earlier that afternoon and learned that evening visiting hours ended at eight o'clock. It was now seven forty-five, and he stood on the river's edge with his coat collar raised, and looked up at the lighted hospital windows and once again went over his plan.

He had thought at first that the whole thing was a cheap cop trick. He had listened attentively while Buddy told him about the visit of the blond cop, the same son of a bitch; Buddy said his name was Kling, Detective Bert Kling. Holding the phone receiver to his ear, he had listened, and his hand had begun sweating on the black plastic. But he had told himself all along that it was only a crumby trick, did they think he was going to fall for such a cheap stunt?

Still, they had known his name; Kling had asked for Cookie. How could they have known his name unless there really *was* a file someplace listing guys who were involved with numbers? And hadn't Kling mentioned something about not being able to locate him at the address they had for him in the file? If anything sounded legit, that sure as hell did. He had moved two years ago, so maybe the file went back before then. And besides, he hadn't been home for the past few days, so even if the file was a *recent* one, well then, they wouldn't have been able to locate him at his address because he simply hadn't been there. So maybe there was some truth in it, who the hell knew?

But a picture? Where would they have gotten a picture of him? Well, that was maybe possible. If the cops really did have such a file, then maybe they also had a picture. He knew goddamn well that they took pictures all the time, mostly trying to get a line on guys in narcotics, but maybe they did it for numbers, too. He had seen laundry trucks or furniture vans parked in the same spot on a street all day long, and had known—together with everybody else in the neighborhood—that it was cops taking pictures. So maybe it was possible they had a picture of him, too. And maybe that little bitch had really pointed him out, maybe so, it was a possibility. But it still smelled a little, there were still too many unanswered questions.

Most of the questions were answered for him when he read the story in the afternoon paper. He'd almost missed it because he had started from the back of the paper, where the racing results were, and then had only turned to the front afterward, sort of killing time. The story confirmed that there *was* a file on numbers racketeers, for one thing, though he was pretty sure about that even before he'd seen the paper. It also explained why Fairchild couldn't make the identification, too. You can't be expected to look at a picture of somebody when you're laying in the hospital with a coma. He didn't think he'd hit the bastard that hard, but maybe he didn't know his own strength. Just to check he'd called Buena Vista as soon as he'd read the story and asked how Patrolman Fairchild was doing. They told him he was still in a coma and on the critical list, so that part of it was true. And, of course, if those jerks in the office where Cindy worked were too scared to identify the picture, well then, Fairchild's condition explained why Cindy was the only person the cops could bank on.

The word "homicide" had scared him. If that son of a bitch *did* die, and if the cops picked him up and Cindy said, yes, that's the man, well, that was it, pal. He thought he'd really made it clear to her, but maybe she was tougher than he thought. For some strange reason, the idea excited him, the idea of her not having been frightened by the beating, of her still having the guts to identify his picture and promise to testify. He could remember being excited when he read the story, and the same excitement overtook him now as he looked up at the hospital windows and went over his plan.

Visiting hours ended at eight o'clock, which meant he had exactly ten minutes to get into the building. He wondered suddenly if they would let him in so close to the deadline, and he immediately began walking toward the front entrance. A wide slanting concrete canopy covered the revolving entrance doors. The hospital was new, an imposing edifice of aluminum and glass and concrete. He pushed through the revolving doors and walked immediately to the desk on the right of the entrance lobby. A woman in white—he supposed she was a nurse—looked up as he approached.

"Miss Cynthia Forrest?" he said.

"Room seven-twenty," the woman said, and immediately looked at her watch. "Visiting hours are over in a few minutes, you know," she said.

"Yes, I know, thanks," he answered, and smiled, and walked swiftly to the elevator bank. There was only one other civilian waiting for an elevator; the rest were all hospital people in white uniforms. He wondered abruptly if there would be a cop on duty outside her door. Well, if there is, he thought, I just call it off, that's all. The elevator doors opened. He stepped in with the other people, pushed the button for the seventh floor, noticed that one of the nurses reached for the same button after he had pushed it, and then withdrew quietly to the rear of the elevator. The doors closed.

"If you ask me," a nurse was saying, "it's psoriasis. Dr. Kirsch said it's blood poisoning, but did you see that man's leg? You can't tell me that's from blood poisoning."

"Well, they're going to test him tomorrow," another nurse said.

"In the meantime, he's got a fever of a hundred and two."

"That's from the swollen leg. The leg's all infected, you know."

"Psoriasis," the first nurse said, "*that's* what it is," and the doors opened. Both nurses stepped out. The doors closed again. The elevator was silent. He looked at his watch. It was five minutes to eight. The elevator stopped again at the fourth floor, and again at the fifth. On the seventh floor, he got off the elevator with the nurse who had earlier reached for the same button. He hesitated in the corridor for a moment. There was a wide-open area directly in front of the elevators. Beyond that was a large room with a bank of windows, the sun-room, he supposed. To the right and left of the elevators were glass doors leading to the patients' rooms beyond. A nurse sat at a desk some three feet before the doors on the left. He walked swiftly to the desk and said, "Which way is seven-twenty?"

The nurse barely looked up. "Straight through," she said. "You've only got a few minutes."

"Yes, I know, thanks," he said, and pushed open the glass door. The room just inside the partition was 700, and the one beyond that was 702, so he assumed 720 was somewhere at the end of the hall. He looked at his watch. It was almost eight o'clock. He hastily scanned the doors in the corridor, walking rapidly, finding the one marked "Men" halfway down the hall. Pushing open the door, he walked immediately to one of the stalls, entered it, and locked it behind him.

In less than a minute, he heard a loudspeaker announcing that visiting hours were now over. He smiled, lowered the toilet seat, sat, lighted a cigarette, and began his long wait.

He did not come out of the men's room until midnight. By that time, he had listened to a variety of patients and doctors as they discussed an endless variety of ills and ailments, both subjectively and objectively. He listened to each of them quietly and with some amusement because they helped to pass the time. He had reasoned that he could not make his move until the hospital turned out the lights in all the rooms. He didn't know what time taps was in this crumby place, but he supposed it would be around ten or ten-thirty. He had decided to wait until midnight, just to be sure. He figured that all of the visiting doctors would be gone by that time, and so he knew he had to be careful when he came out into the corridor. He didn't want anyone to stop him or even to see him on the way to Cindy's room.

It was a shame he would have to kill the little bitch.

She could have really been something.

There was a guy who came back to pee a total of seventeen times between eight o'clock and midnight. He knew because the guy was evidently having some kind of kidney trouble, and every time he came into the john he would walk over to the urinals—the sound of his shuffling slippers carrying into the locked stall—and then he would begin cursing out loud while he peed, "Oh, you son of a bitch! Oh, what did I do to deserve such pain and misery?" and like that. One time, while he was peeing, some other guy yelled out from the stall alongside, "For God's sake, Mandel, keep your sickness to yourself."

And then the guy standing at the urinals had yelled back, "It should happen to *you*, Liebowitz! It should *rot*, and fall off of you, and be washed down the drain into the river, may God hear my plea!"

He had almost burst out laughing, but instead he lighted another cigarette and looked at his watch again, and wondered what time they'd be putting all these sick jerks to bed, and wondered what Cindy would be wearing. He could still remember her undressing that night he'd beat her up, the quick flash of her nudity—he stopped his thoughts. He could not think that way. He had to kill her tonight, there was no sense thinking about—and yet maybe *while* he was doing it, maybe it would be like last time, maybe with her belly smooth and hard beneath him, maybe like last time maybe he could.

The men's room was silent at midnight.

He unlocked the stall and came out into the room and then walked past the sinks to the door and opened it just a bit and looked out into the corridor. The floors were some kind of hard polished asphalt tile, and you could hear the clicking of high heels on it for a mile, which was good. He listened as a nurse went swiftly down the corridor, her heels clicking away, and then he listened until everything was quiet again. Quickly, he stepped out into the hall. He began walking toward the end of the corridor, the steadily mounting door numbers flashing by on left and right, 709, 710, 711 . . . 714, 715, 716 . . .

He was passing the door to room 717 on his left, when it opened and a nurse stepped into the corridor. He was too startled to speak at first. He stopped dead, breathless, debating whether he should hit her. And then, from somewhere, he heard a voice saying, "Good evening, Nurse," and he hardly recognized the voice as his own because it sounded so cultured and pleasant and matter-of-fact. The nurse looked at him for just a moment longer, and then smiled and said, "Good evening, Doctor," and continued walking down the corridor. He did not turn to look back at her. He continued walking until he came to room 720. Hoping it was a private room, he opened the door, stepped inside quickly, closed the door immediately, and leaned against it, listening. He could hear nothing in the corridor outside. Satisfied, he turned into the room.

The only light in the room came from the windows at the far end, just beyond the bed. He could see the silhouette of her body beneath the blankets, the curved hip limned by the dim light coming from the window. The blanket was pulled high over her shoulders and the back of her neck, but he could see the short blond hair illuminated by the dim glow of moonlight from the windows. He was getting excited again, the way he had that night he beat her up. He reminded himself why he was here—this girl could send him to the electric chair. If Fairchild died, this girl was all they needed to convict him. He took a deep breath and moved toward the bed.

In the near darkness, he reached for her throat, seized it between his huge hands, and then whispered, "Cindy," because he wanted her to be awake and looking straight up into his face when he crushed the life out of her. His hands tightened.

She sat erect suddenly. Two fists flew up between his own hands, up and outward, breaking the grip. His eyes opened wide.

"Surprise!" Bert Kling said, and punched him in the mouth.

"Why'd you beat her up?" Kling asked.
"I didn't beat up nobody," Cookie said. "I love that girl."
"You *what*?"
"I love her, you deaf? I loved her from the first minute I ever seen her."

"When was that?"

"The end of the summer. August. It was on the Stem. I just made a collection in a candy store on the corner there, and I was passing this Pokerino place in the middle of the block, and I thought maybe I'd stop in, kill some time, you know? The guy outside was giving his spiel, and I was standing there listening to him, so many games for a quarter, or whatever the hell it was. I looked in and there was this girl in a dark green dress, leaning over one of the tables and rolling the balls, I think she had something like three queens, I'm not sure."

"All right, what happened then?"

"I went in."

"Go ahead."

"What do you want from me?"

"I want to know why you beat her up."

"I didn't beat her up, I told you that!"

"Who'd you think was in that bed tonight, you son of a bitch?"

"I didn't *know* who was in it. Leave me alone. You got nothing on me, you think I'm some snot-nosed kid?"

"Yeah, I think you're some snot-nosed kid," Kling said. "What happened that first night you saw her?"

"Nothing. There was a guy with her, a young guy, one of these advertising types. I kept watching her, that's all. She didn't know I was watching her, she didn't even know I existed. Then I followed them when they left, and found out where she lived, and after that I kept following her wherever she went. That's all."

"That's *not* all."

"I'm telling you that's all."

"Okay, play it your way," Kling said. "Be a wise guy. We'll throw everything but the goddamn kitchen sink at you."

"I'm telling you I never laid a finger on her. I went up to her office to let her know, that's all."

"Let her know what?"

"That she was my girl. That, you know, she wasn't supposed to go out with nobody else or see nobody, that she was *mine*, you dig? That's the only reason I went up there, to let her know. I didn't expect all that kind of goddamn trouble. All I wanted to do was tell her what I expected from her, that's all."

John "Cookie" Cacciatore lowered his head. The brim of his hat hid his eyes from Kling's gaze.

"If you'd all have minded your own business, everything would have been all right."

The squadroom was silent.

"I love that girl," he said.

And then, in a mumble, "You lousy bastard, you almost killed me tonight."

* * *

Morning always comes.

In the morning, Detective Bert Kling went to Elizabeth Rushmore Hospital and asked to see Cynthia Forrest. He knew this was not the normal visiting time, but he explained that he was a working detective, and asked that an allowance be made. Since everyone in the hospital knew that he was the cop who'd captured a hoodlum on the seventh floor the night before, there was really no need to explain. Permission was granted at once.

Cindy was sitting up in bed.

She turned her head toward the door as Kling came in, and then her hand went unconsciously to her short blond hair, fluffing it.

"Hi," he said.

"Hello."

"How do you feel?"

"All right." She touched her eyes gingerly. "Has the swelling gone down?"

"Yes."

"But they're still discolored, aren't they?"

"Yes, they are. You look all right, though."

"Thank you." Cindy paused. "Did . . . did he hurt you last night?"

"No."

"You're sure."

"Yes, I'm sure."

"He's a vicious person."

"I know he is."

"Will he go to jail?"

"To prison, yes. Even without your testimony. He assaulted a police officer." Kling smiled. "Tried to strangle me, in fact. That's attempted murder."

"I'm . . . I'm very frightened of that man," Cindy said.

"Yes, I can imagine."

"But . . ." She swallowed. "But if it'll help the case, I'll . . . I'd be willing to testify. If it'll help, I mean."

"I don't know," Kling said. "The D.A.'s office'll have to let us know about that."

"All right," Cindy said, and was silent. Sunlight streamed through the windows, catching her blond hair. She lowered her eyes. Her hand picked nervously at the blanket. "The only thing I'm afraid of is . . . is when he gets out. Eventually, I mean. When he gets out."

"Well, we'll see that you have police protection," Kling said.

"Mmm," Cindy said. She did not seem convinced.

"I mean . . . I'll *personally* volunteer for the job," Kling said, and hesitated.

Cindy raised her eyes to meet his. "That's . . . very kind of you," she said slowly.

"Well . . ." he answered, and shrugged.

The room was silent.

"You could have got hurt last night," Cindy said.

"No. No, there wasn't a chance."

"You could have," she insisted.

"No, really."

"Yes," she said.

"We're not going to start arguing again, are we?"

"No," she said, and laughed, and then winced and touched her face. "Oh God," she said, "it still hurts."

"But only when you laugh, right?"

"Yes," she said, and laughed again.

"When do you think you'll be out of here?" Kling asked.

"I don't know. Tomorrow, I suppose. Or the day after."

"Because I thought . . ."

"Yes?"

"Well . . ."

"What is it, Detective Kling?"

"I know you're a working girl . . ."

"Yes?"

"And that you don't normally eat out."

"That's right, I don't," Cindy said.

"Unless you're escorted."

Cindy waited.

"I thought . . ."

She waited.

"I thought you'd like to have dinner with me sometime. When you're out of the hospital, I mean." He shrugged. "I mean, *I'd* pay for it," Kling said, and lapsed into silence.

Cindy did not answer for several moments. Then she smiled and said simply, "I'd love to," and paused, and immediately said, "When?"

Eighty Million Eyes, 1966

Bert Kling was in love.

It was not a good time of the year to be in love. It is better to be in love when flowers are blooming and balmy breezes are wafting in off the river, and strange animals come up to lick your hand. There's only one good thing about being in love in March, and that's that it's better to be in love in March than not to be in love at all, as the wise man once remarked.

Bert Kling was madly in love.

He was madly in love with a girl who was twenty-three years old, full-breasted and wide-hipped, her blond hair long and trailing midway down her back or sometimes curled into a honey conch shell at the back of her head, her eyes a cornflower blue, a tall girl who came just level with his chin when she was wearing heels. He was madly in love with a scholarly girl who was studying at night for her master's degree in psychology, while working during the day conducting interviews for a firm downtown on Shepherd Street; a serious girl who hoped to go on for her Ph.D., and then pass the state boards, and then practice psychology; a nutty girl who was capable of sending to the squadroom a six-foot-high heart cut out of plywood and painted red and lettered in yellow with the words "Cynthia Forrest Loves Detective 3rd/Grade Bertram Kling, So Is That a Crime?," as she had done on St. Valentine's Day just last month (and which Kling had still not heard the end of from all his comical colleagues); an emotional girl who could burst into tears at the sight of a blind man playing an accordion on the Stem, to whom she gave a five-dollar bill, merely put the bill silently into the cup, soundlessly, it did not even make a rustle, and turned away to weep into Kling's shoulder; a passionate girl who clung to him fiercely in the night and who woke him sometimes at six in the morning to say, "Hey, cop, I have to go to work in a few hours, are you interested?" to which Kling invariably answered, "No, I am not interested in sex and things like that," and then kissed her until she was dizzy and afterward sat across from her at the kitchen table in her apartment, staring at her, marveling at her beauty, and once caused her to blush when he said, "There's a woman who sells *pidaguas* on Mason Avenue, her name is Iluminada, she was born in Puerto Rico. Your name should be Iluminada, Cindy. You fill the room with light."

Boy, was he in love.

Fuzz, 1968

Kling had come to the apartment to make love.

It was his day off, and that was what he wanted to do. He had been thinking about it all afternoon, in fact, and had finally come over to the apartment at four-thirty, letting himself in with the key Cindy had given him long ago, and then sitting in the darkening living room, waiting for her return.

The city outside was unwinding at day's end, dusk softening her pace, slowing her step. Kling sat in an armchair near the window, watching the sky turn bloodred and then purple and then deepening to a grape-stained silky blackness. The apartment was very still.

Somewhere out there in the city of ten million people, there was a man named Walter Damascus and he had killed Mr. and Mrs. Andrew Leyden, had killed them brutally and viciously, pumping two shotgun blasts into each of their faces.

Kling wanted very much to go to bed with Cindy Forrest.

He did not move when he heard the key in the latch. He sat in the dark with a smile on his face, and then suddenly realized he might frighten her, and moved belatedly to turn on the table lamp. He was too late, she saw or sensed movement in the darkness. He heard her gasp, and immediately said, "It's me, Cind."

"Wow, you scared the hell out of me," she said and turned on the foyer light. "What are you doing here so early? You said . . ."

"I felt like coming over," Kling said, and smiled.

"Yeah?"

"Mmm."

She put her bag down on the hall table, wiggled out of her pumps, and came into the living room.

"Don't you want a light?" she asked.

"No, it's all right."

"Pretty out there."

"Mmm."

"I love that tower. See it there?"

"Yes."

She stared through the window a moment longer, bent to kiss him fleetingly, and then said, "Make yourself a drink, why don't you?"

"You want one, too?"

"Yes. I'm exhausted," Cindy said, and sighed, and padded softly into the bathroom. He heard the water running. He rose, turned on the lamp, and then went to where she kept her liquor in a drop-leaf desk. She was out of bourbon.

"No bourbon," he said.

"What?"

"No bourbon. You're out of bourbon," he shouted.

"Oh, okay, I'll have a little Scotch."

"What?" he shouted.

"Scotch," Cindy shouted. "A little Scotch."

"Okay."

"What?"

"I said *okay*."

"Okay," she said.

He smiled and carried the Scotch bottle into the small kitchenette. He took two short glasses down from the cabinet, poured a liberal shot into each glass, and then nearly broke his wrist trying to dislodge the ice-cube tray from the freezer compartment. He finally chipped the accumulated frost away with a butter knife, dropped two cubes into each glass, and then carried the drinks into the bedroom. Cindy was standing at the closet in half-slip and bra, reaching for a robe. With her back to him, she said, "I think I know what I'm going to write for my thesis, Bert."

"What's that?" he said. "Here's your drink."

"Thank you," she said. Turning, she accepted the drink and tossed her robe onto the bed. She took a long sip, said, "Ahhh," put the glass on the dresser, and then said, "I'll be getting my master's next June, you know. It's time I began thinking about that doctorate."

"Um-huh," Kling said.

"You know what I'd like to do the thesis on?" she asked, and reached behind her to unclasp her bra.

"No, what?"

"The detective as voyeur," she said.

He thought she was kidding, of course, because as she said the words her breasts simultaneously came free of the restraining bra, and he was, in that moment, very *much* the detective as voyeur. But she stepped out of her slip and panties without so much as cracking a smile, and then went to the bed to pick up the robe and put it on. As she was belting it, she said, "What do you think?"

"Are you serious?"

"Yes, of course," she said, looking at him with a somewhat puzzled expression. "Of course I'm serious. Why would I joke about something as important as my thesis?"

"Well, I don't know, I just thought . . ."

"Of *course* I'm serious," she repeated, more strongly this time. She was frowning as she picked up her drink again. "Why? Don't you think it's a good idea?"

"I don't know what you have in mind," Kling said. "You gave me the title, but . . ."

"Well, I don't know if that'd be the *exact* title," Cindy said, annoyed. She sipped some more Scotch and then said, "Let's go into the living room, huh?"

"Why don't we stay in here awhile?" Kling said.

Cindy looked at him. He shrugged and then tried a smile.

"I'm very tired," she said at last. "I've had a lousy day, and I think I'm about to get my period, and I don't . . ."

"All the more reason to . . ."

"No, come on," she said, and walked out of the bedroom. Kling watched her as she went. He kept watching the empty doorframe long after she was out of the room. He took a swallow of his Scotch, set his jaw, and followed her into the living room. She was sitting by the window, gazing out at the distant buildings, her bare feet propped on a hassock. "I think it's a good idea," she said, without turning to look at him.

"Which one?" he asked.

"My thesis," she said testily. "Bert, can we possibly get our minds off . . ."

"*Our* minds?"

"*Your* mind," she corrected.

"Sure," he said.

"It isn't that I don't love you . . ."

"Sure."

"Or even that I don't *want* you . . ."

"Sure."

"It's just that at this particular moment I don't feel like making love. I feel more like crying, if you'd like to know."

"Why?"

"I *told* you. I'm about to get my period. I always feel very depressed a day or two before."

"Okay," he said.

"And also, I've got my mind on this damn thesis."

"Which you don't have to begin work on until next June."

"No, *not* next June. I'll be getting my *master's* next June. I won't start on the doctorate till September. Anyway, what *difference* does it make, would you mind telling me? I have to start thinking about it *sometime*, don't I?"

"Yes, but . . ."

"I don't know what's the matter with you today, Bert."

"It's my day off," he said.

"Well, *that's a non sequitur* if ever I heard one. And anyway, it hasn't been *my* day off. I went to work at nine o'clock this morning and I interviewed twenty-four people, and I'm tired and irritable and about to get . . ."

"Yes, you told me."

"All right, so why are you picking on me?"

"Cindy," he said, "maybe I'd better go home."

"Why?"

"Because I don't want to argue with you."

"Then go home if you want to," she said.

"All right, I will."

"No, don't," she said.

"Cindy . . ."

"Oh, do what you want to do," she said, "I don't care."

"Cindy, I love you very much," he said. "Now cut it out!"

"Then why don't you want to hear about my thesis?"

"I *do* want to hear about your thesis."

"No, all you want to do is make love."

"Well, what's wrong with that?"

"Nothing, except I don't feel like it right now."

"Okay."

"And you don't have to sound so damn offended, either."

"I'm *not* offended."

"And you could at least express a *tiny* bit of interest in my thesis. I *mean*, Bert, you can at least ask what it's going to be about."

"What's it going to be about?" he asked.

"Go to hell, I don't feel like telling you now."

"Okay, fine."

"Fine," she said.

They were both silent.

"Cindy," he said at last, "I don't even *know* you when you're like this."

"Like what?"

"Like a bitch."

"That's too bad, but a bitch is also part of me, I'm awfully sorry. If you love me, you have to love the bitch part, too."

"No, I *don't* have to love the bitch part," Kling said.

"Well, don't, I don't care."

"What's your thesis going to be about?"

"What difference does it make to you?"

"Good night, Cindy," he said, "I'm going home."

"That's right, leave me alone when I'm feeling miserable."

"Cindy . . ."

"It's about you, you know, it was only inspired by you, you know. So go ahead and leave, what difference does it make that I love you so much and think about you day and night and even plan writing my goddamn *thesis* about you? Go ahead, go home, what do I care?"

"Oh boy," he said.

"Sure, oh boy."

"Tell me about your thesis."

"Do you really want to hear it?"

"Yes."

"Well . . ." Cindy said, "I got the idea from *Blow-Up*."

"Mmm?"

"The photographs in *Blow-Up*, you know?"

"Mmm?"

"Do you remember the part of the film where he's enlarging the black-and-white photographs, making them bigger and bigger in an attempt to figure out what happened?"

"Yes, I remember."

"Well, it seemed to me that this entire experience was suggestive of the infantile glimpse of the primal scene."

"The what?"

"The primal scene," Cindy said. "The mother and the father having intercourse."

"If you're going to start talking sexy," Kling said, "I really *am* going home."

"I'm very serious about this, so . . ."

"I'm sorry, go ahead."

"The act of love is rarely understood by the child," Cindy said. "He may witness it again and again, but still remain confused about what's actually happening. The photographer in the film, you'll remember, took a great many pictures of the couple embracing and kissing in the park, do you remember that?"

"Yes, I do."

"Which might possibly relate to the repetitive witnessing of the primal scene. The woman is young and beautiful, you remember, she was played by Vanessa Redgrave, which is how a small boy would think of his mother."

"He would think of his mother as Vanessa Redgrave?"

"No, as young and beautiful. Bert, I swear to God, if you . . ."

"All right, I'm sorry, really. Go on."

"I'm *quite* serious, you know," Cindy said, and took a cigarette from the inlaid box on the table beside the chair. Kling lighted it for her. "Thank you," she said, and blew out a stream of smoke. "Where was I?" she asked.

"The young and beautiful mother."

"Right, which is exactly how a small boy thinks of his mother, as young and beautiful, as the girl he wants to marry. You've heard little boys say they want to marry their mothers, haven't you?"

"Yes," Kling said, "I have."

"All right, the girl in these necking-in-the-park scenes is Vanessa Redgrave, very young, very beautiful. The *man*, however, is an older man, he's got gray hair, he's obviously middle-aged. In fact, Antonioni even inserts some dialogue to that effect, I forget exactly what it was, I think the photographer says something like 'A bit over the hill, isn't he?' Something like that, that's the sense of it, anyway. That this man, her lover, is a much older man. Do you understand?"

"Yes. You're saying he's a father figure."

"Yes. Which means that those scenes in the park, when the photographer is taking pictures of the lovers, *could* be construed as a small boy watching his mother and his father making love."

"All right."

"Which the photographer doesn't quite understand. He's witnessing the primal scene, but he doesn't know what it's really all about. So he takes his pictures home and begins enlarging them, the way a child might enlarge upon vivid memories in an attempt to understand them. But the longer he studies the enlarged pictures, the more confused he becomes, until finally he sees what might be a pistol in one of the blow-ups. A *pistol*, Bert."

"Yes, a pistol," he said.

"I don't have to tell you that the pistol is a fixed psychological symbol."

"For what?"

"For what do you *think*?" Cindy asked.

"Oh," Kling said.

"Yes. And then, to further underscore the Oedipal situation Antonioni has his photographer discover that the older man is dead, he has been *killed*—which is what every small boy wishes would happen to his father. So that he can have the mother all to himself, you do understand?"

"Yes."

"Okay, so that's what started me thinking about the detective as a voyeur. Because, you remember, there was a great deal of suspense in that part of the movie, the part where he's blowing up the photographs. It's really a *mystery* he's working on—and he, in a very real sense, is a *detective*, isn't he?"

"Well, I suppose so."

"Well, of course he is, Bert. The mystery element gets stronger and stronger as he continues with the investigation. And then, of course, we see an actual *corpse*. I mean, there's no question but that a murder *has* been committed. Antonioni leaves it there because he's more interested . . ."

"Leaves what? The corpse?"

"No, not the corpse. Well, yes, he does leave the corpse there, too, as a matter of fact, but I was referring to the mystery element, I meant . . ." She suddenly looked at him suspiciously. "Are you putting me on again?" she asked.

"Yes," he said, and smiled.

"Well, don't be such a wise guy," she said, and returned the smile, which he thought was at least somewhat encouraging. "What I meant was that Antonioni doesn't pursue the *mystery* once it's served his purpose. He's doing a film about illusion and reality and alienation and all, so he's not interested in who done it or why it was done or any of that crap."

"Okay," Kling said. "But I still don't see . . ."

"Well, it occurred to me that perhaps *police* investigation is similarly linked to the primitive and infantile desire to understand the primal scene."

"Boy, that's really reaching, Cindy. How do you get . . ."

"Well, hold it a minute, will you?"

"Okay, let me hear."

"Got you hooked, huh?" she said, and smiled again, this time *very* encouragingly, he thought.

"Go on," he said.

"The police officer . . . the detective . . ."

"Yes?"

". . . is privileged to see the uncensored results of violence, which is what the child *imagines* lovemaking to be. He can think his father is hurting his mother, you know, he can think her moaning is an expression of pain, he can think they're fighting. In any event, he'll often explain it to himself that way because he has neither the experience nor the knowledge to understand it in any other way. He doesn't know *what* they're doing, Bert. It's completely beyond his ken. He knows that he's stimulated by it, yes, but he doesn't know why."

"If you think looking at a guy who's been hit with a meat ax is stimulating . . ."

"No, that's not my point. I'm not trying to make any such analogy, although I do think there's some truth to it."

"What do you mean?"

"Well, violence *is* stimulating. Even the *results* of violence are stimulating."

"The results of violence caused me to throw up last Saturday morning," Kling said.

"That's stimulation of a sort, isn't it? But don't get me away from my point."

"What *is* your point?"

"My point is . . ."

"I don't think I'm going to like it."

"Why not?"

"Because you said I inspired it."

"Antonioni inspired it."

"You said *I* did."

"Not the initial impetus. *Later*, I connected it with you, which is only natural because there was a *homicide* involved, and because I'm madly in love with you and very interested in your work. All right?"

"Well, I like it a little better now, I must admit."

"You haven't even *heard* it yet."

"I'm waiting, I'm waiting."

"Okay. We start with a man—the detective—viewing the results of violence and guessing at what might have happened, right?"

"Well, there's not much guesswork involved when you see two bullet holes in a guy's head. I mean, you can just possibly figure out the violent act was a shooting, you know what I mean?"

"Yes, that's obvious, but the thing you don't know is who did the shooting, or what the circumstances of the shooting were, and so on. You never know what really happened until you catch whoever did it, am I right?"

"No, you're wrong. We usually know plenty before we make an arrest. Otherwise, we don't make it. When we charge somebody, we like to think it'll stick."

"But on what do you base your arrest?"

"On the facts. There're a lot of locked closets in criminal investigation. We open all the doors and look for skeletons."

"*Exactly!*" Cindy said triumphantly. "You search for detail. You examine each and every tiny segment of the picture in an attempt to find a clue that will make the *entire* picture more meaningful, just as the photographer did in *Blow-Up*. And very often your investigation uncovers material that's even more difficult to understand. It only becomes clear later on, the way sexual intercourse eventually becomes clear to the child when he reaches adulthood. He can then say to himself. 'Oh, so *that's* what they were doing in there, they were *screwing* in there."

"I don't recall ever having seen my mother and father doing anything like that," Kling said.

"You've blocked it out."

"No, I just never saw them doing anything like that."

"Like *what*?"

"Like *that*," Kling said.

"You can't even say the *word*," Cindy said, and began giggling. "You've so effectively blocked it out . . ."

"There's one thing I hate about psychologists," Kling said.

"Yeah, what's that?" Cindy asked, still giggling.

"They're all the time analyzing everything."

"Which is exactly what *you* do every day of the week, only *you* call it investigation. Can't you see the possibilities of this, Bert?" she asked, no longer laughing, her face suddenly serious, suddenly very tired-looking again. "Oh, I *know* I haven't really developed it yet, but don't you think it's an awfully good beginning? The detective as voyeur, the detective as privileged observer of a violent scene he can neither control nor understand, frightening by its very nature, confusing at first, but becoming more and more meaningful until it is ultimately understood. It'll make a good thesis. I don't care *what* you think."

"*I* think it'll make a good thesis, too," Kling said. "Let's go work out the primal scene part of it."

He looked down into her face just as she turned hers up, and their eyes met, and held, and neither said a word for several moments. He kept watching her, thinking how much he loved her and wanted her, and seeing the cornflower eyes edged with weariness, her face pale and drawn and drained of energy. Her lips were slightly parted, she took in a deep breath and then released it, and the hand holding the drink slowly lowered to hang limply alongside the arm of the chair. He sensed what she was about to say, Yes, she would say, Yes, she'd make love even though she didn't feel like it, even though she was depressed and tired and felt unattractive, even though she'd much rather sit here and watch the skyline and sip a little more Scotch and then doze off, even though she didn't feel the tiniest bit sexy, Yes, she would, if that was what he wanted. He read this in her eyes and perched on her lips, and he suddenly felt like a hulking rapist who had shambled up out of the sewer, so he shrugged and lightly said, "Maybe we'd better not. Be too much like necrophilia," and smiled. She smiled back at him, wearily and not at all encouragingly. He gently took the glass from her dangling hand and went to refill it for her.

But he was disappointed.

The Roundelay Bar was on Jefferson Avenue, three blocks from the new museum. At five-fifteen that afternoon, when Kling arrived for his business meeting with Anne Gilroy, it was thronged with advertising executives and pretty young secretaries and models, all of whom behaved like guests at a private cocktail party, moving, drinking, chattering, moving on again, hardly any of them sitting at the handful of tables scattered throughout the dimly lit room.

Anne Gilroy was sitting at a table in the far corner, wearing an open crochet dress over what appeared to be a body stocking. At least, Kling *hoped* it was a body stocking, and not just a body. He felt very much out of place in an atmosphere as sleek and as sophisticated as this one, where everyone seemed to be talking about the latest Doyle Dane campaign, or the big Solters and Sabinson coup, or the new Blaine Thompson three-sheet, whatever any of those were. He felt shabbily dressed in his blue plaid jacket, his tie all wrong and improperly knotted, his gun in its shoulder holster causing a very un-Chipplike bulge, felt in fact like a bumbling country hick who had inadvertently stumbled into whatever was making this city tick. And besides, he felt guilty as hell.

Anne waved the moment she saw him. He moved his way through the buzzing crowd and then sat beside her and looked around quickly, certain somehow that Cindy would be standing behind one of the pillars, brandishing a hatchet.

"You're right on time," Anne said, smiling. "I like punctual men."

"Have you ordered yet?" he asked.

"No, I was waiting for you."

"Well, what would you like?"

"Martinis give me a loose, free feeling," she said. "I'll have a martini. Straight up."

He signaled to the waiter and ordered a martini for her and a Scotch and water for himself.

"Do you like my dress?" Anne asked.

"Yes, it's very pretty."

"Did you think it was me?"

"What do you mean?"

"Underneath."

"I wasn't sure."

"It isn't."

"Okay."

"Is something wrong?" she asked.

"No, no. No. No."

"You keep looking around the room."

"Habit. Check it out, you know, known criminals, you know, types. Occupational hazards."

"My, you're nervous," she said. "Does my dress make you nervous?"

"No, it's a very nice dress."

"I wish I had the guts to *really* wear it naked underneath," Anne said, and giggled.

"Well, you'd get arrested," Kling said. "Section 1140 of the Penal Law."

"What do you mean?"

"Exposure of person," Kling said, and began quoting. "A person who willfully and lewdly exposes his person, or the private parts thereof, in any public place, or in any place where others are present, or procures another so to expose himself, is guilty of a misdemeanor."

"Oh, my," Anne said.

"Yes," Kling said, suddenly embarrassed.

"'Private parts,' I love that."

"Well, that's what we call them. I mean, in police work. I mean, that's the way we refer to them."

"Yes, I love it."

"Mmm," Kling said. "Hey, here're the drinks."

"Shall I mix it, sir?" the waiter asked.

"What?"

"Did you want this mixed, sir?"

"Oh. Yes. Yes, just a little water in it, please," he said, and smiled at Anne and almost knocked over her martini. The waiter poured a little water into the Scotch and moved away.

"Cheers," Kling said.

"Cheers," Anne said. "Do you have a girlfriend?"

Kling who was already drinking, almost choked. "What?" he said.

"A girlfriend."

"Yes," he answered glumly, and nodded.

"Is that why you're so worried?"

"Who's worried?" he said.

"You shouldn't be," Anne said. "After all, this is only a business meeting."

"That's right, I'm not worried at all," Kling said.

"What's she like? Your girlfriend?" Anne said.

"Well, I'd much rather discuss the conversation you had with Mrs. Leyden."

"Are you engaged?"

"Not officially."

"What does *that* mean?"

"It means we plan on getting married someday, I guess, but we . . ."

"You *guess*?"

"Well, no, actually there's no guesswork involved. We simply haven't set the date, that's all. Cindy's still in school, and . . ."

"Is that her name? Cindy?"

"Yes. For Cynthia."

"And you say she's still in school? How old is she?"

"Twenty-three. She's finishing her master's this June."

"Oh."

"Yes, and she'll be going on for her doctorate in the fall."

"Oh."

"Yes," Kling said.

"She must be very bright."

"She is."

"I barely finished high school," Anne said, and paused. "Is she pretty?"

"Yes." Kling took another swallow of Scotch and then said, "*I'm* supposed to be the detective, but *you're* asking all the questions."

"I'm a very curious girl," Anne said, and smiled. "But go ahead. What do you want to know?"

"What time did you call Mrs. Leyden last Friday?"

"Oh, I thought you were going to ask some questions about *me*."

"No, actually I . . ."

"I'm twenty-five years old," Anne said, "born and raised right here in the city. My father's a Transit Authority employee, my mother's a housewife. We're all very Irish." She paused and sipped at the martini. "I began working for AT&M right after I graduated high school, and I've been there since. I believe in making love not war, and I think you're possibly the handsomest man I've ever met in my life."

"Thank you," Kling mumbled, and hastily lifted his glass to his lips.

"Does that embarrass you?"

"No."

"What *does* it do?"

"I'm not sure."

"I believe in speaking honestly and frankly," Anne said.

"I see that."

"Would you like to go to bed with me?"

Kling did not answer immediately, because what popped into his mind instantly was the single word *Yes!* and it was followed by a succession of wild images interspersed with blinking neon lights that spelled out additional messages such as *You're goddamn right I'd like to go to bed with you* and *when?* and *Your place or mine?* and things like that. So he waited until he had regained control of his libido, and then he calmly said, "I'll have to think it over. In the meantime, let's talk about Mrs. Leyden, shall we?"

"Sure," Anne said. "What would you like to know?"

"What time did you call her?"

"Just before closing time Friday."

"Which *was?*"

"About ten to five, something like that."

"Do you remember the conversation?"

"Yes. I said, 'Hello, may I please speak to Mrs. Leyden?' and she said, '*This* is Mrs. Leyden.' So I informed her that her husband had wired us from California to ask that she send him a fresh checkbook, and she said she knew all about it, but thanks anyway."

"She knew all about *what?*"

"The checkbook."

"How'd she know?"

"She said her husband had called from the Coast that morning to say he'd be in San Francisco all weekend, and that he'd be moving on to Portland on Monday morning and wanted her to send a fresh checkbook to the Logan Hotel there."

"What time had he called her?"

"She didn't say."

"But if he'd already called her, why'd he bother sending a wire to the company?"

"I don't know. Just double-checking, I guess."

"I wonder if he called her again later to say he'd be coming home instead?"

"She didn't mention getting two calls."

"This was close to five, you said?"

"Yes, just before closing."

"Was he normally so careful?"

"What do you mean?"

"Would he normally make a call and then back it with a wire asking the company to convey the identical information?"

"He may have sent the wire *before* he called his wife."

"Even so."

169

"Besides, the company paid his expenses, so why not?" Anne smiled. "Have you thought it over yet?" she asked.

"No, not yet."

"Think about it. I'd like to. Very much."

"Why?"

"Because you're stunning."

"Oh, come on," Kling said.

"You *are*. I'm not easily impressed, believe me. I think I'm in love with you."

"That's impossible."

"No, it isn't."

"Sure it is. A person can't just fall in love with a person without knowing anything about the person. That only happens in the movies."

"I know everything there is to know about you," Anne said. "Let's have another drink, shall we?"

"Sure," Kling said, and signaled the waiter. "Another round," he said when the waiter came over, and then turned to Anne, who was watching him with her eyes wide and her cheeks flushed, and he suddenly thought, Jesus, I think she really *is* in love with me. "Anyway, as you said, this is a business meeting, and . . ."

"It's a lot more than that," Anne said, "and you *know* it. I think you knew it when you agreed to meet me, but if you didn't know it then, you certainly know it now. I love you and I want to go to bed with you. Let's go to my apartment right this minute."

"Hold it, hold it," Kling said, thinking, What am I, crazy? Say Yes. Pay the check and get out of here, take this luscious little girl to wherever she wants to go, hurry up before she changes her mind. "You don't know me at all," he said, "really. We've hardly even *talked* to each other."

"What's there to talk about? You're a wonderfully good-looking man, and you're undoubtedly brave because you *have* to be brave in your line of work, and you're idealistic because otherwise why would you be involved in crime prevention, and you're bright as hell, and I think it's very cute the way you're so embarrassed because I'm begging you to take me to bed. There's nothing else I have to know, do you have a mole on your thigh, or something?"

"No," he said, and smiled.

"So?"

"Well, I . . . I can't right now, anyway."

"Why not?" Anne paused, and then moved closer to him, covering his hand with hers on the tabletop. "Bert," she whispered, "I love you and I want you."

"Listen," he said, "let's, uh, think this over a little, huh? I'm, uh . . ."

"Don't *you* want *me*?"

"Yes, but . . ."

"Ah, one for our side," she said, and smiled. "What is it, then?"

"I'm, uh, engaged," he said. "I already told you that."

"So what?"

"Well, you, uh, wouldn't want me to . . ."

"Yes, I would," Anne said.

"Well, I couldn't. Not now. I mean, maybe not ever."

"My telephone number is Washington 6-3841. Call me later tonight, after you leave your girlfriend."

"I'm not seeing her tonight."

"You're *not*?" Anne asked astonished.

"No. She goes to school on Wednesday nights."

"Then, that settles it," Anne said. "Pay the check."

"I'll pay the check," Kling said, "but nothing's settled."

"You're coming with me," Anne said. "We're going to make love six times, and then I'm going to cook you some dinner, and then we'll make love another six times. What time do you have to be at work tomorrow morning?"

"The answer is no," Kling said.

"Okay," Anne said breezily. "But write down the telephone number."

"I don't have to write it down."

"Oh, such a smart cop," Anne said. "What's the number?"

"Washington 6-3841."

"You'll call me," she said. "You'll call me later tonight when you think of me all alone in my bed, pining away for you."

"I don't think so," he said.

"Maybe not tonight," she amended. "But soon."

"I can't promise that."

"Anyway," she said, "it doesn't matter. Because if *you* don't call *me*, *I'll* call *you*. I have no pride, Bert. I want you, and I'm going to get you. Consider yourself forewarned."

"You scare hell out of me," he said honestly.

"Good. Do I also excite you just a little bit?"

"Yes," he said, and smiled. "Just a little bit."

"That's *two* for our side," she said, and sqeezed his hand.

It is easy to solve murder cases if you are alert.

It is also easy to get beat up if you are not careful. Bert Kling was not too terribly alert that next afternoon, and so he did not come even close to solving the Leyden case. Being careless, he got beat up.

He got beat up by a woman.

Anne Gilroy marched up the front steps of the station house at ten minutes to three, wearing a blue-and-red-striped mini, her long blond hair caught at the back of her neck with a red ribbon. Her shoes were blue, they flashed with November sunshine as she mounted the steps and walked past the green globes flanking the stoop. She walked directly to where Sergeant Dave Murchison sat behind the high muster desk, beamed a radiant smile at him, batted her blue eyes in a semaphore even desk sergeants understand, and sweetly said, "Is Detective Kling in?"

"He is," Murchison said.

"May I see him, please?"

"Who shall I say is here, whom?" Murchison said.

"Miss Anne Gilroy," she said, and wheeled away from the desk to study first the Wanted posters on the bulletin board, and then the clock on the wall. She sat at last on the wooden bench opposite the muster desk, took a cigarette from her blue bag, glanced inquiringly at Murchison before lighting it (he nodded permission), and then, to his distraction, crossed her legs and sat calmly smoking while he tried to reach Kling, who was at that moment in the lieutenant's office.

"Tied up right now," Murchison said. "Would you mind waiting a moment?"

"Thank you," Anne Gilroy said, and jiggled her foot. Murchison looked at her legs, wondering what the world was coming to, and wondering whether he should give permission to his twelve-year-old daughter, prepubescent and emerging, to wear such short skirts when she entered her teens, see clear up the whole leg, he thought, and then mopped his brow and plugged into the switchboard as a light flashed. He held a brief conversation, pulled out the cord, looked again to where Anne Gilroy sat with crossed legs and smoke-wreathed blond hair, and said, "He'll be right down, miss."

"Oh, can't I go up?"

"He said he'd be down."

"I was hoping to see a squadroom."

"Well," Murchison said, and tilted his head to one side, and thought, What the hell do you hope to see up there except a few bulls working their asses off? The switchboard blinked into life again. He plugged in and took a call from an irate patrolman on Third who said he had phoned in for a meat wagon half an hour ago and there was a lady bleeding on the goddamn sidewalk, when was it gonna *get* there? Murchison told him to calm down, and the patrolman told Murchison he had never seen so much blood in his life, and the lady was gonna die, and the crowd was getting mean. Murchison said he'd call the hospital again, and then yanked out the cord, and gave himself an outside line.

He was dialing the hospital when Kling came down the iron-runged steps leading from the second floor. Kling looked surprised, even though Murchison had told him who was here. Maybe it was the short

skirt that did it. Murchison watched as Kling walked to the bench
("Hello, this is Sergeant Murchison over at the 87th Precinct," he said
into the phone, "where the hell's that ambulance?"), extended his
hand to Anne Gilroy, and then sat on the bench beside her. Murchison
could not hear them from across the room. ("Well, I got a patrolman
screaming at me, and a crowd about to get unmanageable, and a lady
about to bleed to death right on the sidewalk there, so how about it?")
Kling now seemed more embarrassed then surprised, he kept nodding
his head at Anne Gilroy as she smiled and batted her blue eyes, talking
incessantly, her face very close to his as though she were whispering
all the secrets of the universe to him. ("Yeah, well how about breaking
up the goddamn pinochle game and getting somebody over there?"
Murchison shouted into the phone.) Kling nodded again, rose from the
bench, and walked toward the muster desk. ("If I get another call from
that patrolman, I'm going straight to the mayor's office, you got that?"
Murchison yelled, and angrily pulled the cord from the switchboard.)
  "I'm going out for some coffee," Kling said.
  "Okay," Murchison said. "When will you be back?"
  "Half an hour or so."
  "Right," Murchison said, and watched as Kling went back to the
bench. Anne Gilroy stood up, looped her arm through Kling's, smiled
over her shoulder at Murchison, and clickety-clacked on her high
heels across the muster room floor, tight little ass twitching busily,
long blond hair bouncing on her back. The switchboard was glowing
again. Murchison plugged in to find the same patrolman, nearly
hysterical this time because the lady had passed away a minute ago,
and her brother was screaming to the crowd that this was police
negligence, and the patrolman wanted to know what to do. Murchison
said whatever he did, he shouldn't draw his revolver unless it got
really threatening, and the patrolman told him it looked really
threatening right *now*, with the crowd beginning to yell and all, and
maybe he ought to send some reinforcements over. Murchison said
he'd see what he could do and that was when the scream came from
the front steps outside the precinct.
  Murchison was a desk cop, and he wasn't used to reacting too
quickly, but there was something urgent about this scream, and he
put two and two together immediately and realized that the person
screaming must be the girl named Anne Gilroy who had sashayed out
of here just a minute ago on the arm of Bert Kling. He came around
the muster desk with all the swiftness of a corpulent man past fifty,
reaching for his holstered revolver as he puffed toward the main
doors, though he couldn't understand what could possibly be happening on the front steps of a police station, especially to a girl who was in
the company of a detective.
  What was happening—and this surprised Murchison no end be-

cause he expected to find a couple of hoods maybe threatening the girl or something—what was happening was that *another* blond girl was hitting Kling on the head with a dispatch case. It took a moment for Murchison to recognize the other blond girl as Cindy Forrest, whom he had seen around enough times to know that she was Kling's girl, but he had never seen her with such a terrible look on her face. The only time he had ever seen a woman with such a look on her face was the time his Aunt Moira had caught his Uncle John screwing the lady upstairs on the front-room sofa of her apartment. Aunt Moira had gone up to get a recipe for glazed oranges and had got instead her glassy-eyed husband humping the bejabbers out of the woman who until then had been her very good friend. Aunt Moira had chased Uncle John into the hallway and down the steps with his pants barely buttoned, hitting him on the head with a broom she grabbed on the third-floor landing, chasing Uncle John clear into the streets where Murchison and some of his boyhood friends were playing Knuckles near Ben the Kosher Delicatessen. The look on Aunt Moira's face had been something terrible and fiery to see, all right, and the same look was on Cindy Forrest's young and pretty face this very moment as she continued to clobber Kling with the brown leather dispatch case. The blond girl, Anne Gilroy, kept screaming for her to stop, but there was no stopping a lady when she got the Aunt Moira look. Kling, big detective that he was, was trying to cover his face and the top of his head with both hands while Cindy did her demolition work. The girl Anne Gilroy kept screaming as Murchison rushed down the steps yelling, "All right, break it up," sounding exactly like a cop. The only thing Cindy seemed intent on breaking up, however, was Kling's head, so Murchison stepped between them, gingerly avoiding the flailing dispatch case, and then shoved Kling down the steps and out of range, and shouted at Cindy, "You're striking a police officer, miss," which she undoubtedly knew, and the girl Anne Gilroy screamed once again, and then there was silence.

"You rotten son of a bitch," Cindy said to Kling.

"It's all right, Dave," Kling said from the bottom of the steps. "I can handle it."

"Oh, you certainly can handle it, you bastard," Cindy said.

"Are you all right?" Anne Gilroy asked.

"I'm fine, Anne," Kling answered.

"Oh, *Anne*, is it?" Cindy shouted, and swung the dispatch case at her. Murchison stepped into the line of fire, deflected the case with the back of his arm, and then yanked Cindy away from the girl and shouted, "Now, goddamn you, Cindy, do you want to wind up in the cooler?"

By this time a crowd of patrolmen had gathered in the muster room, embarrassing Kling, who liked to maintain a sort of detective superiority over the rank and file. The patrolmen were enormously entertained by the spectacle of Sergeant Murchison trying to keep apart two very dishy blondes, one of whom happened to be Kling's girl, while Kling stood by looking abashed.

"All right, break it up," Kling said to them, also sounding like a cop. The other cops thought this was amusing, but none of them laughed. Neither did any of them break it up. Instead, they crowded into the doorway, ogled the girl in the red and blue mini, ogled Cindy, too (even though she was more sedately dressed in a blue shift), and then glanced first to Kling and then to Murchison to see who would make the next move.

Neither of them did.

Instead, Cindy turned on her heel, tilted her nose up, and marched down the steps and past Kling.

"Cindy, wait, let me explain!" Kling cried, obviously thinking he was in an old Doris Day movie, and immediately ran up the street after her.

"I want to press charges," Anne Gilroy said to Murchison.

"Oh, go home, miss," Murchison said, and then went up the steps and shoved past the patrolmen in the doorway and went back to the switchboard, where the most he'd have to contend with was something like a lady bleeding to death on the sidewalk.

Kling used his own key on the door, and then twisted the knob, and shoved the door inward, but Cindy had taken the precaution of fastening the safety chain, and the door abruptly jarred to a stop, open some two-and-a-half inches, but refusing to budge further.

"Cindy," he shouted, "take off this chain! I want to talk to you."

"I don't want to talk to you!" she shouted back.

"Take off this chain, or I'll break the door off the hinges!"

"Go break your bimbo's door, why don't you?"

"She's not a bimbo!"

"Don't defend her, you louse!" Cindy shouted.

"Cindy, I'm warning you, I'll kick this door in!"

"You do, and I'll call the police!"

"I *am* the police."

"Go police your bimbo, louse."

"Okay, honey, I warned you."

"You'd better have a search warrant," she shouted, "or I'll sue you *and* the city *and* the . . ."

Kling kicked in the door efficiently and effortlessly. Cindy stood facing him with her fists clenched.

"Don't come in here," she said. "You're not wanted here. You're not wanted here ever again. Go home. Go away. Go to hell."

"I want to talk to you."

"I don't want to talk to you ever again as long as I live, that's final."

"What are you so sore about?"

"I don't like liars and cheats and rotten miserable liars. Now get out of here, Bert, I mean it."

"Who's a liar?"

"*You* are."

"How am I . . ."

"You said you loved me."

"I *do* love you."

"Ha!"

"That girl . . ."

"That *slut* . . .."

"She's not a slut."

"That's right, she's a sweet Irish virgin. Go hold her hand a little, why don't you? Get out of here, Bert, before I hit you again."

"Listen, there's nothing . . ."

"That's right, there's nothing, there's absolutely nothing between us ever again, get out of here."

"Lower your voice, you'll have the whole damn building in here."

"All snuggly-cozy, arm in arm, batting her eyes . . ."

"She had information . . ."

"Oh, I'll just *bet* she has information."

". . . about the Leyden case. She came to the squadroom . . ."

"I'll just *bet* she has information," Cindy repeated, a bit hysterically, Kling thought. "I'll bet she has information even *Cleopatra* never dreamt of. Why don't you get out of here and leave me alone, okay? Just get out of here, okay? Go get all that hot information, okay?"

"Cindy . . ."

"I thought we were in love . . ."

"We *are*."

"I thought we . . ."

"We *are*, damnit!"

"I thought we were going to get married one day and have kids and live in the country . . ."

"Cindy . . ."

"So a cheap little floozie flashes a smile and . . ."

"Cindy, she's a nice girl who . . ."

"Don't you *dare*!" Cindy shouted. "If you're here to *defend* that little tramp . . ."

"I'm *not* here to defend her!"

"Then why *are* you here?"

"To tell you I love you."

"Ha!"

"I love you," Kling said.

"Yeah."

"I do."

"Yeah."

"I love you."

"Then why . . ."

"We were going out for a cup of coffee, that's all."

"Sure."

"There's nobody in the whole world I want but you," Kling said. Cindy did not answer.

"I mean it."

She was still silent.

"I love you, honey," he said. "Now come on." He waited. She was standing with her head bent, watching the floor. He did not dare approach her. "Come on," he said.

"I wanted to kill you," Cindy said softly. "When I saw you together, I wanted to kill you." She began weeping gently, still staring at the floor, not raising her eyes to his. He went to her at last and took her in his arms, and held her head cradled against his shoulder, his fingers lightly stroking her hair, her tears wetting his jacket and his shirt.

"I love you so much," she said, "that I wanted to kill you."

Shotgun, 1969

Kling felt pretty lousy.

His condition, he kept telling himself, had nothing to do with the fact that Cindy had broken their engagement three weeks before. To begin with, it had never been a proper engagement, and a person certainly couldn't go around mourning something that had never truly existed. Besides, Cindy had made it abundantly clear that, whereas they had enjoyed some very good times together, and whereas she would always think upon him fondly and recall with great pleasure the days and the months (yea, even years) they had spent together pretending they were in love, she had nonetheless met a very attractive young man who was a practicing psychiatrist at Buenavista Hospital, where she was doing her internship, and seeing as how they shared identical interests, and seeing as how he was quite ready to get married whereas Kling seemed to be married to a .38 Detective's Special, a scarred wooden desk, and a detention cage, Cindy felt it might be best to terminate their relationship immediately rather than court the possibility of trauma induced by slow and painful withdrawal.

That had been three weeks ago, and he had not seen nor called

Cindy since, and the pain of the breakup was equaled only by the pain of the bursitis in his right shoulder, despite the fact that he was wearing a copper bracelet on his wrist. The bracelet had been given to him by none other than Meyer Meyer, whom no one would have dreamed of as a superstitious man given to beliefs in ridiculous claims. The bracelet was supposed to begin working in ten days (well, maybe two weeks, Meyer had said, hedging) and Kling had been wearing it for eleven days now, with no relief for the bursitis, but with a noticeable green stain around his wrist just below the bracelet. Hope springs eternal. Somewhere in his race memory, there lurked a hulking apelike creature rubbing animal teeth by a fire, praying in grunts for a splendid hunt on the morrow. Somewhere also in his race memory, though not as far back, was the image of Cindy Forrest naked in his arms, and the concomitant fantasy that she would call to say she'd made a terrible mistake and was ready to drop her psychiatrist pal. No women's lib man he, Kling nonetheless felt it perfectly all right for Cindy to take the initiative in reestablishing their relationship; it was she, after all, who had taken the first and final step toward ending it.

Early Monday morning, on Kling's day off, he called Cindy. It was only seven-thirty, but he knew her sleeping and waking habits as well as he knew his own, and since the phone was on the kitchen wall near the refrigerator, and since she would at that moment be preparing breakfast, he was not surprised when she answered it on the second ring.

"Hello?" she said. She sounded rushed, a trifle breathless. She always allowed herself a scant half hour to get out of the apartment each morning, rushing from bedroom to kitchen to bathroom to bedroom again, finally rushing for the elevator, looking miraculously well groomed and sleek and rested and ready to do battle with the world. He visualized her standing now at the kitchen phone, only partially clothed, and felt a faint stirring of desire.

"Hi, Cindy," he said. "it's me."

"Oh, hello Bert," she said. "Can you hold just a second? The coffee's about to boil over." He waited. In the promised second, she was back on the line. "Okay," she said. "I tried to reach you the other night."

"Yes, I know. I'm returning your call."

"Right, right," she said. There was a long silence. "I'm trying to remember why I called you. Oh, yes, I found a shirt of yours in the dresser, and I wanted to know what I should do with it. So I called you at home, and there was no answer, and then I figured you probably had night duty, and I tried the squadroom, but Steve said you weren't on. So I decided to wrap it up and mail it. I've already got it all addressed and everything."

There was another silence.

"So I guess I'll drop it off at the post office on my way to work this morning," Cindy said.

"Okay," Kling said.

"If that's what you want me to do," Cindy said.

"Well, what would you *like* to do?"

"It's all wrapped and everything, so I guess that's what I'll do."

"Be a lot of trouble to *un*wrap it, I guess," Kling said.

"Why would I want to unwrap it?"

"I don't know. Why did you call me Saturday night?"

"To ask what you wanted me to do with the shirt."

"What choices did you have in mind?"

"When? Saturday night?"

"Yes," Kling said. "When you called."

"Well, there were several possibilities, I guess. You could have stopped here to pick up the shirt, or I could have dropped it off at your place or the squadroom, or we could have had a drink together or something, at which time . . ."

"I didn't know that was permissible."

"Which?"

"Having a drink together. Or *any* of those things, in fact."

"Well, it's all academic now, isn't it? You weren't home when I called, and you weren't working, either, so I wrapped up the goddamn shirt, and I'll mail it to you this morning."

"What are you sore about?"

"Who's sore?" Cindy said.

"You sound sore."

"I have to get out of here in twenty minutes and I still haven't had my coffee."

"Wouldn't want to be late for the hospital," Kling said. "Might upset your friend Dr. Freud."

"Ha-ha," Cindy said mirthlessly.

"How is he, by the way?"

"He's fine, by the way."

"Good."

"Bert?"

"Yes, Cindy?"

"Never mind, nothing."

"What is it?"

"Nothing. I'll put the shirt in the mail. I washed it and ironed it, I hope it doesn't get messed up."

"I hope not."

"Good-bye, Bert," she said, and hung up.

"87th Squad, Kling."

"Bert, this is Cindy."

"Hi," he said.

"Are you busy?" she asked.

"I was just about to call the I.S."

"Oh."

"But go ahead. It can wait."

Cindy hesitated. Then, her voice very low, she said, "Bert, can I see you tomorrow?"

"Tomorrow?" he said.

"Yes." She hesitated again. "Tomorrow's Christmas Eve."

"I know."

"I bought something for you."

"Why'd you do that, Cindy?"

"Habit," she said, and he suspected she was smiling.

"I'd love to see you, Cindy," he said.

"I'll be working till five."

"No Christmas party?"

"At a *hospital*?" Bert, my dear, we deal here daily with life and death."

"Don't we all," Kling said, and smiled. "Shall I meet you at the hospital?"

"All right. The side entrance. That's near the emergency . . ."

"Yes, I know where it is. At five o'clock?"

"Well, five-fifteen."

"Okay, five-fifteen."

"You'll like what I got you," she said, and then hung up.

He had forgotten, almost, what she looked like.

She came through the hospital's chrome and glass revolving doors, and he saw at first only a tall blond girl, full-breasted and wide-hipped, honey-blond hair clipped close to her head, cornflower-blue eyes, shoving through the doors and out onto the low, flat stoop, and he reacted to her the way he might react to any beautiful stranger stepping into the crisp December twilight, and then he realized it was Cindy, and his heart lurched.

"Hi," he said.

"Hi."

She took his arm. They walked in silence for several moments.

"You look beautiful," he said.

"Thank you. So do you."

He was, in fact, quite aware of the way they looked together, and fell immediately into the Young Lovers syndrome, positive that everyone they passed on the windswept street knew instantly that they were mad about each other. Each stranger (or so he thought) cased them quickly, remarking silently on their oneness, envying their youth and strength and glowing health, longing to be these two on Christmas Eve, Cindy and Bert, American Lovers, who had met cute, and loved long, and fought hard, and parted sadly, and were now together again in the great tradition of the season, radiating love like flashing Christmas bulbs on a sixty-foot-high tree.

They found a cocktail lounge near the hospital, one they had never been to before, either together or separately, Kling sensing that a "first" was necessary to their rediscovery of each other. They sat at a small round table in a corner of the room. The crowd noises were comforting. He suspected an English pub might be like this on Christmas Eve, the voice cadences lulling and soft, the room itself warm and protective, a good place for nurturing a love that had almost died and was now about to redeclare itself.

"Where's my present?" he said, and grinned in mock, evil greediness.

She reached behind her to where she had hung her coat on a wall peg, and dug into the pocket, and placed a small package in the exact center of the table. The package was wrapped in bright blue paper and tied with a green ribbon and bow. He felt a little embarrassed; he always did when receiving a gift. He went into the pocket of his own coat, and placed his gift on the table beside hers, a slightly larger package wrapped in jingle-bells paper, red and gold, no bow.

"So," she said.

"So," he said.

"Merry Christmas."

"Merry Christmas."

They hesitated. They looked at each other. They both smiled.

"You first," he said.

"All right."

She slipped her fingernail under the Scotch tape and broke open the wrapping without tearing the paper, and then eased the box out, and moved the wrapping aside, intact, and centered the box before her, and opened its lid. He had bought her a plump gold heart, seemingly bursting with an inner life of its own, the antiqued gold chain a tether that kept it from ballooning ecstatically into space. She looked at the heart, and then glanced quickly into his expectant face and nodded briefly and said, "Thank you, it's beautiful."

"It's not Valentine's Day . . ."

"Yes." She was still nodding. She was looking down at the heart again, and nodding.

"But I thought . . ." He shrugged.

"Yes, it's beautiful," she said again. "Thank you, Bert."

"Well," he said, and shrugged again, feeling vaguely uncomfortable and suspecting it was because he hated the ritual of opening presents.

He ripped off the bow on her gift, tore open the paper, and lifted the lid off the tiny box. She had bought him a gold tie tack in the form of miniature handcuffs, and he read meaning into the gift immediately, significance beyond the fact that he was a cop whose tools of the trade included real handcuffs hanging from his belt. His gift had told her something about the way he felt, and he was certain that her gift was telling him the very same thing—they were together again, she was binding herself to him again.

"Thank you," he said.

"Do you like it, Bert?"

"I love it."

"I thought . . ."

"Yes, I love it."

"Good."

They had not yet ordered drinks. Kling signaled for the waiter, and they sat in curious silence until he came to the table. The waiter left, and the silence lengthened, and it was then that Kling began to suspect something was wrong, something was terribly wrong. She had closed the lid on his gift, and was staring at the closed box.

"What is it?" Kling asked.

"Bert . . ."

"Tell me, Cindy."

"I didn't come here to . . ."

He knew already, there was no need for her to elaborate. He knew, and the noises of the room were suddenly too loud, the room itself too hot.

"Bert, I'm going to marry him," she said.

"I see."

"I'm sorry."

"No, no," he said. "No, Cindy, please."

"Bert, what you and I had together was very good . . ."

"I know that, honey."

"And I just couldn't end it the way . . . the way we were ending it. I had to see you again, and tell you how much you'd meant to me. I had to be sure you knew that."

"Okay," he said.

"Bert?"

"Yes, Cindy. Okay," he said. He smiled and touched her hand reassuringly. "Okay," he said again.

They spent a half hour together, drinking only the single round, and then they went into the cold, and they shook hands briefly, and Cindy said, "Good-bye, Bert," and he said, "Good-bye, Cindy," and they walked off in opposite directions.

Sadie When She Died, 1972

AUGUSTA BLAIR

T he lady was sitting on the living room sofa.

The lady had long red hair and green eyes and a deep suntan. She was wearing a dark green sweater, a short brown skirt, and brown boots. Her legs crossed, she kept staring at the wall as Kling came into the room, and then turned to face him. His first impression was one of total harmony, a casual perfection of color and design, russet and green, hair and eyes, sweater and skirt, boots blending with the smoothness of her tan, the long sleek grace of crossed legs, the inquisitively angled head, the red hair cascading in clean vertical descent. Her face and figure came as residuals to his brief course in art appreciation. High cheekbones, eyes slanting up from them, fiercely green against the tan, tilted nose gently drawing the upper lip away from partially exposed, even white teeth. Her sweater swelled over breasts firm without a bra, the wool cinched tightly at her waist with a brown, brass-studded belt, hip softly carving an arc against the nubby sofa back, skirt revealing a secret thigh as she turned more fully toward him.

He had never seen a more beautiful woman in his life.

"I'm Detective Kling," he said. "How do you do?"

185

"Hullo," she said dully. She seemed on the edge of tears. Her green eyes glistened, she extended her hand to him, and he took it clumsily, and they exchanged handshakes, and he could not take his eyes from her face. He realized all at once that he was still holding her hand. He dropped it abruptly, cleared his throat, and reached into his pocket for his pad.

"I don't believe I have your name, miss," he said.

"Augusta Blair," she said. "Did you see the mess inside? In the bedroom?"

"I'll take a look in a minute," Kling said. "When did you discover the theft, Miss Blair?"

"I got home about half an hour ago."

"From where?"

"Austria."

"Nice thing to come home to," Ingersoll said, and shook his head.

"Was the door locked when you got here?" Kling asked.

"Yes."

"You used your key to get in?"

"Yes."

"Anybody in the apartment?"

"No."

"Did you hear anything? Any sound at all?"

"Nothing."

"Tell me what happened."

"I came in, and I left the door open behind me because I knew the doorman was coming up with my bags. Then I took off my coat and hung it in the hall closet, and then I went to the john, and then I went into the bedroom. Everything looked all right until then. The minute I stepped in there, I felt . . . invaded."

"You'd better take a look at it, Bert," Ingersoll said. "The guy went sort of berserk."

"That it?" Kling asked, indicating a doorway across the room.

"Yes," Augusta said, and rose from the couch. She was a tall girl, at least five-seven, perhaps five-eight, and she moved with swift grace, preceding him to the bedroom door, looking inside once again, and then turning away in dismay. Kling went into the room, but she did not follow him. She stood in the doorframe instead, worrying her lip, her shoulder against the jamb.

The burglar had slashed through the room like a hurricane. The dresser drawers had all been pulled out and dumped onto the rug—slips, bras, panties, sweaters, stockings, scarves, blouses, spilling across the room in a dazzle of color. Similarly, the clothes on hangers had been yanked out of the closet and flung helter-skelter—coats, suits, skirts, gowns, robes strewn over the floor, bed, and chairs. A jewelry box had been overturned in the center of the bed, and bracelets, rings, beads, pendants, chokers glittered amid a swirl of chiffon, silk, nylon, and wool. A white kitten sat on the dresser top, mewing.

"Did he find what he was looking for?" Kling asked.

"Yes," she answered. "My good jewelry was wrapped in a red silk scarf at the back of the top drawer. It's gone."

"Anything else?"

"Two furs. A leopard and an otter."

"He's selective," Ingersoll said.

"Mmm," Kling said. "Any radios, phonographs, stuff like that?"

"No. The hi-fi equipment's in the living room. He didn't touch it."

"I'll need a list of the jewelry and coats, Miss Blair."

"What for?"

"Well, so we can get working on it. Also, I'm sure you want to report this to your insurance company."

"None of it was insured."

"Oh boy," Kling said.

"I just never thought anything like this would happen," Augusta said.

"How long have you been *living* here?" Kling asked incredulously.

"The city or the apartment?"

"Both."

"I've lived in the city for a year and a half. The apartment for eight months."

"Where are you from originally?"

"Seattle."

"Are you presently employed?" Kling said, and took out his pad.

"Yes."

"Can you give me the name of the firm?"

"I'm a model," Augusta said. "I'm represented by the Cutler Agency."

"Were you in Austria on a modeling assignment?"

"No, vacation. Skiing."

"I thought you looked familiar," Ingersoll said. "I'll bet I've seen your picture in the magazines."

"Mmm," Augusta said without interest.

"How long were you gone?" Kling asked.

"Two weeks. Well, sixteen days, actually."

"Nice thing to come home to," Ingersoll said again, and again shook his head.

"I moved here because it had a doorman," Augusta said. "I thought buildings with doormen were safe."

"*None* of the buildings on this side of the city are safe," Ingersoll said.

"Not many of them, anyway," Kling said.

"I couldn't afford anything across the park," Augusta said. "I haven't been modeling a very long time, I don't really get many bookings." She saw the question on Kling's face and said, "The furs were gifts from my mother, and the jewelry was left to me by my aunt. I saved six goddamn months for the trip to Austria," she said, and suddenly burst into tears. "Oh, shit," she said, "why'd he have to do this?"

Ingersoll and Kling stood by awkwardly. Augusta turned swiftly, walked past Ingersoll to the sofa, and took a handkerchief from her handbag. She noisily blew her nose, dried her eyes, and said, "I'm sorry."

"If you'll let me have the complete list . . ." Kling said.

"Yes, of course."

"We'll do what we can to get it back."

"Sure," Augusta said, and blew her nose again.

At ten minutes to one on Wednesday afternoon, Augusta Blair called the squadroom and asked to talk to Detective Kling, who was on his lunch hour and down the hall in the locker room, taking a nap. Meyer asked if Kling could call her back and she breathlessly told him she had only a minute and would appreciate it if he could be called to the phone. It had to do with the burglary, she said. Meyer went down the hall and reluctantly awakened Kling, who did not seem to mind at all. In fact, he hurried to his desk, picked up the receiver, and said, quite cheerfully, "Hello, Miss Blair, how are you?"

"Fine, thank you," she said. "I've been trying to call you all day long, Mr. Kling, but this is the first break we've had. We started at nine this morning, and I didn't know if you got to work that early."

"Yes, I was here," Kling said.

"I guess I should have called then. Anyway, here I am now. And I've got to be back in a minute. Do you think you can come down here?"

"Where are you, Miss Blair?"

"Schaeffer Photography at 580 Hall Avenue. The fifth floor."

"What's this about?"

"When I was cleaning up the mess in the apartment, I found something that wasn't mine. I figure the burglar may have dropped it."

"I'll be right there," Kling said. "What was it you found?"

"Well, I'll show you when you get here," she said. "I've got to run, Mr. Kling."

"Okay," he said, "I'll . . ."

But she was gone.

Schaeffer Photography occupied the entire fifth floor of 580 Hall. The receptionist, a pert blonde with a marked German accent, informed Kling that Augusta had said he would be coming, and then directed him to the studio, which was at the end of a long hallway hung with samples of Schaeffer's work. Judging from the selection, Schaeffer did mostly fashion photography; no avid reader of *Vogue*, Kling nonetheless recognized the faces of half the models, and searched in vain for a picture of Augusta. Apparently she had been telling the truth when she said she'd been in the business only a short while.

The door to the studio was closed. Kling eased it open, and found himself in an enormous room overhung by a skylight. A platform was at the far end of the room, the wall behind it hung with red backing paper. Four power packs rested on the floor, with cables running to strobe lights on stands, their gray, umbrella-shaped reflectors angled toward the platform. Redheaded Augusta Blair, wearing a red blouse, a short red jumper, red knee socks, and red patent-leather pumps, stood before the red backing paper. A young girl in jeans and a Snoopy sweatshirt stood to the right of the platform, her arms folded across her chest. The photographer and his assistant were hunched over a tripod-mounted Polaroid. They took several pictures, strobe lights flashing for a fraction of a second each time they pressed the shutter release, and then, apparently satisfied with the exposure setting, removed the Polaroid from its mount and replaced it with a Nikon. Augusta spotted Kling standing near the door, grinned, and waggled the fingers of her right hand at him. The photographer turned.

"Yes?" he said.

"He's a friend of mine," Augusta said.

"Oh, okay," the photographer said in dismissal. "Make yourself comfortable, keep it quiet. You ready, honey? Where's David?"

"David!" the assistant called, and a man rushed over from where he'd been standing at a wall phone, partially hidden by a screen over which was draped a pair of purple panty hose. He went directly to Augusta, combed her hair swiftly, and then stepped off the platform.

"Okay?" the photographer asked.

"Ready," Augusta said.

"The headline is 'Red on Red,' God help us, and the idea—"

"What's the matter with the headline?" the girl in the Snoopy sweatshirt asked.

"Nothing, Helen, far be it from me to cast aspersions on your magazine. Gussie, the idea is to get this big *red* feeling, you know what I mean? Everything bursting and screaming and, you know, *red* as hell, okay? You know what I want?"

"I think so," Augusta said.

"We want *red*," Helen said.

"What the hell's this proxar doing on here?" the photographer asked.

189

"I thought we'd be doing close stuff," his assistant said.

"No, Eddie, get it off here, will you?"

"Sure," Eddie said, and began unscrewing the lens.

"David, get that hair off her forehead, will you?"

"Where?"

"Right there, hanging over her eye, don't you see it there?"

"Oh, yeah."

"Yeah, that's it, thank you. Eddie, how we doing?"

"You've got it."

"Gussie?"

"Yep."

"Okay, then, here we go, now give me that big *red*, Gussie, that's what I want, I want this thing to yell *red* all over town, that's the girl, more of that, now tilt the head, that's good, Gussie, smile now, more teeth, honey, red, *red*, throw your arms wide, good, good, that's it, now you're beginning to feel it, let it bubble up, honey, let it burst out of your fingertips, nice, I like that, give me that with a, that's it, good, now the other side, the head the other way, no, no, keep the arms out, fine, that's good, all right now come toward me, no, honey, don't slink, this isn't blue, it's *red*, you've got to *explode* toward, *yes*, that's it, yes, *yes*, good, now with more hip, Gussie, fine, I like that, I like it, eyes wider, toss the hair, good, honey . . ."

For the next half hour Kling watched as Augusta exhibited to the camera a wide variety of facial expressions, body positions, and acrobatic contortions, looking nothing less than beautiful in every pose she struck. The only sounds in the huge room were the photographer's voice and the clicking of his camera. Coaxing, scolding, persuading, approving, suggesting, chiding, cajoling, the voice went on and on, barely audible except to Augusta, while the tiny clicking of the camera accompanied the running patter like a soft-shoe routine. Kling was fascinated. In Augusta's apartment the other night, he had been overwhelmed by her beauty, but had not suspected her vitality. Reacting to the burglary, she had presented a solemn, dispirited façade, so that her beauty seemed unmarred but essentially lifeless. Now, as Kling watched her bursting with energy and ideas to convey the concept of red, the camera clicking, the photographer circling her and talking to her, she seemed another person entirely, and he wondered suddenly how many faces Augusta Blair owned, and how many of them he would get to know.

"Okay, great, Gussie," the photographer said, "let's break for ten minutes. Then we'll do those sailing outfits, Helen. Eddie, can we get some coffee?"

"Right away."

Augusta came down off the platform and walked to where Kling was standing at the back of the room. "Hi," she said. "I'm sorry I kept you waiting."

"I enjoyed it," Kling said.

"It *was* kind of fun," Augusta said. "Most of them aren't."

"Which of these do you want her in first, Helen?" the photographer asked.

"The one with the striped top."

"You *do* want me to shoot both of them, right?"

"Yes. The two *tops*. There's only one pair of pants," Helen said.

"Okay, both tops, the striped one first. You going to introduce me to your friend, Gussie?" he said, and walked to where Kling and Augusta were standing.

"Rick Schaeffer," she said, "this is Detective Kling. I'm sorry, I don't know your first name."

"Bert," he said.

"Nice to meet you," Schaeffer said, and extended his hand. The men shook hands briefly, and Schaeffer said, "Is this about the burglary?"

"Yes," Kling said.

"Well, look, I won't take up your time," Schaeffer said. "Gussie, honey, we'll be shooting the striped top first."

"Okay."

"I want to go as soon as we change the no-seam."

"I'll be ready."

"Right. Nice meeting you, Bert."

He walked off briskly toward where two men were carrying a roll of blue backing paper to the platform.

"What did you find in the apartment?" Kling asked.

"I've got it in my bag," Augusta said. She began walking toward a bench on the side of the room, Kling following. "Listen, I must apologize for the rush act, but they're paying me twenty-five dollars an hour, and they don't like me sitting around."

"I understand," Kling said.

Augusta dug into her bag and pulled out a ballpoint pen, which she handed to Kling and which, despite the fact that her fingerprints were already all over it, he accepted on a tented handkerchief. The top half of the pen was made of metal, brass-plated to resemble gold. The bottom half of the pen was made of black plastic. The pen was obviously a give-away item. Stamped onto the plastic in white letters were the words:

Sulzbacher Realty
1142 Ashmead Avenue
Calm's Point

"You're sure it isn't yours?" Kling asked.

"Positive. Will it help you?"

"It's a start."

"Good." She glanced over her shoulder toward where the men were rolling down the blue seamless. "What time is it, Bert?"

Kling looked at his watch. "Almost two. What do I call you? Augusta or Gussie?"

"Depends on what we're doing," she said, and smiled.

"What are we doing tonight?" Kling asked immediately.

"I'm busy," Augusta said.

"How about tomorrow?"

She looked at him for a moment, seemed to make a swift decision, and then said, "Let me check my book." She reached into her bag for an appointment calendar, opened it, said, "What's tomorrow, Thursday?" and without waiting for his answer, flipped open to the page marked Thursday, April 22. "No, not tomorrow, either," she said, and Kling figured he had got the message loud and clear. "I'm free Saturday night, though," she said, surprising him. "How's Saturday?"

"Saturday's fine," he said quickly. "Dinner?"

"I'd love to."

"And maybe a movie later."

"Why don't we do it the other way around? If you won't mind how I look, you can pick me up at the studio . . ."

"Fine . . ."

"Around six, six-fifteen, and we can catch an early movie, and then maybe grab a hamburger or something later on. What time do you quit work?"

"I'll certainly be free by six."

"Okay, the photographer's name is Jerry Bloom, and he's at 1204 Concord. The second floor, I think. Aren't you going to write it down?"

"Jerry Bloom," Kling said, "1204 Concord, the second floor, at six o'clock."

"Gussie, let's go!" Schaeffer shouted.

"Saturday," she said and, to Kling's vast amazement, touched her fingers to her lips, blew him an unmistakable kiss, grinned, and walked swiftly to where Rick Schaeffer was waiting.

Kling blinked.

The trouble was, Kling could not stop staring at her.

He had picked up Augusta at six o'clock sharp, and whereas she had warned him about the way she might look after a full day's shooting, she looked nothing less than radiant. Red hair still a bit damp (she confessed to having caught a quick shower in Jerry Bloom's own executive washroom), she came into the reception room to meet Kling, extended her hand to him, and then offered her cheek for a kiss he only belatedly realized was expected. Her cheek was cool and smooth, there was not a trace of makeup on her face except for the pale green shadow on her eyelids, the brownish liner just above her lashes. Her hair was brushed straight back from her forehead, falling to her shoulders without a part. She was wearing blue jeans, sandals, and a ribbed jersey top without a bra. A blue leather bag was slung over her right shoulder, but she shifted it immediately to the shoulder opposite, looped her right hand through his arm, and said, "Were you waiting long?"

"No, I just got here."

"Is something wrong?"

"No. What do you mean?"

"The way you're looking at me."

"No. No, no, everything's fine."

But he could not stop staring at her. The film they went to see was *Bullitt*, which Kling had seen the first time it played the circuit, but which Augusta was intent on seeing in the presence of a *real* cop. Kling hesitated to tell her that, real cop or not, the first time he'd seen *Bullitt* he hadn't for a moment known what the hell was going on. He had come out of the theater grateful that he hadn't been the cop assigned to the case, partially because he wouldn't have known where to begin unraveling it, and partially because fast car rides made him dizzy. He didn't know what the movie was about *this* time either, but not because of any devious motivation or complicated plot twists. The simple fact was that he didn't *watch* the picture; he watched Augusta instead.

It was dark when they came out into the street. They walked in silence for several moments, and then Augusta said, "Listen, I think we'd better get something straight right away."

"What's that?" he said, afraid she would tell him she was married, or engaged, or living with a high-priced photographer.

"I *know* I'm beautiful," she said.

"What?" he said.

"Bert," she said, "I'm a model, and I get *paid* for being beautiful. It makes me very nervous to have you staring at me all the time."

"Okay, I won't . . ."

"No, please let me finish . . ."

"I thought you *were* finished."

"No. I want to get this settled."

"It's settled," he said. "Now we *both* know you're beautiful." He hesitated just an instant, and then added, "And modest besides."

"Oh boy," she said. "I'm trying to relate as a goddamn *person*, and you're . . ."

"I'm sorry I made you uncomfortable," he said. "But the truth is . . ."

"Yes, what's the truth?" Augusta said. "Let's at least *start* with the truth, okay?"

"The truth is I've never in my life been out with a girl as beautiful as you are, that's the truth. And I can't get over it. So I keep staring at you. That's the truth."

"Well, you'll have to get over it."

"Why?"

"Because I think you're beautiful, too," Augusta said, "and we'd have one hell of a relationship if all we did was sit around and *stare* at each other all the time."

She stopped dead in the middle of the sidewalk. Kling searched her face, hoping she would recognize that this was not the same as staring.

"I mean," she said, "I expect we'll be seeing a lot of each other, and I'd like to think I'm permitted to *sweat* every now and then. I *do* sweat, you know."

"Yes, I suppose you do," he said, and smiled.

"Okay?" she said.

"Okay."

"Let's eat," she said. "I'm famished."

In the dim silence of Augusta Blair's bedroom, they made love. It was not so good.

"What's the matter?" Augusta whispered.

"I don't know," Kling whispered back.

"Am I doing something wrong?"

"No, no."

"Because if I am . . ."

"No, Augusta, really."

"Then what is it?"

"I think I'm a little afraid of you."

"Afraid?"

"Yes. I keep thinking, What's a dumb kid from Riverhead doing in bed with a beautiful model?"

"You're not a dumb kid," Augusta said, and smiled, and touched his mouth with her fingertips.

"I feel like a dumb kid."

"Why?"

"Because you're so beautiful."

"Bert, if you start that again, I'll hit you right on the head with a hammer."

"How'd you know about a hammer?"

"What?"

"A hammer. About it being the best weapon for a woman."

"I didn't know."

They were both silent for several moments.

"Relax," she said.

"I think that's exactly the problem," Kling said.

"If you want me to be ugly, I can be ugly as hell. Look," she said, and made a face. "How's that?"

"Beautiful."

"Where's my hammer?" she said, and got out of bed naked and padded out of the room. He heard her rummaging around in the kitchen. When she returned, she was indeed carrying a hammer. "Have you ever been hit with a hammer?" she asked, and sat beside him, pulling her long legs up onto the bed, crossing them Indian fashion, her head and back erect, the hammer clutched in her right hand.

"No," he said. "Lots of things, but never a hammer."

"Have you ever been shot?"

"Yes."

"Is that what this is?" she asked, and pointed with the hammer at the scar on his shoulder."

"Yes."

"Did it hurt?"

"Yes."

"Think I'll kiss it," she said, and bent over from the waist and kissed his shoulder lightly, and then sat up again. "You're dealing with the Mad Hammer Hitter here," she said. "One more word about how good-looking I am and, pow, your friends'll be investigating a homicide. You got that?"

"Got it," Kling said.

"This is the obligatory sex scene," she said. "I'm going to drive you to distraction in the next ten minutes. If you fail to respond, I'll cleave your skull with a swift single blow. In fact," she said, "a swift single blow might not be a bad way to start," and she bent over swiftly, her tongue darting. "I think you're beginning to get the message," she murmured. "Must be the goddamn hammer."

"Must be," Kling whispered.

Abruptly, she brought her head up to the pillow, stretched her legs, and rolled in tight against him, the hammer still in her right hand. "Listen, you," she whispered.

"I'm listening."

"We're going to be very important to each other."

"I know that."

"I'm scared to death," she said, and caught her breath. "I've never felt this way about any man. Do you believe me, Bert?"

"Yes."

"We're going to make love now."

"Yes, Augusta."

"We're going to make beautiful love."

"Yes."

"Yes, touch me," she said, and the hammer slipped from her grasp.

The telephone rang four times while they were in bed together. Each time, Augusta's answering service picked it up on the first ring.

"Might be someone important," Kling whispered after the last call.

"No one's more important than you," she whispered back, and immediately got out of bed and went into the kitchen. When she returned, she was carrying a split of champagne.

"Ah, good," he said. "How'd you know I was thirsty?"

"You open it while I think up a toast."

"You forgot glasses."

"Lovers don't need glasses."

"My grandmother does. Blind as a bat without them."

"Is she a lover?"

"Just ask Grandpa."

Kling popped the cork with his thumbs.

"Got that toast?" he asked.

"You're getting the bed wet."

"Come on, think of some people we can drink to."

"How about John and Martha Mitchell?"

"Why not? Here's to . . ."

"How about us?" Augusta said. She gently took the bottle from him, lifted it high, and said, "To Bert and Augusta. And to . . ." She hesitated.

"Yes?"

Solemnly, she studied his face, the bottle still extended. "And to at least the possibility of always," she said, and quickly, almost shyly, brought the bottle to her lips, drank from the open top, and handed it back to Kling. He did not take his eyes from her face. Watching her steadily, he said, "To us. And to always," and drank.

"Excuse me," Augusta said, and started out of the room.

"Leaving already, huh?" Kling said. "After all that sweet talk about . . ."

"I'm only going to the bathroom," Augusta said, and giggled.

"In that case, check the phone on the way back."

"Why?"

"I'm a cop."

"Hell with the phone," Augusta said.

Let's Hear It for the Deaf Man, 1973

196

"**"Y**eah?" Carella said, surprised.

"Yeah," Kling said, and nodded.

Carella knew better than to make some wise-ass remark when Kling was apparently so serious. The squadroom banter about the frequent calls from "Gussie" (as Kling's colleagues called her) had achieved almost monumental proportions in the past two months, but they hardly seemed appropriate in the one-to-one intimacy of an automobile whose windows, except for the windshield, were entirely covered with rime. Carella busied himself with the heater.

"What do you think?" Kling asked.

"Well, I don't know. Do you think she'll say yes?"

"Oh, yeah, I think she'll say yes."

"Well, then, ask her."

"Well," Kling said, and fell silent.

They had come through the tollbooth. Behind them, Isola thrust its jagged peaks and minarets into a leaden sky. Ahead, the terrain consisted of rolling smoke-colored hills through which the road to Turman snaked its lazy way.

"The thing is," Kling said at last, "I'm a little scared."

"Of what?" Carella asked.

"Of getting married. I mean, it's . . . well . . . it's a serious commitment, you know."

"Yes, I know," Carella said. He could not quite understand Kling's hesitancy. If he really wanted to marry Gussie, why the doubts? And if there were doubts, then did he really want to marry her?

"What's it like?" Kling asked.

"What's *what* like?"

"Being married."

"I can only tell you what it's like being married to Teddy," Carella said.

"Yeah, what's it like?"

"It's wonderful."

"Mmm," Kling said. "Because, suppose you get married and then you find out it isn't the same as when you weren't married."

"*What* isn't the same?"

"Everything."

"Like what?"

"Like, well, for example, suppose, well, that, well, the sex isn't the same?"

"Why should it be any different?"

"I don't know," Kling said, and shrugged.

"What's the marriage certificate got to do with it?"

197

"I don't know," Kling said, and shrugged again. "*Is* it the same? The sex?"

"Sure," Carella said.

"I don't mean to get personal . . ."

"No, no."

"But it's the same, huh?"

"Sure, it's the same." ·

"And the rest? I mean, you know, do you still have fun?"

"Fun?"

"Yeah."

"Sure, we have fun."

"Like before?"

"Better than before."

"Because we have a lot of fun together," Kling said. "Augusta and I. A lot of fun."

"That's good," Carella said.

"Yes, it's very good. That two people can enjoy things together. I think that's very good, Steve, don't you?"

"Yes, I think it's very good when that happens between two people."

"Not that we don't have fights," Kling said.

"Well, everybody has fights. Any two people . . ."

"Yes, but not too many."

"No, no."

"And our . . . our personal relationship is very good. We're very good together."

"Mmm."

"The sex, I mean," Kling said quickly, and suddenly seemed very intent on the road ahead. "That's very good between us."

"Mmm, well, good. That's good."

"Though not always. I mean, sometimes it's not as good as other times."

"Yes, well, that's natural," Carella said.

"But *most* of the time . . ."

"Yes, sure."

"Most of the time, we really do enjoy it."

"Sure," Carella said.

"And we love each other. That's important."

"That's the single most important thing," Carella said.

"Yes, I think so."

"No question."

"It *is* the single most important thing," Kling said. "It's what makes everything else seem right. The decisions we make together, the things we do together, even the fights we have together. It's the fact that we love each other . . . well . . . that's what makes it *work*, you see."

"Yes," Carella said.

"So you think I should marry her?"

"It sounds like you're married already," Carella said.

Kling turned abruptly from the wheel to see whether or not Carella was smiling. Carella was not. He was hunched on the seat with his feet propped up against the clattering heater, and his hands tucked under his arms, and his chin ducked into the upturned collar of his coat.

"I suppose it *is* sort of like being married," Kling said, turning his attention to the road again. "But not exactly."

"Well, how's it any different?" Carella said.

"Well, I don't know. That's what I'm asking you."

"Well, I don't see any difference."

"Then why should we get married?" Kling asked.

"Jesus, Bert, *I* don't know," Carella said. "If you want to get married, get married. If you don't, then stay the way you are."

"Why'd *you* get married?"

Carella thought for a long time. Then he said, "Because I couldn't bear the thought of any other man ever touching Teddy."

Kling nodded.

He said nothing more all the way to Turman.

Kling was about to propose to her.

It was almost nine-thirty, and they had finished their meal and their coffee, and Kling had ordered cognac for both of them, and they were waiting for it to arrive. There was a candle in a red translucent holder on the tabletop, and it cast a gentle glow on Augusta's face, softening her features, not that she needed any help. There was a time when Kling had been thoroughly flustered by Augusta's beauty. In her presence he had been speechless, breathless, awkward, stupid, and incapable of doing anything but stare at her in wonder and gratitude. Over the past nine months, however, he had not only grown accustomed to her beauty, and comfortable in its presence, but had also begun to feel somehow responsible for it—like the curator of a museum beginning to think that the rare paintings on the walls had not only been discovered by him, but had in fact been *painted* by him.

"Augusta," he said, "there's something serious I'd like to ask you."

"Yes, Bert?" she said, and looked directly into his face, and he felt again what he had first felt nine months ago when he'd walked into her burglarized apartment and seen her sitting on the couch, her eyes glistening with tears about to spill. He had clumsily shaken hands with her, and his heart had stopped.

"I've been doing a lot of thinking," he said.

"Yes, Bert?" she said.

The waiter brought the cognac. Augusta lifted her snifter and rolled it between her palms. Kling picked up his snifter and almost dropped it, spilling some of the cognac on the tablecloth. He dabbed at it with his napkin, smiled weakly at Augusta, put the napkin back on his lap and the snifter back on the table before he spilled it all over his shirt and his pants and the rug and maybe the silk-brocaded walls of this very fancy French joint he had chosen because he thought it would be a suitably romantic setting for a proposal, even though it was costing him half a week's pay. "Augusta," he said, and cleared his throat.

"Yes, Bert?"

"Augusta, I have something very serious to ask you."

"Yes, Bert, you've said that already." There seemed to be a slight smile on her mouth. Her eyes looked exceedingly merry.

"Augusta?"

"Yes, Bert?"

"Excuse me, Mr. Kling," the waiter said. "There's a telephone call for you."

"Oh, sh—" Kling started, and then nodded, and said, "Thank you, thank you." He shoved his chair back, dropping his napkin to the floor as he rose. He picked up the napkin, said, "Excuse me, Augusta," and was heading away from the table when she very softly said, "Bert?"

He stopped and turned.

"I will, Bert," she said.

"You will?" he asked.

"I'll marry you," she said.

"Okay," he said, and smiled. "I'll marry you, too."

"Okay," she said.

"Okay," he said.

Hail to the Chief, 1973

"If that guy takes one more picture . . ." Kling said.

"He's doing a conscientious job," Augusta said.

They had changed into street clothes and were at the front desk of the hotel now, registering for the room they had reserved. Across the lobby, Pike was standing with his camera to his eye, focusing for a long shot of the couple at the desk.

"Does he plan to sleep with us tonight?" Kling asked.

"Who plans on sleeping?" Augusta asked, and smiled slyly.

"I mean—"

"I'll gently suggest that maybe he's taken enough pictures, okay?" Augusta said. "He's a dear friend, Bert. I don't want to hurt his feelings."

"Okay."

"And it *will* be nice to have a record afterward."

"Yes, I know. Gus, are you happy?"

"Yes, darling, I'm very happy."

"It was a real nice wedding, wasn't it?"

"Yes."

"I mean, the ceremony itself."

"Yes, darling, I know."

"There's something awesome about those words," Kling said. "When you come to think of it, that's one hell of a frightening contract."

"Are you frightened?"

"Sure, aren't you? I take this very seriously, Gus."

"So do I."

"I mean, I really *do* want it to last so long as we both shall live."

"I do, too."

"So . . . so let's just make sure it *does* last, Gus."

"Are you worried about it?"

"No, but—well, yes, in a way. I love you so much, Gus, I just want to do everything I can to make you happy and to see you grow and to—"

"Your key, sir," the night clerk said.

"Thank you," Kling said.

"That's room 824, the bellhop will show you up."

"Thank you," Kling said again.

Across the lobby, Pike was sitting on one of the sofas, putting a fresh roll of film into his camera. The moment he saw them moving away from the desk, he snapped the back of the camera shut, and rose, and began walking swiftly toward them.

"I just want one more picture," he said in immediate apology.

"You've really been an angel," Augusta said. "Did you get a chance to enjoy the wedding, or were you just working all day long?"

"I had a marvelous time," he said. "But I still need another picture."

"Which one is that?" Kling asked apprehensively.

"I haven't got a single shot of Augusta and me. Bert, I would appreciate it greatly if you took a picture of Augusta and me."

Kling smiled broadly. "I'd be happy to," he said.

"I just put in a fresh roll," Pike said, and handed Kling the camera and the strobe pack, then looked around the lobby and maneuvered Augusta to a potted palm just inside the revolving entrance doors, where a steady trickle of people moved in and out of the hotel. Kling brought the camera to his eye, focusing from a distance of some three feet, and then held up the strobe as though he were the Statue of Liberty. "Smile," he said, and pressed the shutter-release button. The shutter clicked, the strobe light flashed. Pike and Augusta blinked.

"That's got it," Kling said.

"Thank you," Pike said.

As Kling handed the camera and strobe back to him, he noticed there were tears in Pike's eyes.

"Alex," he said, "we can't thank you enough for what you did today."

"It was my pleasure," Pike said. He kissed Augusta on the cheek, said, "Be happy, darlin'," and then turned to Kling and took his hand and said, "Take good care of her, Bert."

"I will," Kling promised.

"Good night, then, and the best to both of you," Pike said, and turned swiftly away.

In the elevator, the bellhop said, "Are you newlyweds or something?"

"That's right," Kling said.

"You're the third newlyweds I had today. Is this some kind of special day or something?"

"What do you mean?" Augusta asked.

"Everybody getting married today. Is it a religious holiday or something? What's today, anyway? The ninth, ain't it?"

"Yes."

"So what's the ninth? Is it something?"

"It's our wedding day," Augusta said.

"Well, I know that, but is it *something*?"

"That *is* something," Augusta said.

"Right, I appreciate that," the bellhop said, "but you know what I mean, don't you? I'm trying to figure out, is it a day of some special significance where I've already had three couples who got married today, that's what I'm trying to figure out." They were on the eighth floor now, and walking down the corridor to room 824. When they reached the room, the bellhop put down their bags, and then unlocked the door and stepped aside for them to enter.

In the room, they both fell suddenly silent.

The bellhop wondered aloud why all the double-bedded rooms were always at the end of the hall, but neither of them said a word in answer, and the bellhop speculated that maybe all the hotels were trying to discourage romance, and still they said nothing in response. He put their bags up on the luggage racks, and showed them the bathroom, and the thermostat, and explained how the red light on the phone would indicate there was a message for them, and made himself generally busy and visible while waiting for his tip. And then he did something rare for a bellhop in that city—he touched his fingers to his cap in a sort of salute and silently left the room. Kling put the "Do Not Disturb" sign on the knob and locked the door, and silently he and Augusta hung up their coats, and then began unpacking their bags.

They were neither of them kids. Their silence had nothing to do with virginal apprehension or fears of physical incompatibility or frigidity or impotence or anything even mildly related to sex, which they had been enjoying together and almost incessantly for quite some time now. Instead, their silence was caused by what they both recognized to be a rather serious commitment. They had talked about this peripherally in the lobby, but now they thought about it gravely and solemnly, and decided separately that they'd been speaking the truth when they said they wanted this to last forever. They both knew that no one had forced them into marriage: they could have gone on living together forever. They had each and separately agonized over taking the plunge, in fact, and had each and separately arrived at the same conclusion almost at the same time. When Kling had finally asked her to marry him, Augusta had said yes at once. He'd asked her because he'd decided simply and irrevocably that he wanted to spend the rest of his life with her. And she'd accepted because she'd made the same decision concerning him. They were now married, the man had spoken the words this afternoon at a little past four o'clock, the man had said, "For as you both have consented in wedlock, and have acknowledged it before this company, I do by virtue of the authority invested in me by the church and the laws of this state now pronounce you husband and wife. And may God bless your union." The word "union" had thrilled them both. Union. That was what they wanted their marriage to be, a true union, and that was what each was separately thinking now.

There wasn't much to unpack. They would be here at the hotel only for the night, and would be flying to Guadeloupe in the morning. When Kling finished he asked if he should call down for a nightcap, and Augusta said no, she'd had enough to drink tonight. He asked if she wanted to use the bathroom first, and she said, "No, go ahead, Bert, I want to lay out some clothes for the morning." She looked at both her bags then, trying to remember in which one she'd packed what she would be wearing on the plane tomorrow, a perplexed look on her face, her lower lip caught between her teeth as she pondered this very serious and weighty problem.

"I love you," Kling said suddenly.

She turned to look at him, a slight smile of surprise on her face. "I love you, too," she said.

"I mean, I *really* love you."

"Yes," she said quietly, and went into his arms and held him close. They stood that way for several moments, locked in silent embrace, not kissing, just standing very close to each other, hugging each other fiercely. Then Augusta looked up into his face, and touched his lips gently with her fingers, and he nodded, and they broke apart. "Now go take your shower," Augusta said, and Kling smiled and went into the bathroom, and closed the door behind him. When he came out ten minutes later, Augusta was gone.

He had planned something of a big male macho entrance, and he stood now in the bathroom doorway with a towel wrapped around his waist, and saw immediately that she was not in the room, and then saw that the door to the corridor was open. He assumed Augusta had gone out into the corridor for something, perhaps in search of a chambermaid, though he couldn't understand why she hadn't simply picked up the phone if she needed anything. He went to the door and looked out into the corridor, and saw no trace of her. Puzzled, he closed the door to the room and then went to the closet where he'd hung his robe. He didn't expect to find Augusta hiding in there or anything stupid like that; Augusta just wasn't the type to play such childish games. He went to the closet only because he felt suddenly naked with just the towel around his waist, and he wanted to put on his robe. He had begun thinking, in fact, that perhaps the boys of the 87th were up to some mischief. As Parker had explained, a traditional wedding-night prank was to spirit a bride away from her groom and return her later when a ransom was paid, the ransom usually consisting of a nightcap shared with the newlyweds amidst much guffawing and slapping on the back. Kling had never heard of a bride being kidnapped from her honeymoon suite, but the boys of the 87th were professionals, after all, and could be expected to come up with something more inventive than simply snatching a girl from a wedding reception. As Kling grabbed the knob on the closet door, it all began to seem not only possible but likely. They had undoubtedly found out which room Kling and Augusta were in, and then either loided the door lock with the plastic "Do Not Disturb" sign, or actually used a pick and tension bar on it, cops being just as good as burglars when it came to such matters. Wearily he opened the closet door. He liked the guys on the squad a lot, but he and Augusta had to get up early in the morning to catch their plane, and he considered the prank not only foolish but inconsiderate as well. As he reached for his robe he realized that he'd now have to sit around here twiddling his thumbs till those crazy bastards decided to call with their ransom demand. And then, when they finally *did* bring Augusta back, there'd be another half hour of drinking and laughing before he finally got rid of them. He noticed then that Augusta's overcoat was still on the clothes bar, just where she'd hung it when they first entered the room.

He was still not alarmed—but a quiet, reasoning, deductive part of his mind told him that this was November and the temperature outside was somewhere in the low thirties, and whereas the boys of the 87th might be spirited, they certainly weren't stupid or cruel; they would never have taken Augusta out of the hotel without a coat. Well, now, wait a minute, he thought. Who says they had to take her out of the hotel? They may be sitting in the lobby, or better yet, the bar, right this very minute, having a few drinks with her, laughing it up while they watch the clock till it's time to call me. Very funny, he thought. You've got some sense of humor, fellows. He went to the phone, picked up the receiver, and then sat on the edge of the bed while he dialed the front desk. He told the clerk who answered that this was Mr. Kling in 824, he'd just checked in with his wife, a tall girl with auburn hair . . .

"Yes, sir, I remember," the clerk said.

"You don't see her anywhere in the lobby, do you?" Kling asked.

"Sir?"

"My wife. Mrs. Kling. She isn't down there in the lobby, is she?"

"I don't see her anywhere in the lobby, sir."

"We were expecting some friends, you see, and I thought she might have gone down to meet them."

"No, sir, she's not in the lobby."

"*Would* you have seen her if she'd come down to the lobby?"

"Well, yes, sir, I suppose so. The elevators are just opposite the desk, I suppose I would have seen her if she'd taken the elevator down."

"What about the fire stairs? Suppose she'd taken those down?"

"The fire stairs are at the rear of the building, sir. No, I wouldn't have seen her if she'd taken those down. Unless she crossed the lobby to leave the building."

"Any other way to leave the building?" Kling asked.

"Well, yes, there's the service entrance."

"Fire stairs come anywhere near that?"

"Yes, sir, they feed into both the lobby *and* the service courtyard."

"What floor's the bar on?"

"The lobby floor, sir."

"Can you see the bar from the front desk?"

"No, sir. It's at the other end of the lobby. Opposite the fire stairs."

"Thank you," Kling said, and hung up, and immediately dialed the bar. He described Augusta to the bartender and said she might be sitting there with some fellows who looked like detectives. He was a detective himself, he explained, and these friends of his, these colleagues, might be playing a joke on him, this being his wedding night and all. So would the bartender please take a look around and see if they were down there with his wife? "And, listen, if they *are* there, don't say a word to them, okay? I'll just come down and surprise them, okay?"

"I don't *have* to take a look around, sir," the bartender said. "There's only two people in here, and they're both old men, and they don't look nothing like what you described your wife to me."

"Okay," Kling said.

"They kidnapped *my* wife on our wedding night, too," the bartender said dryly. "I wish now they woulda kept her."

"Well, thanks a lot," Kling said, and hung up.

It was then that he saw Augusta's shoe. Just the one shoe. Lying alongside the wastebasket on the floor there. Near the dresser. Just to the left of the door, near one of the dressers. The pair she'd put on when she changed out of her bridal costume. But no longer a pair. Just one of them. One high-heeled pump lying on its side near the wastebasket. He went to it and picked it up. As he looked at the shoe (telling himself there was still no reason to become alarmed, this was just a prank, this *had* to be just a prank) he was suddenly aware of a cloying scent that seemed to be coming from the wastebasket at his feet. He put the shoe on the dresser top, and then knelt and looked into the wastebasket. The aroma was sickeningly sweet. He immediately turned his head away, but not before he'd seen a large wad of absorbent cotton on the bottom of the otherwise empty basket. He realized at once the smell was emanating from the cotton, and suddenly recognized it for what it was: chloroform.

It was then that he became alarmed.

She had lost all track of time and did not know how long she'd been conscious; she suspected, though, that hours and hours had passed since the moment he'd clamped the chloroform-soaked piece of cotton over her nose and mouth. She lay on the floor with her wrists bound behind her back, her ankles bound together. Her eyes were closed, she could feel what she supposed were balls of absorbent cotton pressing against the lids, held firmly in place by either adhesive tape or a bandage of some kind. A rag had been stuffed into her mouth (she could taste it, she hoped she would not choke on it), and then a gag, again either adhesive tape or bandage, had been wound over it. She could neither see nor speak, and though she listened intently for the slightest sound, she could hear nothing at all.

She remembered . . . he had a scapel in his right hand. She turned when she heard the hotel door clicking open, and saw him striding toward her across the room, the scapel glittering in the light of the lamp on the dresser. He was wearing a green surgical mask, and his eyes above the mask scanned the room swiftly as he crossed to where she was already moving from the suitcase toward the bathroom door, intercepting her, grabbing her from behind and pulling her in against him. She opened her mouth to scream, but his left arm was tight around her waist now, and suddenly his right hand, the hand holding the scapel, moved to her throat, circling up from behind. She felt the blade against her flesh and heard him whisper just the single word "Silence," and the formative scream became only a terrified whimper drowned by the roar of the shower.

He was pulling her backward toward the door, and then suddenly he swung her around and shoved her against the wall, the scalpel coming up against her throat again, his left hand reaching into his coat pocket. She saw the wad of absorbent cotton an instant before he clamped it over her nose and mouth. She had detested the stench of chloroform ever since she was six and had her tonsils removed. She twisted her head to escape the smothering aroma, and then felt the scalpel nudging her flesh, insistently reminding her that it was there and that it could cut. She became fearful that if she lost consciousness, she might fall forward onto the sharp blade, and she tried to keep from becoming dizzy, but the sound of the shower seemed magnified, an ocean surf pounding against some desolate shore, waves crashing and receding in endless repetition, foam bubbles dissolving, and far overhead, so distant it could scarcely be heard, the cry of a gull that might have been only her own strangled scream.

She listened now.

She could hear nothing, she suspected she was alone. But she could not be certain. Behind the blindfold, she began to weep soundlessly.

His voice startled her.

She had not known he was in the room until she heard him speak, and she reacted sharply to the sound of his voice, almost as though someone had suddenly slapped her in the dark.

"You must be hungry," he said. "It is almost three-thirty."

She wondered instantly whether it was three-thirty in the morning or three-thirty in the afternoon, and then she wondered how long he had been standing there, watching her silently.

"Are you hungry?" he asked.

There was a faint foreign accent to his speech; she suspected his first language was German. In response to his question, she shook her head from side to side. She was violently hungry, but she dared not eat anything he might offer her.

"Well, then," he said.

She listened. She could not hear him breathing. She did not know whether he had left the room or not. She waited.

"I will have something to eat," he said.

Again there was silence. Not a board creaked, not a footfall sounded. She assumed he had left the room, but she did not know for certain. In a while she smelled the aroma of coffee perking. She listened more intently, detected sounds she associated with bacon crisping in a pan, heard a click that might have been a toaster popping, and then a sound she identified positively as that of a refrigerator door being opened and then closed again not a moment later. There was another click, and then a hum, and then a man's voice saying, ". . . in the low thirties, dropping to below freezing tonight. The present temperature here on Hall Avenue is thirty-four degrees." There was a brief, static-riddled pause, and then the sound of canned music, and then another click that cut off the music abruptly—he had apparently been hoping to catch the three-thirty news report, had only got the last few seconds of it, and had now turned off the radio. From the kitchen (she assumed it was the kitchen), she heard the sound of cutlery clinking against china. He was eating. She suddenly became furious with him. Struggling against her bonds, she tried to twist free of them. The air in the room was stale, and the cooking smells from the kitchen, so tantalizing a few minutes before, now began to sicken her. She warned herself against becoming nauseated; she did not want to choke on her own vomit. She heard dishes clattering in the kitchen; he was cleaning up after himself. There, yes, the sound of water running. She waited, certain he would come into the room again.

She did not hear his approach. She assumed that he walked lightly and that the apartment or the house or the hotel suite (or whatever it was) had thickly carpeted floors. Again, she did not know how long he'd been standing there. She had heard the water being turned off, and then silence, and now, suddenly, his voice again.

"Are you sure you are not hungry? Well, you will be hungry sooner or later," he said.

She visualized a smile on his face. She hated him intensely, and could think only that Bert would kill him when he found them. Bert would draw his revolver and shoot the man dead. Lying on her back sightless and speechless, she drew strength from the knowledge that Bert would kill him. But she could not stop trembling because his unseen presence frightened her, and she did not know what he might do next, and she could remember the fanatic intensity in those blue eyes above the green surgical mask, and the speed with which he had crossed the room and put the scalpel to her throat. She kept listening for his breathing. His silence was almost supernatural, he appeared and disappeared as soundlessly as a vampire. Was he still there watching her? Or had he left the room again?

"Would you like to talk?" he said.

She was ready to shake her head; the last thing on earth she wanted was to *talk* to him. But she realized that he would have to remove the gag if he expected her to speak, and once her mouth was free . . .

She nodded.

"If you plan to scream . . ." he said, and let the warning dangle.

She shook her head in a vigorous lie; she planned to scream the moment he took off the gag.

"I still have the scalpel," he said. "Feel?" he said, and put the cold blade against her cheek. The touch was sudden and unexpected, and she twisted her head away sharply, but he followed her with the blade, laying it flat against her cheek and saying again, "Feel?"

She nodded.

"I do not want to cut you, Augusta. It would be a pity to cut you."

He knew her name.

"Do you understand, Augusta? I'm going to remove the tape from your mouth now, I'm going to allow you to speak. But if you scream, Augusta, I will use the scalpel not only on the tape but on you as well. Is that clear?"

She nodded.

"I hope that is clear, Augusta. Sincerely, I do not want to cut you."

She nodded again.

"Very well, then. But please remember, yes?"

She felt the scalpel sliding under the gag. He twisted the blade and she heard the tape tearing, and suddenly the pressure on her mouth was gone, the tape was cut through, he was ripping the ends of it loose. As he lifted her head and pulled the remainder of the tape free, she spat out the cotton wad that had been in her mouth.

"Now, do not scream," he said. "Here. Feel the blade," he said, and put it against her throat. "That is so you will not scream, Augusta."

"I won't scream," she said very softly.

"Ah," he said. "That is the first time I hear your voice. It is a lovely voice, Augusta. As lovely as I knew it would be."

"Who are you?" she asked.

"Ah," he said.

"Why are you doing this?" she asked. "My husband's a policeman, do you know that?"

"Yes, I know."

"A detective."

"I know."

"Do you know what happens when a cop or his family is injured or threatened or . . . ?"

"Yes, I can imagine. Augusta, you are raising your voice," he chided, and she felt him increase the pressure against her throat, moving his hand so that *it* and not the scapel exerted the force, but the gesture nonetheless threatening in that she *knew* what was in his hand, and knew how sharp the instrument was—it had sliced through the tape with a simple twist of the blade.

"I'm sorry," she said, "I didn't realize . . ."

"Yes, you must be more calm."

"I'm sorry."

"Yes," he said. "Augusta, I know your husband is a detective, that is what it said in the newspaper article announcing your wedding. Detective Third/Grade Bertram A. Kling. That is his name, is it not?"

"Yes," Augusta said.

209

"Yes. Bertram A. Kling. I was very distressed when I read that in the newspaper, Augusta. That was in October, do you remember?"

"Yes," she said.

"October the fifth. It said you were to be wed the following month. To this man Betram A. Kling. This policeman. This detective. I was very distressed. I did not know what to do, Augusta. It took me a long while to understand what I must do. Even to yesterday morning, I was not sure I would do it. And then, at the church, I knew it was right what I wished to do. And now you are here. With me. Now you are going to be mine," he said, and she suddenly realized he was insane.

He was sitting just inside the door.

Augusta had heard him entering the room some ten minutes ago. He had not said anything in all that time, but she knew he was sitting there, watching her. When his voice came, it startled her.

"Your husband has blond hair," he said.

She nodded. She could not answer him because he had replaced the gag the moment they'd concluded their earlier conversation, though he had not bothered to stuff anything into her mouth this time, had only wrapped the thick adhesive tape tightly across it and around the back of her head. That had been sometime after three-thirty; he had mentioned the time to her. She was ravenously hungry now, and knew she would accept food if he offered it to her. She made a sound deep in her throat to let him know she wished him to remove the gag again. He either did not hear her or pretended not to.

"What color do you think my hair is?" he asked.

She shook her head. She knew what color his hair was, of course; she had seen it when he'd burst hatless into the hotel room. His hair was blond. And his eyes above the surgical mask . . .

"You do not know?" he asked.

Again she shook her head.

"Ah, but you *saw* me," he chided gently. "At the hotel. *Surely* you noticed the color of my hair."

She made a sound behind the gag again.

"Something?" he asked.

She lifted her chin, twisted her head, tried to indicate to him that she wished the gag removed from her mouth. And in doing so, felt completely dependent upon him, and felt again a helpless rage.

"Ah, the adhesive," he said. "Do you wish the adhesive removed? Is that it?"

She nodded.

"You wish to talk to me?"

She nodded again.

"I will not talk to you if you continue to lie," he said, and she heard

210

him rising from the chair. A moment later she heard him closing and locking the door to the room.

He did not return for what seemed like a very long time.

"Augusta?" he whispered. "Are you asleep?"

She shook her head again.

"It's two o'clock in the morning. You should try to sleep, Augusta. Or would you prefer to talk?"

She nodded.

"But you must not lie to me again. You lied to me earlier. You said you didn't know what color my hair is. You *do* know what color it is, don't you?"

Wearily, she nodded.

"Shall I remove the adhesive? You must promise not to scream. Here," he said, "feel." He had moved to her side, and she felt now the cold steel of the scalpel against her throat. "You know what this is," he said. "I will use it if you scream. So," he said, and slid the blade flat under the adhesive, and then twisted it, and cut the tape, and pulled it free.

"Thank you," she said.

"You're quite welcome," he said. "Are you hungry?"

"Yes."

"I thought you might be. You need not be afraid of me, Augusta."

"I'm not afraid of you," she lied.

"I shall prepare you something to eat in a moment."

"Thank you."

"What color is my hair, Augusta? Please don't lie this time."

"Blond," she said.

"Yes. And my eyes?"

"Blue."

"You had a very good look at me."

"Yes."

"Why did you lie? Were you worried that if you could identify me, I might harm you?"

"Why would you want to harm me?" she asked.

"Is that what you thought? That I might harm you?"

"Why am I here?" she asked.

"Augusta, please, you are making me angry again," he said. "When I ask you something, please answer it. I know you have many questions, but *my* questions come first, do you understand that?"

"Yes," she said.

"*Why* do my questions come first?" he asked.

"Because . . ." She shook her head. She did not know what answer he wanted from her.

"Because I am the one who has the scalpel," he said.

"Yes," she said.

"And you are the one who is helplessly bound."

"Yes."

"Do you realize *just* how helpless you are, Augusta?"

"Yes."

"I *could* in fact harm you if I wished to."

"But you said . . ."

"Yes, what did I say?"

"That you wouldn't harm me."

"No, I did not say that, Augusta."

"I thought . . ."

"You must listen more carefully."

"I thought that was what you said."

"No. If you weren't so intent on asking questions of your own, then perhaps you would listen more carefully."

"Yes, I'll try to listen," she said.

"You must."

"Yes."

"I did *not* say I wouldn't harm you. I asked if you *thought* I might harm you. Isn't that so?"

"Yes, I remember now."

"And you did not answer my question. Would you like to answer it now? I'll repeat it for you. I asked if—"

"I remember what you asked."

"Please don't interrupt, Augusta. You make me very impatient."

"I'm sorry, I . . ."

"Augusta, do you want me to put the adhesive on again?"

"No. No, I don't."

"Then please speak only when I *ask* you to speak. All right?"

"Yes, all right."

"I asked you why you lied to me. I asked whether you were worried that I might harm you if you could identify me."

"Yes, I remember that."

"Is that why you lied to me, Augusta?"

"Yes."

"But surely I *had* to know you'd seen me."

"Yes, but you were wearing a surgical mask. I still don't really know what you look like. The mask covered—"

"You're trying to protect yourself again, aren't you?" he said. "By saying you still don't know what I look like?"

"I suppose so, yes. But it's true, you know. There *are* lots of people with blond hair and . . ."

"But you *are* trying to protect yourself?"

"Yes. Yes, I am. Yes."

"Because you still feel I might harm you."

"Yes."

"I might indeed," he said, and laughed. He seized her chin then, and taped her mouth again, and swiftly left the room.

On the floor, Augusta began trembling violently.

She heard the key turning in the lock, and then the door opened. He came to where she was lying near the wall, and stood there silently for what seemed like a very long time.

"Augusta," he said at last, "I do not wish to keep you gagged. Perhaps if I explain your situation, you will realize how foolish it would be to scream. We are in a three-story brownstone, Augusta, on the top floor of the building. The first two floors are rented by a retired optometrist and his wife. They go to Florida at the beginning of November each year. We are quite alone in the building, Augusta. The room we are in was a very large pantry at one time. I have used it for storage ever since I moved into the apartment. It is quite empty now. I emptied it last month, after I decided what had to be done. Do you understand?"

She nodded.

"Fine," he said, and cut the tape and pulled it free. She did not scream, but only because she was afraid of the scalpel. She did not believe for a moment that they were alone together in a three-story brownstone; if indeed he did not gag her again, she would scream as soon as he left her alone in the room.

"I've made you some soup," he said. "You shall have to sit up. I shall have to untie your hands."

"Good," she said.

"You wish your hands untied?"

"Yes."

"And your feet, too?"

"Yes."

"No," he said, and laughed. "Your feet will stay as they are. I'm going to cut the adhesive that is holding your hands behind your back. Please don't try to strike out at me when your hands are free. Seriously, I will use the scalpel if I have to. I want your promise. Otherwise, I'll throw the soup in the toilet bowl and forget about feeding you."

"I promise," she said.

"And about screaming. Seriously, no one will hear you but me. I advise you not to scream. I become violent."

He said the words so earnestly, so matter-of-factly that she believed him at once.

"I won't scream," she said.

"It will be better," he said, and cut the tape on her hands. She was

213

tempted to reach up for the blindfold at once, pull the blindfold loose—but she remembered the scalpel again.

"Is that better?" he said.

"Yes, thank you."

"Come," he said, and pulled her to the wall, and propped her against it. She sat with her hands in her lap while he spoon-fed her. The soup was delicious. She did not know what kind of soup it was, but she tasted what she thought were meatballs in it, and noodles, and celery. She kept her hands folded in her lap, opening her mouth to accept the spoon each time it touched her lips. He made small sounds of satisfaction as she ate the soup, and when at last he said, "All gone, Augusta," it was rather like a father talking to a small child.

"Thank you," she said. "That was very good."

"Am I taking good care of you, Augusta?"

"Yes, you are. The soup was very good," she said.

"Thank you. I'm trying to take very good care of you."

"You are. But . . ."

"But you would like to be free."

She hesitated. Then, very softly, she said, "Yes."

"Then I will free you," he said.

"What?"

"Did you not hear me?"

"Yes, but . . ."

"I will free you, Augusta."

"You're joking," she said. "You're trying to torment me."

"No, no, I will indeed free you."

"Please, will you?" she said.

"Yes."

"Thank you," she said. "Oh God, thank you. And when you let me go, I promise I won't—"

"Let you go?" he said.

"Yes, you—"

"No, I didn't say I would let you go."

"You said—"

"I said I would *free* you. I meant I would untie your feet."

"I thought—"

"You're interrupting again, Augusta."

"I'm sorry, I—"

"Why did you marry him, Augusta?"

"I . . . please, I . . . please, let me go. I promise I won't tell anyone what you—"

"I'm going to untie your feet," he said. "The door has a dead bolt on it. From either side, it can be opened only with a key. Do not run for the door when I untie you."

"No. No, I won't," she said.

She heard the tape tearing, and suddenly her ankles were free.

"I'm going to take off the blindfold now," he said. "There are no windows in the room, there is only the door, that is all. It would be foolish for you to try to escape before the ceremony, Augusta, but—"

"What ceremony?" she asked at once.

"You constantly interrupt," he said.

"I'm sorry. But what—"

"I don't think you will try to escape," he said.

"That's right, I won't try to escape. But what cere—"

"Still, I must be gone part of the day, you know. I'm a working man, you know. And though the door will be locked, I could not risk your somehow opening it, and getting out of the room, and running down to the street."

"I wouldn't do that. Really," she said, "I—"

"Still, I must protect myself against that possibility," he said, and laughed.

She smelled a familiar aroma, and started to back away from the sound of his voice, and collided with the wall, and was trying to rip the tape from her eyes when he pulled her hands away and clapped the chloroform-soaked rag over her nose and her mouth again. She screamed. She screamed at the top of her lungs.

But no one came to help her.

There were no windows in the room, just as he had promised.

The only source of illumination was a light bulb screwed into a ceiling fixture and operated from a switch just inside the door. The light was on now. The lock on the door was a key-operated dead bolt; it could not be unlocked from either side without a key. She walked to the door and examined the lock, and realized it had been installed only recently; there were jagged splinters of unpainted wood around the lock in the otherwise white-painted door. Against the wall opposite the door, a plastic bowl of water rested on the floor, and alongside that a bowl with what appeared to be some sort of hash in it. She went to the bowl, picked it up, sniffed at the contents, and then put the bowl down on the floor again. It was cold in the room, there was no visible source of heat. She shivered with a sudden chill and crossed her arms over her breasts, hugging herself. In the apartment outside, she heard footsteps approaching the door. She backed away from it.

"Augusta?" he called.

She did not answer. She debated lying on the floor again, pretending to be still unconscious so that she could make a run for the door when he unlocked it. But would he enter the room without the scalpel in his hand? She doubted it. She knew the sharpness of that blade, and she feared it. But she feared he might use it, anyway, whether she

215

attempted escape or not. She waited. She was beginning to tremble again, and she knew it was not from the cold.

"May I come in, Augusta? I know you're conscious, I heard you moving about."

His idiotic politeness infuriated her. She was his prisoner, he could do with her whatever he wished, and yet he asked permission to enter the room.

"You *know* you can come in, why do you bother asking?" she said.

"Ah," he said, and she heard a key being inserted into the lock. The door opened. He stepped into the room and closed and locked the door behind him. "How are you?" he asked pleasantly. "Are you all right?"

"Yes, I'm fine," she said. She was studying his face more closely than she had in the hotel room. She was memorizing the straight blond hair, and the slight scar in the blond eyebrow over his left eye, and the white flecks in the blue eyes, and the bump on the bridge of his nose, where perhaps the nose had once been broken, and the small mole at the right-hand corner of his mouth. He was wearing dark blue trousers and a pale blue turtleneck shirt. There was a gold ring on his right hand, with a violet-colored stone that might have been amethyst; it appeared to be either a college or a high school graduation ring. He wore a wristwatch on his left wrist. His feet were encased in white socks and sneakers.

"I have a suprise for you," he said, and smiled. He turned abruptly then, and left the room without explanation, locking the door behind him. She moved into a corner of the room the moment he was gone, as though her position was more protected there in the right angle of two joining walls. In a little while she heard the key turning in the lock again. She watched the knob apprehensively. It turned, the door opened. He came into the room carrying a half-dozen or more garments on wire hangers. Holding these in his left hand, he extricated the key from the outside of the lock, and then closed the door and locked it from the inside. The clothing looked familiar. He saw her studying the garments, and smiled.

"Do you recognize them?" he asked.

"I'm . . . not sure."

"These were some of my favorites," he said. "I want you to put them on for me."

"What are they?" she asked.

"You'll remember."

"I've worn them before, haven't I?" she said.

"Yes. Yes, you have."

"I've modeled them."

"Yes, that's it exactly."

She recognized most of the clothing now—the chambray-blue safari jacket and matching shorts she had modeled for *Mademoiselle*, the ruffle-edged cotton T-shirt and matching wraparound skirt she had posed in for *Vogue*, yes, and wasn't that the high-yoked chemise she had worn for *Harper's Bazaar*? And there, the robe that—

"Would you hold these, please?" he asked. "The floor is clean, I scrubbed it before you came, but I would rather not put them down." He shrugged apologetically and extended the clothes to her. "It will only be for a moment," he said.

She held out her arms and he draped the garments across them, and turned and went to the door. She watched as he unlocked it again. He left the key in the keyway this time, and he left the door open behind him. But he did not go very far from the room. Just outside the door, Augusta could see a standing clothes rack and a straight-backed wooden chair. He carried the clothes rack into the room first, taking it to the far corner where Augusta had earlier retreated. Then he carried the chair in, and closed and locked the door, and set the chair down just inside it, and was preparing to sit when he said abruptly, "Oh, I almost forgot." He moved the chair away from the door again, and again inserted his key into the lock. "Would you hang the clothes on the rack, please?" he said. "I won't be a moment." He unlocked the door, opened it, and went out. She heard him locking the door again from the other side.

The clothes rack was painted white, a simple standing rack with one vertical post to which were attached, at slanting angles and at varying heights, a series of pegs. She carried the clothes to the rack and hung them on the pegs. She noticed as she did so that at least one of the garments—the safari jacket—was in her size, and she quickly checked the others and learned that *all* of them were exactly her size. She wondered how he had known the size, and guessed he had got it from the suit she'd been wearing—but had he bought all this clothing *after* he'd taken her from the hotel room? One of the garments on the rack was a robe she had modeled for *Town & Country*. She took it down, and was putting it on when the door opened again.

"What are you doing?" he said. He spoke the words very softly. "Take that off."

"I was a little chilly, I thought—"

"Take it off!" he said, his voice rising. "Take it off this instant!"

Silently, she took off the robe, put it back on the hanger, and hung it on the rack. He was standing just inside the open door now. In his left hand he was holding a paper bag with the logo of one of the city's most expensive department stores on it.

"I did not give you permission," he said.

"I didn't know I needed permission," Augusta said. "I was cold. It's cold in here."

"You will do only what I tell you to do, when I tell you to do it. Is that clear?"

She did not answer.

"Is it?"

"Yes, yes," she said.

"I don't believe I like that note of impatience in your voice, Augusta."

"I'm sorry."

He locked the door behind him, put the key into his pocket, moved the chair so that its back was against the door again, and then said, "We are to have a fashion show." He smiled and extended the small parcel he was holding. "Here," he said. "Take it."

She walked to where he was sitting, and took the paper bag from his hands. Inside the bag, she found a pair of pale blue bikini panties and a blue bra. The panties were a size 5, the bra was a 34B.

"How did you know my sizes?" she asked.

"They were in *Vogue*," he said. "The April issue. Last year, don't you remember? 'All About Augusta.' Don't you remember?"

"Yes."

"That was a very good article, Augusta."

"Yes, it was."

"It didn't mention Detective Bert Kling, though."

"Well . . ."

"In an article titled 'All About Augusta,' it would hardly seem honest to neglect mentioning—"

"I guess the agency felt—"

"You're interrupting, Augusta."

"I'm sorry."

"That is truly a vile habit. In my home, if I ever interrupted, I was severely thrashed."

"I won't interrupt again. I was only trying to explain why the article didn't mention Bert."

"Ah, is that what you call him? Bert?"

"Yes."

"And what does he call you?"

"Augusta. Or sometimes Gus. Or Gussie."

"I prefer Augusta."

"Actually, I do, too."

"Good. We are at least in agreement on something. Blue is your favorite color, the article said. Is that true?"

"Yes."

"Does the blue please you?"

"Yes, it's fine. When did you buy these clothes?"

"Last month," he said. "When I knew what had to be done."

"You still haven't told me—"

"The ceremony will take place tomorrow evening," he said.

"What ceremony?"

"You will see," he said. "My mother was a model, you know. In Europe, of course. But she was quite well known."

"What was her name?" Augusta said.

"You would not know it," he said. "This was long before your time. She was murdered," he said. "Yes. I was a small boy at the time. Someone broke into the house, a burglar, a rapist, who knows? I awakened to the sounds of my mother screaming."

Augusta watched him. He seemed unaware of her presence now, seemed to be talking only to himself. His eyes were somewhat out of focus, as though he were drifting off to another place, a place he knew only too well—and dreaded.

"My father was a leather-goods salesman, he was away from home. I leaped out of bed, she was screaming, screaming. I ran across the parlor toward her bedroom—and the screaming stopped." He nodded. "Yes." He nodded again. "Yes," he said, and fell silent for several moments, and then said, "She was on the floor in a pool of her own blood. He had slit her throat." He closed his eyes abruptly, squeezed them shut, and then opened them almost immediately. "Well, that was a long time ago," he said. "I was just a small boy."

"It must have been horrible for you."

"Yes," he said, and then shrugged, seemingly dismissing the entire matter. "I think the pants suit will suit you nicely," he said, and grinned. "Do you understand the pun, Augusta?"

"What? I . . ."

"The suit. The suit will suit you," he said, and laughed. "That's good, don't you think? The hardest thing to do in a second language is to make a pun."

"What's your *first* language?" she asked.

"I come from Austria," he said.

"Where in Austria?"

"Vienna. Do you know Austria?"

"I've skied there."

"Yes, of course, how stupid of me! In the article—"

"Yes."

"—it said you skied in Zürs one time. Yes, I remember now."

"Do you ski?"

"No. No, I have never skied. Augusta," he said, "I wish you to take off the clothes you are now wearing and put on first the panties and brassiere, and then the suit."

"If you'll leave the room . . ."

"No," he said, "I'll stay here while you change. It will be more *intime, n'est-ce pas?* Do you speak French?"

"A little. I'll put on the clothes only if you—"

"No, no," he said, and laughed. "Really, Augusta, you are being quite ridiculous. I could have done to you whatever I wished while

219

you were unconscious. You'll be pleased to learn I took no liberties. So now, when you—"

"I would like to go to the toilet," she said.

"What?"

"I have to move my bowels," she said.

A look of total revulsion crossed his face. He kept staring at her in utter disbelief, and then he rose abruptly and shoved the chair aside, and unlocked the door and went out of the room. She heard the lock clicking shut again, and rather suspected the fashion show had suddenly been canceled. Smiling, she went to the wall opposite the door, and sat on the floor with her back against it. She felt a bit warmer now.

There was no time in the room.

He was her clock, she realized.

She dozed and awakened again. She sipped water from the bowl. She nibbled at the meat in the other bowl. When she grew cold again, she put on the long white robe over her clothes, and sat huddled on the floor, hugging herself. She dozed again.

When he came into the room again, he left the door open. He was wearing a dark brown overcoat, and in the open V of the coat, she could see the collar of a white shirt, and a dark tie with a narrow knot. Behind him, from a window somewhere in the apartment, there was the faint wintry light of early morning.

"I must go to work now," he said. His tone was colder than it had been.

"What time is it?" she asked.

"It's six-thirty A.M."

"You go to work early," she said.

"Yes," he said.

"What sort of work do you do?"

"That is no concern of yours," he said. "I will return by three-thirty at the latest. I will prepare you for the ceremony then."

"What sort of ceremony is it to be?" she asked.

"I see no harm in telling you," he said.

"Yes, I'd really like to know."

"We are to be married, Augusta," he said.

"I'm already married."

"Your marriage has not taken effect."

"What do you mean?"

"It has not been consummated."

She said nothing.

"Do you remember the wedding gown you wore in *Brides* magazine?"

"Yes."

"I have it. I bought it for you."

"Look I . . . I appreciate what—"

"No, I don't think so," he said.

"What?"

"I don't think you *do* appreciate the trouble I've gone to."

"I do, really I do. But . . ."

"I didn't know your shoe size, that's why I didn't buy any shoes. The article about you didn't mention your shoe size."

"Probably because I have such big feet," she said, and smiled.

"You shall have to be married barefoot," he said.

"But, you see," she said, refusing to enter into his delusion, "I'm *already* married. I got married on Sunday afternoon. I'm Mrs. Bertram . . ."

"I was there at the church, you don't have to tell me."

"Then you know I'm married."

"Are you angry about the shoes?"

"You have a trick," she said.

"Oh? What trick is that?"

"Of refusing to face reality."

"There is only one reality," he said. "You are here, and you are mine. That is reality."

"I'm *here*, that's reality, yes. But I'm not yours."

"I'll be late for work," he said, and looked at his watch.

"There's your trick again. I'm *mine*," she said. "I belong to *me*."

"You *were* yours. You are no longer yours. You are mine. This afternoon, after the ceremony, I will demonstrate that to you."

"Let's talk about reality again, okay?"

"Augusta, that *is* the reality. I will be home at three-thirty. I will take you to the bathroom, where you will bathe yourself and anoint yourself with the perfume I've purchased—L'Oriel *is* your favorite, am I correct? That's what the article said. And then you will put on the white undergarments I bought, and the blue garter, and the gown you modeled in *Brides*. And then we shall have a simple wedding ceremony, uniting us in the eyes of God."

"No," she said, "I'm already—"

"Yes," he insisted. "And then we shall make love, Augusta. I have been waiting a long time to make love to you. I have been waiting since I first saw your photograph in a magazine. That was more than two years ago, Augusta, you should not have *dared* give yourself to another man. Two long years, Augusta! I've loved you all that time, I've been waiting all that time to possess you, yes, Augusta. When I saw you on television doing a hair commercial—do you remember the Clairol commercial?—saw you *moving*, Augusta, saw your photographs suddenly coming to *life*, your hair floating on the wind as you ran, how beautiful you looked, Augusta—I waited for the commercial again. I sat before the set, waiting for you to appear again, and finally I was rewarded—but ah, how brief the commercial was, how long *are* those commercials? Thirty seconds? Sixty seconds?"

"They vary," she answered automatically, and was suddenly aware of the lunatic nightmare proportions of the conversation. She was discussing the length of television commercials with a man who planned to marry her today in a fantasy ceremony. . .

"I abuse myself with your photographs," he said suddenly. "Does that excite you? The thought of my doing such things with your pictures?"

She did not answer him.

"But this afternoon I will actually possess you. We will be married, Augusta, and then we will make love together."

"No, we—"

"Yes," he said. "And then I will slit your throat."

She was alone in the apartment.

The entire place was still.

She had listened very carefully after he'd gone out of the room and locked the door. She had gone to the door instantly, and put her ear against it, listening the way Bert had told her *he* listened before entering a suspect premises. She had heard the front door of the apartment closing behind him, and then she had continued listening, her ear pressed to the wooden door, listening for footsteps approaching the storage room again, suspecting a trick. She did not have a watch, he had taken that from her, but she counted to sixty, and then to sixty again, and again, and over again until she estimated that she'd been standing inside the door with her ear pressed to the wood for about fifteen minutes. In all that time, she heard nothing. She had to assume he was really and truly gone.

He had left the clothing behind.

More important than that, he had left the wire hangers and the wooden clothes rack. He was a very careful man, he had installed a double keyway dead bolt on the door as soon as he'd decided to abduct her, a most methodical, most fastidious, foresighted person. But he had forgotten that he was dealing with a cop's wife, and he had neglected to notice that the door opened *into* the room, and that the hinge pins were on Augusta's side of the door. Quickly, she removed all the clothing from the rack and tossed it into one corner of the room. Then she dragged the rack over to the door, and opened up one of the wire hangers by twisting the curved hook away from the body.

She was ready to go to work.

The hinge pins had been painted into the hinges.

Augusta had broken off one of the pegs on the clothes rack, and tried using that as a makeshift mallet, hoping to chip away the paint. But the peg wasn't heavy enough, and however hard she struck at the hinge, the paint remained solidly caked to it. She had no idea what time it was, but she'd been working on just that single hinge for what seemed like hours. She had made no headway, and there were three hinges on the door, and he had told her he would be back in the apartment by three-thirty. She picked up the clothes rack now, picked it up in both hands, and using it like a battering ram, she began smashing at the middle hinge on the door.

A chip of paint flaked off.

She stepped out of the storage room into a narrow corridor painted white. She turned to her left and walked into a kitchen similarly painted white, its single window slanting wintry sunlight onto the white vinyl-tile floor. There was a swinging door at the opposite end of the kitchen, just to the right of the refrigerator, and she walked to that now, and pushed it open, and that was when the sterile whiteness ended.

She almost backed away into the kitchen again.

She was inside a shrine.

The entire apartment was a shrine. Augusta was the wallpaper and Augusta was the floor covering and Augusta was the ceiling decoration and Augusta obliterated any light that ordinarily might have filtered through the windows because Augusta covered all the windows as well. It was impossible to look anywhere without seeing Augusta. Standing there in the corridor just outside the kitchen door, she felt as though she were being reflected by thousands upon thousands of mirrors, tiny mirrors and large ones, mirrors that threw back images in color or in black and white, mirrors that caught her in action or in repose. The corridor, and the living room beyond that, and the bedroom at the far end of the hall together formed a massive collage of photographs snipped from every magazine in which she'd ever appeared, some of them going back to the very beginning of her career. She could not possibly estimate how many copies of each edition of each magazine had been purchased and scrutinized and finally cut apart to create this cubistic monument. There were photographs everywhere. Those on the walls alone would have suffice to create an overwhelming effect, meticulously pasted up to cover every inch of space, forming an interlocking, overlapping, overflowing vertical scrapbook. But the pictures devoured the walls, and then consumed the ceilings and dripped onto the floors as well, photographs of Augusta running rampant overhead and below, and flanking her on every side. Some of the photographs were duplicates, she saw, triplicates, quadruplicates, so that the concept of a myriad reflecting mirrors now seemed to multiply dangerously—there were mirrors reflecting other mirrors and Augusta stood in the midst of this visual reverberating photographic chamber and suddenly doubted her own reality, suddenly wondered whether she herself, standing there at the center of an Augusta-echoing-Augusta universe, was not simply an echo of another Augusta somewhere on the walls. The entire display had been shellacked, and the artificial illumination in the apartment cast a glow onto the shiny surfaces, pinpoint pricks of light seeming to brighten a photographed eye as she moved past it, hair as dead as the paper upon which it was printed suddenly seeming to shimmer with life.

There was a king-sized bed in the bedroom. It was covered with white sheets; there were white pillowcases on the pillows. A white lacquered dresser was against one wall, and a chair covered with white vinyl stood against the adjoining wall. There was no other furniture in the bedroom. Just the bed, the dresser, and the chair— stark and white against the photographs that rampaged across the floor and up the walls and over the ceilings.

She wondered suddenly what time it was.

She had lost all track of time while working on the door, but she surmised it was a little past noon now. She went quickly to the front door, ascertained that the lock on it was a key-operated dead bolt, and then went immediately into the kitchen. The unadorned white of the room came as a cool oasis in a blazing desert. She was moving toward the wall telephone when she saw the clock above the refrigerator. The time came as a shock, as chilling as the touch of the scalpel had been on her throat. She could not possibly imagine the hours having gone by that swiftly, and yet the hands of the clock told her it was now three twenty-five . . . was it possible the clock had stopped? But no, she could hear it humming on the wall, could see the minute hand moving almost imperceptibly as she stared at it. The clock was working; it was three twenty-five and he'd told her he would return at three-thirty.

She immediately lifted the telephone receiver from the hook, waited for a dial tone, and then jiggled the bar impatiently, lifted it again, listened for a dial tone again, and got one just as she heard the lock turning in the front door. She dropped the phone, reached for the latch over the kitchen window, and discovered at once that the window was painted shut.

She turned, moved swiftly to the kitchen table, pulled a chair from under it, lifted the chair, and was swinging it toward the window when she heard his footsteps coming through the apartment. The glass shattered, exploding into the shaftway and cascading in shards to the interior courtyard below. He was running through the apartment now. She remembered his admonition about screaming, remembered his admonition about screaming, remembered that it made him violent. But he was running through the apartment toward her, and he had promised her a wedding ceremony, and a nuptial consummation, and a slit throat—and at the moment she couldn't think of anything more violent than a slit throat.

She screamed.

He was in the kitchen now. She did not see his face until he pulled her from the window and twisted her toward him and slapped her with all the force of his arm and shoulder behind the blow. His face was distorted, the blue eyes wide and staring, the mouth hanging open. He kept striking her repeatedly as she screamed, the blows becoming more and more fierce until she feared he would break her jaw or her cheekbones. She cut off a scream just as it was bubbling onto her lips, strangled it, but he kept striking her, his arm flailing as though he were no longer conscious of its action, the hand swinging to collide with her face, and then returning to catch her backhanded just as she reeled away from the earlier blow. "Stop," she said, "please," scarcely daring to give voice to the words lest they infuriate him further and cause him to lose control completely. She tried to cover her face with her hands, but he yanked first one hand away and then the other, and he kept striking her till she felt she would lose consciousness if he hit her one more time. But she did not faint, she sank deliberately to the floor instead, breaking the pattern of his blows, crouching on all fours with her head bent, gasping for breath. He pulled her to her feet immediately, but he did not strike her again. Instead, he dragged her out of the kitchen and across the corridor into the living room, where he hurled her angrily onto the floor again. Her lip was beginning to swell from the repeated blows. She touched her mouth to see if it was bleeding. Standing in the doorway, he watched her calmly now, and took off his overcoat, and placed it neatly over the arm of the sofa. There was only one light burning in the room, a floor lamp that cast faint illumination on the shellacked pictures that covered the walls, the ceiling, and the floor. Augusta lay on her own photographs like a protectively colored jungled creature hoping to fade out against a sympathetic background.

"This was to be a surprise," he said. "You spoiled the surprise."

He made no mention of the fact that she had broken the window and screamed for help. As she had done earlier, she insisted now on bringing him back to reality. "You'd better let me go," she said. "While there's still time. This may be the goddamn city, but someone's *sure* to have heard—"

"I wanted to be with you when you saw it for the first time. Do you like what I've done?"

"Somebody's going to report those screams to the police, and they'll come busting in here—"

"I'm sorry I struck you," he said. "I warned you about screaming, though. It truly does make me violent."

"Do you understand what I'm saying?"

"Yes, you're staying someone will have heard you."

"Yes, and they'll come looking for this apartment, and once they find you—"

"Well, it doesn't matter," he said.

"What do you mean?"

"The ceremony will be brief. By the time they locate the apartment, we'll have finished."

"They'll find it sooner than you think," Augusta said. "The kitchen window is broken. They'll look for a broken window, and once they locate it on the outside of the building—"

"*Who*, Augusta?"

"Whoever heard me screaming. There's a building right across the way, I saw windows on the wall there . . ."

"Yes, it used to be a hat factory. And, until recently, an artist was living there. But he moved out six months ago. The loft has been empty since."

"You're lying to me."

"No."

"You want me to think no one heard me."

"Someone *may* have heard you, Augusta, it's quite possible. But it really doesn't matter. As I say, it will be quite some time before we're found, even if you *were* heard. Augusta, do you like what I've done with your photographs? This didn't just happen overnight, you know, I've been working on it for quite some time. Do you like it?"

"Why did you do all this?" she asked.

"Because I love you," he said simply.

"Then let me go."

"No."

"Please. *Please* let me go. I promise I won't—"

"No, Augusta, that's impossible. Really, it's quite impossible. We mustn't even discuss it. Besides, it's almost time for the ceremony, and if someone heard you screaming, as you pointed out—"

"If you really love me . . ."

"Ah, but I do."

"Then let me go."

"Why? So you can go back to him? No, Augusta. Come now. It's time for your bath."

"I don't *want* a bath."

"The article about you—"

"The hell with the article about me!"

"It said you bathed twice daily. You haven't had a bath since I brought you here, Augusta."

"I don't want a goddamn bath!"

"Don't you feel dirty, Augusta?"

"No."

"You must bathe, anyway."

"Leave me alone."

"You must be clean for the ceremony. Get up, Augusta."

"No."

"Get off the floor."

"Go fuck yourself," she said.

The scapel appeared suddenly in his hand. He smiled.

"Go ahead, use it," she said. "You're going to kill me, anyway, so what difference—?"

"If I use it now," he said, "it will not be pleasant. I prefer not to use it in anger, Augusta. Believe me, if you provoke me further, I can make it very painful for you. I love you, Augusta, don't force me to hurt you."

They stared at each other across the length of the room.

"Please believe me," he said.

"But *however* you kill me—"

"I do not wish to talk about killing you."

"You said you were going to kill me."

"Yes. I do not want to talk about it."

"Why? Why are you going to kill me?"

"To punish you."

"Punish me? I thought you loved me."

"I do love you."

"Then why do you want to punish me?"

"For what you did."

"What did I do?"

"This is pointless. You are angering me. You should not have screamed. You frightened me."

"When?"

"When? Just now. When I came into the apartment. You were screaming. You frightened me. I thought someone—"

"Yes, what did you think?"

"I thought someone had got in here and was . . . was trying to harm you."

"But you *yourself* are going to harm me."

"No," he said, and shook his head.

"You're going to kill me. You said you're—"

"I want to bathe you now," he said. "Come." He held out his left hand. In the right hand he was holding the scalpel. "Come, Augusta."

She took his hand, and he helped her to her feet. As they went through the apartment to the bathroom, she thought she should not have broken the window, she should not have screamed, she should not have done either of those things. The only thing to do with this man was humor him, listen to everything he said, nod, smile pleasantly, agree with him, tell him how nice it was to be in an apartment papered with pictures of herself. Stall for time, wait for Bert to get a line on him, because surely they were working on it right this minute. Wait it out, that was all. Patience. Forbearance. They'd be here eventually. She knew them well enough to know they'd be here.

"I could so easily hurt you," he said.

She did not answer him. Calm and easy, she thought. Cool. Wait it out. Humor him.

"It is so easy to hurt someone," he said. "Did I tell you my mother was killed by an intruder?"

"Yes."

"That was a long time ago, of course. Come, we must bathe you, Augusta."

In the bathroom, he poured bubble bath into the tub, and she watched the bubbles foaming up, and heard him behind her, tapping the blade of the scalpel against the edge of the sink.

"Do you know why I bought the bubble bath?" he asked.

"Yes, because of the magazine article."

"Is it true that you like bubble baths?"

"Yes."

"I am going to bathe you now," he said.

She suffered his hands upon her.

There were six buttons on the bodice of the gown, spaced between the square neckline and the Empire waist. The gown was made of cotton, with rows and rows of tucked white lace, and more lace on the cuffs of the full sleeves. A silk-illusion veil crowned Augusta's auburn hair, and she was carrying a small bouquet of red roses. He had dressed her himself, fumbling with the delicate lace-edged panties and bra, sliding the lacy blue garter up over her left thigh, adjusting the veil on her head, and then presenting her with the bouquet. He led her barefoot into the living room now, and asked her to sit on the sofa, facing him. She sat, and he told her to clasp both hands around the shaft of the bouquet, and to hold the flowers on her lap and to look straight ahead of her, neither to the right nor to the left, but straight ahead. He was standing directly in front of her, some six feet away, as he began his recitation.

"We are witnesses here," he said, "the two of us alone, we are witnesses to this holy sacrament, we are witnesses. You and I, man and woman, and child asleep in innocence, we are witnesses. We are witnesses to the act, we have seen, we have seen. I have seen her before, yes, I have witnessed her before, I have seen photographs, yes, she knew this, she was a famous model, there would be roses at the door, roses from strangers, they would often arrive without warning. I have seen photographs of her, yes, she was quite famous, I have seen her dressing too, I have sometimes witnessed—the bedroom door ajar, I have sometimes in her underthings, yes, she was quite beautiful, I have witnessed, but never naked, never that way, *das Blut, ach!*"

He shook his head. Though Augusta knew no German, she instantly understood the word "*Blut*." He repeated the word in English now, still shaking his head, his eyes on the roses in Augusta's lap.

"Blood. So much blood. Everywhere. On the floor, on her legs, *nackt und offen*, do you understand? My own mother, *meine Mutter*. To expose herself that way, but ah, it was so very long ago, we must forget, *nein*? And in fairness, she was dead, you know, he had cut her throat, you know, forgive them their trespasses, they know not what they do. So much blood, though . . . so much. He had cut her so bad, yes, even before her throat, she was so . . . so many cuts . . . she . . . everywhere she had touched, there was blood. Running away from him, you know. Touching the walls, and the bureau, and the closet door, and the chairs, blood everywhere. Screaming, *Ach, ach*, I covered my ears with my hands, *Bitte, bitte*, she kept screaming again and again, Please, please, *Bitte, bitte*, where is my father to let this happen to her, where? There is blood everywhere I look. Her legs are open wide when I go into the bedroom, there is blood on the inside of her legs, shameless, like a cheap whore, to let him *do* this to her? Why did she allow it, *why*? Always so careful with *me*, of course, always so modest and chaste—Now, now, Klaus, you must not stay in the bedroom when I am dressing, you must not peek on your mother, eh? Run along now, run along, there's a good boy—petticoats and lace, and once in her bloomers, with nothing on top, smelling of perfume, I wanted so much to touch you that day, Augusta, but of course I am too small—you are too small, Augusta, your breasts. You are really quite a disappointment to me, I don't know why I bother loving you at all, when you give yourself so freely to another. Ah, well, it was a long time ago, *nein*? Forgive and forget, let bygones be bygones, we are here today to change all that, we are here today as witnesses."

He smiled abruptly, and looked up from the roses, directly into Augusta's face.

"Johanna, my love," he said, "we are here to be married today, you and I, we are here to celebrate our wedding. We are here to sanctify our union that will be, we are here to witness and to obliterate. The other, I mean. Your union with another, we will obliterate that, Johanna, we will forget that shameless performance—why did you let him *do* it?" he shouted, and then immediately said, "Forgive me, Augusta," and walked to where she was sitting on the sofa, and took the bouquet from her hands and placed it on the floor. Then, kneeling before her, he took both her hands between his own, and said, simply, "I take you for my wife, I take you for my own."

He kissed her hands then, first one and then the other, and rose, and gently lifted her from the couch and led her into the bedroom.

The scalpel was in his hand.

He had tried to make love to her, and had failed, and now he rose from the bed angrily, and said, "Put on your underthings! Are you a whore? Is that what you are?" and watched as she lifted the long bridal gown and put on the white lace-edged panties, the only garment he had earlier asked her to remove.

"You do not have to answer," he said. "I *know* what you are, I have known for a long time."

She said nothing.

"I suppose you are disappointed in me," he said. "Someone like you, who knows so many men. I suppose my performance was less than satisfying."

Still, she said nothing.

"Have you known others like me?" he asked. "In your experience, have you known others who could not perform?"

"I want you to let me go," she said.

"Answer me! Have you known others like me?"

"Please let me go. Give me the key to the front door, and—"

"I'm sure you have known a great many men who had medical problems such as mine. This is entirely a medical problem, I will see a doctor one day, he will prescribe a pill, it will vanish. I myself was almost a doctor, did you know that? I was Phi Beta Kappa at Ramsey University, did you know that? Yes. I was an undergraduate there, Phi Beta Kappa. And I was accepted at one of the finest medical schools in the country. Yes. I went for two years to medical school. Would you like to know what happened? Would you like to know why I am not a doctor today? I could have been a doctor, you know."

"I want to leave here," she said. "Please give me the key."

"Augusta, you are being absurd," he said. "You cannot leave. You will *never* leave. I am going to kill you, Augusta."

"Why?"

"I told you why. Would you like to know what happened in medical school, Augusta? Would you like to know why I was expelled? I mutilated a cadaver," he said. "I mutilated a female cadaver. With a scalpel."

She backed away from him.

He was coming for her with the scalpel in his hand. He was between her and the doorway. The bed was in the center of the room, she backed toward it, and then climbed onto the mattress, and stood in the middle of the bed, ready to leap to the floor on the side opposite whichever one he approached.

"I urge you not to do this," he said.

She did not answer. She watched him, waiting for his move, poised to leap. She would use the bed as a wall between them. If he approached it from the side closest to the door, the right-hand side, she would jump off onto the floor on the left. If he crawled onto the bed in an attempt to cross it, she would run around the end of it to the other side. She would keep the bed between them forever if she had to, use it as a barrier and a—

He thrust the scalpel at her, and seemed about to reach across the bed, and she jumped to the floor away from him, and realized too late that his move had been a feint. He was coming around the side of the bed, it was too late for her to maneuver her way to the door, she backed into the corner as he came toward her.

She would remember always the sound of the door being kicked in, would remember, too, the swift shock of recognition that darted into his eyes and the way his head turned sharply away from her. She could see past him to the front door, could see the bolt shattering inward, and Steve Carella bursting into the room, a very fat man behind him, and then Bert—and the scalpel came up, the scalpel came toward her.

They were all holding guns, but the fat man was the only one who fired. Steve and Bert, they just stood there looking into the room, they saw the scalpel in his hand, they saw her in a wedding gown, crouched in the corner of the room, the scalpel coming toward her face—*I mutilated a female cadaver*—the fat man taking in the situation at once, his gun coming level, and two explosions erupting from the muzzle.

She would realize later that the fat man was the only one who did not love her. And she would vow never to ask either Steve or Bert why they had not fired instantly, why they had left it to Fat Ollie Weeks to pump the two slugs into the man who was about to slit her throat.

WEEKS: We just told you your rights, and you just told us you understood your rights and didn't need no lawyer here to tell us what this whole thing is about. Now, I just want you to understand one more thing, you shithead, and that's you're in no danger of dying, the doctor says you're gonna be fine. So I don't want no trouble later, I want it clear on the record when we get to court that nobody said you were going to die or anything. We didn't get you to make a statement by saying you were a dying man or nothing like that.

SCHEINER: That's true.

WEEKS: So that's why the stenographer's taking all this down if you want to tell us about it.

SCHEINER: What do you want to know?

WEEKS: Why'd you kidnap the lady?

SCHEINER: Because I love her.

WEEKS: You love her, huh? You were ready to f'Christ's sake *kill* her when we—

SCHEINER: *And* myself.

WEEKS: You were going to kill yourself, too?

SCHEINER: Yes.

WEEKS: Why?

SCHEINER: With her dead, what would be the sense of living?

WEEKS: You're crazier'n a fuckin' bedbug, you know that? *You're* the one was gonna kill her.

SCHEINER: To punish her for what she did.

WEEKS: What'd she do?

SCHEINER: She allowed him.

WEEKS: She allowed him, huh? You fuckin' lunatic, you're a fuckin' lunatic, you know that? How'd you know what hotel they were at?

SCHEINER: I followed them from the church.

WEEKS: Were you at the reception?

SCHEINER: No. I waited downstairs for them.

WEEKS: All the while the reception was going on?

SCHEINER: Yes. Except for when I moved the ambulance.

WEEKS: When was that?

SCHEINER: About eleven o'clock, I think it was. I moved it into the alley behind the hotel. That was after I learned where the service courtyard was.

WEEKS: Then what?

SCHEINER: Then I came around to the front again—because the alley door was locked, I couldn't get in that way. And I was just coming through the revolving doors when I saw them standing there, just inside the doors—he was taking a picture of her and another man. I turned away, I walked toward the phone booths.

WEEKS: How'd you find out what room they were in?

SCHEINER: I picked up a house phone in the lobby, and asked.

WEEKS: You see that? You see what they'll tell you? You walk in any hotel in this city, you ask them what room Mr. so-and-so is in, they'll tell you. Unless he's a celebrity. How'd you get into the room, Scheiner?

SCHEINER: I used a slat from a venetian blind.

WEEKS: How come you know how to do that? What *are* you, a burglar?

SCHEINER: No, no. I drive an ambulance.

WEEKS: Then how'd you learn about that?

SCHEINER: I have read books.

WEEKS: And you learned how to loid a door, huh?

SCHEINER:	I learned how to force a door, to push back the bolt.
WEEKS:	That's loiding.
SCHEINER:	I don't know what you call it.
WEEKS:	But you know how to *do* it pretty good, don't you, you shithead? Didn't you know there was a *cop* in that room? He could've blown your head off the minute you opened the door.
SCHEINER:	I did not think he would have a gun on his wedding day. Besides, I was prepared.
WEEKS:	For what?
SCHEINER:	To kill him.
WEEKS:	Why?
SCHEINER:	For taking her from me.

They put Kling and Augusta into a taxi, and then they went out for hamburgers and coffee. Fat Ollie Weeks ate six hamburgers. He did not say a word all the while he was eating. He had finished his six hamburgers and three cups of coffee before Meyer and Carella finished what they had ordered, and then he sat back against the red Leatherette booth, and belched, and said, "That man was a fuckin' lunatic. I'da cracked the case earlier if only we hadn't been dealing with a lunatic. Lunatics are very hard to fathom." He belched again. "I'll bet old Augusta ain't gonna forget *this* for a while, huh?"

"I guess not," Meyer said.

"I wonder if he got in her pants," Ollie said.

"Ollie," Carella said very softly, "if I were you, I wouldn't ever again wonder anything like that aloud. *Ever*, Ollie. You understand me?"

"Oh, sure," Ollie said.

"*Ever*," Carella said.

"Yeah, yeah, relax already, will ya?" Ollie said. "I think I'll have another hamburger. You guys feel like another hamburger?"

So Long as You Both Shall Live, 1976

The car windows were open, the heat ballooned around the two men as Carella edged the vehicle through the heavy lunch-hour traffic. He glanced sidelong at Kling, who was staring straight ahead through the windshield, and then said, "Tell me."

"I'm not sure I want to talk about it," Kling said.

"Then why'd you bring it up?"

" 'Cause it's been driving me crazy for the past month."

"Let's start from the beginning, okay?" Carella said.

The beginning, as Kling painfully and haltingly told it, had been on the Fourth of July, when he and Augusta were invited out to Sands Spit for the weekend. Their host was one of the photographers with whom Augusta had worked many times in the past. Carella, listening, remembered the throng of photographers, agents, and professional models, like Augusta, who had been guests at their wedding almost four years ago.

". . . on the beach out there in Westphalia," Kling was saying. "Beautiful house set on the dunes, two guest rooms. We went out on the third, and there was a big party the next day, models, photographers . . . well, you know the crowd Gussie likes to run with. That was when I got the first inkling, at the party."

He had never felt too terribly close to his wife's friends and associates, Kling said; they had, in fact, had some big arguments in the past over what he called her "tinsel crowd." He supposed much of his discomfort had to do with the fact that as a Detective/Third he was earning $24,600 a year, whereas his wife was earning $100 an hour as a top fashion model; the joint IRS return they'd filed in April had listed their combined incomes as a bit more than $100,000 for the previous year. Moreover, most of Augusta's friends were *also* earning that kind of money, and whereas he felt no qualms about inviting eight or ten of them for dinner at any of the city's most expensive restaurants and signing for the tab afterward ("She keeps telling me they're business associates, it's all deductible," Kling said), he always felt somewhat inadequate at such feasts, something like a poor relative visiting a rich city cousin, or—worse—something like a kept man. Kling himself preferred small dinner parties at their apartment with friends of his from the police force, people like Carella and his wife, Teddy, and Cotton Hawes and any one of his dozens of girlfriends, or Artie and Connie Brown, or Meyer Meyer and his wife, Sarah—people he knew and liked, people he could feel relaxed with.

The party out there on the beach in Westphalia, some hundred and thirty miles from the city in Sagamore County, was pretty much the same as all the parties Augusta dragged him to in the city. She'd get through with a modeling job at four, five in the afternoon, and if he'd been working the Day Tour, he'd be off at four and would get back to the apartment at about the same time she did, and she'd always have a cocktail party to go to, either at a photographer's studio or the offices of some fashion magazine, or some other model's apartment, or her agent's—always someplace to go. There were times he'd be following some cheap hood all over the city, walking the pavements flat and getting home exhausted and wanted nothing more than a bottle of beer, and the place would be full of flitty photographers or gorgeous models talking about the latest spread in *Vogue* or *Harper's Bazaar*, drinking the booze Augusta paid for out of her earnings, and wanting to know all about how it felt to shoot somebody ("Have you ever actually *killed* a person, Bert?"), as if police work were the same kind of empty game modeling was. It irked him every time Augusta referred to herself as a "mannequin." It made her seem as shallow as the work she did, a hollow store-window dummy draped in the latest Parisian fashions.

"Well, what the hell," Kling said, "you make allowances, am I right? I'm a cop, she's a model, we both knew that before we got married. So, okay, you compromise. If Gussie doesn't like to cook, we'll send out for Chink's whenever anybody from the squad's coming over with his wife. And if I've just been in a shoot-out with an armed robber, the way I was two weeks ago when that guy tried to hold up the bank on Culver and Third, then I can't be expected to go to a gallery opening or a cocktail party, or a benefit, or whatever the hell, Gussie'll just have to go alone, am I right?"

Which is just the way they'd been working it for the past few months now. Augusta running off to this or that glittering little party while Kling took off his shoes, and sat wearily in front of the television set drinking beer till she got home, when generally they'd go out for a bite to eat. That was if he was working the Day Tour. If he was working the Night Watch, he'd get home bone weary at nine-thirty in the morning, and *maybe*, if he was lucky, catch breakfast with her before she ran off to her first assignment. A hundred dollars an hour was not pumpkin seeds, and—as Augusta had told him time and again—in her business it was important to make hay while the sun was shining; how many *more* years of successful modeling could she count on? So off she'd run to this or that photographer's studio, rushing out of the apartment with a kerchief on her head and her shoulder bag flying, leaving Kling to put the dishes in the dishwasher before going directly to bed, where he'd sleep till six that night and then go out to dinner with her when she got home from her usual cocktail party. After dinner, *maybe*, and nowadays less and less frequently, they'd make love before he had to leave for the station house again at twelve-thirty in the morning. But that was only on the two days a month he caught the Night Watch.

In fact, he'd been looking forward to going out to Sands Spit, not because he particularly cared for the photographer they'd be visiting (or *any* of Augusta's friends, for that matter) but only because he was exhausted and wanted nothing more than to collapse on a beach for two full days—his days off. Nor was he due back at work till Saturday afternoon at 1600—and that's where the trouble started. Or, at least, that's where the *argument* started. He didn't think of it as trouble until later that night, when he got into a conversation with a twerpy little blond model who opened his eyes for him while their photographer-host was running up and down the beach touching off the fireworks he'd bought illegally in Chinatown.

The argument was about whether or not Augusta should stay at the beach for the entire long weekend, instead of going back to the city with Kling on Saturday. They'd been married for almost four years now; she should have realized by this time that the police department respected no holidays, and that a cop's two successive days off sometimes fell in the middle of the week. He was lucky this year, in fact, to have caught the Glorious Fourth and the day preceding it, and he felt he was within his rights to ask his own *wife*, goddamnit, to accompany him back to the city when he left at ten tomorrow morning. Augusta maintained that the Fourth of July rarely was bracketed by an entire long weekend, as it was this year, and it was senseless for her to go back to what would be essentially a ghost town when *he* had to go to work anyway. What was she supposed to do while he was out chasing crooks? Sit in the empty apartment and twiddle her thumbs? He told her she was coming *back* with him, and *that* was that. She told him she was *staying*, and that was *that*.

They barely spoke to each other all through dinner, served on their host's deck overlooking the crashing sea, and by the time the fireworks started at 9:00 P.M., Augusta had drifted over to a group of photographers with whom she'd immediately begun a spirited, and much too animated, conversation. The little blonde who sat down next to Kling while the first of the fireworks erupted was holding a martini glass in her hand, and it was evident from the first few words she spoke that she'd had at least *four* too many of them already. She was wearing very short white shorts and an orange blouse Kling had seen in *Glamour* (Augusta on the cover) the month before, slashed deep over her breasts and exposing at least one of them clear to the nipple. She said, "Hi," and then tucked her bare feet up under her, her shoulder touching Kling's as she performed the delicate maneuver, and then asked him in a gin-slurred voice where he'd been all afternoon, she hadn't seen him around, and she thought sure she'd seen every good-looking man there. The fireworks kept exploding against the blackness of the sky.

The girl went on to say that she was a junior model with the Cutler Agency (the same agency that represented Augusta) and then asked whether he was a model himself, he was so good-looking, or just a mere photographer (she made photographers sound like child molesters), or did he work for one of the fashion magazines, or was he perhaps that lowest of the low, an agent? Kling told her he was a cop, and before she could ask to see his pistol (or anything else) promptly informed her that he was here with his wife. His wife, at the moment, was ooohing and aaahing over a spectacular swarm of golden fish that erupted overhead and swam erratically against the sky, dripping sparks as they fell toward the ocean. The girl, who seemed no older than eighteen or nineteen, and who had the largest blue eyes Kling had ever seen in his life, set in a pixie face with a somewhat lopsided chipmunk grin, asked Kling who his wife might be, and when he pointed her out and said, "Augusta Blair," the name she still used when modeling, the girl raised her eyebrows and said, "Don't shit me, man, Augusta's not married."

Well, Kling wasn't used to being told he wasn't married to Augusta, although at times he certainly felt that way. He explained, or *started* to explain, that he and Augusta had been married for—but the girl cut him off and said, "I see her all over town," and shrugged and gulped at her martini. She was just drunk enough to have missed the fact that Kling was a cop, which breed (especially of the detective variety) are prone to ask all sorts of pertinent questions, and further too drunk to realize that she didn't necessarily have to add, "with *guys*" after she'd swallowed the gin and vermouth, two words which—when coupled with her previous statement and forgiving the brief hiatus—came out altogether as "I see her all over town with guys."

Kling knew, of course, that Augusta went to quite a few cocktail parties without him, and he also knew that undoubtedly she *talked* to people at those parties, and that some of those people were possibly *men*. But the blonde's words seemed to imply something more than simple cocktail chatter, and he was about to ask her what she meant, exactly, when a waiter in black trousers and a white jacket came around with a refill, apparently having divined her need from across the wide expanse of the crowded deck. The blonde deftly lifted a fresh martini glass from the tray the waiter proffered, gulped down half its contents, and then—compounding the felony—said, "*One* guy especially."

"What do you mean, exactly?" Kling managed to say this time.

"Come on, what do I mean?" the blonde said, and winked at him.

"Tell me about it," Kling said. His heart was pounding in his chest.

"Go ask Augusta, you're so interested in Augusta," the blonde said.

"Are you saying she's been seeing some guy?"

"Who *cares*? Listen, would you like to go inside with me? Don't fireworks bore you to death? Let's go inside and find someplace, okay?"

"No, tell me about Augusta."

"Oh, *fuck* Augusta," the blonde said, and untangled her legs from under her bottom and got unsteadily to her feet, and then said, "And you, *too*," and tossed her hair and went staggering into the house through the French doors.

The last time he saw her that night, she was curled up, asleep in the master bedroom, her blouse open to the waist, both cherry-nippled breasts recklessly exposed. He was tempted to wake her and question her further about this "*one* guy especially," but his host walked into the room at that moment, and cleared his throat, and Kling had the distinct impression he was being suspected of rape or at least sexual molestation. The blonde later disappeared into the night, as suddenly as she had materialized. But before leaving the next day (Augusta stayed behind, as she had promised, or perhaps threatened) Kling asked some discreet questions and learned that her name was Monica Thorpe. On Monday morning he called the Cutler Agency, identified himself as Augusta's husband, said they wanted to invite Monica to a small dinner party, and got her unlisted number from them. When he called her at home, she said she didn't know who he was, and didn't remember saying anything about Augusta, who was anyway her dearest friend and one of the sweetest people on earth. She hung up before Kling could say another word. When he called back a moment later, she said, "Hey, knock it off, okay, man? I don't know what you're talking about," and hung up again.

"So that's it," Kling said.

"That's it, huh?" Carella said. "Are you telling me . . . ?"

"I'm telling you what happened."

"*Nothing* happened," Carella said. "Except some dumb blonde got drunk and filled your head with—"

"She said she saw Augusta all over town. With *guys*, Steve. With *one* guy *especially*, Steve."

"Uh-huh. And you believe her, huh?"

"I don't know *what* to believe."

"Have you talked to Augusta about it?"

"No."

"Why not?"

"What am I supposed to do? Ask her if there's some guy she's been seeing? Suppose she tells me there *is*? Then what? Shit, Steve . . ."

"If I were in a similar situation, I'd ask Teddy in a minute."

"And what if she said it was true?"

"We'd work it out."

"Sure."

"We would."

Kling was silent for several moments. His face was beaded with sweat, he appeared on the verge of tears. He took a handkerchief from his back pocket and dabbed at his forehead. He sucked in a deep breath, and said, "Steve . . . is it . . . is it still good between you and Teddy?"

"Yes."

"I mean—"

"I know what you mean."

"In bed, I mean."

"Yes, in bed. And everywhere else."

"Because . . . I, I don't think I'd have believed a word that blonde was saying if, if I, if I didn't already think something was wrong. Steve, we . . . these past few months . . . ever since June it must be . . . we . . . you know, it used to be we couldn't keep our hands off each other, I'd come home from work, she'd be all over me. But lately . . ." He shook his head, his voice trailed.

Carella said nothing. He stared through the windshield ahead, and then blew the horn at a pedestrian about to step off the curb against the light. Kling shook his head again. He took out his handkerchief again, and again dabbed at his brow with it.

"It's just that lately . . . well, for a long time now . . . there hasn't been anything between us. I mean, not like before. Not the way it used to be, when we, when we couldn't stand being apart for a minute. Now it's . . . when we make love, it's just so . . . so cut-and-dried, Steve. As if she's . . . *tolerating* me, you know what I mean? Just doing it to, to, to get it *over* with. Aw, shit, Steve," he said, and ducked his face into the handkerchief, both hands spread over it, and began sobbing.

"Come on," Carella said.

"I'm sorry."

"That's okay, come on."

"What an asshole," Kling said, sobbing into the handkerchief.

"You've got to talk to her about it," Carella said.

"Yeah." The handkerchief was still covering his face. He kept sobbing into it, his head turned away from Carella, his shoulders heaving.

"Will you do that?"

"Yeah."

"Bert? Will you talk to her?"

"Yeah. Yeah, I will."

"Come on, now."

"Yeah, okay," Kling said, and sniffed, and took the handkerchief from his face, and dried his eyes, and sniffed again, and said, "Thanks," and stared straight ahead through the windshield again.

She did not get home until almost eleven.

He was watching the news on television when she came into the apartment. She was wearing a pale green, silk chiffon jumpsuit, the flimsy top slashed low over her naked breasts, the color complementing the flaming autumn of her hair, swept to one side of her face to expose one ear dotted with an emerald earring that accentuated the jungle green of her eyes, a darker echo of her costume. As always, he caught his breath at the sheer beauty of her. He had been tongue-tied the first time he'd seen her in her burglarized apartment on Richardson Drive. She had just come back from a skiing trip to find the place ransacked; he had never been skiing in his life, he'd always thought of it as a sport for the very rich. He supposed they were very rich now. The only problem was that he never felt any of it was really his.

"Hi, sweetie," she said from the front door, and took her key from the lock, and then came to where he was sitting in front of the television set, a can of warm beer in his hand. She kissed him fleetingly on top of his head, and then said, "I have to pee, don't go away."

On the television screen, the newscaster was detailing the latest trouble in the Middle East. Sometimes Kling thought the Middle East had been invented by the government, the way the war in Orwell's novel had been invented by Big Brother. Without the Middle East to occupy their thoughts the people would have to worry about unemployment and inflation and crime in the streets and racial conflict and corruption in high places and tsetse flies. He sipped at his beer. He had eaten a TV dinner consisting of veal parmigiana with apple slices, peas in seasoned sauce, and a lemon muffin. He had also consumed three cans of beer; this was his fourth. The thawed meal had been lousy. He was a big man, and he was hungry again. He heard her flushing the toilet, and then heard the closet door in their bedroom sliding open. He waited.

When she came back into the living room, she was wearing a wraparound black nylon robe belted at the waist. Her hair fell loose around her face. She was barefoot. The television newscaster droned on.

"Are you watching that?" she asked.

"Sort of," he said.

"Why don't you turn it off?" she said, and, without waiting for his reply, went to the set and snapped the switch. The room went silent. "Another scorcher today, huh?" she said. "How'd it go for you?"

"So-so."

"What time did you get home?"

"Little after six."

"Did you forget the party at Bianca's?"

"We're working a complicated one."

"When *aren't* you working a complicated one?" Augusta asked, and smiled.

He watched as she sat on the carpet in front of the blank television screen, her legs extended, the flaps of the nylon robe thrown back, and began doing her situps, part of her nightly exercise routine. Her hands clasped behind her head, she raised her trunk and lowered it, raised it and lowered it.

"We had to go see this lady," Kling said.

"I told you this morning about the party."

"I know, but Steve wanted to hit her this afternoon."

"First twenty-four hours are the most important," Augusta said by rote.

"Well, that's true, in fact. How was the party?"

"Fine," Augusta said.

"She still living with that photographer, what's his name?"

"Andy Hastings. He's only the most important fashion photographer in America."

"I have trouble keeping them straight," Kling said.

"Andy's the one with the black hair and blue eyes."

"Who's the bald one?"

"Lamont."

"Yeah. With the earring in his left ear. Was he there?"

"*Everybody* was there. Except my husband."

"Well, I do have to earn a living."

"You didn't have to earn a living after four P.M. today."

"Man dies of an overdose of Seconal, you can't just let the case lay there for a week."

"First twenty-four hours are the most important, right," Augusta said again, and rolled her eyes.

"They are."

"So I've been told."

"You mind if I turn this on again?" he asked. "I want to see what the weather'll be tomorrow."

She did not answer. She rolled onto her side, and began lifting and lowering one leg, steadily, methodically. He put the beer can down, rose from where he was sitting in the leather easy chair, and snapped on the television set. As he turned to go back to his chair, the auburn hair covering her crotch winked for just an instant, and then her legs closed, and opened again, the flaming wink again, and closed again. He sat heavily in the leather chair and picked up the beer can. The female television forecaster was a brunette with the cutes. Smiling idiotically, bantering with the anchorman, she finally relayed the information that there was no relief in sight; the temperature tomorrow would hit a high of somewhere between ninety-eight and ninety-nine ("That's normal *body* temperature, isn't it?" the anchorman asked. "Ninety-eight point six?") with the humidity hovering at sixty-four percent, and the pollution index unsatisfactory.

"So what *else* is new?" Augusta said to the television screen, her leg moving up and down, up and down.

"Marty Trovaro is next with the sports," the anchorman said. "Stay tuned."

"Now we get what all the baseball teams did today," Augusta said. "Can't you turn that off, Bert?"

"I like baseball," he said. "Where'd you go after the party?"

"To a Chinese joint on Boone."

"Any good?"

"So-so."

"How many of you went?"

"About a dozen. Eleven, actually. *Your* chair was empty."

"On Boone, did you say?"

"Yes."

"In Chinatown?"

"Yes."

"All the way down there, huh?"

"Bianca lives in the Quarter, you know that."

"Oh, yeah, right."

The television sportscasters in America all had the same barber. Kling had thought the distinctive haircut was indigenous only to this part of the country, but he'd once gone down to Miami to pick up a guy on an extradition warrant, and the television sportscaster there had his hair cut the same way, as if someone had put a bowl over his head and trimmed all around it. He sometimes wondered if every sportscaster in America was bald and wearing a rug. Meyer Meyer had begun talking lately about buying a hairpiece. He tried to visualize Meyer with hair. He felt that hair would cost Meyer his credibility. Augusta was doing push-ups now. She did twenty-five of them every night. As the sportscaster read off the baseball scores, he watched her pushing against the carpet, watched the firm outline of her ass under the nylon robe, and unconsciously counted along with her. She stopped when he had counted only twenty-three; he must have missed a few. He got up and turned off the television set.

"Ah, blessed silence," Augusta said.

"What time did the party break up?" he asked.

Augusta got to her feet. "Would you like some coffee?" she asked.

"Keep me awake," he said.

"What time are you going in tomorrow?"

"It's my day off."

"Hallelujah," she said. "You sure you don't want any?"

"I'm sure."

"I think I'll have some," she said, and started for the kitchen.

"What time did you say?" he asked.

"What time what?" she said over her shoulder.

"The party."

She turned to him. "At Bianca's, do you mean?"

"Yeah."

"We left about seven-thirty."

"And went across to Chinatown, huh?"

"Yes," she said.

"By cab, or what?"

"Some of us went by cab, yes. I got a lift over."

"Who with?"

"The Santessons," she said, "you don't know them," and turned and walked out into the kitchen.

He heard her puttering around out there, taking the tin of coffee from the cabinet over the counter, and then opening one of the drawers, and moving the percolator from the stove to set it down noisily on the counter. He knew he would have to discuss it with her, knew he had to stop playing detective here, asking dumb questions about where she'd been and what time she got there and who she'd been with, had to ask her flat out, *discuss* the damn thing with her, the way he'd promised Carella he would. He told himself he'd do that the moment she came back into the room, ask her whether she was seeing somebody else, some other man. And maybe lose her, he thought. She went back into the bathroom again. He heard her opening and closing the door on the medicine cabinet. She was in there a long time. When finally she came out, she went into the kitchen and he heard her pouring the coffee. She came back into the living room then, holding a mug in her hand, and sat cross-legged on the carpet, and began sipping at the coffee.

He told himself he would ask her now.

He looked at her.

"What time did you leave the restaurant?" he asked.

"What *is* this?" she said suddenly.

"What do you mean?" he said. His heart had begun to flutter.

"I mean . . . what *is* this? What time did I leave *Bianca's*, what time did I leave the *restaurant*—what the hell *is* this?"

"I'm just curious."

"Just curious, huh? Is that some kind of occupational hazard? Curiosity? Curiosity killed the cat, Bert."

"Oh? Is that right? *Did* curiosity . . . ?"

"If you're so damn interested in what time I *got* someplace, then why don't you come *with* me next time, instead of running around the city looking for pills?"

"Pills?"

"You said Seconal, you said—"

"It was capsules."

"I don't give a damn *what* it was. I left Bianca's at seven twenty-two and fourteen seconds, okay? I entered a black Buick Regal bearing the license plate . . ."

"Okay, Augusta."

". . . double-oh-seven, a license to *kill*, Bert, owned and operated by one Philip Santesson, who is the art director at . . ."

"I said okay."

". . . Winston, Loeb and Fields, accompanied by his wife, June

Santesson, whereupon the suspect vehicle proceeded to Chinatown to join the rest of the party at a place called Ah Wong's. We ordered—"

"Cut it out, Gussie!"

"No, goddammit, *you* cut it out! I left that fucking restaurant at ten-thirty and I caught a cab on Aqueduct, and came straight home to my loving husband who's been putting me through a third-degree from the minute I walked through that door!" she shouted, pointing wildly at the front door. "Now, what the hell is it, Bert? If you've got something on your mind, let me know what it is! Otherwise, just shut up! I'm tired of playing cops and robbers "

"So am I."

"Then, what is it?"

"Nothing," he said.

"I *told* you about the party, I *told* you we were supposed to . . ."

"I know you—"

". . . be there at six, six-thirty."

"All right, I know."

"All right," she said, and sighed, her anger suddenly dissipating. "I'm sorry," he said.

"I wanted to make love," she said softly. "I came home wanting to make love."

"I'm sorry, honey."

"Instead . . ."

"I'm sorry." He hesitated. Then, cautiously, he said, "We can still make love."

"No," she said, "we can't."

"Wh—?"

"I just got my period."

He looked at her. And suddenly he knew she'd been lying about the party at Bianca's and the ride crosstown with the Santessons and the dinner at Ah Wong's and the cab she'd caught on Aqueduct, knew she'd been lying about all of it and putting up the same brave blustery front of a murderer caught with a smoking pistol in his fist.

"Okay," he said, "some other time," and went to the television set and snapped it on again.

Kling should have realized his marriage was doomed the moment he began tailing his wife.

Carella could have told him that in any marriage there was a line either partner simply could not safely cross. Once you stepped over that line, once you said or did something that couldn't possibly be taken back, the marriage was irretrievable. In any good marriage, there were arguments and even fights—but you fought fair if you wanted the marriage to survive. The minute you started hitting below the belt, it was time to call the divorce lawyers. That's why Carella had asked him to *discuss* this with Augusta.

Instead, Kling decided he would find out for himself whether she was seeing another man. He made his decision after a hot, sleepless night. He made it on the steamy morning of August 11, while he and Augusta were eating breakfast. He made it ten minutes before she left for her first assignment of the week.

He was a cop. Tailing a suspect came easily and naturally to him. Standing together at the curb outside their building, Augusta looking frantically at her watch, Kling trying to get a taxi at the height of the morning rush hour, he told her there was something he wanted to check at the office, and would probably be gone all day. Even though this was his day off, she accepted the lie; all too often in the past, he had gone back to the station house on his day off. He finally managed to hail a taxi, and when it pulled in to the curb, he yanked open the rear door for her.

"Where are you going, honey?" he asked.

"Ranger Photography, 1201 Goedkoop."

"Have you got that?" Kling asked the cabbie through the open window on the curb side.

"Got it," the cabbie said.

Augusta blew a kiss at Kling, and the taxi pulled away from the curb and into the stream of traffic heading downtown. It took Kling ten minutes to find another cab. He was in no hurry. He had checked Augusta's appointment calendar while she was bathing before bed last night, when he was still mulling his decision. It had showed two sittings for this morning: one at Ranger Photography for nine, the other at Coopersmith Creatives for eleven. Her next appointment was at two in the afternoon at Fashion Flair, and alongside this she had penned in the words "Cutler if time." Cutler was the agency representing her.

Goedkoop Avenue was in the oldest section of town, its narrow streets and gabled waterfront houses dating back to when the Dutch were still governing. The area lay cheek by jowl with the courthouses and municipal buildings in the Chinatown Precinct, but whereas the illusion was one of overlap, the business here was neither legal nor administrative. Goedkoop was in the heart of the financial district, an area of twentieth-century skyscrapers softened by the old Dutch warehouses and wharves, the later British churches and graveyards. Here and there in lofts along the narrow side streets, the artists and photographers had taken up residence, spilling over from the Quarter and the more recently voguish "Hopscotch" area, so called because the first gallery to open there was on Hopper Street, overlooking the Scotch Meadows Park. Standing across the street from 1201 Goedkoop, where he had asked the cabbie to let him out, Kling looked around for a pay phone, and then went into a cigar store on the corner of Goedkoop and Fields, where he looked up the phone number for Ranger Photography. From a phone booth near the magazine rack, he dialed the number and waited.

"Ranger," a man's voice said.

"May I speak to Augusta Blair, please?" he said. It rankled every time he had to use her maiden name, *however* damn professionally necessary it was.

"Minute," the man said.

Kling waited.

When she came onto the line, he said, "Gussie, hi, I'm sorry to break in this way."

"We haven't started yet," she said. "I just got here a few minutes ago. What is it, Bert?"

"I wanted to remind you, we're having dinner with Meyer and Sarah tonight."

"Yes, I know."

"Oh, okay, then."

"We talked about it at breakfast," she said. "Don't you remember?"

"Right, right. Okay, then. They're coming by at seven for drinks."

"Yes," she said, "I have it in my book. Where are you now, Bert?"

"Just got here," he said. "You want to try that new Italian joint on Trafalgar?"

"Yes, sure. Bert, I have to go. They're waving frantically."

"I'll make a reservation," he said. "Eight o'clock sound okay?"

"Yes, fine. 'Bye, darling, I'll talk to you later."

There was a click on the line. Okay, he thought, she's where she's supposed to be. He put the phone back on the hook, and then went out into the street again. It was blazing hot already, and his watch read only nine twenty-seven. He crossed the street to 1201 Goedkoop, and entered the building, checking to see if there was a side or a back entrance. Nothing. Just the big brass doors through which he'd entered, and through which Augusta would have to pass when she left. He looked at his watch again, and then went across the street to take up his position.

She did not come out of the building until a quarter to eleven.

He had hailed a taxi five minutes earlier, and flashed the tin, and had told the cabbie he was a policeman on assignment and would want him to follow a suspect vehicle in just a few minutes. That was when he was still allowing Augusta at least twenty minutes to get to her next sitting, crosstown and uptown. Her calendar had listed it for eleven sharp; she would be late, that was certain. The cabbie had thrown his flag five minutes ago; he now sat picking his teeth and reading the *Racing Form*. As Augusta came out of the building, another taxi pulled in some three feet ahead of her. She raised her arm, yelled "Taxi!" and then sprinted for the curb, her shoulder bag flying.

"There she is," Kling said. "Just getting in that cab across the street."

"Nice dish," the cabbie said.

"Yeah," Kling said.

"What'd she do?"

"Maybe nothing," Kling said.

"So what's all the hysteria?" the cabbie asked, and threw the taxi in gear and made a wide U-turn in an area posted with "No U-Turn" signs, figuring, What the hell, he had a cop in the backseat.

"Not too close now," Kling said. "Just don't lose her."

"You guys do this all the time?" the cabbie asked.

"Do what?"

"Ride taxis when you're chasing people?"

"Sometimes."

"So who pays for it?"

"We have a fund."

"Yeah, I'll just *bet* you have a fund. It's the *taxpayers* are footing the bill, that's who it is."

"Don't lose her, okay?" Kling said.

"I never lost nobody in my life," the cabbie said. "You think you're the first cop who ever jumped in my cab and told me to follow somebody? You know what I hate about cops who jump in my cab and tell me to follow somebody? What I hate is I get *stiffed*! They run out chasing the guy, and they forget to pay even the tab, never mind a tip."

"I won't stiff you, don't worry about it."

"Sure, it's only the taxpayers' money, right?"

"You'd better pick it up a little," Kling said.

The melodramatic chase (Kling could not help thinking of it as such) might have been more meaningful if Augusta's taxi hadn't taken her to 21 Lincoln Street, where Coopersmith Creatives had its studios—as he'd learned from the Isola directory the night before, while Augusta was still in the tub. Kling wanted nothing more than to prove his wife was innocent of any wrongdoing. Innocent till proved guilty, he reminded himself; the basic tenet of American criminal law. Beyond a resonable doubt, he reminded himself. But at the same time, something inside him longed perversely for a confrontation with her phantom lover. Had the taxi taken her anywhere else in the city, her elaborate lie would have been exposed. Write down an appointment at Coopersmith Creatives for 11:00 A.M., and then fly off to meet some tall, handsome bastard at his apartment in a more fashionable section of town. But no, here she was at 21 Lincoln Street, getting out of the taxi and handing a wad of bills through the open window, and then dashing across the sidewalk to a plate-glass door decorated with a pair of thick diagonal red and blue stripes, the huge numerals 21 worked into the slanting motif. He handed the cabbie the fare and a fifty-cent tip. The cabbie said, "Will wonders never?" and pocketed the money.

Kling walked past the building, and glanced through the plate-glass door. She was no longer in the small lobby. He yanked open the door and walked swiftly to the single elevator at the rear of the building. The needle of the floor indicator was still moving, 5, 6, 7—it stopped at 8. He found the directory for the building's tenants on the wall just inside the entrance door. Coopersmith Creatives was on the eighth floor. No need to call her again with a trumped-up story reminding her of a dinner date. She was exactly where she was supposed to be.

The sitting was a short one. She came out of the building again at a little past noon, and walked directly to a plastic pay-phone shell on the corner. Watching from a doorway across the street, he saw her fishing in her bag for a coin, and dialing a number. He wondered if she was calling the squadroom. He kept watching. She was on the phone for what seemed a long time. When finally she hung up, she did not immediately step out of the shell. Puzzled, he kept watching, and then realized she had run out of coins and had asked the person on the other end to call her back. He did not hear the telephone when it rang, the street traffic was too noisy. But he saw her snatch the receiver from the hook and immediately begin talking again. She talked even longer this time. He saw her nodding. She nodded again, and then hung up. She was smiling. He expected her to hail another taxi, but instead she began walking uptown, and it took him another moment to realize she was heading for the subway kiosk on the next corner. He thought, protectively, Jesus, Gussie, don't you know better than to ride the subways in this city? and then he quickened his pace and started down the steps after her, catching sight of her at the change booth. A train was pulling in. He flashed his shield at the attendant in the booth and pushed through the gate to the left of the stiles just as Augusta entered one of the cars.

Someone had once told Kling that one of America's celebrity novelists considered graffiti an art form. Maybe the celebrity novelist never had to ride the subways in this city. The graffiti covered the cars inside and out, obscuring the panels that told you where the train was headed and where it had come from, obfuscating the subway maps that told you where the various station stops were, obliterating the advertising placards, the windows, the walls, and even many of the seats. The graffiti spelled out the names of the spray-can authors (maybe *that's* why the celebrity novelist considered it an art form), the streets on which they lived, and sometimes the "clubs" to which they belonged. The graffiti were a reminder that the barbarians were waiting just outside the gates and that many of the barricades had already fallen and wild ponies were galloping in the streets. The graffiti were an insult and a warning: we do not *like* your city, it is *not* our city, we *shit* on your city. Trapped in a moving cage of violent steel walls shrieking color upon color, Kling stood at the far end of the car, his back to Augusta, and prayed she would not recognize him if she chanced to glance in his direction.

On a normal subway tail, there'd have been two of them, one in each of the cars flanking the suspect's car, standing close to the glass panels on the doors separating the cars, a classic bookend tail. In recent years, you couldn't *see* too easily through the glass panel because it had been spray-painted over, but the idea was to squint through the graffiti, and keep your eye on your man, one of you on either side of him, so that you were ready to move out when he came to his station stop. Today, and curiously, the spray paint worked *for* Kling. Facing the glass panel in the door at the end of the car, he noticed that it had been spray-painted only on the outside, with a dark blue paint that made through-visibility impossible but that served to create a mirror effect. Even with his back to Augusta, he could clearly see her reflection.

She had taken a seat facing the station stops, and she craned for a look through the spray-painted squiggles and scrawls each time the train slowed. He counted nine stops before she rose suddenly at the Hopper Street station and moved toward the opening doors. He stepped out onto the platform the instant she did. She turned left and began walking swiftly toward the exit steps, her high heels clicking; his wife was in a goddamn hurry. He followed at a safe distance behind her, reached the end of the platform, pushed through the gate, and saw her as she reached the top of the stairs leading to the street, her long legs flashing, the shoulder bag swinging.

He took the steps up two at a time. The sunlight was blinding after the gloom of the subterranean tunnel. He looked swiftly toward the corner, turned to look in the opposite direction, and saw her standing and waiting for the traffic light to change. He stayed right where he was, crossing the street when she did, keeping a block's distance between them. A sidewalk clock outside a savings and loan association told him it was already twelve-thirty. Augusta's next appointment was uptown, at two. He guessed she planned to skip lunch. He hoped against hope that he was wrong. He'd have given his right arm if only she walked into any one of the delicatessens or restaurants that lined the streets in this part of the city. But she continued walking, swiftly, not checking any of the addresses on the buildings, seeming to know exactly where she was going. The area was a mélange of art galleries, boutiques, shops selling antiques, drug paraphernalia, sandals, jewelry, and unpainted furniture. She was heading toward the Scotch Meadows Park in the heart of the Hopscotch artists' quarter. He's an artist, Kling thought. The son of a bitch is an artist.

He followed her for two blocks, to the corner of Hopper and Matthews. Then suddenly, without breaking her stride for an instant, without looking up at the numerals over the door—she was surely familiar with the address—she walked into one of the old buildings that had earlier been factories but which now housed tenants paying astronomical rents. He gave her a minute or two, checked out the hallway to make sure it was empty, and then entered the lobby. The walls were painted a dark green. There was no elevator in the building, only a set of iron-runged steps at the end of the lobby, reminiscent of the steps that climbed to the squadroom at the station house uptown. He listened, the way a good cop was taught to do, and heard the faint clatter of her heels somewhere on the iron rungs above. There was a directory of tenants in the lobby. He scanned it briefly, afraid Augusta might suddenly decide to reverse her direction and come down to discover him in the lobby.

He went outside again, and stood on the sidewalk. In addition to the street-level floor of the building, there were five floors above it. Four windows fronted the street on each of these upper stories, but he supposed most of the loft space was divided, and he couldn't even *guess* how many apartments there might be. He jotted the address into his notebook—641 Hopper Street—and then went into a luncheonette on the corner across the street, and sat eating a soggy hamburger and drinking a lukewarm egg cream while he watched the building. The clock on the grease-spattered wall read twelve-forty. He checked the time against his own watch.

It was one o'clock when he orderd another egg cream. It was one-thirty when he asked the counterman for an iced coffee. Augusta did not come out of the building until a quarter to two. She walked immediately to the curb and signaled to a cruising taxi. Kling finished his coffee, and then went into the building again and copied down all the names on the lobby directory. Six of them in all. Six suspects. There was no rush now; he suspected the damage had already been done. He took the subway uptown to Jefferson and Wyatt, where his wife had a two o'clock appointment at Fashion Flair. He waited outside on the sidewalk across the street from the building till she emerged at a little past five, and then followed her on foot crosstown to her agency on Carrington Street. He watched as she climbed the steps to the first floor of the narrow building.

Then he took the subway again, and went home.

The air conditioner was humming in the second-floor bedroom of the brownstone. The room was cool, but Kling could not sleep. It was two in the morning, and he wasn't due back at work till four this afternoon, but he'd hoped to get up early again in the morning, in time to leave the apartment when Augusta did. He wanted to see if she visited her pal on Hopper Street again. Wanted to see if visiting her pal was a regular lunch-hour thing with her, quick matinee every day of the week when she wasn't out screwing around instead of eating in a Chinese restaurant. He was tempted to confront her with it now, tell her he'd followed her to Hopper Street, tell her he'd seen her go into the building at 641 Hopper Street, ask her what possible business she could have had in that building. Get it over with here and now. He remembered what Carella had advised him.

"Augusta?" he whispered.

"Mm."

"Gussie?"

"Mm."

"You awake?"

"No," she said, and rolled over.

"Gussie, I want to talk to you."

"Go t'sleep," Augusta mumbled.

"Gussie?"

"Sleep," she said.

"Honey, this is important," he said.

"Shit."

"Honey . . ."

"Shit, shit, *shit*," she said, and sat up and snapped on the bedside lamp. "What is it?" she said, and looked at the clock on the table. "Bert, it's two o'*clock*, I have a sitting at eight-thirty, can't this wait?"

"I really feel I have to talk to you now," he said.

"I have to get up at *six*-thirty!" she said.

"I'm sorry," he said, "but, Gussie, this has really been bothering me."

"All right, what is it?" she said, and sighed. She took a pack of cigarettes from beside the clock, shook one free, and lighted it.

"I'm worried," he said.

"Worried? What do you mean?" she said.

"About us," he said.

"Us?"

"I think we're drifting apart."

"That's ridiculous," she said.

"I think we are."

"What makes you think so?"

"Well, we . . . for one thing, we don't make love as often as we used to."

"I've got my period," Augusta said. "You know that."

"I know that, but . . . well, that didn't used to matter in the past. When we were first married."

"Well," she said, and hesitated. "*I* thought we were doing fine."

"I don't think so," he said, shaking his head.

"Is it the sex, is that it? I mean, that you think we don't have enough sex?"

"That's only part of it," he said.

"Because if you, you know, if you'd like me to . . ."

"No, no."

"I thought we were doing fine," she said again, and shrugged, and stubbed out the cigarette.

"You know this girl who's with the agency?" he said. Here it is, he thought. Here we go.

"What girl?"

"Little blond girl. She models junior stuff."

"Monica?"

"Yeah."

"Monica Thorpe? What about her?"

"She was out there at the beach that night of the party. On the Fourth. Do you remember?"

"So?"

"We got to talking," Kling said.

"Uh-huh," Augusta said, and reached for the pack of cigarettes again. Lighting one, she said, "Must've been fascinating, talking to that nitwit."

"You smoke an awful lot, do you know that?" Kling said.

"Is that another complaint?" Augusta asked. "No sex, too much smoking, are we going to go through a whole *catalogue* at two in the morning?"

"Well, I'm only thinking of your health," Kling said.

"So what about Monica? What'd you talk about?"

"You."

"Me? Now, *there's* a switch, all right. I thought Monica never talked about anything but her own cute little adorable self. What'd she have to say? Does *she* think I smoke too much?"

"She said she's seen you around town with a lot of guys," Kling said in a rush, and then caught his breath.

"What?"

"She said—"

"Oh, that rotten little *bitch*!" Augusta said, and angrily stubbed out the cigarette she'd just lighted. "Seen me *around*, seen me—"

"One guy in particular," Kling said.

"Oh, *one* guy in particular, uh-huh."

"That's what she said."

"Which guy?"

"I don't know. You tell me, Gussie."

"This is ridiculous," Augusta said.

"I'm only repeating what she said."

"And you believed her."

"I . . . listened to her. Let's put it that way."

"But she couldn't tell you *which* guy, in *particular*, I'm supposed to have been seen around town with, is that it, Bert?"

"No. I asked her, but—"

"Oh, you *asked* her. So you *did* believe her, right?"

"I was listening, Gussie."

"To a juvenile delinquent who's only been laid by every photographer in the entire city, and who has the gall—"

"Calm down," he said.

"—to suggest that *I'm*—"

"Come on, Gussie."

"I'll kill that little bitch. I swear to God, I'll *kill* her!"

"Then it isn't true, right?"

"Right, it isn't true. Did you think it *was*?"

"I guess so."

"Thanks a lot," Augusta said.

They were silent for several moments. He was thinking he would have to ask her about 641 Hopper Street, about why she'd gone this afternoon to 641 Hopper Street. He was thinking he'd done what Carella had suggested he should do, but he still wasn't satisfied, he still didn't have the answers that would set his mind at ease. He had only opened the can of peas, and now he had to spill them all over the bed.

"Gussie . . ." he said.

"I love you, Bert," she said, "you know that."

"I thought you did."

"I do."

"But you keep going places without me . . ."

"That was *your* idea, Bert, you know it was. You *hate* those parties."

"Yeah, but still . . ."

"I won't go anywhere else without you, okay?"

"Well . . ."

What about during the day? he wondered. What about when I'm out chasing some cheap thief, what about then? What about when I have the night watch? What will you be doing *then*? he wondered. The parties don't mean a damn, he thought, except when you tell me you had dinner at a Chinese restaurant with a whole bunch of people, and Mr. Ah Wong himself tells me there was no redhead in Miss Mercier's party. You should have been a brunette, Gussie, they don't stand out as much in a crowd.

"I promise," she said. "No place else without you. Now lie down."

"There are still some things . . ."

"Lie down," she said. "On your back."

She pulled the sheet off of him.

"Just lie still," she said.

"Gussie . . ."

"Quiet."

"Honey . . ."

"Shh," she said. "Shh, baby. I'm gonna take care of you. Poor little neglected darling, Mama's gonna take good care of you," she said, and her mouth descended hungrily.

She came into the apartment at a little after midnight. He was sitting before the television set watching the beginning of an old movie.

"Hi," she said from the front door, and then took her key from the lock, and came into the living room, and kissed him on top of his head.

"How'd it go?" he asked.

"It was called off," she said.

"Oh?"

"Some trouble with the hospital. They didn't want us shooting outside. Said it would disturb the patients."

"So where'd you end up shooting?" Kling asked.

"We didn't. Had a big meeting instead. Up at Chelsea."

"Chelsea?"

"Chelsea TV, Inc. Would you like a sandwich or something? I'm famished," she said, and walked out to the kitchen.

He watched her as she went, kept watching her as she unwrapped a loaf of sliced bread at the kitchen counter. He could remember the first time they'd met, could remember all of it as if it were happening here and now, the call from Murchison on the desk downstairs, a Burglary Past at 657 Richardson Drive, Apartment 11D, see the lady. He had never seen a more beautiful woman in his life.

"Who are they?" he asked.

"What?" Augusta said from the kitchen.

"Chelsea TV."

"The ad firm shooting the commercial."

"Oh," he said. "So what was the meeting about?"

"Rewriting, rescheduling, picking a new location—the same old jazz." She licked the knife with which she'd been spreading peanut butter and said, "Mmm, you sure you don't want some of this?"

"They needed you for that, huh?"

"For what?"

"Rewriting, and rescheduling, and—"

"Well, Larry wants me for the spot."

"Larry?"

"Patterson. At Chelsea. He wrote the spot, and he's directing it."

"Oh, yeah, right."

"So we had to figure out my availability and all that."

He found himself staring at her as she came back into the living room, the sandwich in her hand, just the way he'd stared at her on their first date so long ago, couldn't stop staring at her. When finally she'd told him to stop it, he was forced to admit he'd never been out with a girl as beautiful as she was, and she simply said he'd have to get over it, he could still remember her exact words.

Well, you'll have to get over it. Because I think you're beautiful, too, and we'd have one hell of a relationship if all we did was sit around and stare at each other all the time. I mean, I expect we'll be seeing a lot of each other, and I'd like to think I'm permitted to sweat every now and then. I do sweat, you know.

Yes, Gussie, he thought, you do sweat, I know that now, and you belch and you fart, too, and I've seen you sitting on the toilet bowl, and once when you got drunk with all those flitty photographer friends of yours, I held your head while you vomited, and I put you to bed afterward and wiped up the bathroom floor, yes, Gussie, I *know* you sweat, I *know* you're human, but Jesus, Gussie, do you have to . . . do you have to *do* this to me, do you have to behave like . . . like a goddamn bitch in heat?

". . . thinking of going down to South America to do it," Augusta said.

"What?" Kling said.

"Larry. Shoot the spot down there. There's snow down there now. Forget the *symbolic* mountain, do it on a *real* mountain instead."

"What symbolic mountain?"

"Long General. Have you ever seen it? It looks like—"

"Yeah, a mountain."

"Well, you know what I mean."

"So you'll be going to South America, huh?"

"Just for a few days. If it works out."

"When?"

"Well, I don't know yet."

"When do you *think* it might be?"

"Pretty soon, I guess. While there's still snow. This is like their winter, you know."

"Yeah," Kling said. "Like when? This month sometime?"

"Probably."

"Did you tell him you'd go?"

"I don't get many shots at television, Bert. This is a full minute, the exposure'll mean a lot to me."

"Oh, sure, I know that."

"It'll just be for a few days."

"Who'll be going down there?" he asked.

"Just me, and Larry, and the crew."

"No other models?"

"He'll pick up his extras on the spot."

"I don't think I've met him," Kling said. "Have I met him?"

"Who?"

"Larry Patterson."

"No, I don't think so," Augusta said, and looked away. "You sure you don't want me to fix you something?"

"Nothing," Kling said. "Thanks."

He wanted to make sure he'd given her enough time to get here.

She had called him at the squadroom at nine o'clock, to say she was going to the movies after all, if he wouldn't mind, and would be catching the nine twenty-seven show, just around the corner, he didn't have to worry about her getting home safe, the avenue was well lighted. She had then gone on to reel off the name of the movie she'd be seeing, the novel upon which it was based, the stars who were in it, and had even quoted from a review she'd read on it. She had done her homework well.

It was now a little past ten.

The windows on the first floor of the Hopper Street building were lighted; Michael Lucas, the painter, was home. On the second floor, only the lights to the apartment shared by Martha and Michelle were on; Franny next door was apparently uptown with her Zooey. The lights on the third and fourth floors were out, as usual. Only one light burned on the fifth floor, at the northernmost end of Bradford Douglas's apartment—the bedroom light, Kling thought.

He waited.

In a little while, the light went out.

He crossed the street and rang the service bell. Henry Watkins, the superintendant he'd talked to this past Tuesday, opened the door when he identified himself.

"What's it now?" Watkins asked.

"Same old runaway," Kling said. "Have to ask a few more questions."

"Help yourself," Watkins said, and shrugged. "Let yourself out when you're finished, just pull the door shut hard behind you."

"Thanks," Kling said.

He waited until Watkins went back into his own ground-floor apartment, and then he started up the iron-runged steps. On the first floor, a stereo was blaring rock and roll music behind Lucas's closed door. On the second floor, he heard nothing as he passed the door to the apartment shared by the two women. He walked past the studio belonging to Peter Lang, the photographer on the third floor, and then took the steps up to the fourth floor. The light was still out in the hallway there. He picked his way through the dark again, and went up the stairs to the fifth floor.

His heart was pounding.

He stood outside the door to apartment 51 and listened.

Not a sound.

He took his gun from his shoulder holster. Holding it in his right hand, he backed away from the door, and then leveled a kick at the lock. The door sprang open, wood splinters flying. He moved into the room swiftly, slightly crouched, the gun fanning the air ahead of him, light filtering into the room from under a door at the end of the hall, to his left. He was moving toward the crack of light when the door flew open and Bradford Douglas came into the hall.

He was naked, and holding a baseball bat in his right hand. He stood silhouetted in the lighted rectangle of the doorway, hesitating there before taking a tentaive step into the gloom beyond.

"Police," Kling said, "hold it right there!"

"Wh—?"

"Don't move!" Kling said.

"What the hell? Who . . . ?"

Kling moved forward into the light spilling from the bedroom. Douglas recognized him at once, and the fear he'd earlier felt—when he'd thought a burglar had broken in—was replaced by immediate indignation. And then he saw the gun in Kling's hand, and a new fear washed over him, struggling with the indignation. The indignation triumphed. "What the hell do you mean, breaking down my door?" he shouted.

"I've got a warrant," Kling said. "Who's in that bedroom with you?"

"None of your business," Douglas said. He was still holding the bat in his right hand. "*What* warrant? What the hell *is* this?"

"Here," Kling said, and reached into his pocket. "Put down that bat."

Without turning, Douglas tossed the bat back into the bedroom. Kling waited while he read the warrant. The bedroom fronted Hopper Street, and there were no fire escapes on that side of the building. Unless Augusta decided to *jump* all the way down to the street below, there was no hurry. He looked past Douglas, into the bedroom. He could not see the bed from where he was standing, only a dresser, an easy chair, a floor lamp.

"Attempted murder?" Douglas said, reading from the warrant. "*What* attempted murder?" He kept reading. "I don't have this gun you describe, I don't have *any* gun. Who the hell said I—?"

"I haven't got all night here," Kling said, and held out his left hand. "The warrant gives me the right to search both you and the apartment. It's signed by—"

"No, just wait a goddamn *minute*," Douglas said, and kept reading. "Where'd you get this information? Who told you I've got this gun?"

"That doesn't matter, Mr. Douglas. Are you finished with that?"

"I *still* don't—"

"Let me have it. And let's take a look inside."

"I've got somebody with me," Douglas said.

"Who?"

"Your warrant doesn't give you the right to—"

"We'll worry about that later."

"No, we'll worry about it *now*," Douglas said.

"Look, you prick," Kling said, and brought the pistol up close to Douglas's face, "I want to search that bedroom, do you understand?"

"Don't get excited," Douglas said, backing away.

"I *am* excited," Kling said, "I'm *very* excited. Get out of my way."

He shoved Douglas aside and moved into the bedroom. The bed was against the wall at the far end of the room. The sheets were thrown back. The bed was empty.

"Where is she?" Kling said.

"Maybe the bathroom," Douglas said.

"Which door?"

"I thought you were looking for a gun."

"Which *door*?" Kling said tightly.

"Near the stereo there," Douglas said.

Kling went across the room. He tried the knob on the door there. The door was locked.

"Open up," he said.

From behind the door, he could hear a woman weeping.

"Open up, or I'll kick it in," he said.

The weeping continued. He heard the small oiled click of the lock being turned. He caught his breath and waited. The door opened.

She was not Augusta.

She was a small dark-haired girl with wet brown eyes, holding a bath towel to cover her nakedness.

"He's got a warrant, Felice," Douglas said behind him.

The girl kept weeping.

"Anybody else here?" Kling asked. He felt suddenly like a horse's ass.

"Nobody," Douglas said.

"I want to check the other rooms."

"Go ahead."

He went through the apartment, turning on lights ahead of him. He checked each room and every closet. There was no one else in the apartment. When he went back into the bedroom again, both Douglas and the girl had dressed. She sat on the edge of the bed, still weeping. Douglas stood beside her, trying to comfort her.

"When I was here Tuesday night, you told me you'd had a visitor the day before," Kling said. "Who was your visitor?"

"Where does it say in your warrant . . . ?"

"Mr. Douglas," Kling said, "I don't want to hear anymore bullshit about the warrant. All I want to know is who was here in this apartment between twelve-thirty and one forty-five last Monday."

"I . . . I'd feel funny telling you that."

"You'll feel a lot funnier if I have to ask a grand jury to subpoena you," Kling said. "Who was it?"

"A friend of mine."

"Male or female?"

"Male."

"What was he doing here?"

"I told him he could use the apartment."

"What for?"

"He's . . . there's a girl he's been seeing."

"Who?"

"I don't know her name."

"Have you ever met her?"

"No."

"Then you don't know what she looks like."

"Larry says she's gorgeous."

"Larry?"

"My friend."

"Larry *who*?" Kling said at once.

"Larry Patterson."

Kling nodded.

"He's married, so's the broad," Douglas said. "He needed a place to shack up, I've been lending him the pad here. I do a lot of work for him. He's one of the creative people at—"

"Chelsea TV," Kling said. "Thanks, Mr. Douglas, I'm sorry for the intrusion." He looked at the weeping girl. "I'm sorry, miss," he mumbled, and quickly left the apartment.

So now it was all over.

Face her down when she got home tonight after the "movie" she'd gone to see, tell her he knew she'd been with this man named Larry Patterson last Monday, enjoying a quick roll in the hay in a borrowed apartment, tell her he knew all about her and her little married playmate, had seen through the lie about the never-scheduled television commercial outside Long General, confront her with the indisputable fact that the man she'd be accompanying to South America was this man Larry Patterson, her lover, tell her, get it over with, end it. End it.

It was almost eleven-thirty when he got back to the apartment.

He inserted his key into the lock, and then opened the door. The apartment was dark, he reached for the switch just inside the door, and turned on the lights. He was bone-weary and suddenly very hungry. He was starting toward the kitchen when he heard the sound in the bedroom.

The sound was stealthy, the sound a burglar might make when suddenly surprised by an unexpected arrival home, nothing more than a whisper really, a rustle beyond the closed bedroom door; he reached for the shoulder holster and pulled his gun. The gun was a .38 Smith & Wesson Centennial Model with a two-inch barrel and a capacity of five shots. He knew this was not a burglar in there, this was Augusta in there, and he also knew that she was not alone, and hoped he was wrong, and his hand began sweating on the walnut grip of the pistol.

He almost turned and left the apartment. He almost holstered the gun, and turned his back on that closed bedroom door, on what was beyond that closed bedroom door, almost walked out of the apartment and out of their life as it had been together, once, too long ago, almost avoided the confrontation, and knew it could not be avoided, and became suddenly frightened. As he crossed the room to the bedroom door, the gun was trembling in his fist. There could have been a hatchet murderer beyond that door, the effect would have been much the same.

And then the fear of confrontation gave way to something alien and even more terrifying, a blind, unreasoning anger, the stranger here in his own home, the intruder in his bedroom, the lover, who was Larry Patterson, here with his wife, the trap sprung, she thought he would be working the night watch, she knew she would be safe till morning, there hadn't been a movie at all, there was only the movie here in this bedroom, *his* bedroom, an obscene pornographic movie behind that closed door.

He took the knob in his left hand, twisted it, and opened the door. And he hoped, in that final instant, that he would be wrong again, he would not find Augusta in this room, not find Augusta with her lover but instead find a small brown-eyed girl who went by the name of Felice or Agnes or Charity, a mistake somehow, a comedy of errors they would all laugh about in later years.

But of course it was Augusta.

And Augusta was naked in their bed, absurdly clutching the sheet to her breasts, hiding her shame, protecting her nakedness from the prying eyes of her own husband, her green eyes wide, her hair tousled, a fine sheen of perspiration on the marvelous cheekbones that were her fortune, her lip trembling the way the gun in his hand was trembling. And the man with Augusta was in his undershorts and reaching for his trousers folded over a bedside chair, the man was short and wiry, he looked like Genero, with curly black hair and brown eyes wide in terror, he looked just like Genero, absurdly like Genero, but he was Larry Patterson, he was Augusta's lover, and as he turned from the chair where his trousers were draped, he said only, "Don't shoot," and Kling leveled the gun at him.

He almost pulled the trigger. He almost allowed his anger and his humiliation and his despair to rocket into his brain and connect there with whatever nerve endings might have signaled to the index finger of his right hand, cause it to tighten on the trigger, cause him to squeeze off one shot and then another and another at this stranger who was in that moment a target as helpless as any of the cardboard ones on the firing range at the Academy—do it, *end* it!

But then—and this was against every principle that had ever been drilled into him throughout the years he'd spent on the force, never give up your gun, hang on to your gun, your gun is your life, save the gun, keep the gun—he suddenly hurled it across the room as though it had become malevolently burning in his hand, threw it with all his might, surprised when it collided with a vase on the dresser top, smashing it, porcelain shards splintering the air like debris of his own dead marriage.

His eyes met Augusta's.

Their eyes said everything there was to say, and all there was to say was nothing.

Heat, 1981

EILEEN BURKE

The girl's legs were crossed.

She sat opposite Willis and Byrnes in the lieutenant's office on the second floor of the 87th Precinct. They were good legs. The skirt reached to just a shade below her knees, and Willis could not help noticing they were good legs. Sleek and clean, full-calved, tapering to slender ankles, enhanced by the high-heeled black patent pumps.

The girl was a redhead, and that was good. Red hair is obvious hair. The girl had a pretty face, with a small Irish nose and green eyes. She listened to the men in serious silence, and you could feel intelligence on her face and in her eyes. Occasionally she sucked in a deep breath, and when she did, the severe cut of her suit did nothing to hide the sloping curve of her breast.

The girl earned $5,555 a year. The girl had a .38 in her purse.

The girl was a Detective 2nd/Grade, and her name was Eileen Burke, as Irish as her nose.

"You don't have to take this one if you don't want it, Miss Burke," Byrnes said.

"It sounds interesting," Eileen answered.

"Hal—Willis'll be following close behind all the way, you under-

265

stand. But that's no guarantee he can get to you in time should anything happen."

"I understand that, sir," Eileen said.

"And Clifford isn't such a gentleman," Willis said. "He's beaten, and he's killed. Or at least we think so. It might not be such a picnic."

"We don't think he's armed, but he used something on his last job, and it wasn't his fist. So you see, Miss Burke . . ."

"What we're trying to tell you," Willis said, "is that you needn't feel any compulsion to accept this assignment. We would understand completely were you to refuse it."

"Are you trying to talk me *into* this or *out* of it?" Eileen asked.

"We're simply asking you to make your own decision. We're sending you out as a sitting duck, and we feel—"

"I won't be such a sitting duck with a gun in my bag."

"Still, we felt we should present the facts to you before—"

"Will we be the only pair?" Eileen asked Willis.

"To start, yes. We're not sure how this'll work. I can't follow too close or Clifford'll panic. And I can't lag too far behind or I'll be worthless."

"Do you think he'll bite?"

"We don't know. He's been hitting in the precinct and getting away with it, so chances are he won't change his m.o.—unless this killing has scared him. And from what the victims have given us, he seems to hit without any plan. He just waits for a victim and then pounces."

"I see."

"So we figured an attractive girl walking the streets late at night, apparently alone, might smoke him out."

"I see." Ellen let the compliment pass. There were about four million attractive girls in the city, and she knew she was no prettier than most. "Has there been any sex motive?" she asked.

Willis glanced at Byrnes. "Not that we can figure. He hasn't molested any of his victims."

"I was only trying to figure what I should wear," Eileen said.

"Well, no hat," Willis said. "That's for sure. We want him to spot that red hair a mile away."

"All right," Eileen said.

"Something bright, so I won't lose you—but nothing too flashy," Willis said. "We don't want the Vice Squad picking you up."

Eileen smiled. "Sweater and skirt?" she asked.

"Whatever you'll be most comfortable in."

"I've got a white sweater," she said. "That should be clearly visible to both you and Clifford."

"Yes," Willis said.

"Heels or flats?"

"Entirely up to you. You may have to—well, he may give you a rough time. If heels will hamper you, wear flats."

"He can hear heels better," Eileen said.

"It's up to you."

"I'll wear heels."

"All right."

"Will anyone else be in on this? I mean, will you have a walkie-talkie or anything?"

"No," Willis said, "it'd be too obvious. There'll be just the two of us."

"And Clifford, we hope."

"Yes," Willis said.

Eileen Burke sighed. "When do we start?"

"Tonight?" Willis asked.

"I was going to get my hair done," Eileen said, smiling, "but I suppose that can wait." The smile broadened. "It isn't every girl who can be sure at least *one* man is following her."

"Can you meet me here?"

"What time?" Eileen asked.

"When the shift changes. Eleven forty-five?"

"I'll be here," she said. She uncrossed her legs and rose. "Lieutenant," she said, and Byrnes took her hand.

"Be careful, won't you?" Byrnes said.

"Yes, sir. Thank you." She turned to Willis. "I'll see you later."

"I'll be waiting for you."

"Good-bye, now," she said, and she left the office.

When she was gone, Willis asked, "What do you think?"

"I think she'll be okay," Byrnes said. "She's got a record of fourteen subway-masher arrests."

"Mashers aren't muggers," Willis said.

Byrnes nodded reflectively. "I think she'll be okay."

Willis smiled. "I think so, too," he said.

At two o'clock on the morning of Thursday, September 21, Eileen walked the streets of Isola in a white sweater and a tight skirt.

She was a tired cop.

She had been walking the streets of Isola since eleven forty-five the previous Saturday night. This was her fifth night of walking. She wore high-heeled pumps, and they had definitely not been designed for hikes. During the course of her early morning promenades, she had been approached seven times by sailors, four times by soldiers, and twenty-two times by civilians in various styles of male attire. The approaches had ranged from polite remarks such as, "Nice night, ain't it?" to more direct opening gambits like, "Walking all alone, honey?" to downright unmistakable business inquiries like, "How much, babe?"

All of these, Eileen had taken in stride.

They had, to be truthful, broken the monotony of her otherwise lonely and silent excursions. She had never once caught sight of Willis behind her, though she knew with certainty that he was there. She wondered now if he was as bored as she, and she concluded that he was possibly not. He did, after all, have the compensating sight of a backside which she jiggled jauntily for the benefit of any unseen, observant mugger.

Where are you, Clifford? she mentally asked.

Have we scared you off? Did the sight of the twisted and bloody young kid whose head you split open turn your stomach, Clifford? Have you decided to give up this business, or are you waiting until the heat's off?

Come on Clifford.

See the pretty wiggle? The bait is yours, Clifford. And the only hook is the .38 in my purse.

Come on, Clifford!

From where Willis jogged doggedly along behind Eileen, he could make out only the white sweater and occasionally a sudden burst of bright red when the lights caught at her hair.

He was a tired cop.

It had been a long time since he'd walked a beat, and this was worse than walking any beat in the city. When you had a beat, you also had bars and restaurants and sometimes tailor shops or candy stores. And in those places you could pick up, respectively, a quick beer, cup of coffee, snatch of idle conversation, or warmth from a hissing radiator.

This girl Eileen liked walking. He had followed behind her for four nights now, and this was the fifth, and she hadn't once stopped walking. This was an admirable attitude, to be sure, a devotion to duty which was not to be scoffed aside.

But good Christ, man, did she have a motor?

What propelled those legs of hers? (Good legs, Willis. Admit it.)

And why so fast? Did she think Clifford was a cross-country track star? He had spoken to her about her speed after their first night of breakneck pacing. She had smiled easily, fluffed her hair like a virgin at a freshman tea, and said, "I always walk fast."

That, he thought now, had been the understatement of the year. What she meant, of course, was "I always *run* slow."

He did not envy Clifford. Whoever he was, wherever he was, he would need a motorcycle to catch this redhead with the paperback-cover bazooms.

Well, he thought, she's making the game worth the candle.

Wherever you are, Clifford, Miss Burke's going to give you a run for your money.

* * *

He had first heard the tapping of her heels.

The impatient beaks of woodpeckers riveting at the stout mahogany heart of his city. Fluttering taps, light-footed, strong legs and quick feet.

He had then see the white sweater, a beacon in the distance, coming nearer and nearer, losing its two-dimensionality as it grew closer, expanding until it had the three-sidedness of a work of sculpture, then taking on reality, becoming woolen fiber covering firm high breasts.

He had seen the red hair then, long, lapped by the nervous fingers of the wind, enveloping her head like a blazing funeral pyre. He had stood in the alleyway across the street and watched her as she pranced by, cursing his station, wishing he had posted himself on the other side of the street instead. She carried a black patent-leather sling bag over her shoulder, the strap loose, the bag knocking against her left hipbone as she walked. The bag looked heavy.

He knew that looks could be deceiving, that many women carried all sorts of junk in their purses, but he smelled money in this one. She was either a whore drumming up trade or a society bitch out for a late evening stroll—it was sometimes difficult to tell them apart. Whichever she was, the purse promised money, and money was what he needed pretty badly right now.

The newspapers shrieking about Jeannie Paige, Jesus!

They had driven him clear off the streets. But how long can a murder remain hot? And doesn't a man have to eat?

He watched the redhead swing past, and then he ducked into the alleyway, quickly calculating a route which would intersect her apparent course.

There are three lampposts on each block, Eileen thought.

It takes approximately one and one-half minutes to cover the distance between lampposts. Four and a half minutes a block. That's plain arithmetic.

Nor is that exceptionally fast. If Willis thinks that's fast, he should meet my brother. My brother is the type of person who rushes through everything—breakfast, dinner . . .

Hold it now!

She was reaching for the .38 in her purse when the strap left her shoulder. She felt the secure weight of the purse leaving her hipbone, and then the bag was gone. And just as she planted her feet to throw the intruder over her shoulder, he spun her around and slammed her against the wall of the building.

"I'm not playing around," he said in a low, menacing voice, and she realized instantly that he wasn't. The collision with the wall of the building had knocked the breath out of her. She watched his face, dimly lighted in the alleyway. He was not wearing sunglasses, but she could not determine the color of his eyes. He was wearing a hat, too, and she cursed the hat because it hid his hair.

His fist lashed out suddenly, exploding just beneath her left eye. She had heard about purple and yellow globes of light which followed a punch in the eye, but she had never experienced them until this moment. She tried to move away from the wall, momentarily blinded, but he shoved her back viciously.

"That's just a warning," he said. "Don't scream when I'm gone, you understand?"

"I understand," she said levelly. *Willis, where are you?* her mind shrieked. *For God's sake, where are you?*

She had to detain this man. She had to hold him until Willis showed. Come on, Willis.

"Who are you?" she asked.

His hand went out again, and her head rocked from his strong slap.

"Shut up!" he warned. "I'm taking off now."

If this was Clifford, she had a chance. If this was Clifford, she would have to move in a few seconds, and she tensed herself for the move, knowing only that she had to hold the man until Willis arrived.

There!

He was going into it now.

"Clifford thanks you, madam," he said, and his arm swept across his waist, and he went into a low bow, and Eileen clasped both hands together, raised them high over head, and swung them at the back of his neck as if she were wielding a hammer.

The blow caught him completely by surprise. He began to pitch forward, and she brought up her knee, catching him under the jaw. His arms opened wide. He dropped the purse and staggered backward, and when he lifted his head again, Eileen was standing with a spike-heeled shoe in one hand. She didn't wait for his attack. With one foot shoeless, she hobbled forward and swung out at his head.

He backed away, missing her swing, and then he bellowed like a wounded bear, and cut loose with a roundhouse blow that caught her just below her bosom. She felt the sharp knifing pain, and then he was hitting her again, hitting her cruelly and viciously now. She dropped the shoe, and she caught at his clothes, one hand going to his face, trying to rip, trying to claw, forgetting all her police knowledge in that one desperate lunge for self-survival, using a woman's weapons—nails.

She missed his face, and she stumbled forward, catching at his jacket again, clawing at the breast pocket. He pulled away, and she felt the material tear, and then she was holding the torn shield of his pocket patch in her hands, and he hit her again, full on the jaw, and she fell back against the wall and heard Willis's running footsteps.

The mugger stooped down for the fallen purse, seizing it by the shoulder straps as Willis burst into the alley, a gun in his fist.

Clifford came erect, swinging the bag as he stood. The bag caught Willis on the side of the head, and he staggered sideward, the gun going off in his hand. He shook his head, saw the mugger taking flight, shot without aiming, shot again, missing both times. Clifford turned the corner, and Willis took off after him, rounding the same bend.

The mugger was nowhere in sight.

He went back to where Eileen sat propped against the wall of the building. Her knees were up, and her skirt was pulled back, and she sat in a very unladylike position, cradling her head. Her left eye was beginning to throb painfully. When she lifted her head, Willis winced.

"He clipped you," he said.

"Where the hell were you?" Eileen answered.

The Mugger, 1956

T he black lunch pail containing approximately fifty thousand scraps of newspaper was placed in the center of the third bench on the Clinton Street footpath into Grover Park by Detective Cotton Hawes, who was wearing thermal underwear and two sweaters and a business suit and an overcoat and earmuffs. Hawes was an expert skier, and he had skied on days when the temperature at the base was four below zero and the temperature at the summit was thirty below, had skied on days when his feet went and his hands went and he boomed the mountain nonstop not for fun or sport but just to get near the fire in the base lodge before he shattered into a hundred brittle pieces. But he had never been this cold before. It was bad enough to be working on Saturday, but it was indecent to be working when the weather threatened to gelatinize a man's blood.

Among the other people who were braving the unseasonable winds and temperatures that Saturday were:

(1) A pretzel salesman at the entrance to the Clinton Street footpath.
(2) Two nuns saying their beads on the second bench into the park.
(3) A passionate couple necking in a sleeping bag on the grass behind the third bench.
(4) A blind man sitting on the fourth bench, patting his Seeing Eye German shepherd and scattering bread crumbs to the pigeons.

The pretzel salesman was a detective named Stanley Faulk, recruited from the 88th across the park, a man of fifty-eight who wore a gray handlebar mustache as his trademark. The mustache made it quite simple to identify him when he was working in his own territory, thereby diminishing his value on plants. But it also served to strike terror into the hearts of hoods near and wide, in much the same way that the green and white color combination of a radio motor patrol car is supposed to frighten criminals and serve as a deterrent. Faulk wasn't too happy about being called into service for the 87th on a day like this one, but he was bundled up warmly in several sweaters over which was a black cardigan-type candy-store-owner sweater over which he had put on a white apron. He was standing behind a cart that displayed pretzels stacked on long round sticks. A walkie-talkie was set into the top of the cart.

The two nuns saying their beads were Detectives Meyer Meyer and Bert Kling, and they were really saying what a son of a bitch Byrnes had been to bawl them out that way in front of Hawes and Willis, embarrassing them and making them feel very foolish."

"I feel very foolish right now," Meyer whispered.

"How come?" Kling whispered.

"I feel like I'm in drag," Meyer whispered.

The "passionate couple" assignment had been the choice assignment, and Hawes and Willis had drawn straws for it. The reason it was so choice was that the other half of the passionate couple was herself quite choice, a policewoman named Eileen Burke, with whom Willis had worked on a mugging case many years back.

"We're supposed to be kissing," he said, and held her close in the warm sleeping bag.

"My lips are getting chapped," she said.

"Your lips are very nice," he said.

"We're supposed to be here on business," Eileen said.

"Mmm," he answered.

"Get your hand off my behind," she said.

"Oh, is that your behind?" he asked.

"Listen," she said.

"I hear it," he said. "Somebody's coming. You'd better kiss me."

She kissed him. Willis kept one eye on the bench. The person passing was a governess wheeling a baby carriage. God knew who would send an infant out on a day when the glacier was moving south. The woman and the carriage passed. Willis kept kissing Detective 2nd/Grade Eileen Burke.

"Mm frick sheb bron," Eileen mumbled.

"Mmm?" Willis mumbled.

Eileen pulled her mouth away and caught her breath. "I *said* I think she's gone."

"What's that?" Willis asked suddenly.

"Do not be afraid, *guapa*, it is only my pistol," Eileen said, and laughed.

"I meant on the path. Listen."

They listened.

Someone else was approaching the bench.

From where Patrolman Richard Genero sat in plain clothes on the fourth bench, wearing dark glasses and patting the head of the German shepherd at his feet, tossing crumbs to the pigeons, wishing for summer, he could clearly see the young man who walked rapidly to the third bench, picked up the lunch pail, looked swiftly over his shoulder, and began walking not *out* of the park, but *into* it.

Genero didn't know quite what to do at first.

He had been pressed into duty only because there was a shortage of available men that afternoon (crime prevention being an arduous and difficult task on any given day, but especially on Saturday), and he had been placed in the position thought least vulnerable, it being assumed the man who picked up the lunch pail would immediately reverse direction and head out of the park again, onto Grover Avenue, where Faulk the pretzel man and Hawes, parked in his own car at the curb, would immediately collar him. But the suspect was coming into the park instead, heading for Genero's bench, and Genero was a fellow who didn't care very much for violence, so he sat there wishing he was home in bed, with his mother serving him hot minestrone and singing old Italian arias.

The dog at his feet had been trained for police work, and Genero had been taught a few hand signals and voice signals in the squadroom before heading out for his vigil on the fourth bench, but he was also afraid of dogs, especially big dogs, and the idea of giving this animal a kill command that might possibly be misunderstood filled Genero with fear and trembling. Suppose he gave the command and the dog leaped for his *own* jugular rather than for the throat of the young man who was perhaps three feet away now and walking quite rapidly, glancing over his shoulder every now and again? Suppose he did that and this beast tore him to shreds, what would his mother say to that? *Che bella cosa*, you hadda to become a police, hah?

Willis, in the meantime, had slid his walkie-talkie up between Eileen's breasts and flashed the news to Hawes, parked in his own car on Grover Avenue, good place to be when your man is going the other way. Willis was now desperately trying to lower the zipper on the bag, which zipper seemed to have become somehow stuck. Willis didn't mind being stuck in a sleeping bag with someone like Eileen Burke, who wiggled and wriggled along with him as they attempted to extricate themselves, but he suddenly fantasized the lieutenant chewing him out the way he had chewed out Kling and Meyer this morning and so he really *was* trying to lower that damn zipper while entertaining the further fantasy that Eileen Burke was beginning to enjoy all this adolescent tumbling. Genero, of course, didn't know that Hawes had been alerted, he only knew that the suspect was abreast of him now, and passing the bench now, and moving swiftly beyond the bench now, so he got up and first took off the sunglasses, and then unbuttoned the third button of his coat the way he had seen detectives do on television, and then reached in for his revolver and then shot himself in the leg.

The suspect began running.

Genero fell to the ground and the dog licked his face.

Willis got out of the sleeping bag and Eileen Burke buttoned her blouse and her coat and then adjusted her garters, and Hawes came running into the park and slipped on a patch of ice near the third bench and almost broke his neck.

"Stop, police!" Willis shouted.

And, miracle of miracles, the suspect stopped dead in his tracks and waited for Willis to approach him with his gun in his hand and lipstick all over his face.

Fuzz, 1968

"Who raped who *this* time?" Eileen asked.

"Don't talk dirty in my squadroom," Meyer said, and winked at Willis.

"Where do you want to discuss this?" Willis asked Eileen.

"Oh, the old 'Your place or mine?' ploy," Meyer said. "Is this the laundromat case?"

"It's the laundromat case," Willis said.

"A rapist in a *laundromat*?" Eileen asked, and stubbed our her cigarette.

"No, a guy who's been holding up laundromats late at night. We figured we'd plant you in the one he's gonna hit next—"

"How do you know which one he'll hit next?" Eileen asked.

"Well, we're guessing," Willis said. "But there's sort of a pattern."

"Oh, the old modus operandi ploy," Meyer said, and actually burst out laughing. Willis looked at him. Meyer shrugged and stopped laughing.

"Dress you up like a lady with dirty laundry," Willis said.

"Sounds good to me," Eileen said. "You're the backup, huh?"

"I'm the backup."

"Where will *you* be?"

"In a sleeping bag outside," Willis said, and grinned.

"Sure," she said, and grinned back.

"Remember?" he said.

"Memory like a judge," she said.

"When do we start?" Ellen asked, and lit another cigarette.

"Tonight?" Willis said.

The laundromat was on the corner of Culver and Tenth, a neighborhood enclave that for many years had been exclusively Irish but that nowadays was a rich melting-pot mixture of Irish, black, and Puerto Rican. The melting pot here, as elsewhere in this city, never seemed to come to a precise boil, but that didn't bother any of the residents; they all knew it was nonsense, anyway. Even though they all shopped the same supermarkets and clothing stores; even though they all bought gasoline at the same gas stations and rode the same subways; even though they washed their clothes at the same laundromats and ate hamburgers side by side in the same greasy spoons, they all knew that when it came to socializing it was the Irish with the Irish and the blacks with the blacks and the Puerto Ricans with the Puerto Ricans and never mind that brotherhood-of-man stuff.

Eileen, what with her peaches-and-cream complexion and her red hair and green eyes, could have passed for any daughter of Hibernian descent in the neighborhood—which, of course, was exactly what they were hoping for. It would not do to have the Dirty Panties Bandit, as the boys of the Eight-Seven had wittily taken to calling him, pop into the laundromat with his .357 Magnum in his fist, spot Eileen for a policewoman, and put a hole the size of a bowling ball in her ample chest. No, no. Eileen did not want to become a dead heroine. Eileen wanted to become the first lady Chief of Detectives in this city, but not over her own dead body. For the job tonight, she was dressed rather more sedately than she would have been if she'd been on the street trying to flush a rapist. Her red hair was pulled to the back of her head, held there with a rubber band, and covered with a dun-colored scarf knotted under her chin and hiding the pair of gold loop earrings she considered her good-luck charms. She was wearing a cloth coat that matched the scarf, and knee-length brown socks and brown rubber boots, and she was sitting on a yellow plastic chair in the very cold laundromat, watching her dirty laundry (or rather the dirty laundry supplied by the Eight-Seven) turn over and over in one of the washing machines while the neon sign in the window of the place flashed "Laundromat" first in orange, and then "Lavandería" in green.

In the open handbag on her lap, the butt of a .38 Detective's Special beckoned from behind a wad of Kleenex tissues.

The manager of the place did not know Eileen was a cop. The manager of the place was the night man, who came on at four and worked through till midnight, at which time he locked up the place and went home. Every morning, the owner of the laundromat would come around to unlock the machines, pour all the coins into a big gray sack, and take them to the bank. That was the owner's job: emptying the machines of coins. The owner had thirty-seven laundromats all over the city, and he lived in a very good section of Majesta. He did not empty the machines at closing time because he thought that might be dangerous, which in fact it would have been. He preferred that his thirty-seven night men all over the city simply lock the doors, turn on the burglar alarms, and go home. That was part of their job, the night men. The rest of their job was to make change for the ladies who brought in their dirty clothes, and to call for service if any of the machines broke down, and also to make sure nobody stole any of the cheap plastic furniture in the various laundromats, although the owner didn't care much about that since he'd got a break on the stuff from his brother-in-law. Every now and then it occurred to the owner that his thirty-seven night men each had keys to the thirty-seven separate burglar alarms in the thirty-seven different locations and if they decided to go into cahoots with one of the crazies in this city, they could open the stores and break open the machines—but so what? Easy come, easy go. Besides, he liked to think all of his night men were pure and innocent.

Detective Hal Willis knew for damn sure that the night man at the laundromat on Tenth and Culver was as pure and as innocent as the driven snow so far as the true identity of Eileen Burke was concerned. The night man did not know she was a cop, nor did he know that Willis himself, angle-parked in an unmarked green Toronado in front of the bar next door to the laundromat, was *also* a cop. In fact, the night man did not have the faintest inkling that the Eight-Seven had chosen his nice little establishment for a stakeout on the assumption that the Dirty Panties Bandit would hit it next. The assumption seemed a good educated guess. The man had been working his way straight down Culver Avenue for the past three weeks, hitting laundromats on alternate sides of the avenue, inexorably moving farther and farther downtown. The place he'd hit three nights ago had been on the south side of the avenue. The laundromat they were staking out tonight was eight blocks farther downtown, on the north side of the avenue.

The Dirty Panties Bandit was no small-time thief, oh, no. In the two months during which he'd operated unchecked along Culver Avenue, first in the bordering precinct farther uptown, and then moving lower

into the Eight-Seven's territory, he had netted—or so the police had
estimated from what the victimized women had told them—six
hundred dollars in cash, twelve gold wedding bands, four gold lockets,
a gold engagement ring with a one-carat diamond, and a total of
twenty-two pairs of panties. These panties had not been lifted from
the victims' laundry baskets. Instead, the Dirty Panties Bandit—and
hence his name—had asked all those hapless laundromat ladies to
please remove their panties for him, which they had all readily agreed
to do since they were looking into the rather large barrel of a .357
Magnum. No one had been raped—yet. No one had been harmed—yet.
And whereas there was something darkly humorous, after all, about
an armed robber taking home his victims' panties, there was nothing
at all humorous about the potential of a .357 Magnum. Sitting in the
parked car outside the bar, Willis was very much aware of the caliber
of the gun the laundromat robber carried. Sitting inside the laundromat, flanked by a Puerto Rican woman on her left and a black
woman on her right, Eileen was even more aware of the devastating
power of that gun.

She looked up at the wall clock.

It was only ten-fifteen, and the place wouldn't be closing till
midnight.

She was having a splendid time watching her laundry go round and
round. The night man thought she was a little crazy, but then again
everybody in this town was a little crazy. She had put the same batch
of laundry through the machine five times already. Each time, she sat
watching the laundry spinning in the machine. The night man didn't
notice that she alternately watched the front door of the place or
looked through the plate-glass window each time a car pulled in. The
neon fixture splashed orange and green on the floor of the laundromat:
Lavendería . . . Laundromat . . . Lavendería . . . Laundromat.
The laundry in the machines went round and round.

A woman with a baby strapped to her back was at one of the
machines, putting in another load. Eileen guessed she was no older
than nineteen or twenty, a slender attractive blue-eyed blond who
directed a nonstop flow of soft chatter over her shoulder to her near-
dozing infant. Another woman was sitting on the yellow plastic chair
next to Eileen's, reading a magazine. She was a stout black woman, in
her late thirties or early forties, Eileen guessed, wearing a bulky knit
sweater over blue jeans and galoshes. Every now and then, she flipped
a page of the magazine, looked up at the washing machines, and then
flipped another page. A third woman came into the store, looked
around frantically for a moment, seemed relieved to discover there
were plenty of free machines, dashed out of the store, and returned a
moment later with what appeared to be the week's laundry for an

entire Russian regiment. She asked the manager to change a five-dollar bill for her. He changed it from a coin dispenser attached to his belt, thumbing and clicking out the coins like a streetcar conductor. Eileen watched as he walked to a safe bolted to the floor and dropped the bill into a slot on its top, just as though he were making a night deposit at a bank. A sign on the wall advised any prospective holdup man: "Manager does not have combination to safe. Manager cannot change bills larger than five dollars." Idly, Eileen wondered what the manager did when he ran out of coins. Did he run into the bar next door to ask the bartender for change? Did the bartender next door have a little coin dispenser attached to *his* belt? Idly, Eileen wondered why she wondered such things. And then she wondered if she'd ever meet a man who wondered the same things she wondered. That was when the Dirty Panties Bandit came into the store.

Eileen recognized him at once from the police-artist composites Willis had shown her back at the squadroom. He was a short slender white man wearing a navy pea coat and watch cap over dark brown, wide-wale corduroy trousers and tan suede desert boots. He had darting brown eyes and a very thin nose with a narrow mustache under it. There was a scar in his right eyebrow. The bell over the door tinkled as he came into the store. As he reached behind him with his left hand to close the door, Eileen's hand went into the bag on her lap. She was closing her fingers around the butt of the .38 when the man's right hand came out of his coat pocket. The Magnum would have looked enormous in any event. But because the man was so small and so thin, it looked like an artillery piece. The man's hand was shaking. The gun in it flailed the room.

Eileen looked at the Magnum, looked at the man's eyes, and felt the butt of her own pistol under her closing fingers. If she pulled the gun out now, she had maybe a thirty/seventy chance of bringing him down before he sprayed the room with bullets that could tear a man's head off his body. In addition to herself and the robber, there were five other people in the store, three of them women, one of them an infant. Her hand froze motionless around the butt of the gun.

"All right, all right," the man said in a thin, almost girlish voice, "nobody moves, nobody gets hurt." His eyes darted. His hand was still shaking. Suddenly, he giggled. The giggle scared Eileen more than the gun in his hand did. The giggle was high and nervous and just enough off center to send a shiver racing up her spine. Her hand on the butt of the .38 suddenly began sweating.

"All I want is your money, all your money," the man said. "And your—"

"I don't have the combination to the safe," the manager said.

"Who asked *you* for anything?" the man said, turning to him. "You just shut up, you hear me?"

"Yes, sir," the manager said.

"You hear me?"

"Yes, sir."

"I'm talking to the ladies here, not you, you hear me?"

"Yes, sir."

"So shut up."

"Yes, sir."

"You!" the man said, and turned to the woman with the baby strapped to her back, jerking the gun at her, moving erratically, almost dancing across the floor of the laundromat, turning this way and that as though playing to an audience from a stage. Each time he turned, the woman with the baby on her back turned with him, so that she was always facing him, her body forming a barricade between him and the baby. She doesn't know, Eileen thought, that a slug from that gun can go clear through her *and* the baby *and* the wall behind them, too.

"Your money!" the man said. "Hurry up! Your rings, too, give me your rings!"

"Just don't shoot," the woman said.

"Shut up! Give me your panties!"

"What?"

"Your panties, take off your panties, give them to me!"

The woman stared at him.

"Are you deaf?" he said, and danced toward her, and jabbed the gun at her. The woman already had a wad of dollar bills clutched in one fist and her wedding ring and engagement ring in the other, and she stood there uncertainly, knowing she had heard him say he wanted her panties, but not knowing whether he wanted her to give him the money and the jewelry *first* or—

"Hurry up!" he said. "Take them off! Hurry up!"

The woman quickly handed him the bills and rings and then reached up under her skirt and lowered her panties over her thighs and down to her ankles. She stepped out of them, picked them up, handed them to him, and quickly backed away from him as he stuffed them into his pocket.

"All of you!" he said, his voice higher now. "I want all of you to take off your panties. Give me your money! Give me all your money! And your rings! And your panties, take them off, hurry up!"

The black woman sitting on the chair alongside Eileen kept staring at the man as though he had popped out of a bottle, following his every move around the room, her eyes wide, disbelieving his demands, disbelieving the gun in his hand, disbelieving his very existence. She just kept staring at him and shaking her head in disbelief.

"You!" he said, dancing over to her. "Give me that necklace! Hurry up!"

"Ain't but costume jewelry," the woman said calmly.

"Give me your money!"

"Ain't got but a dollar an' a quarter in change," the woman said.

"Give it to me!" he said, and held out his left hand.

The woman rummaged in her handbag. She took out a change purse. Ignoring the man, ignoring the gun not a foot from her nose, she unsnapped the purse, and reached into it, and took out coin after coin, transferring the coins from her right hand to the palm of her left hand, three quarters and five dimes, and then closing her fist on the coins, and bringing her fist to his open palm, and opening the fist and letting the coins fall (disdainfully, it seemed to Eileen) onto his palm.

"Now your panties," he said.

"Nossir."

"Take off your panties," he said.

"Won't do no such thing," the woman said.

"What?"

"Won't do no such thing. Ain't just a matter of reachin' up under m'skirt way that lady with the baby did, nossir. I'd have to take off fust m'galoshes and then m'jeans, an' there ain't no way I plan to stan' here naked in front of two men I never seen in my life, nossir."

The man waved the gun.

"Do what I tell you," he said

"Nossir," the woman said.

Eileen tensed.

She wondered if she should make her move now, a bad situation could only get worse, she'd been taught that at the Academy and it was a rule she'd lived by and survived by all the years she'd been on the force, but a rule she'd somehow neglected tonight when this silly little son of a bitch walked through the door and pulled the cannon from his pocket, a bad situation can only get worse, make your move now, do it now, go for the money, go for broke, but now, *now*! And she wondered, too, if he would bother turning to fire at *her* once she pulled the gun from her handbag or would he instead fire at the black woman who was willing to risk getting shot and maybe killed rather than take off her jeans and then her panties in a room containing a trembling night man and an armed robber who maybe was or maybe wasn't bonkers, make your move, stop thinking, stop wondering—but what if the baby gets shot?

It occurred to her that maybe the black woman would actually succeed in staring down the little man with the penchant for panties, get him to turn away in defeat, run for the door, out into the cold and into the waiting arms of Detective Hal Willis—which reminds me, where the hell *are* you, Willis? It would not hurt to have my backup come in *behind* this guy right now, it would not hurt to have his attention diverted from me to you, two guns against one, the good guys against the bad guys, where the hell *are* you? The little man was trembling violently now, the struggle inside him so intense that it seemed he would rattle himself to pieces, crumble into a pile of broken pink chalk around a huge weapon—he's a closet rapist, she thought suddenly, the man's a closet rapist!

The thought was blinding in its clarity. She knew now, or felt she knew, why he was running around town holding up laundromats. He was holding up laundromats because there were *women* in laundromats and he wanted to see those women taking off their panties. The holdups had nothing at all to do with money or jewelry, the man was after *panties!* The rings and the bracelets and the cash were all his cover, his beard, his smoke screen, the man wanted ladies' panties, the man wanted the aroma of women on his loot, the man probably had a garageful of panties wherever he lived, the man was a closet rapist and she knew how to deal with rapists, she had certainly dealt with enough rapists in her lifetime, but that was her alone in a park, that was when the only life at stake had been her own, make your move, she thought, make it *now!*

"You!" she said sharply.

The man turned toward her. The gun turned at the same time.

"Take mine," she said.

"What?" he said.

"Leave her alone. Take *my* panties."

"What?"

"Reach under my skirt," she whispered. "Rip off my panties."

She thought for a terrifying moment that she'd made a costly mistake. His face contorted in what appeared to be rage, and the gun began shaking even more violently in his fist. Oh God, she thought, I've forced him out of the closet, I've forced him to see himself for what he is, that gun is his cock as sure as I'm sitting here, and he's going to jerk it off into my face in the next ten seconds! And then a strange thing happened to his face, a strange smile replaced the anger, a strange secret smile touched the corners of his mouth, a secret communication flashed in his eyes, his eyes to her eyes, *their* secret, a secret to share, he lowered the gun, he moved toward her.

"Police!" she shouted, and the .38 came up out of the bag in the same instant that she came up off the plastic chair, and she rammed the muzzle of the gun into the hollow of his throat and said so quietly that only he could hear it, "Don't even *think* it or I'll shoot you dead!" And she would remember later and remember always the way the shouted word "Police!" had shattered the secret in his eyes, their shared secret, and she would always wonder if the way she'd disarmed him hadn't been particularly cruel and unjust.

She clamped the handcuffs onto his wrists and then stooped to pick up the Magnum from where he'd dropped it on the laundromat floor.

Willis was trying to explain why he hadn't happened to notice the Dirty Panties Bandit when he entered the laundromat. They had sent down for pizza, and now they sat in the relative 1:00 A.M. silence of the squadroom, eating Papa Joe's really pretty good combination anchovies and pepperoni and drinking Miscolo's really pretty lousy Colombian coffee; Detective Bert Kling was sitting with them, but he wasn't eating or saying very much.

Eileen remembered him as a man with a huge appetite, and she wondered now if he was on a diet. He looked thinner than she recalled—well, that had been several years back—and he also looked somewhat drawn and pale and, well, unkempt. His straight blond hair was growing raggedly over his shirt collar and ears, and the collar itself looked a bit frayed, and his suit looked unpressed, and there were stains on the tie he was wearing. Eileen figured he was maybe coming in off a stakeout someplace. Maybe he was *supposed* to look like somebody who was going to seed. And maybe those dark shadows under his eyes were all part of the role he was playing out there on the street, in which case he should get not only a commendation but an Academy Award besides.

Willis was very apologetic.

"I'll tell you the truth," he said, "I figured we didn't have a chance of our man showing. Because on the other jobs, he usually hit between ten and ten-thirty, and it was almost eleven when this guy came running out of the bar—"

"Wait a minute," Eileen said. "*What* guy?"

"Came running out of the bar next door," Willis said. "Bert, don't you want some of this?"

"Thanks," Kling said, and shook his head.

"Yelling, 'Police, police,'" Willis said.

"When was this?" Eileen asked.

"I told you, a little before eleven," Willis said. "Even so, if I thought we had a chance of our man showing I'd have said screw it, let some other cop handle whatever it is in the bar there. But I mean it, Eileen, I figured we'd had it for tonight."

"So you went in the bar?"

"No. Well, yes. But not right away, no. I got out of the car, and I asked the guy what the trouble was, and he asked me did I see a cop anywhere because there was somebody with a knife in the bar and I told him I was a cop and he said I ought to go in there and take the knife away before somebody got cut."

"So naturally you went right in," Eileen said, and winked at Kling. Kling did not wink back. Kling lifted his coffee cup and sipped at it.

He seemed not to be listening to what Willis was saying. He seemed almost comatose. Eileen wondered what was wrong with him.

"No, I still gave it a bit of thought," Willis said. "I would have rushed in *immediately*, of course—"

"Of course," Eileen said.

"To disarm that guy . . . who by the way turned out to be a girl . . . but I was worried about you being all alone there in the laundromat in case Mr. Bloomers *did* decide to show up."

"Mr. Bloomers!" Eileen said, and burst out laughing. She was still feeling very high after the bust, and she wished that Kling wouldn't sit there like a zombie but would instead join in the general postmortem celebration.

"So I looked through the window," Willis said.

"Of the bar?"

"No, the laundromat. And saw that everything was still cool, you were sitting there next to a lady reading a magazine and this other lady was carrying about seven tons of laundry into the store, so I figured you'd be safe for another minute or two while I went in there and settled the thing with the knife, *especially* since I didn't think our man was going to show up anyway. So I went in the bar, and there's this very nicely dressed middle-class-looking lady wearing eyesglasses and her hair swept up on her head and a dispatch case sitting on the bar as if she's a lawyer or an accountant who stopped in for a pink lady on the way home and she's got an eight-foot-long switchblade in her right hand and she's swinging it in front of her like this, back and forth, slicing the air with it, you know, and I'm surprised first of all that it's a lady and next that it's a switchblade she's holding, which is not exactly a lady's weapon. Also, I do not wish to get cut," Willis said.

"Naturally," Eileen said.

"Naturally," Willis said. "In fact, I'm beginning to think I'd better go check on you again, make sure the panties nut hasn't shown up after all. But just then the guy who came out in the street yelling 'Police, police,' now says to the crazy lady with the stiletto, 'I warned you, Grace, this man is a policeman.' Which means I now have to uphold law and order, which is the last thing on earth I wish to do."

"What'd you do?" Eileen asked.

She was really interested now. She had never come up against a woman wielding a dangerous weapon, her line of specialty being men, of sorts. Usually she leveled her gun at a would-be rapist's privates, figuring she'd threaten him where he lived. Tonight, she had rammed the gun into the hollow of the man's throat. The barrel of the gun had left a bruise there, she had seen the bruise when she was putting the cuffs on him. But how do you begin taking a knife away from an angry *woman*? You couldn't threaten to shoot her in the balls, could you?

"I walked over to her and I said, 'Grace, that's a mighty fine knife you've got there, I wonder if you'd mind giving it to me.'"

"That was a mistake," Eileen said. "She might've given it to you, all right, she might've *really* given it to you."

"But she didn't," Willis said. "Instead, she turned to the guy who'd run out of the bar—"

"The 'Police, police' guy?"

"Yeah, and she said, 'Harry,' or whatever the hell his name was, 'Harry, how can you keep cheating on me this way?' and then she burst into tears and handed the knife to the *bartender* instead of to *me*, and Harry took her in his arms—"

"Excuse me, huh?" Kling said, and got up from behind the desk, and walked out of the squadroom.

"Oh God," Willis said.

"Huh?" Eileen said.

"I forgot," Willis said. "He probably thinks I told that story on purpose. I'd better go talk to him, Excuse me, okay? I'm sorry, Eileen, excuse me."

"Sure," she said, puzzled, and watched while Willis went through the gate in the slatted rail divider and down the corridor after Kling. There were some things she would never in a million years understand about the guys who worked up here. Never. She picked up another slice of pizza. It was cold. And she hadn't even got a chance to tell anyone about how absolutely brilliant and courageous and deadly forceful she'd been in that laundromat.

It was beginning to snow again. Lightly. Fat fluffy flakes drifting down lazily from the sky. Arthur Brown was driving. Bert Kling sat beside him on the front seat of the five-year-old unmarked sedan. Eileen was sitting in the back. She had still been in the squadroom when the homicide squeal came in, and she'd asked Kling if he'd mind dropping her off at the subway on his way to the scene. Kling had merely grunted. Kling was a charmer, Eileen thought.

Brown was a huge man who looked even more enormous in his bulky overcoat. The coat was gray and it had a fake black fur collar. He was wearing black leather gloves that matched the black collar. Brown was supposed to be what people nowadays called a "black" man, but Brown knew that his complexion did not match the color of either the black collar or the black gloves. Whenever he looked at himself in the mirror, he saw someone with a chocolate-colored skin looking back at him, but he did not think of himself as a "chocolate" man. Neither did he think of himself as a Negro anymore; somehow, if a black man thought of himself as a Negro, he was thinking obsequiously. *Negro* had become a derogatory term, God alone knew when or how. Brown's father used to call himself "a person of color" which Brown thought was a very hoity-toity expression even when it was still okay for black men to call themselves Negroes. (Brown noticed that *Ebony* magazine capitalized the word *Black*, and he often wondered why.) He guessed he still thought of himself as colored, and he sincerely hoped there was nothing wrong with that. Nowadays, a nigger didn't know *what* he was supposed to think.

Brown was the kind of black man white men crossed the street to avoid. If you were white, and you saw Brown approaching on the same side of the street, you automatically assumed he was going to mug you, or cut you with a razor, or do something else terrible to you. That was partially due to the fact that Brown was six feet four inches tall and weighed two hundred and twenty pounds. It was also partially (*mostly*) due to the fact that Brown was black, or colored, or whatever you chose to call him, but he certainly was not white. A white man approaching Brown might not have crossed the street if Brown had also been a white man; unfortunately, Brown never had the opportunity to conduct such an experiment. The fact remained that when Brown was casually walking down the street minding his own business, white people crossed over to the other side. Sometimes even white *cops* crossed over to the other side. Nobody wanted trouble with someone who looked the way Brown looked. Even *black* people sometimes crossed the street when Brown approached, but only because he looked so bad-ass.

Brown knew he was, in fact, very handsome.

Whenever Brown looked in the mirror, he saw a very handsome chocolate-colored man looking back at him out of soulful brown eyes. Brown liked himself a lot. Brown was very comfortable with himself. Brown was glad he was a cop because he knew that the *real* reason white people crossed the street when they saw him was because they thought all black people were thieves or murderers. He frequently regretted the day he was promoted into the Detective Division because then he could no longer wear his identifying blue uniform, the contradiction to his identifying brown skin. Brown especially liked to bust people of his own race. He especially liked it when some black dude said, "Come on, brother, give me a break." That man was no more Brown's brother than Brown was brother to a hippopotamus. In Brown's world, there were the good guys and the bad guys, white or black, it made no difference. Brown was one of the good guys. All those guys breaking the law out there were the bad guys. Tonight, one of the bad guys had left somebody dead and bleeding on the floor of a garage under a building on fancy Silvermine Road, and Kling had caught the squeal, and Brown was his partner, and they were two good guys riding out into the gently falling snow, with another good guy (who happened to be a girl) sitting on the backseat—which reminded him: He had to drop her off at the subway station.

"The one on Culver and Fourth okay?" he asked her.

"That'll be fine, Artie," Eileen said.

Kling was hunkered down inside his coat, looking out at the falling snow. The car heater rattled and clunked, something wrong with the fan. The car was the worst one the squad owned. Brown wondered how come whenever it was his turn to check out a car, he got *this* one. Worst car in the entire *city*, maybe. Ripe tomato accelerator, rattled like a two-dollar whore, something wrong with the exhaust, the damn car always smelled of carbon monoxide, they were probably *poisoning* themselves on the way to the homicide.

"Willis says you nabbed the guy who was running around pulling down bloomers, huh?" Brown said.

"Yeah," Eileen said, grinning.

"Good thing, too," Brown said. "This kind of weather, lady *needs* her underdrawers." He began laughing. Eileen laughed, too. Kling sat staring through the windshield.

"Will you be all right on the subway, this hour of the night?" Brown asked.

"Yeah, I'll be fine," Eileen said.

He pulled the car into the curb.

"You sure now?"

"Positive. G'night, Artie," she said, and opened the door. "G'night, Bert."

"Good night," Brown said. "Take care."

Kling said nothing. Eileen shrugged and closed the door behind her. Brown watched as she went down the steps into the subway. He pulled the car away from the curb the moment her head disappeared from sight.

"Hey, hi!" the voice said.

He was approaching the elevators, his head bent, his eyes on the marble floor. He did not recognize the voice, nor did he even realize at first that it was he who was being addressed. But he looked up because someone had stepped into his path. The someone was Eileen Burke. She was wearing a simple brown suit with a green blouse that was sort of ruffly at the throat, the green the color of her eyes, her long red hair swept efficiently back from her face, standing tall in high-heeled brown pumps a shade darker than the suit. She was carrying a shoulder bag, and he could see into the bag to where the barrel of a revolver seemed planted in a bed of crumpled Kleenexes. The picture on her plastic I.D. card, clipped to the lapel of her suit, showed a younger Eileen Burke, her red hair done in the frizzies. She was smiling—in the picture, and in person.

"What are you doing down *here*?" she asked. "Nobody comes here on a Sunday."

"I need a picture from the I.S.," he said. She seemed waiting for him to say more. "How about you?" he added.

"I work here. Special Forces is here. Right on this floor, in fact. Come on in for a cup of coffee," she said, and her smile widened.

"No, thanks, I'm sort of in a hurry," Kling said, even though he was in no hurry at all.

"Okay," Eileen said, and shrugged. "Actually, I'm glad I ran into you. I was going to call later in the day, anyway."

"Oh?" Kling said.

"I think I lost an earring up there. Either there or in the laundromat with the panty perpetrator. If it *was* the laundromat, good-bye, Charlie. But if it was the squadroom, or maybe the car—when you were dropping me off last night, you know . . ."

"Yeah," Kling said.

"It was just a simple gold hoop earring, about the size of a quarter. Nothing ostentatious when you're doing dirty laundry, right?"

"Which ear was it?" he asked.

"The right," she said. "Huh? What difference does it make? I mean, it *was* the right ear, but earrings are interchangeable, so—"

"Yeah, that's right," Kling said. He was looking at her right ear, or at the space beyond her right ear or wherever. He was certainly not looking at her face, certainly not allowing his eyes to meet her eyes. What the hell is *wrong* with him? she wondered.

"Well, take a look up there, okay?" she said. "If you find it, give me a call. I'm with Special Forces—well, you know that—but I'm in and out all the time, so just leave a message. That is, if you happen to find the earring." She hesitated, and then said, "The *right* one, that is. If you find the *left* one, it's the *wrong* one." She smiled. He did not return the smile. "Well, see you around the pool hall," she said, and spread her hand in a farewell fan, and turned on her heel, and walked away from him.

Kling pressed the button for the elevator.

The phone on Kling's desk began ringing just as he and Brown were leaving the squadroom. He leaned over the slatted rail divider and picked up the receiver.

"Kling," he said.

"Bert, it's Eileen."

"Oh, hi," he said. "I was going to call you later today."

"Did you find it?"

"Just where you said it was. Backseat of the car."

"You know how many earrings I've lost in the backseats of cars?" Eileen said.

Kling said nothing.

"Years ago, of course," she said.

Kling still said nothing.

"When I was a teenager," she said.

The silence lengthened.

"Well," she said, "I'm glad you found it."

"What do you want me to do with it?" Kling asked.

"I don't suppose you'll be coming down this way for anything, will you?"

"Well . . ."

"Court? Or the lab? D.A.'s office? Anything like that?"

"No, but . . ."

She waited.

"Actually, I live down near the bridge," Kling said.

"The Calm's Point Bridge?"

"Yes."

"Oh, well, good! Do you know A View From the Bridge?"

"What?"

"It's *under* the bridge, actually, right on the Dix. A little wine bar."

"Oh."

"It's just . . . I don't want to take you out of your way."

"Well . . ."

"Does five sound okay?" Eileen asked.

"I was just leaving the office, I don't know what time—"

"It's just at the end of Lamb Street, under the bridge, right on the river, you can't miss it. Five o'clock, okay? My treat, it'll be a reward, sort of."

"Well—"

"Or have you made other plans?" Eileen asked.

"No. No other plans."

"Five o'clock, then?"

"Okay," he said.

"Good," she said, and hung up.

Kling had a bewildered look on his face.

"What was that?" Brown asked.

"Eileen's earring," Kling said.

"What?" Brown said.

"Forget it," Kling said.

The ceiling of A View From the Bridge was adorned with wineglasses, the foot of each glass captured between narrow wooden slats, the stem and bowl hanging downward to create an overall impression of a vast, wall-to-wall chandelier glistening with reflected light from the fireplace on one wall of the room. The fireplace wall was made of brick, and the surrounding walls were wood-paneled except for the one facing the river, a wide expanse of glass through which Kling could see the water beyond and the tugboats moving slowly through the rapidly gathering dusk. It was five-thirty by the clock over the bar facing the entrance doorway.

The wine bar, at this hour, was crowded with men and women who, presumably, worked in the myriad courthouses, muncipal buildings, law offices, and brokerage firms that housed the judicial, economic, legal, and governmental power structure in this oldest part of the city. There was a pleasant conversational hum in the place, punctuated by relaxed laughter, a coziness encouraged by the blazing fire and the flickering glow of candles in ruby-red holders on each of the round tables. Kling had never been to England, but he suspected that a pub in London might have looked and sounded exactly like this at the end of a long working day. He recognized an assistant D.A. he knew, said hello to him, and then looked for Eileen.

She was sitting at a table by the window, staring out over the river. The candle in its ruby holder cast flickering highlights into her hair, red reflecting red. Her chin was resting on the cupped palm of her hand. She looked pensive and contained, and for a moment he debated intruding on whatever mood she was sharing with the dark waters of the river beyond. He took off his coat, hung it on a wall rack just inside the door, and then moved across the room to where she was sitting. She turned away from the river as he moved toward her, as though sensing his approach.

"Hi," he said, "I'm sorry I'm late, we ran into something."

"I just got here myself," she said.

He pulled out the chair opposite her.

"So," she said. "You found it."

"Right where you said it'd be." He reached into his jacket pocket. "Let me give it to you before it gets lost again," he said, and placed the shining circle of gold on the table between them. He noticed all at once that she was wearing the mate to it on her right ear. He watched as she lifted the earring from the table, reached up with her left hand to pull down the lobe of her left ear, and crossed her right hand over her body to fasten the earring. The gesture reminded him suddenly and painfully of the numberless times he had watched Augusta putting on or taking off earrings, the peculiarly female tilt of her head, her hair falling in an auburn cascade. Augusta had pierced ears; Eileen's earrings were clip-ons.

"So," she said, and smiled, and then suddenly looked at him with something like embarrassment on her face, as though she'd been caught in an intimate act when she thought she'd been unobserved. The smile faltered for an instant. She looked quickly across the room to where the waiter was taking an order at another table. "What do you prefer?" she asked. "White or red?"

"White'll be fine," he said. "But listen, *I* want to pay for this. There's no need—"

"Absolutely out of the question," she said. "After all the trouble I put you to?"

"It was no trouble at—"

"No way," she said, and signaled to the waiter.

Kling fell silent. She looked across at him, studying his face, a policewoman suddenly alerted to something odd.

"This really *does* bother you, doesn't it?" she said.

"No, no."

"My paying, I mean."

"Well . . . no," he said, but he meant yes. One of the things that had been *most* troubling about his marriage was the fact that Augusta's exorbitant salary had paid for most of the luxuries they'd enjoyed.

The waiter was standing by the table now, the wine list in his hand. Clued by the fact that she was the one who'd signaled him, and no longer surprised by women who did the ordering and picked up the tab, he extended the leather-covered folder to her. "Yes, miss?" he said.

"I believe the gentleman would like to do the ordering," Eileen said. Kling looked at her. "He'll want the check, too," she added.

"Whatever turns you on," the waiter said, and handed the list to Kling.

"I'm not so good at this," he said.

"Neither am I," she said.

"Were you thinking of a white or a red?" the waiter asked.

"A white," Kling said.

"A *dry* white?"

"Well . . . sure."

"May I . . . suggest the Pouilly-Fumé, sir? It's a nice dry white with a somewhat smoky taste."

"Eileen?"

"Yes, that sounds fine," she said.

"Yes, the . . . uh . . . Pooey Foo May, please," Kling said, and handed the wine list back as if it had caught fire in his hands. "Sounds like a Chinese dish," he said to Eileen as the waiter walked off.

"Did you see the French movie, it's a classic," she said. "I forget the title. With Gerard Philippe and . . . Michele Morgan, I think. She's an older woman and he's a very young man, and he takes her to a fancy French restaurant—"

"No, I don't think so," Kling said.

"Anyway, he's trying to impress her, you know, and when the wine steward brings the wine he ordered, and pours a little into his glass to taste it, he takes a little sip—she's watching him all the while, and the steward is watching him, too—and he rolls it around on his tongue, and says, 'This wine tastes of cork.' The wine steward looks at him—

they're all supposed to be such bastards, you know, French waiters—and he pours a little of the wine into his little silver tasting cup, whatever they call it, and *he* takes a sip, and rolls it around in his mouth, and everybody in the place is watching them because they know they're lovers, and there's nothing in the world a Frenchman likes better than a lover. And finally, the steward nods very solemnly, and says, 'Monsieur is correct, this wine *does* taste of cork,' and he goes away to get a fresh bottle, and Gerard Philippe smiles, and Michele Morgan smiles, and everybody in the entire place smiles."

Eileen was smiling now.

"It was a very lovely scene," she said.

"I don't much care for foreign movies," Kling said. "I mean, the ones with subtitles."

"This one had subtitles," Eileen said. "But it was beautiful."

"That scene *did* sound very good," Kling said.

"*Le Diable au Corps*, that was it."

Kling looked at her, puzzled.

"The title," she said. "It means 'Devil in the Flesh.'"

"That's a good title," Kling said.

"Yes," Eileen said.

"The Pouilly-Fumé," the waiter said, and pulled the cork. He wiped the lip of the bottle with his towel, and then poured a little wine into Kling's glass. Kling looked at Eileen, lifted the glass, brought it to his lips, sipped at the wine, rolled the wine around in his mouth, raised his eyebrows, and said, "This wine tastes of cork."

Eileen burst out laughing.

"Cork?" the waiter said.

"I'm joking," Kling said, "it's really fine."

"Because, *really*, if it's—"

"No, no, it's fine, really."

Eileen was still laughing. The waiter frowned at her as he poured the wine into her glass, and then filled Kling's. He was still frowning when he walked away from the table. They raised their glasses.

"Here's to golden days and purple nights," Eileen said, and clinked her glass against his.

"Cheers," he said.

"My Uncle Matt always used to say that," Eileen said. "He drank like a fish." She brought the glass to her lips. "Be funny if it *really* tasted of cork, wouldn't it?" she said, and then sipped at the wine.

"*Does* it?" Kling asked.

"No, no, it's very good. Try it," she said. "For *real* this time."

He drank.

"Good?" she said.

"Yes," he said.

"Actually, it was Micheline Presle, I think," she said. "The heroine."

They sat silently for several moments. Out on the river, a tugboat hooted into the night.

"So," she said, "what are you working on?"

"That homicide we caught when you were up there Saturday night."

"How does it look?"

"Puzzling," Kling said.

"That's what makes them interesting," Eileen said.

"I suppose."

"*My* stuff is hardly ever puzzling. I'm always the bait for some lunatic out there, hoping he'll take the hook."

"I wouldn't want to be in your shoes," Kling said.

"It does get scary every now and then."

"I'll bet."

"So listen, who asked me to become a cop, right?"

"How'd you happen to get into it?"

"Uncle Matt. He of the golden days and purple nights, the big drinker. He was a cop. I loved him to death, so I figured *I'd* become a cop, too. He worked out of the old Hundred and Tenth in Riverhead. That is, till he caught it one night in a bar brawl. He wasn't even on duty. Just sitting there drinking his sour-mash bourbon when some guy came in with a sawed-off shotgun and a red plaid kerchief over his face. Uncle Matt went for his service revolver and the guy shot him dead." Eileen paused. "The guy got fifty-two dollars and thirty-six cents from the cash register. He also got away clean. I keep hoping I'll run into him one day. Sawed-off shotgun and red plaid kerchief. I'll blow him away without batting an eyelash."

She batted both eyelashes now.

"Tough talk on the lady, huh?" she said, and smiled. "So how about *you*?" she said. "How'd *you* get into it?"

"Seemed like the right thing to do at the time," he said, and shrugged.

"How about now? Does it *still* seem like the right thing?"

"I guess so." He shrugged again. "You get sort of . . . it wears you down, you know."

"Mm," she said.

"Everything out there," he said, and fell silent.

They sipped some more wine.

"What are *you* working on?" he asked.

"Thursday," she said. "I won't start till Thursday night."

"And what's that?"

"Some guy's been raping nurses outside Worth Memorial. On their way to the subway, when they're crossing that park outside the hospital, do you know the park? In Chinatown?"

"Yes," Kling said, and nodded.

292

"Pretty big park for that part of the city. He hits the ones coming off the four-to-midnight, three of them in the past three months, always when there's no moon."

"I gather there'll be no moon this Thursday night."

"No moon at all," she said. "Don't you just *love* that song?"

"What song?"

"'No Moon at All.'"

"I don't know it," Kling said. "I'm sorry."

"Well, this certainly isn't the 'We both like the same things' scene, is it?"

"I don't know what scene that is," Kling said.

"In the movies. What's your favorite color? Yellow. Mine, too! What's your favorite flower? Geraniums. Mine, too! Gee, we both like the same things!" She laughed again.

"Well, at least we both like the *wine*," Kling said, and smiled, and poured her glass full again. "Will you be dressed like a nurse?" he asked.

"Oh, sure. Do you think that's sexy?"

"What?"

"Nurses. Their uniforms, I mean."

"I've never thought about it."

"Lots of men have things for nurses, you know. I guess it's because they figure they've seen it all, nurses. Guys lying around naked on operating tables and so forth. They figure nurses are experienced."

"Mm," Kling said.

"Somebody once told me—this man I used to date, he was an editor at a paperback house—he told me if you put the word *nurse* in a title, you're guaranteed a million-copy sale."

"Is that true?"

"It's what he told me."

"I guess he would know."

"But nurses don't turn you on, huh?"

"I didn't say that."

"I'll have to show you what I look like," Eileen said. Her eyes met his. "In my nurse's outfit."

Kling said nothing.

"It must have something to do with white, too," Eileen said. "The fact that a nurse's uniform is white. Like a bride's gown, don't you think?"

"Maybe," Kling said.

"The conflicting image, do you know? The *experienced* virgin. Not that too many brides today are virgins," she said, and shrugged. "Nobody would even *expect* that today, would they? A man, I mean. That his bride's going to be a virgin?"

"I guess not," Kling said.

"You've never been married, have you?" she said.

"I've been married," he said.

"I didn't know that."

"Yes," he said.

"And?"

Kling hesitated.

"I was recently divorced," he said.

"I'm sorry," she said.

"Well," he said, and lifted his wineglass, avoiding her steady gaze. "How about you?" he said. He was looking out over the river now.

"Still hoping for Mr. Right," she said. "I keep having this fantasy . . . well, I really shouldn't tell you this."

"No, go ahead," he said, turning back to her.

"Well . . . really, it's *silly*," she said, and he could swear that she was blushing, but perhaps it was only the red glow of the candle in its holder. "I keep fantasizing that one of those rapists out there will *succeed* one night, do you know? I won't be able to get my gun on him in time, he'll do whatever he *wants* and—*surprise*—he'll turn out to be Prince *Charming*! I'll fall madly in love with him, and we'll live happily ever after. Whatever you do, don't tell that to Betty Friedan or Gloria Steinem. I'll get drummed out of the women's movement."

"The old rape fantasy," Kling said.

"Except that I happen to deal with *real* rape," Eileen said. "And I know it isn't fun and games."

"Mm," Kling said.

"So why should I fantasize about it? I mean, I've come within a *hairs*breadth so *many* times . . ."

"Maybe that's what accounts for the fantasy," Kling said. "The fantasy makes it seem less frightening. Your work. What you have to do. Maybe," he said, and shrugged.

"We've just had our 'I don't know why I'm telling you all this' scene, haven't we?"

"I suppose so," he said, and smiled.

"Somebody ought to write a book about all the different kinds of clichéd scenes," she said. "The one I like best, I think, is when the killer has a gun on the guy who's been chasing him, and he says something like, 'It's safe to tell you this now because in three seconds flat you'll be dead,' and then proceeds to brag about all the people he killed and how and why he killed them."

"I wish it was that easy," Kling said, still smiling.

"Or what I call the '*Uh*-oh!' scene. Where we see a wife in bed with her lover, and then we cut away to the husband putting his key in the door latch, and we're all supposed to go, '*Uh*-oh, here it comes!' Don't you just *love* that scene?"

The smile dropped from his face.

She looked into his eyes, trying to read them, knowing she'd somehow made a dreadful mistake, and trying to understand what she'd said that had been so terribly wrong. Until that moment, they'd seemed—

"I'd better get the check," he said.

She knew better than to press it. If there was one thing she'd learned as a decoy, it was patience.

"Sure," she said, "I've got to run, too. Hey, thanks for bringing the earring back, really. I appreciate it."

"No problem," Kling said, but he wasn't looking at her, he was signaling to the waiter instead.

They sat in silence while they waited for the check. When they left the place, they shook hands politely on the sidewalk outside and walked off in opposite directions.

When the telephone rang, it startled Kling.

The phone was on an end table beside the bed, and the first ring slammed into the silence of the room like a pistol shot, causing him to sit bolt upright, his heart pounding. He grabbed for the receiver.

"Hello?" he said.

"Hi, this is Eileen," she said.

"Oh, hi," he said.

"You sound out of breath."

"No, I . . . it was very quiet in here. When the phone rang, it surprised me." His heart was still pounding.

"You weren't asleep, were you? I didn't—"

"No, no, I was just lying here."

"In bed?"

"Yes."

"I'm in bed, too," she said.

He said nothing.

"I wanted to apologize," she said.

"What for?"

"I didn't know about the divorce," she said.

"Well, that's okay."

"I wouldn't have said what I said if I'd known."

What she meant, he realized, was that she hadn't known about the *circumstances* of the divorce. She had found out since yesterday, it was common currency in the department, and now she was apologizing for having described what she'd called an "*Uh*-oh!" scene, the wife in bed with her lover, the husband coming up the steps, the very damn thing that had happened to Kling.

"That's okay," he said.

It was not okay.

"I've just made it worse, haven't I?" she said.

He was about to say, "No, don't be silly, thanks for calling," when he thought, unexpectedly, Yes, you *have* made it worse, and he said, "As a matter of fact, you have."

"I'm sorry. I only wanted—"

"What'd they tell you?" he asked.

"Who?"

"Come on," he said. "Whoever told you about it."

"Only that there'd been some kind of problem."

"Uh-huh. What kind of problem?"

"Just a problem."

"My wife was playing around, right?"

"Well, yes, that's what I was told."

"Fine," he said.

There was a long silence on the line.

"Well," she said, and sighed. "I just wanted to tell you I'm sorry if I upset you yesterday."

"You didn't upset me," he said.

"You sound upset."

"I *am* upset," he said.

"Bert . . ." she said, and hesitated. "Please don't be mad at *me*, okay? Please *don't*!" and he could swear that suddenly she was crying. The next thing he heard was a click on the line.

He looked at the phone receiver.

"What?" he said to the empty room.

Had she been crying?

He hadn't wanted to make her *cry*, he hardly *knew* the girl. He went to the window and stared out at the cars moving steadily across the bridge, their headlights piercing the night. It was snowing again. Would it ever stop snowing? He had not wanted to make her cry. What the hell was *wrong* with him? *Augusta* is wrong with me, he thought, and went back to the bed.

It might have been easier to forget her if only he didn't have to see her face everywhere he turned. Your average divorced couple, especially if there were no kids involved, you hardly ever ran into each other after the final decree. You started to forget. Sometimes you forgot even the *good* things you'd shared, which was bad but which was the nature of the beast called divorce. With Augusta, it was different. Augusta was a model. You couldn't pass a magazine rack without seeing her face on the cover of at least one magazine each and every month, sometimes two. You couldn't turn on television without seeing her in a hair commercial (she had such beautiful hair) or a toothpaste commercial, or just last week in a nail-polish commercial, Augusta's hands fanned out in front of her gorgeous face, the nails long and bright red, as if they'd been dipped in fresh blood, the smile on her face—ahh, Jesus, that wonderful smile. It got so he didn't want to turn on the TV set anymore, for fear Augusta would leap out of the tube at him, and he'd start remembering again, and begin crying again.

He lay fully dressed on the bed in the small apartment he was renting near the bridge, his hands behind his head, his head turned so that he could see through the window, see the cars moving on the bridge to Calm's Point—the theater crowd, he guessed; the shows had all broken by now, and people were heading home. People going home together. He took a deep breath.

His gun was in a holster on the dresser across the room.

He thought about the gun a lot.

Whenever he wasn't thinking about Augusta, he was thinking about the gun.

He didn't know why he'd let Brown take all that stuff home with him, he'd have welcomed the opportunity to go through it himself, give him something to do tonight instead of thinking about either Augusta or the gun. He knew Brown hated paperwork, he'd have been happy to take the load off his hands. But Brown had tiptoed around him, they all tiptoed around him these days, No, Bert, that's fine, you just go out and have a good time, hear? I'll be through with this stuff by morning, we'll talk it over then, okay? It was as if somebody very close to him had died. They all knew somebody had died, and they were uncomfortable with him, the way people are always uncomfortable with mourners, never knowing where to hide their hands, never knowing what to say in condolence. He'd be doing them all a favor, not only himself. Take the gun and . . .

Come on, he thought.

He turned his head on the pillow, and looked up at the ceiling.

He knew the ceiling by heart. He knew every peak and valley in the rough plaster, knew every smear of dirt, every cobweb. He didn't know some *people* the way he knew that ceiling. Sometimes, when he thought of Augusta, the ceiling blurred, he could not see his old friend the ceiling through his own tears. If he used the gun, he'd have to be careful of the angle. Wouldn't want to have the bullet take off the top of his skull and then put a hole in the ceiling besides, not his old friend the ceiling. He smiled. He figured somebody smiling wasn't somebody about to eat his own gun. Not yet, anyway.

Damnit, he really *hadn't* wanted to make her cry.

He sat up abruptly, reached for the Isola directory on the end table, and thumbed through it, not expecting to find a listing for her, and not surprised when he didn't. Nowadays, with thieves getting out of prison ten minutes after you locked them up, not too many cops were eager to list their home numbers in the city's telephone books. He dialed Communications downtown, a number he knew by heart, and told the clerk who answered the phone that he wanted extension 12.

"Departmental Directory," a woman's voice said.

"Home number for a police officer," Kling said.

"Is *this* a police officer calling?"

"It is," Kling said.

"Your name, please?"

"Bertram A. Kling."

"Your rank and shield number, please?"

"Detective/Third, seven-four-five-seven-nine."

"And the party?"

"Eileen Burke."

There was a silence on the line.

"Is this a joke?" the woman said.

"A joke? What do you mean?"

"*She* called here ten minutes ago, wanting *your* number."

"We're working a case together," Kling said, and wondered why he'd lied.

"So did she *call* you?"

"She called me."

"So why didn't you ask *her* what her number was?"

"I forgot," Kling said.

"This isn't a *dating* service," the woman said.

"I told you, we're working a case together," Kling said.

"Sure," the woman said. "Hold on, let me run this through."

He waited. He knew she was making a computer check on him verifying that he was a bona fide cop. He looked through the window. It was snowing more heavily now. Come *on*, he thought.

"Hello?" the woman said.

"I'm still here," Kling said.

"Our computers are down, I had to do it manually."

"Am I a real cop?" Kling said.

"Who knows nowadays?" the woman answered. "Here's the number, have you got a pencil?"

He wrote down the number, thanked her for her time, and then pressed one of the receiver rest buttons on top of the phone. He released the button, got a dial tone, was about to dial, and then hesitated. What am I starting here? he wondered. I don't want to start anything here. I'm not *ready* to start anything. He put the phone back on the cradle. He owed her an apology, didn't he? Or did he? What the hell, he thought, and went back to the phone, and dialed her number.

"Hello?" she said. Her voice sounded very small and a trifle sniffly.

"This is Bert," he said.

"Hello," she said. The same small sniffly voice.

"Bert Kling," he said.

"I know," she said.

"I'm sorry," he said. "I didn't mean to yell at you."

"That's okay," she said.

"Really, I'm sorry."

"That's okay," she said again.

There was a long silence on the line.

"So . . . how are you?" he said.

"Fine, I guess," she said.

There was another long silence.

"Is your apartment cold?" she asked.

"No, it's fine. Nice and warm."

"I'm freezing to death here," she said. "I'm going to call the Ombudsman's Office first thing tomorrow morning. They're not supposed to turn off the heat so early, are they?"

"Eleven o'clock, I thought."

"Is it eleven already?"

"It's almost midnight."

"Another day, another dollar," Eileen said, and sighed. "Anyway, they're not supposed to turn it off *entirely*, are they?"

"Sixty-two, I think."

"The radiators here are ice-cold," she said. "I have *four* blankets on the bed."

"You ought to get an electric blanket," Kling said.

"I'm afraid of them. I'm afraid I'll catch on fire or something."

"No, no, they're very safe."

"Do *you* have an electric blanket?"

"No. But I'm told they're very safe."

"Or electrocuted," she said.

"Well," he said, "I just wanted to make sure you're okay. And really, I *am* sorry for—"

"Me, too." She paused. "This is the 'I'm-Sorry-You're-Sorry' scene, isn't it?" she said.

"I guess so."

"Yeah, that's what it is," she said.

Silence again.

"Well," he said, "it's late, I don't want to—"

"No, don't go," she said. "Talk to me."

She had asked him not to go, she had asked him to talk to her, and suddenly he could think of nothing else to say. The silence on the line lengthened. On the street outside, he heard the distinctive wail of a 911 Emergency truck, and wondered which poor bastard had jumped off a bridge or got himself pinned under a subway train.

"Do you ever get scared?" she asked.

"Yes," he said.

"I mean, on the job."

"Yes."

"I'm scared," she said.

"What about?"

"Tomorrow night."

"The nurse thing?"

"Yeah."

"Well, just don't—"

"I mean, I'm always a *little* scared, but not like this time." She hesitated. "He blinded one of them," she said. "One of the nurses he raped."

"Boy," Kling said.

"Yeah."

"Well, what you have to do . . . just be careful, that's all."

"Yeah, I'm always careful," she said.

"Who's your backup on this?"

"*Two* of them. I've got two of them."

"Well, that's good."

"Abrahams and McCann, do you know them?"

"No."

"They're out of the Chinatown Precinct."

"I don't know them."

"They seem okay, but . . . well, a backup can't stay *glued* to you, you know, otherwise he'll scare off the guy you're trying to catch."

"Yeah, but they'll be there if you need them."

"I guess."

"Sure, they will."

"How long does it take to put out somebody's eyes?" she asked.

"I wouldn't worry about that, really, that's not going to help, worrying about it. Just make sure you've got your hand on your gun, that's all."

"In my bag, yeah."

"Wherever you carry it."

"That's where I carry it."

"Make sure it's in your hand. And keep your finger inside the trigger guard."

"Yeah, I always do."

"It wouldn't hurt to carry a spare, either."

"Where would I carry a spare?"

"Strap it to your ankle. Wear slacks. Nurses are allowed to wear slacks, aren't they?"

"Oh, sure. But they like a leg show, you see. I'll be wearing the uniform, you know, like a dress. The white uniform."

"Who do you mean? Rank? They told you to wear a dress?"

"I'm sorry, what—"

"You said they like a leg show . . ."

"Oh. I meant the lunatics out there. They like a little leg, a little ass. Shake your boobs, lure them out of the bushes."

"Yeah, well," Kling said.

"I'll be wearing one of those starched things, you know, with a little white cap, and white panty hose, and this big black cape. I already tried it on today, it'll be at the hospital when I check in tomorrow night."

"What time will that be?"

"When I get to the hospital, or when I go out?"

"Both?"

"I'm due there at eleven. I'll be hitting the park at a little after midnight."

"Well, be careful."

"I will."

They were silent for a moment.

"Maybe I could tuck it in my bra or something. The spare."

"Yeah, get yourself one of those little guns . . ."

"Yeah, like a derringer or something."

"No, that won't help you, that's Mickey Mouse time. I'm talking about something like a Browning or a Bernardelli, those little pocket automatics, you know?"

"Yeah," she said, "tuck it in my bra."

"As a spare, you know."

"Yeah."

"You can pick one up anywhere in the city," Kling said. "Cost you something like thirty, forty dollars."

"But those are small-caliber guns, aren't they?" she asked. "Twenty-twos? Or twenty-fives?"

"That doesn't mean anything, the caliber. A gun like a twenty-two can do more damage than a thirty-eight. When Reagan got shot, everybody was saying he was lucky it was only a twenty-two the guy used, but that was wrong thinking. I was talking to this guy at Ballistics . . . Dorfsman, do you know Dorfsman?"

"No," Eileen said.

"Anyway, he told me you have to think of the human body like a room with furniture in it. You shoot a thirty-eight or a forty-five through one wall of the room, the slug goes right out through another wall. But you shoot a twenty-two or a twenty-five into that room, it hasn't got the power to *exit*, you understand? It hits a sofa, it ricochets off and hits the television set, it ricochets off that and hits a lamp—those are all the organs inside the body, you understand? Like the heart, or the kidneys, or the lungs, the bullet just goes bouncing around inside there doing a lot of damage. So you don't have to worry about the caliber, I mean it. Those little guns can really hurt somebody."

"Yeah," Eileen said, and hesitated. "I'm *still* scared," she said.

"No, don't be. You'll be fine."

"Maybe it's because of what I told you yesterday," she said. "My fantasy, you know. I never told that to anyone in my life. Now I feel as if I'm tempting God or something. Because I said it out loud. About . . . you know, *wanting* to get raped."

"Well, you don't *really* want to get raped."

"I know I don't."

"So that's got nothing to do with it."

"Except for fun and games," she said.

"What do you mean?"

"Getting raped."

"Oh."

"You know," she said. "You tear off my panties and my bra, I struggle a little . . . like that. Pretending."

"Sure," he said.

"To spice it up a little," she said.

"Yeah."

"But not for real."

"No."

She was quiet for a long time. Then she said, "It's too bad tomorrow night is for real."

"Take the spare along," Kling said.

"Oh, I *will*, don't worry."

"Well," he said, "I guess—"

"No, don't go," she said. "Talk to me."

Suddenly, and again, he could think of nothing else to say.

"Tell me what happened," she said. "The divorce."

"I'm not sure I want to," he said.

"*Will* you tell me one day?"

"Maybe."

"Only if you want to," she said. "Bert . . ." She hesitated. "Thank you. I feel a lot better now."

"Well, good," he said. "Listen, if you *want* to . . ."

"Yes?"

"Give me a call tomorrow night. When you come in, I mean. When it's all over. Let me know how it went, okay?"

"Well, that's liable to be pretty late."

"I'm usually up late."

"Well, if you'd like me to."

"Yes, I would."

"It'll be after midnight, you know."

"That's okay."

"Maybe later, if we make the collar. Time we book him—"

"Whenever," Kling said. "Just call me whenever."

"Okay," she said. "Well," she said.

"Well, good night," he said.

"Good night, Bert," she said, and hung up.

She felt stupid with a gun in her bra.

The gun was a .22-caliber Llama with a six-shot capacity, deadly enough, she supposed, if push came to shove. Its overall length was four and three-quarter inches, just small enough to fit cozily if uncomfortably between her breasts. It weighed only thirteen and a half ounces, but it felt like thirteen and a half *pounds* tucked there inside her bra, and besides, the metal was cold. That was because she had left the top three buttons of the uniform unfastened, in case she needed to get in there in a hurry. The wind was blowing up under the flapping black cape she was wearing, straight from the North Pole and directly into the open V-necked wedge of the uniform. Her breasts were cold, and her nipples were cold and erect besides—but maybe that was because she was scared to death.

She did not like the setup, she had told them that from the start. Even after the dry run this afternoon, she had voiced her complaints. It had taken her eight minutes to cross the park on the winding path that ran more or less diagonally through it, walking at a slightly faster than normal clip, the way a woman alone at midnight would be expected to walk through a deserted park. She had argued for a classic bookend surveillance, one of her backup men ahead of her, the other behind, at reasonably safe distances. Both of her backups were old-timers from the Chinatown Precinct, both of them Detectives/First. Abrahams ("Call me Morrie," he said back at the precinct, when they were laying out their strategy) argued that anybody walking point would scare off their rapist if he made a head-on approach. McCann ("I'm Mickey," he told her) argued that if the guy made his approach from *behind*, he'd spot the follow-up man and call it all off. Eileen could see the sense of what they were saying, but she still didn't like the way *they* were proposing to do it. What *they* wanted to do was plant one of them at either end of the path, at opposite ends of the park. That meant that if their man hit when she was midway through the park, the way he'd done on his last three outings, she'd be four minutes away from either one of them—okay, say three minutes, if they came at a gallop.

"If I'm in trouble," she said, "you won't be able to reach me in time. Why can't we put you under the trees someplace, hiding under those trees in the middle of the park? That's where he hit the last three times. If you're under the trees there, we won't have four minutes separating us."

"Three minutes," Abrahams said.

"That's where he hit the last three times," she said again.

"Suppose he scouts the area this time?" McCann said.

"And spots two guys hiding under the trees there?" Abrahams said.

"He'll call it off," McCann said.

"You'll have the transmitter in your bag," Abrahams said.

"A lot of good *that'll* do if he decides to stick an ice pick in my eye," Eileen said.

"Voice-activated," McCann said.

"Terrific," Eileen said. "Will that get you there any faster? I could yell bloody murder, and it'll still take you three minutes—*minimum*—to get from either end of that park. In three minutes, I can be a statistic."

Abrahams laughed.

"Very funny," Eileen said. "Only it's *my* ass we're talking about here."

"I dig this broad," Abrahams said, laughing.

"That radio can pick up a whisper from twenty-five feet away," McCann said.

"So what?" Eileen said. "It'll *still* take you three minutes to reach me from where you guys want to plant yourselves. Look, Morrie, why don't *you* go in? How about you, Mickey? Either one of you in drag, how does that sound? *I'll* sit outside the park, listening to the radio, okay?"

"I really dig this broad," Abrahams said, laughing.

"So what do you want to do?" McCann asked her.

"I told you. The trees. We hide you under the trees."

"Be pointless. The guy combs the park first, he spots us, he knows we've got it staked out. That's what you want to do, we might as well forget the whole thing."

"Let him go on raping those nurses there," Abrahams said.

Both men looked at her.

So that was what it got down to at last, that was what it always got down to in the long run. You had to show them you were just as good as *they* were, willing to take the same chances *they'd* have taken in similar circumstances, prove to them you had *balls*.

"Okay," she said, and sighed.

"Better take off those earrings," McCann said.

"I'm wearing the earrings," she said.

"Nurses don't wear earrings. I never seen a nurse wearing earrings. He'll spot the earrings."

"I'm wearing the earrings," she said flatly.

So here I am, she thought, ball-less to be sure, but wearing my good-luck earrings, and carrying one gun tucked in my bra, and another gun in my shoulder bag alongside the battery-powered, voice-activated FM transmitter that can pick up a whisper from twenty-five feet away—according to McCann, who, by her current estimate, was now two and a half minutes away at the southeast corner of the park, with Abrahams *three* and a half minutes away at the northwest corner.

If he's going to make his move, she thought, this is where he'll make it, right here, halfway through the park, far from the streetlights. Trees on either side of the path, spruces, hemlocks, pines, snow-covered terrain beyond them. Jump out of the trees, drag me off the path the way he did with the others, this is where he hit the last three times, this is where he'll do it now. The descriptions of the man had been conflicting, they always seemed to be when the offense was rape. One of the victims had described him as being black, another as white. The girl he'd blinded had sobbingly told the investigating officer that her assailant was short and squat, built like a gorilla. The other two nurses insisted that he was very tall, with the slender, muscular body of a weight lifter. He'd been variously described as wearing a business suit, a black leather jacket and blue jeans, and a jogging suit. One of the nurses said he was in his mid-forties, another said he was no older than twenty-five, the third had no opinion whatever about his age. The first nurse he'd raped said he was blond. The second one said he'd been wearing a peaked hat, like a baseball cap. The one he'd blinded—her hand began sweating on the butt of the .38 in her shoulder bag.

It was funny the way her hands always started sweating whenever she found herself in a tight situation. She wondered if McCann's hands were sweating. Three minutes behind her now, Abrahams equidistant at the other end of the park. She wondered if the transmitter was picking up the clicking of her boots on the asphalt path. The path was shoveled clear of snow, but there were still some patches of ice on it, and she skirted one of those now, and looked into the darkness ahead, her eyes accustomed to the dark, and thought she saw something under the trees ahead, and almost stopped dead in her tracks—but that was not what a good decoy was supposed to do. A good decoy marched right into it, a good decoy allowed her man to make his move, a good decoy—

She thought at first she was hearing things.

Her hand tightened on the butt of the gun.

Somebody whistling?

What?

She kept walking, peering into the darkness ahead, past the midway point now, McCann a bit more than three and a half minutes behind her, Abrahams two and a half minutes away in the opposite direction, *still* too far away, and saw a boy on a skateboard coming up the path, whistling as he curved the board in graceful arcs back and forth across the path. He couldn't have been older than thirteen or fourteen, a hatless youngster wearing a blue ski parka and jeans, sneakered feet expertly guiding the skateboard, arms akimbo as he balanced himself, a midnight whistler enjoying the dark silence of the empty park, closer now, still whistling. She smiled, and her hand relaxed on the butt of the gun.

And then, suddenly, he swerved the board into her, bending at the knees, leaning all his weight to one side so that the board slid out from under him, the wheels coming at her, the underside slamming her across the shins. She was pulling the gun from her bag when he punched her in the face. The gun went off while it was still inside the bag, blowing out leather and cigarettes and chewing gum and Kleenex tissues—but not the radio, she hoped, Jesus, not the radio!

In the next thirty seconds, it couldn't have been longer than that, her finger tightening in reflex on the trigger again, the gun's explosion shattering the stillness of the night again, their breaths pluming brokenly from their mouths, merging, blowing away on the wind, she thought, remembered, *Force part of psychological interplay*, he punched her over the breast, *Attendant danger of being severely beaten or killed*, the gun went off a third time, his fist smashed into her mouth, *But he's just a kid.* She tasted blood, felt herself going limp, he was grabbing her right arm, turning her, behind her now, forcing her to her knees, he was going to break her arm, "Let go of it!" yanking on the arm, pulling up on it, "Let *go!*" her hand opened, the gun clattered to the asphalt.

She tried to get to the feet as he came around her, but he shoved her back onto the path, hard, knocking the wind out of her. As he started to straddle her, she kicked out at him with her booted left foot, white skirts flying, the black heel of the boot catching him on the thigh, a trifle too low for the money. She wondered how many seconds had gone by now, wondered where McCann and Abrahams were, she'd *told* them the setup was no good, she'd *told* them—he began slapping her. Straddling her, slapping her, both hands moving, the slaps somehow more painful than the punches had been, dizzying, big callused hands punishing her cheeks and her jaw, back and forth, her head flailing with each successive slap, his weight on her chest, pressing on her breasts—the gun. She remembered the gun in her bra.

She tried to twist away from him, her arms pinioned by his thighs on either side of her, tried to turn her head to avoid the incessant slaps, and idiotically noticed the nurse's cap lying white and still on the path where it had fallen. She could not free her arms or her hands she could not get to the gun.

The slapping stopped abruptly.

There was only the darkness now, and the sound of his vaporized breath coming in short, ragged bursts from his mouth. His hands reached for the front of the uniform. He grasped the fabric. He tore open the front, buttons flying, reached her bra and her breasts—and stopped again. He had seen the gun, he must have seen the gun. His silence now was more frightening than his earlier fury had been. *One* gun might have meant a streetwise lady who knew the city's parks were dangerous. *Another* gun, this one hidden in a bra, could mean only one thing. The lady was a cop. He shifted his weight. She knew he was reaching for something in his pants pocket. She knew the something would be a weapon, and she thought, *He's going to blind me.*

In that moment, fear turned to ice. Cold, crystalline, hard. In that moment, she knew she couldn't count on the cavalry or the marines getting here in time, there was nobody here but us chickens, boss, and nobody to look after little Eileen but little Eileen herself. She took advantage of the shift of his body weight to the left, his right hand going into his pocket, the balance an uneasy one for the barest fraction of a second, enough time for her to emulate the movement of his own body, her left shoulder rising in easy symmetry with his own cant, their bodies in motion together for only a fraction of a second, movement responding to movement as though they were true lovers, and suddenly she lurched, every ounce of strength concentrated in that left shoulder, adding her own weight and momentum to his already off-center tilt—and he toppled over.

His right hand was still in his pocket as she scrambled to her feet. He rolled over onto the path, his right hand coming free of his pocket, the switchblade knife snapping open just as she pulled the Llama out of her bra. She knew she would kill him if he moved. He saw the gun in her hand, steady, leveled at his head, and perhaps he saw the look in her eyes as well, though there was no moon. She liked to think later that what happened next had nothing to do with the sound of footsteps pounding on the path from the north and south, nothing to do with the approach of either Abrahams or McCann.

He dropped the knife.

First he said, "Don't hurt me."

Then he said, "Don't tell on me."

"You okay?" Abrahams asked.

She nodded. She couldn't seem to catch her breath. The gun in her hand was trembling now.

"I would've killed him," she whispered.

"What?" Abrahams said.

"A kid," she whispered.

"We better call for a meat wagon," McCann said. "It looks to me like she's—"

"I'm all *right!*" she said fiercely, and both men stared at her. "I'm all right," she said more softly, and felt suddenly faint, and hoped against hope that she wouldn't pass out in front of these two hairbags from the Chinatown Precinct, and stood there sucking in great gulps of air until the queasiness and the dizziness passed, and then she smiled weakly and said, "What kept you?"

He was exhausted, but the first thing he did when he came into the apartment was dial Eileen's number. There was no answer. He let the phone ring a dozen times, hung up, dialed it again, slowly and carefully this time, and let it ring another dozen times. Still no answer. He thumbed through the R's in his directory, and found the listing for Frank Riley, a man who'd gone through the Academy with him, and who was now a Detective/Second working out of the Chinatown Precinct. He dialed the precinct, told the desk sergeant who he was, and then asked if he had any information on the stakeout outside Worth Memorial earlier that night. The desk sergeant didn't know anything about any stakeout. He put Kling through to the squadroom upstairs, where he talked to a weary detective on the graveyard shift. The detective told him he heard it had gone down as scheduled, but he didn't know all the details. When Kling asked him if Detective Burke was okay, he said there was nobody by that name on the Chinatown Squad.

He was wondering who to try next when the knock sounded on his door. He went to the door.

"Who is it?" he asked.

"Me," she answered. Her voice sounded very weary and very small.

He took off the night chain, unlocked the dead bolt, and opened the door. She was wearing a navy pea jacket over blue jeans and black boots. Her long red hair was hanging loose around her face. In the dim illumination of the hallway light bulb, he could see that her face was discolored and bruised, her lip swollen.

"Okay to come in?" she asked.

"Come in," he said, and immediately, "Are you okay?"

"Tired," she said.

He locked the door behind her, and put on the night chain. When he turned from the door, she was sitting on the edge of the bed.

"How'd it go?" he asked.

"We got him," she said. "Fourteen years old," she said. "I almost killed him," she said.

Their eyes met.

"Would you mind very much making love to me?" she said.

Ice, 1983

T he two women were sizing each other up.

Annie Rawles had been told that Eileen Burke was the best decoy in Special Forces. Eileen had been told that Annie Rawles was a hard-nosed Rape Squad cop who'd once worked out of Robbery and had shot down two hoods trying to rip off a midtown bank. Eileen was looking at a woman with eyes the color of loam behind glasses that gave her a scholarly look, wedge-cut hair the color of midnight, firm cupcake breasts, and a slender boy's body. They were both about the same age, Eileen guessed, give or take a year or so. Eileen kept wondering how somebody who looked so much like a bookkeeper could have pulled her service revolver and blown away two desperate punks facing a max of twenty years hard time.

"What do you think?" Annie asked.

"You say this isn't the only repeat?" Eileen said.

They were still sizing each other up. Eileen figured this wasn't a matter of choice. If Annie Rawles had asked for her, and if her lieutenant had assigned Eileen to the job, then that was it, they both outranked her. Still, she liked to know whom she'd be working with. Annie was wondering if Eileen was really as good at the job as they'd said she was. She looked a little flashy for a decoy. Spot her strutting along in high heels with those tits bouncing, a rapist would make her in a minute and run for the hills. This was a very special rapist they were dealing with here; Annie didn't want an amateur screwing it up.

"We've got three women say they were raped more than once by this same guy. Fits the description in each case," Annie said. "There may be more, we haven't run an m.o. cross-check."

"When will you be doing that?" Eileen asked; she liked to know whom she was working with, how efficient they were. It wouldn't be Annie Rawles's ass out there on the street, it would be her own.

"Working on that now," Annie said. She liked Eileen's question. She knew she was asking Eileen to put herself in a dangerous position. The man had already slashed one of the victims, left her face scarred. At the same time, that was the job. If Eileen didn't like Special Forces, she should ask for transfer to something else. Annie didn't know that Eileen was considering just that possibility, but not for any reason Annie might have understood.

"All over the city, or any special location?" Eileen asked.

"Anyplace, anytime."

"I'm only one person," Eileen said.

"There'll be other decoys. But what I have in mind for you . . ."

"How many?"

"Six, if I can get them."

"Counting me?"

"Yes."

"Who are the others?"

"I've got their names here, you want to look them over," Annie said, and handed her a typewritten sheet.

Eileen read it over carefully. She knew all of the women on the list. Most of them knew their jobs. One of them didn't. She refrained from voicing this opinion; no sense bad-mouthing anybody.

"Uh-huh," she said.

"Look okay to you?"

"Sure." She hesitated. "Connie needs a bit more experience," she said tactfully. "You might want to save her for something less complicated. Good cop, but this guy's got a knife, you said . . ."

"And he's *used* it," Annie said.

"Yeah, so save Connie for something a little less complicated." Both women understood the euphemism. "Less complicated" meant "less dangerous." Nobody wanted a lady cop slashed because she was incapable of handling something like this.

"What age groups?" Eileen asked. "The victims."

"The three we know about for sure . . . let me look at this a minute." Annie picked up another typewritten sheet. "One of them is forty-six. Another is twenty-eight. This last one—Mary Hollings, the one last Saturday night—is thirty-seven. He's raped her three times already."

"Same guy each time, huh? You're *positive* about that?"

"According to the descriptions."

"What do they say he looks like?"

"In his thirties, black hair and blue eyes . . ."

"White?"

"White. About six feet tall . . . well, it varies there. We've got him ranging from five-ten to six-two. About a hundred and eighty pounds, very muscular, very strong."

"Any identifying marks? Scars? Tattoos?"

"None of the victims mentioned any."

"Same guy each time," Eileen said, as if trying to lend credibility to it by repeating it. "That's unusual, isn't it? Guy coming back to the same victim?"

"Very," Annie said. "Which is why I thought . . ."

"With your rapists, usually . . ."

"I know."

"They don't care *who* they get, it's got nothing to do with lust."

"I know."

"So the m.o. would seem to indicate he has *favorites* or something. That doesn't jibe with the *psychology* of it."

"I know."

"So what's the plan? Cover these victims or cruise their neighborhoods?"

"We don't think they're random victims," Annie said. "That's why I'd like you to . . ."

"Then cruising's out, right?"

Annie nodded. "This last one—Mary Hollings—is a redhead."

"Oh," Eileen said. "Okay, I get it."

"About your size," Annie said. "A little shorter. What are you, five-ten, five-eleven?"

"I *wish*," Eileen said, and smiled. "Five-nine."

"She's five-seven."

"Built like me?"

"Zoftig, I'd say."

"Bovine, *I'd* say," Eileen said, and smiled.

"Hardly," Annie said, and returned the smile.

"So you want me to be Mary Hollings, is that it?"

"If you think you can pass."

"You know the lady, I don't," Eileen said.

"It's a reasonable likeness," Annie said. "Up close, he'll tip in a minute. But by that time, it should be too late."

"Where does she live?" Eileen asked.

"1840 Laramie Crescent."

"Up in the Eight-Seven?"

"Yes."

"Does she work, this woman?" 'Cause if she runs a computer terminal or something . . ."

"She's divorced, living on alimony payments."

"Lucky her," Eileen said. "I'll need her daily routine . . ."

"You can get that directly from her," Annie said.

"Where do we hide *her*, meanwhile?"

"She'll be leaving for California day after tomorrow. She has a sister out there."

"Better give her a wig, case he's watching the apartment when she leaves."

"We will."

"How about other tenants in the building? Won't they know I'm not . . . ?"

"We figured you could pass yourself off as the sister. I doubt he'll be talking to any of the tenants."

"Any security there?"

"No."

"Elevator operator?"

"No."

"So it's just between me and them. The tenants, I mean."

"And *him*," Annie said.

"What about boyfriends and such? What about social clubs or other places where they know her?"

"She'll be telling all her friends she's going out of town. If anyone calls while you're in the apartment, you're the sister."

"Suppose *he* calls?"

"He hasn't yet, we don't think he will. He's not a heavy breather."

"Different psychology," Eileen said, nodding.

"We figure you can go wherever she was in the habit of going, we don't think he'll follow you inside. Go in, hang around, do your nails, whatever, then come out again. If he's watching, he'll pick up the trail again outside. It should work. I *hope*."

"I never had one like this before."

"Neither have I."

"I'll need a cross-checked breakdown," Eileen said. "On Mary Hollings and the other two victims."

"We're working that up now. We didn't think there was a pattern until now. I mean . . ."

Eileen detected a crack in the hard-nosed veneer.

"It's just . . ."

Again Annie hesitated.

"These other two . . . one's out in Riverhead, the other's in Calm's Point, it's a big city. I didn't realize till Saturday, after I talked to Mary Hollings . . . I mean, it just didn't *register* before then. That these were serial rapes. That he's hitting the same women more than once. Came to me like a bolt out of the blue. Now that we *know* there's a pattern, we're cross-checking similarities on these three victims we're *sure* were attacked by the same guy, see if we can't come up with anything in their backgrounds that might have singled them out. It's a place to start."

"You using the computer?"

"Not only for the three," Annie said, nodding. "We're running a check on every rape reported since the beginning of the year. If there are *other* victims who were serially raped . . ."

"When do I get the printouts?" Eileen asked.

"As soon as I get them."

"And when's that?"

"I know it's your ass out there," Annie said softly.

Eileen said nothing.

"I know he has a knife," Annie said.

Eileen still said nothing.

"I'd no more risk your life than I would my own," Annie said, and Eileen thought of her facing down two armed robbers in the marbled lobby of a midtown bank.

"When do I start?" she asked.

* * *

A musician roamed from table to table, strumming his guitar and singing Mexican songs. When he got to Eileen's table, he played "Cielito Lindo" for her, optimistically, she thought; the sky outside had been bloated with threatening black clouds when she'd entered the restaurant. The rain had stopped entirely at about four in the afternoon, but the clouds had begun building again at dusk, piling up massively and ominously overhead. By six-fifteen, when she'd left the apartment to walk here, she could already hear the sound of distant thunder in the next state, beyond the river.

She was having her coffee—the wall clock read twenty minutes past seven—when the first lightning flash came, illuminating the curtained window facing the street. The following boom of thunder was ear-shattering; she hunched her shoulders in anticipation, and even so its volume shocked her. The rain came then, unleashed in fury, enforced by a keening wind, battering the window and pelting the sidewalk outside. She lighted a cigarette and smoked it while she finished her coffee. It was almost seven-thirty when she paid her bill and went to the checkroom for the raincoat and umbrella she'd left there.

The raincoat was Mary's. It fit her a bit too snugly, but she thought it might be recognizable to him, and if the rain came—as it most certainly had—visibility might be poor; she did not want to lose him because he couldn't *see* her. The umbrella was Mary's, too, a delicate little red plaid thing that was more stylish than protective, especially against what was raging outside just now. The rain boots were Eileen's. Rubber with floppy tops. She had chosen them exactly because the tops *were* floppy. Strapped to her ankle inside the right boot was a holster containing a lightweight Browning .380 automatic pistol, her spare. Her regulation pistol was a .38 Detective's Special, and she was carrying that in a shoulder bag slung over her left shoulder for an easy cross-body draw.

She tipped the checkroom girl a dollar (wondering if this was too much), put on the raincoat, reslung the shoulder bag, and then walked out into the small entry alcove. A pair of glass doors, with the word *Ocho* engraved on one and *Ríos* on the other, faced the street outside, lashed with rain now. Lightning flashed as she pushed open one of the doors. She backed inside again, waited for the boom of thunder to fade, and then stepped out into the rain, opening the umbrella.

A gust of wind almost tore the umbrella from her grasp. She turned into the wind, fighting it, refusing to allow it to turn the umbrella inside out. Angling it over her face and shoulders, using it as a shield to bully her way through the driving rain, she started for the corner. The route she had traced out this afternoon would take her one block west on a brightly lighted avenue—deserted now because of the storm—and then two blocks north on less well lighted streets to

Mary's apartment. She did not expect him to make his move while she was on the avenue. But on that two-block walk to the apartment—
She suddenly wished she'd asked for a backup.
Stupid, playing it this way.
And yet, if she'd planted her backups, say, on the other side of the street, one walking fifty feet ahead of her, the other fifty feet behind, he'd be sure to spot them, wouldn't he? Three women walking out here in the rain in the classic triangle pattern? Sure to spot them. Or suppose she'd planted them in any one of the darkened doorways or alleyways along the route she'd walked this afternoon, and suppose he checked out that same route, saw two ladies lurking in doorways—not many hookers up here, and certainly none on the side streets where there wasn't any business—no, he'd tip, he'd run, they'd lose him. Better without any backups. And still, she wished she had one.
She took a deep breath as she turned the corner off the avenue. The blocks would be longer now.
Your side streets were always longer than your streets on the avenue. Maybe twice as long. Plenty of opportunity for him in there. Two long blocks.
It was raining inside the floppy tops of the boots. She could feel the backup pistol inside the right boot, the butt cold against the nylon of her panty hose. She was wearing panties *under* the panty hose, great protection against a knife, oh, sure, great big chastity belt he could slash open in a minute. She was holding the umbrella with both hands now, trying to keep it from being carried away by the wind. She wondered suddenly if she shouldn't just throw the damn thing away, put her right hand onto the butt of the .38 in her bag—*He pulls that knife, don't ask questions, just blow him away.* Annie's advice. Not that she needed it.
Alley coming up on her right. Narrow space between two of the buildings, stacked with garbage cans when she'd passed it this afternoon. *Too* narrow for action? The guy wasn't looking to *dance*, he was looking to *rape*, and the width of the alley seemed to preclude the space for that. Ever get raped on top of a garbage can? she asked herself. *Don't ask questions, just blow him away.* Dark doorway in the building beyond the alley. Lights in the next building and the one after that. Lamppost on the corner. The sky suddenly split by a streak of lightning. Thunder booming on the night. A gust of wind turned the umbrella inside out. She threw it into the garbage can on the corner and felt the immediate onslaught of the rain on her naked head. Should have worn a hat, she thought. Or one of those plastic things you tie under your chin. Her hand found the butt of the .38 in her shoulder bag.
She crossed the street.
Another lamppost on the corner opposite.

314

Darkness beyond that.

An alley coming up, she knew. Wider than the first had been, a car's width across, at least. Nice place to tango. Plenty of room. Her hand tightened on the gun butt. Nothing. Nobody in the alley that she could see, no footsteps behind her after she passed it. Lighted buildings ahead now, looking potbelly warm in the rain. Another alley way up ahead, two buildings down from Mary's. What if they'd been wrong? What if he *didn't* plan to hit tonight? She kept walking, her hand on the gun butt. She skirted a puddle on the sidewalk. More lightning, she winced; more thunder, she winced again. Passing the only other alley now, dark and wide, but not as wide as the last one had been. Garbage cans. A scraggly wet cat sitting on one of the cans, peering out at the falling rain. Cat would've bolted if somebody was in there, no? She was passing the alley when he grabbed her.

He grabbed her from behind, his left arm looping around her neck and yanking her off her feet. She fell back against him, her right hand already yanking the pistol out of her bag. The cat shrieked and leaped off the garbage can, skittering underfoot as it streaked out into the rain.

"Hello, Mary," he whispered, and she pulled the gun free.

"This is a knife, Mary," he said, and his right hand came up suddenly, and she felt the sharp tip of the blade against her ribs, just below her heart.

"Just drop the gun, Mary," he said. "You still have the gun, huh, Mary? Same as last time. Well, just drop it, nice and easy, drop it on the ground, Mary."

He prodded her with the knife. The tip poked at the lightweight raincoat, poked at the thin fabric of her blouse beneath it, poked at her ribs. His left arm was still looped around her neck, holding her tight in the crook of his elbow. The pistol was in her hand, but he was behind her, and powerless in his grip, and the pressure of the knife blade was more insistent now.

"*Do* it!" he said urgently, and she dropped the pistol.

It clattered to the alleyway floor. Lightning shattered the night. There was an enormous boom of thunder. He dragged her deeper into the alley, into the darkness, past the garbage cans to where a loading platform was set in the wall some three feet above the floor. A pair of rusted iron doors were behind the platform. He threw her onto the platform, and her hand went immediately into the top of her floppy rubber boot, groping for the butt of the Browning.

"Don't force me to cut you," he said.

She yanked the pistol out of its holster.

She was bringing it up into firing position when he slashed her.

She dropped the gun at once, her hand going up to her face where sudden fire blazed a trail across her cheek. Her hand came away wet, she thought it was the rain at first, but the wet was sticky and thick, and she knew it was blood—he had cut her cheek, she was bleeding from the cheek! And suddenly she was overcome by a fear she had never before known in her life.

"Good girl," he said.

There was another flash of lightning, more thunder. The knife was under her dress now, she dared not move, he was picking at the nylon of the panty hose with the knife, catching at it, plucking at it; she winced below, tightened there in horrified reaction, afraid of the knife, fearful he would use it again where she was infinitely more vulnerable. The tip of the blade caught the fabric, held. There was a sound of the nylon ripping, the whisper of the knife as it opened the panty hose over her crotch and the panties underneath. He laughed when he realized she was also wearing panties.

"Expecting a rape?" he asked, still laughing, and then slashed the panties, too, and now she was open to the cold of the night, her legs spread and trembling, the rain beating down on her face and mingling there with the blood, washing the blood from her cheek burning hot where the gash crossed it, her eyes widening in terror when he placed the cold flat of the knife against her vagina and said, "Want me to cut you here, too, Mary?"

She shook her head, *No, please.* Mumbled the words incoherently. Said them aloud at last, "No, please," trembling beneath him as he moved between her legs and put the knife to her throat again. "Please," she said. "Don't . . . cut me again. Please."

"Want me to fuck you instead?" he said.

She shook her head again. *No!* she thought. But she said instead, "Don't cut me again."

"You want to get fucked instead, isn't that right, Mary?"

No! she thought. "Yes," she said. *Don't cut me,* she thought. Please.

"Say it, Mary."

"Don't cut me," she said.

"*Say* it, Mary!"

"Fuck me in . . . instead," she said.

"You want my baby, don't you, Mary?"

Oh God, no, she thought, *oh God,* that's *it*! "Yes," she said, "I want your baby."

"The hell you do," he said, and laughed.

Lightning tore the night close by. Thunder boomed into the alleyway, immediately overhead, echoing.

She knew all the things to do, knew all about going for the eyes, clawing at the jelly of the eyes, blinding the bastard, she knew all about that. She knew what to do if he forced you to blow him, knew all about fondling his balls and taking him in your mouth, and then biting down hard on his cock and squeezing his balls tight at the same time, knew all about how to send a rapist shrieking into the night in pain. But a knife was at her throat.

The tip of the sharp blade was in the hollow of her throat where a tiny pulse beat wildly. He had slashed her face, she could still feel the slow steady ooze of blood from the cut, fire blazing along the length of the cut from one end to the other. The rain pelted her face and her legs, her skirt up around her thighs, the cold, wet concrete of the platform beneath her, the rusted iron doors behind her. And then—suddenly— she felt the rigid thrust of him below, against her unreceptive lips, and thought he would tear her with the force of his penetration, rip her as if with the knife itself, still at her throat, poised to cut.

She trembled in fear, and in shame, and in helpless desperation, suffering his pounding below, sobbing now, repeatedly begging him to stop, afraid of screaming lest the knife pierce the flesh of her throat as surely as he himself was piercing her flesh below. And when he shuddered convulsively—the knife tip trembling against her throat— and then lay motionless upon her for several moments, she could only think, *It's over, he's done*, and the shame washed over her again, the utter sense of degradation caused by his invasion, and she sobbed more scathingly. And realized in that instant that this was not a working cop here in a dark alley, her underwear torn, her legs spread, a stranger's sperm inside her. No. This was a frightened *victim*, a helpless violated *woman*. And she closed her eyes against the rain and the tears and the pain.

"*Now* go get your abortion," he said.

He rolled off her.

She wondered where her gun was. Her guns.

She heard him running out of the alley on the patter of the rain.

She lay there in pain, above and below, her eyes closed tight.

She lay there for a very long while.

Then she stumbled out of the alley, and found the nearest patrol box, and called in the crime.

And fainted as lightning flashed again, and did not hear the following boom of thunder.

She was sitting up in bed, her hands flat on the sheet, when Kling entered the room. Her head was turned away from him. The window oozed raindrops, framed a gray view of buildings beyond.

"Hi," he said.

When she turned toward the door, he saw the bandage on her left cheek. A thick wad of cotton layers covered with adhesive plaster tape. She'd been crying; the flesh around her eyes was red and puffy. She smiled and lifted one hand from the sheet in greeting. The hand dropped again, limply, white against the white sheet.

"Hi," she said.

317

He came to the bed. He kissed her on the cheek that wasn't bandaged.

"You okay?" he asked.

"Yeah, fine," she said.

"I was just talking to the doctor, he says they'll be releasing you later today."

"Good," she said.

He did not know what else to say. He knew what had happened to her. He did not know what to say.

"Some cop, huh?" she said. "Let him scare me out of both my guns, let him . . ." She turned her face away again. Rain slithered down the windowpanes.

"He raped me, Bert."

"I know."

"How . . . ?" Her voice caught. "How do you feel about that?"

"I want to kill him," Kling said.

"Sure, but . . . how do . . . how do you feel about me getting raped?"

He looked at her, puzzled. Her head was still turned away from him, as though she were trying to hide the patch on her cheek and by extension the wound that testified to her surrender.

"About letting him rape me," she said.

"You didn't *let* him do *anything*."

"I'm a cop," she said.

"Honey . . ."

"I should have . . ." She shook her head. "I was too scared, Bert," she said. Her voice was very low.

"I've been scared," he said.

"I was afraid he'd kill me."

She turned to look at him.

Their eyes met. Tears were forming in her eyes. She blinked them back.

"A cop isn't *supposed* to get that scared, Bert. A cop is supposed to . . . to . . . . I threw away my *gun*! The minute he stuck that knife in my ribs, I panicked, Bert, I threw away my *gun*! I had it in my hand but I threw it away!"

"I'd have done the same . . ."

"I had a spare in my boot, a little Browning. I reached into the boot, I had the gun in my hand, ready to fire, when he . . . he . . . cut me."

Kling was silent.

"I didn't think it would hurt that much, Bert. Getting cut. You cut yourself shaving your legs or your armpits, it stings for a minute but this was my *face*, Bert, he cut my *face*, and oh *Jesus*, how it *hurt*! I'm no beauty, I know that, but it's the only face I have, and when he . . ."

"You're gorgeous," he said.

"Not anymore," she said, and turned away from him again. "That was when I—when he cut me and I lost the second gun—that was when I knew I . . . I'd do . . . I'd do anything he wanted me to do. I *let* him rape me, Bert. I *let* him do it."

"You'd be dead otherwise," Kling said.

"So damn helpless," she said, and shook her head again.

He said nothing.

"So now . . ." Her voice caught again. "I guess you'll always wonder whether I was asking for it, huh?"

"Cut it out," he said.

"Isn't that what men are supposed to wonder when their wives or their girlfriends get . . . ?"

"You *were* asking for it," Kling said. "That's why you were out there, that was your job. You were doing your job, Eileen, and you got hurt. And that's . . ."

"I also got *raped*!" she said, and turned to him, her eyes flashing.

"That was part of getting hurt," he said.

"No!" she said. "*You've* been hurt on the job, but nobody ever *raped* you afterward! There's a difference, Bert."

"I understand the difference," he said.

"I'm not sure you do," she said. "Because if you did, you wouldn't be giving me this 'line of duty' bullshit!"

"Eileen . . ."

"He didn't rape a *cop*, he raped a *woman*! He raped *me*, Bert! *Because* I'm a woman!"

"I know."

"No, you *don't* know," she said. "How *can* you know? You're a man, and men don't get raped."

"Men get raped," he said softly.

"Where?" she said. "In prison? Only because there aren't any women handy."

"Men get raped," he said again, but did not elaborate.

She looked at him. The pain in his eyes was as deep as the pain she had felt last night when the knife ripped across her face. She kept studying his eyes, searching his face. Her anger dissipated. This was Bert sitting here with her, this was not some vague enemy named Man, this was Bert Kling—and *he*, after all, was not the man who'd raped her.

"I'm sorry," she said.

"That's okay."

"I shouldn't be taking it out on you."

"Who else?" he said, and smiled.

"I'm sorry," she said. "Really."

She searched for his hand. He took her hand in both his own.

"I never thought this could happen to me," she said, and sighed. "Never in a million years. I've been scared out there, you're always a little scared . . ."

"Yes," he said.

"But I never thought *this* could happen. Remember how I used to kid around about my rape fantasies?"

"Yes."

"It's only a fantasy when it isn't *real*," she said. "I used to think . . . I guess I thought . . . I mean, I was *scared*, Bert, even with backups I was scared. But not of being *raped*. Hurt, maybe, but not *raped*. I was a *cop*, how could a cop possibly . . . ?"

"You're still a cop," he said.

"You better believe it," she said. "Remember what I was telling you? About feeling degraded by decoy work? About maybe asking for a transfer?"

"I remember."

"Well, now they'll have to blast me out of this job with dynamite."

"Good," he said, and kissed her hand.

" 'Cause I mean . . . doesn't *somebody* have to be out there? To make sure this doesn't happen to *other* women? I mean, there has to be *somebody* out there, doesn't there?"

"Sure," he said. "You."

"Yeah, me," she said, and sighed deeply.

He held her hand to his cheek.

They were silent for several moments.

She almost turned her face away again.

Instead, she held his eyes with her own and said, "Will you . . . ?" Her voice caught again.

"Will you love me as much with a scar?"

Lightning, 1984

Ed McBain
Jigsaw £2.99

There's nothing like a little homicide to give the 87th Precinct a shot in the arm. Or the chest, as the case may be ... Detectives Brown and Carella had themselves a puzzle with six missing pieces. Put it together and there's $750,000 for the taking. In this case bodies were easy to find – clues came a little harder ...

'McBain's so far ahead of police-procedural writers that it's virtually a one-horse race ... Hyper-readable, witty, credible'
THE SCOTSMAN

Lightning £2.99

The night was almost balmy for October. But Carella felt suddenly cold when he saw the woman's body hanging from the lamppost ... That same night, a woman was raped – for the *Third* time in succession, by the *same* man each time. This was turning out to be the worst autumn Carella had ever known.

'The best McBain of recent vintage ... Repetitive rape, multiple killings, blood, sex, toil, autopsies, the whole stitched together by the daddy of the police-procedural until you can almost taste those greasy French fries in the 87th Precinct's canteen' OBSERVER

Ice £3.50

It was snowing again on the frozen sidewalks when the girl dancer walked out of the stage door and straight into the gunsight of the man hidden in the nearby doorway. When they pulled the .38 Smith & Wesson slug out of her corpse, Ballistics noticed that it matched the one they'd found in a Puerto Rican dope dealer just three days before. Carella knew which direction he was taking. Ice means winter on the Precinct streets, and ice means killing. But ice means something else too, something every bit as deadly ...

Ed McBain
Ghosts £2.99

The dead woman on the snowy sidewalk was a little early for a
Christmas Eve suicide. She wasn't a suicide, she was a murder victim
– and so was the ghost-story writer who died of nineteen stab
wounds only minutes later. This Precinct murder hunt, taking in
mediums and haunted houses, was one set to give Steve Carella the
biggest scare of his life.

'In *Ghosts* the maestro is near the top of his form' CURRENT CRIME

Doll £1.95

A man grasping a kitchen knife slashed relentlessly at lovely Tinka
Sachs. Obscenities and blade enveloped her in blood and spittle.
In the next room, the child Anna clung fiercely to her doll all night
long.

Looking for the murderer, Carella found himself the prisoner of a
lush brunette who would kill a man as easily as she could
seduce him . . .

Ed McBain
Blood Relatives £2.50

Saturday night, and party night on the Precinct – the perfect
backdrop for a knife-carrying sex attacker. Seventeen-year-old
Muriel was stabbed to death and her cousin Patricia got away with a
slashed cheek. When she ran into the station house Kling watched
the bloody hand-prints appear on the glass panel. A messy start to a
case that got messier – every time Patricia changed her story...

'Totally gripping ... he rivets the reader throughout'
JILL NEVILLE, BBC KALEIDOSCOPE

Axe £2.99

January brought a sunless lack of cheer to the 87th Precinct. There
would be no happy new year for George Lasser. An axe had split his
skull wide open. Then someone killed a cop. It looked like being a
lousy month for Detectives Hawes and Carella...

Heat £2.50

In the heat of the city summer, Jerry Newman, failed painter and
twice-failed husband, died. Suicide they said, but Carella knew that
suicides left notes and didn't turn the air-conditioning off on the
hottest night of the year. Which puts Carella on the trail of a killer,
while Kling's on the trail of a lovely wife he can't trust, and someone
nasty is on Kling's trail.

'Tense, gripping and stylish ... by the best modern American crime
writer' SUNDAY EXPRESS

Colin Forbes
Terminal £3.50

When international news correspondent Bob Newman gets a tip-off
about a mysterious package smuggled across an eastern border it's
yet another link in a chain of sinister incidents that have one thing in
common – they are all connected with the Berne Clinic and
Terminal. But what is Terminal? And why are the British SIS so
desperate to find out?

Double Jeopardy £2.99

A British agent inexplicably murdered on Lake Konstanz; his
replacement, Keith Martel, must move swiftly. The neo-Nazi Delta
organization are fighting dirty, and maybe someone else is fighting
the same way. A nightmare bloodbath in Zurich, a sudden attempt
on Martel's life, and close to midnight on 2 June the Summit
Express takes the top four western leaders to meet the Soviet premier
in Vienna. One of them is targeted. Which one and how to save him
are Martel's problem.

'One of the top half-dozen British thriller writers' DAILY MIRROR

The Leader and the Damned £3.99

In 1943 Hitler was at the height of his power. At his side, Martin
Bormann. And constantly on his mind, the war against the
beleaguered might of Stalin's Russia. After 13 March of that year,
records show a drastic change in the Führer's behaviour and
personality: 13 March 1943 was the date of a bomb attack on the
Führer's private aircraft. If Hitler was destroyed on that fateful date,
who was the man in the Berlin Bunker two years later? And how
did Bormann succeed in keeping the anti-Nazi generals from seizing
the Reich?

'It is easy to forget this is fiction' DAILY MAIL

All Pan books are available at your local bookshop or newsagent, or can be ordered direct from the publisher. Indicate the number of copies required and fill in the form below.

Send to: **CS Department, Pan Books Ltd., P.O. Box 40, Basingstoke, Hants. RG21 2YT.**

or phone: 0256 469551 (Ansaphone), quoting title, author and Credit Card number.

Please enclose a remittance* to the value of the cover price plus: 60p for the first book plus 30p per copy for each additional book ordered to a maximum charge of £2.40 to cover postage and packing.

*Payment may be made in sterling by UK personal cheque, postal order, sterling draft or international money order, made payable to Pan Books Ltd.

Alternatively by Barclaycard/Access:

Card No. ☐☐☐☐☐☐☐☐☐☐☐☐☐☐☐☐☐☐☐

Signature:

Applicable only in the UK and Republic of Ireland.

While every effort is made to keep prices low, it is sometimes necessary to increase prices at short notice. Pan Books reserve the right to show on covers and charge new retail prices which may differ from those advertised in the text or elsewhere.

NAME AND ADDRESS IN BLOCK LETTERS PLEASE:

....

Name ————————————————————————

Address ————————————————————————

————————————————————————

————————————————————————

————————————————————————

3/87